Two Penn'orth of Sky

Also by Katie Flynn

A Liverpool Miss
The Girl From Penny Lane
Liverpool Taffy
The Mersey Girls
Strawberry Fields
Rainbow's End
Rose of Tralee
No Silver Spoon
Polly's Angel
The Girl from Seaforth Sands
The Liverpool Rose
Poor Little Rich Girl
The Bad Penny
Down Daisy Street
A Kiss and a Promise

Two Penn'orth of Sky

KATIE FLYNN

WILLIAM HEINEMANN : LONDON

William Heinemann,
The Random House Group Limited
20 Vauxhall Bridge Road, London, SW1V 2SA

Random House Australia (Pty) Limited
20 Alfred Street, Milsons Point, Sydney, New South Wales 2061, Australia

Random House New Zealand Limited
18 Poland Road, Glenfield
Auckland 10, New Zealand

Random House South Africa (Pty) Limited
Endulini, 5a Jubilee Road, Parktown, 2193, South Africa

Random House UK Limited Reg. No. 954009

www.randomhouse.co.uk

A CIP catalogue record for this book is available from the British Library

Papers used by Random House are natural, recyclable products made
from wood grown in sustainable forests. The manufacturing processes conform
to the environmental regulations of the country of origin

Typeset by Palimpsest Book Production Limited, Polmont, Stirlingshire
Printed and bound in the United Kingdom by
Mackays of Chatham plc, Chatham, Kent

ISBN 0 434 01239 4

For Angharad and Patrick Williams, because I used their town (though not the lifeboat).

Acknowledgements

As usual, the Liverpool Central Library found me some useful material, this time from the audio department, but heartfelt thanks must go to Walter McIlhagga, whose knowledge of Llandudno – and the trams – in the thirties was of inestimable value.

Chapter One

[illegible]

[illegible]

Chapter One
June 1919

'Emmy, time's getting on, queen. I know they say brides always ought to be a bit late, but you don't want to leave poor Peter standing in the church, thinking you're not coming.'

Emmy heard her friend Beryl's voice coming up the stairwell and smiled at her mother, who had been fussing over the pearl beads which she had lent for the occasion. That was the 'something borrowed'; 'something blue' was the garters, which held up Emmy's silk stockings. She took a last glance at herself in the mirror. Her ash-blonde hair was almost hidden by the floating white veil and the wreath of tiny white rosebuds that held everything in place, but she knew she was looking her best. Her dress had been made by her mother; Mrs Dickens was a noted needlewoman and the gown was perfect, showing off Emmy's slender figure to best advantage. Downstairs, Emmy knew, her bouquet waited for her: cream roses, gypsophila, and a few sprigs of sweet-smelling myrtle, chosen because her mother considered it lucky.

Mrs Dickens finished fastening the beads and stood back, eyes misting. 'You look radiant, my dear,' she said softly. 'The most beautiful bride Nightingale Court has ever known. And this is going to be the sort of wedding that folk will remember. Not one person has refused the invitation and we've enough food and drink to feed an army. Oh aye, people will be talking about this day for years to come.'

'Oh, Mam, if they do, it's you I've got to thank,' Emmy said sincerely. 'You've been the best mother in the world and I'm a lucky girl, I know I am. Why, Peter loves you as much as I do, or he would never have suggested that you should come and live with us in Lancaster Avenue. Oh, Mam . . .'

Beryl's voice came closer; clearly, she was mounting the stairs. 'Come *on*, Emmy!'

Emmy went out to the head of the stairs and found Beryl Fisher halfway up, smiling at her. Beryl was her oldest friend, a tall, well-built young woman, four years Emmy's senior. At first glance, one might have thought her plain, for she had a broad face with high cheekbones and rather small, twinkling eyes, but a second glance would show that her thick brown hair was naturally curly and when she smiled her face was transformed. Beryl would have been Emmy's bridesmaid, except that she had been married to Wally Fisher for three years and had a small son, Charlie. Emmy had suggested that Beryl might be matron-of-honour, but her friend had laughed and told her not to be so daft. 'You have me niece, Susie,' she advised. 'You won't have to buy her a dress 'cos the pink one you wore when you were my bridesmaid will fit her nicely.' So now Susie waited in the kitchen downstairs, pretty as a picture in the pink silk dress, her dark hair and eyes a foil for Emmy's fragile fairness.

'The car's arrived,' Beryl said, retreating down the stairs. 'My, you look good enough to eat! Wait till you see the crowd in the court. Everyone wants to catch a glimpse before you leave . . . them that can't come to the church, that is. So mind you go slowly so's they can all get an eyeful.'

Emmy smiled. For years, her mother had been

saving for this day, because she had always been certain that her daughter would marry well. 'A good marriage is the only way to shake the dust of Nightingale Court off your feet,' she had said, as soon as Emmy was old enough to understand. 'When I married your dear father, we told ourselves we'd give the court a year and then move on to somewhere better. He was ambitious, was Sam, and would have gone places and taken us with him. Only then he got consumption and couldn't work full-time and you were born . . .' She sighed. 'Your poor dad! But you'll do better, I know it in me bones.'

Since Sam Dickens had been dead a dozen years, Mrs Dickens was going to give her daughter away, so now Emmy picked up her bouquet and placed her hand lightly on her mother's arm, and the two of them went out of the front doorway, into the court. Beryl had been right. The place was crowded, and as the two women appeared a ragged cheer went up. Emmy glanced quickly towards the arch which led into Raymond Street; yes, she could see the June sunlight out there, so she was to have good weather on this, the most important day of her life so far. Satisfied, she allowed her blue gaze to sweep the crowd and for a moment she was all smiles, until she saw the tall young man who stood nearest. Johnny Frost! He was staring at her steadily and she could read the hunger in his dark blue eyes, and the pain.

Hastily, Emmy turned away from him and began to walk towards the archway, beyond which the wedding car waited. She tried to tell herself that Johnny had no right to come and stare at her, no right to be in the court at all. He had not been invited to the wedding and lived a couple of streets away, so he had come deliberately, knowing that his presence could only embarrass her.

She had been very close to Johnny Frost once, had truly meant to marry him. Oh, there had been no engagement ring, no public promises, but they had been childhood sweethearts and she knew Johnny had taken it for granted that they would wed one day. But Johnny wasn't ambitious, had no desire to better himself. Marriage to Johnny, she thought bitterly now, would have meant a baby every year, a flat over a grocer's shop, and herself taking in washing to make ends meet. Her mother had warned her, but being a headstrong girl of seventeen she had taken no notice – until Peter Wesley had come into her life, that was. Peter was a dozen years older than she and First Officer on a liner. His parents were well-to-do people living in Southampton. Mr and Mrs Wesley, senior, had come up for the wedding but had refused Mrs Dickens's shyly offered hospitality and had booked themselves rooms at the Adelphi instead.

The little party had reached the car, but it was not until the uniformed chauffeur set his vehicle in motion that Emmy felt safe from Johnny's burning gaze. Her mother was fussing with her dress again, smoothing down the rich material, whilst Susie leaned forward and tweaked the veil, which had caught on her headdress.

'Not long now, Emmy, and you'll be Mrs Wesley, livin' in a posh house,' she said encouragingly. 'And it ain't as if you'll be alone there when Peter goes back to sea, because you'll have your mam, won't you? My, we're goin' to miss you in Nightingale Court.'

Emmy smiled affectionately at her mother. Mrs Dickens had promised faithfully to move herself and her belongings to Lancaster Avenue a month after the wedding, and Emmy knew her mother was as excited as a young girl over the prospect of moving house. Emmy was doubly grateful to Peter, for was he not rescuing both of them from Nightingale Court?

Sunshine never penetrated as far as the courts, because the tottery, three-storey houses were too close to each other, and too tall, to allow much natural light to enter. Mrs Dickens was fond of remarking that all you got in Nightingale Court was two penn'orth of sky, and in order to see that, you had to stand in the middle of the court and tilt your head back, staring up till your eyes watered.

All the houses in the court were in constant need of maintenance. The landlord was mean and greedy, never reducing the rents but always promising repairs and renovations, though he never did anything which was not absolutely essential. Consequently, the paving was uneven, the paintwork peeling; doors never fitted, letting in howling draughts in winter; and roof tiles were missing, so attics were often damp. And then there was the grime from the surrounding factories and from the smoke which belched, blackly, from every chimney.

Some of the inhabitants of the court kept their homes nice and did repairs themselves, but others were feckless, living in conditions of total squalor. Mrs Dickens had always tried to keep herself to herself and Emmy, even as a small child, had known better than to mix with what Mrs Dickens called 'the lower elements', though with Beryl – then Pritchard – as her friend, she had really needed no other.

Beryl was the youngest of a large family, most of whom had left home long before Emmy's birth. Despite the difference in their ages the two girls had always got on well, Beryl being protective towards the blue-eyed, blonde-haired scrap from the first moment Emmy had managed to toddle out into the court, attracted by the presence of so many other children.

'Here we are then, Emmy,' Mrs Dickens said, as the car drew up in front of the church. 'Today you are starting a new life; a wonderful life which will give you all the things you want and deserve. Peter is a fine young man, though I'm afraid his parents think we are . . . rather ordinary, but after seeing you today they'll be bound to realise how very, very special you are. Why, if your father could see you now, his heart would burst with pride.'

The car had halted and the chauffeur came round to open the nearside door for them. One of Peter's fellow officers, clearly deputed for this task, came forward to help the three women out of the car. He was tall and handsome, though not as handsome as Peter, Emmy reminded herself quickly. Peter was six foot tall, with thick, tawny hair and eyes of exactly the same colour. He was very tanned and had a crooked grin which showed off his white teeth, and he had a charm to which most females were susceptible, and an air of command and of knowing exactly what he wanted, which had been lacking in all Emmy's previous admirers.

Walking slowly up to the church, Emmy remembered how they had first met, though it was an uncomfortable recollection, for she had been with Johnny at the time. They had gone to the Daulby Hall, as they often did on a Saturday night, and had been twirling around the floor when a young man had tapped Johnny smartly on the shoulder, given both of them a brilliant smile, and said, 'Excuse me,' in a deep, amused voice. Johnny had opened his mouth to argue – not seriously, just in fun – but by then she was already in the officer's arms. After the 'Excuse me' dance had finished he had asked if he might walk her home, and when she began to explain that she was with Johnny he had suggested she might like to give him her name and address.

She had laughed and complied, and from that moment on she had been swept off her feet into a whirlwind courtship, because Peter had only taken a fortnight's leave of absence and had told her, on their very first date, that he meant to have her promise to marry him before he returned to sea. She had laughed again but had felt her pulses flutter with excitement at this frank avowal and, very soon, Peter filled not only all her time, but all her thoughts as well. He was so romantic, so different from shy, unassuming Johnny. He made her laugh, paid her the prettiest compliments, took her to theatres, and to dances in smart hotels, and invited her to dine in restaurants she had not known existed. He hired a motor car and they had a long weekend touring Wales. Despite having lived in Liverpool all her life, she had never before seen the glories of Snowdonia, or visited the beautiful coastal resorts of North Wales and the Lleyn Peninsula. They had spent the nights in small hotels or guest houses and Peter had been a perfect gentleman, never even kissing her good night when they parted outside their separate rooms.

At the end of his fortnight's leave, as he had promised, Peter asked her to marry him and when she accepted gave her a beautiful sapphire ring because he said the stone was the same colour as her eyes.

Now, Emmy entered the church on her mother's arm with Susie holding up her long, silken train.

Ahead of her she could see Peter, incredibly smart in his uniform, with his best man, Second Officer on board SS *Queen of the South*, standing beside him. Emmy glided forward, reached Peter and turned to smile up at him. It was no longer a dream. This was really happening; the wonderful life which Peter had promised her was about to begin. She handed her bouquet to Susie and just touched Peter's fingers. He gripped her hand warmly, reassuringly, and the two of them moved forward to where the priest in charge waited.

'Dearly beloved, we are gathered together here, in the sight of God, and in the face of this congregation, to join together this man and this woman in holy matrimony, which is an honourable estate . . .'

Emmy listened to the words which would make her Peter's wife in a daze of happiness. He was the best, the nicest man she had ever known and they were going to be the happiest couple in the history of the world. When the time came for her to make her vows, her voice rang out, as clear and confident as his. 'I take thee, Peter Albert, to my wedded husband, to have and to hold from this day forward, for better for worse, for richer for poorer, in sickness and in health, to love, cherish, and to obey, till death us do part, according to God's holy ordinance; and thereto I give thee my troth.'

Peter took the ring from the bible, and placed it on Emmy's finger. 'With this ring I thee wed, with my body I thee worship . . .'

Emmy felt the warm blood steal across her face and, for the first time, she remembered that weddings are followed by parties and parties by honeymoons. Tonight, she and Peter would share not only a room, but a bed. For a whole week, they would live in a smart hotel, sharing everything. Yet now that she thought about it, she had only known Peter for a few short months, and most of that time they had been separated by many miles of ocean. Loving him was all very well, she told herself, but what would living with him be like? They had kissed, and even cuddled, but he had never seen her with her hair hanging loose down her back, never seen her in her brand new white lawn nightgown with its low neckline threaded with pale blue ribbon, and its tiny sleeves made of creamy lace. Heavens, would he expect to see her out of it?

Suddenly, Emmy wanted to turn and run. Peter was wonderful, of course he was, but he was unfamiliar country. His upbringing had been totally different from her own; his parents seemed to despise her own mother, and his home was actually called Epsley Manor and was situated in the village of Epsley, somewhere on the South Downs. She glanced wildly to right and left, aware of the cold of the gold ring on her finger, feeling suddenly lost, alone.

Then the priest ushered them away from the altar and into the vestry where they were to sign the register, Emmy using her maiden name for the last time, and suddenly it was all right. Peter was exuberant, beaming at everyone. His parents were smiling, his mother telling Emmy in a stage whisper that she looked truly beautiful, that Peter was a very lucky man. Peter's father harrumphed and nodded in agreement and Emmy's own mother simply smiled and smiled. Emmy felt proud of her. She was wearing a well-cut grey jacket and matching skirt over a blouse so white and crisp that it dazzled the eye, and the black court shoes on her feet shone like glass.

'Well, Mrs Wesley? How does it feel to be married to my old friend Peter, eh?'

Emmy turned to smile at the speaker. It was Carl Johansson, Peter's best man. She had met him only once before, but with his thick fair hair and slight foreign accent he was impossible to forget. 'It feels wonderful, Mr Johansson,' Emmy said, predictably; after all, he could scarcely have expected her to say anything else and besides, she now realised that it was true. All her silly fears had fled. She might not have known Peter for long but she felt she knew him better than almost anyone else in her life, apart from her mother.

Presently, when all the signing and official business was over, the bridal entourage formed up and re-entered the church to the swelling chorus of the Wedding March. Emmy and Peter began to walk towards the west door, smiling and nodding to friends and relatives as they passed them.

In the very last pew, Johnny Frost sat alone. She thought he was going to ignore her, to continue to stare straight ahead, but at the last moment he turned towards her, giving her a brilliant smile. Beneath his breath, as she drew level, he whispered: 'You look beautiful, queen, and I wish you everything you wish yourself.'

Emmy felt tears prick her eyes but banished them resolutely and whispered, 'Thank you, Johnny,' praying that he had heard her above the crashing chords of the Wedding March. She thought, remorsefully, that she had underrated her old friend; he was kind and generous, for she knew she had treated him badly and did not deserve the forgiveness which was implicit in his words.

But then they were out of the church and into the

June sunshine. Above them the bells were pealing out their message of happiness and hope. All around her were smiling faces and Emmy saw a large group of girls from the big department store in which she worked, friends from school, neighbours from the court . . . even the wife of the butcher who had made all the pies and pasties for the wedding feast, wearing her best blue hat with the feathers, and beaming as though Emmy were her own daughter, instead of just a good customer.

And then they were throwing rice and Peter was pretending to threaten reprisals as it caught in his thick mop of hair and fell down the neck of his uniform jacket. Laughing and shaking the clinging little pieces out of her veil, Emmy climbed into the waiting car and pulled Peter in after her. Everyone else would walk because it was really only a step, but the car would drive three or four times round the block so that everyone could see the bride and groom, and to give everyone involved in the catering a chance to get back to the court and set out the long tables with white paper cloths and all the food and drink to which practically every woman in the court had contributed in some way, though the actual cost had been largely borne by Peter's parents. They had insisted upon paying for ingredients and so on, since they were in no position to help with either shopping or cooking, and Mrs Dickens had been very grateful. It had enabled her to spend some of her carefully hoarded money on kitting her daughter out for married life in a style which, otherwise, would not have been possible. Silk stockings, filmy underwear – including such items as camiknickers and camisoles – drawers decorated with pink and blue ribbon. And there were dresses in poplin and cotton, with the new double sleeve, and a white muslin gown with a long front panel and a pink sash, which would be donned on special occasions. There were pleated skirts and bright woollen jumpers which could be worn under an overall when she was doing her housework, or with some colourful beads, or a scarf round the neck, when entertaining.

'I say, look at that, Emmy!' Peter's voice sounded genuinely delighted. 'They've decorated the arch; doesn't it look grand? They must have done it whilst we were in the church.' Emmy smiled, but said nothing. Peter had not visited the court before going to the church because it was not the done thing, but in fact Emmy had joined practically everyone else to help with the decorating very early that morning. It was June, and flowers were relatively cheap, so the previous evening they had bargained cheerfully with the stallholders and flower ladies in Byrom Street and Clayton Place, and the boys and young men had trekked off into the country – or, more likely, into the local parks – and helped themselves to leafy branches. These, and the flowers, had been fastened on to the grimy brickwork, turning the arch into a thing of real beauty. The flowers and foliage had been sprayed with water so that they would stay fresh, and Emmy knew that the court itself was decorated likewise, with even the poorest families making some sort of show, since everyone, from the oldest grandfather to the youngest child, would partake of the wedding feast.

The car drew to a halt and Emmy and Peter climbed out, Emmy holding up her skirts, for though the court had been cleaned down and whitewashed the pavement outside was as filthy as ever, and she had no desire to walk around for the rest of the day in a gown with a stained hem. Susie, who had arrived well ahead of them, rushed forward to pick up Emmy's long ruched train, and the small procession moved into the court. Beside her, Peter bent his head to whisper into her ear. 'What would have happened, sweetheart, if it had rained? There's far too much food – and far too many people – to cram into any of the houses.'

Emmy giggled. She had wondered the same herself, wondered it many times when she had attended as a guest on similar occasions, but for some reason weddings seemed to be especially blessed, so that even if the sun did not shine, neither did the rain fall. She said as much to Peter, adding that her mother had once told her that the church hall would have to be hired if it rained, which was probably why, when someone in Nightingale Court married, they chose to do so in late spring or summer.

'I see,' Peter said gravely. 'And I thought this weather was a special dispensation from above to show us that God and all his angels think we're doing the right thing.'

Emmy laughed again. 'Who's to say you're not right?' she said, rather challengingly. 'I suppose God – and the priests – must want people to marry instead of living tally, so that's why we get the good weather.'

Peter's eyes widened in pretended surprise. 'Living tally indeed? It's called living in sin where I come from, so don't you forget it, young lady. My mama would be shocked to hear such an expression on your lips.'

Emmy glanced at him suspiciously, not sure whether he was joking or serious, but then her mother came over and led the young couple to a beautiful bower of lilies. 'You must greet your guests now, my dears,' she said instructively. 'And you must introduce everyone to Mr and Mrs Wesley, though Peter will have to perform the introductions for his shipmates, since you can't possibly know them all.'

'They'll just want to meet the pretty girls,' Peter said, grinning. 'Carl, my best man, has already got his eye on Susie.'

But Mrs Dickens had already bustled away to fetch the Wesleys to take their place in the receiving line. The first guests began a rather awkward, shuffling approach, but Peter soon put them at their ease and presently Mr Cubley, who was presiding over the beer barrel, began to hand out foaming mugs of ale and the covers were ripped off the food. Immediately, shyness was forgotten. The adults picked up plates from the pile laid out ready and began to move slowly along the laden table, helping themselves as they went. Soon everyone was seated, the children carrying their plates to the various doorsteps, the adults taking their places on the long wooden benches. Emmy chuckled; the court had been positively raucous until the food was served, but now a comfortable hush fell on the company as they enjoyed the sort of food which was not often seen in Nightingale Court.

She and Peter were seated side by side at the top table, flanked by their parents. On a small separate table stood the wedding cake, a masterpiece of the confectioner's art, all glistening white icing, the purity of it enhanced rather than broken by the miniature bride and groom on the top tier, standing in a bed of sugar flowers. When the meal was over, she and Peter would cut that cake, and after it was eaten and the tables cleared away, the musical trio her mother had engaged would appear and the dancing would begin.

Not that we'll see much of the dancing, because our train leaves from Lime Street Station at three o'clock, Emmy reminded herself. Most brides aren't lucky enough to have a proper honeymoon and just go away for a night somewhere local, but we're off to Llandudno, to stay in a real hotel for a whole week! And then we'll come back to the beautiful house in Lancaster Avenue. She could see it clearly in her head: the tree-lined avenue, the neat little garden, bright with flowers, the gleaming windows and cheery red brick façade, the four well-whited steps leading up to the green-painted front door. Oh, I'm such a lucky girl! Mam said this was the start of a new life and I mean to make it the sort of life I've always dreamed of.

Emmy had looked forward to dancing with Peter, knowing how the skirt of her dress would sway like the bell of a great flower, but the musicians had barely begun to tune their instruments before she had to run up to her room to change for her train journey. Susie, who seemed to be getting on extremely well with one of Peter's fellow officers, offered to accompany her, but Beryl stepped forward, telling Susie that, in the bride's absence, her attendant should start the dancing. 'I'll see to Emmy, same as she saw to me when I were a bride,' she said firmly. Then she turned to her friend. 'It's a shame you can't wear the dress for a while longer, queen, because I've never seen anything lovelier. But there you are, you're having a honeymoon which is more'n most do. Where's you off to now? I forget the name of the resort.'

Emmy, entering her bedroom, shook her head chidingly at her friend. 'Peter said we weren't to tell anyone where we were going or they would be certain to play tricks on us,' she reminded her friend. 'But I'll send you a postcard, Bee, honest to God I will.'

Beryl laughed and began to remove Emmy's head-dress and veil, draping the veil over a coat hanger and placing it carefully in the wardrobe. Then she undid the dozens of tiny buttons which fastened the bride's dress from the nape of her neck to her hips, and began easing it off. Emmy stepped out of the froth of lace and silk and began to put on the pale blue muslin dress, the long, white, elbow-length gloves, and the smart little shoes in blue kid, which she had bought from Blackler's only a week before. Then she sat down and began to unpin her hair, brush it out and coil it into a big, soft chignon at the base of her neck. Beryl tutted disapprovingly and took over, smoothing the hair back from her friend's face until not a strand was loose, and then settling the gold straw hat with its wreath of blue cornflowers on Emmy's head. 'I'm going to miss you like anything, queen,' she said heavily. 'D'you realise, we've never been apart since you could toddle? And now you're going away and leaving me, Wally and Charlie and—well, you're leaving us behind,' she finished, rather awkwardly.

Absorbed as she was at this moment by her own affairs, Emmy still heard the hesitation in Beryl's voice. She had been examining her reflection critically in the small mirror, but now she swung round to face her friend. 'Oh, Beryl, you're expecting another baby!' she said, and, realising that it had sounded like an accusation, hastily added: 'Isn't that just wonderful? I'm so happy for you, queen. Can I be godmother?'

She was watching Beryl's face as she spoke and

saw the anxious, defensive look melt into a beam of pure pleasure. 'Oh, Em, I'm so glad you're pleased. The baby's due in a couple of months which is another reason why I wouldn't be your matron-of-honour. Folk think it's just fat, but it's really the baby. My mam were quite cross; said there were enough of us in the house already and she could do without a second bawling brat. But our Charlie's nearly two, and we thought it were time he had a little brother or sister. As for being a godmother, who else would I choose?'

'Well? I know you're all packed, but are you ready, dear? The car to take you to the station arrived a few minutes ago and you don't want to miss that train!' It was Mrs Dickens, very flushed in the face, with her elegant hat tipped rather further forward than it should have been and a sausage roll in one hand. Emmy leaned down and kissed her cheek. 'Yes, I'm ready,' she said, a trifle breathlessly. 'Oh, Mam, now that the time has come to leave I feel sad and . . . well, lonely, in a way. I wish you were coming to Llandudno with us.'

Her mother gave her arm a consoling pat and Beryl uttered a crow of delight. 'Llandudno! Me and Wally will gerron a train an' come and visit you. We'll bring a heap o' rice an' chuck it all over you so's everyone'll know you're newly-weds. Oh, an' we'll tie tin cans to your wedding car . . . I guess Wally's doin' that this minute, come to think of it.'

Emmy clapped her hands to her hot cheeks. 'Oh, don't let on I've given the game away,' she said imploringly. 'I never meant to say a word, honest to God I didn't.'

Beryl laughed and gave her a squeeze. 'Don't you fret yourself, chuck,' she said kindly. 'Off with you now; it may be tradition to keep the bridegroom waiting, but trains stick to their timetable, no matter what.' She picked up Emmy's suitcase as she spoke and the three of them headed down the stairs.

'Be good, an' if you can't be good, be careful,' Beryl shrieked after them, as the hired car drew away from the kerb, the tins clattering behind it.

'An' may all your troubles be little ones,' someone else bawled. 'Oh, don't I wish I were you, Peter Wesley, you lucky sod.'

Emmy laughed but Peter looked a trifle tight-lipped, though he had begun to relax once more by the time the car drew up outside Lime Street Station. He hurried Emmy on to the concourse, scarcely giving her time to glance around, for they only had five minutes to catch their train. But something made Emmy look to her left. There was Johnny, leaning against a sooty brick wall, smiling at her, as a group of other young men, all in uniform, rushed forward and began to pelt them with more rice.

'What a send-off,' Peter gasped, as the two of them sank on to the plush seats of a first-class carriage. 'I don't suppose there's much point in trying to get rid of this rice before the train leaves the station, because—'

Even as he spoke, he was proved right. A long arm reached through the half-open window, opening it fully, and then handful upon handful of rice showered into the carriage. Emmy thought, apprehensively, that the young officers were going to get inside as well, for one of them, red-faced and obviously the worse for drink, kept shouting that he had not yet kissed the bride and what was a wedding if one did not kiss the bride at least once on her wedding day. But whilst he was still fumbling with the handle, the train began to move and his friends dragged him away. Peter went across and pulled the strap which closed the window, then turned back to Emmy, smiling ruefully. 'I might have guessed they'd follow us to the station,' he said. 'But now we can settle ourselves down for a bit of peace and quiet before we reach our destination. Would you like to take off your coat and hat? Only it's quite warm in here.'

Obeying, Emmy removed the garments and placed them carefully on the string rack overhead. They had the carriage to themselves – it was not a corridor train – so she settled back in one corner and put her feet up, smiling with as much gaiety as she could muster at her new husband. But in the back of her mind there was a little niggle of discontent. Johnny had come to the station but he had neither thrown rice nor taken any part in the boisterous horseplay of the young officers. Emmy thought that he might have at least pretended to be cheerful, have accepted that she was happily marrying someone else, for she was sure his disappointment and misery must have been as obvious to everyone else as they were to her. But I won't feel guilty, she told herself defiantly, turning her head to look out of the window at the June countryside flashing past. I know Johnny believed I'd marry him, one day, but I never actually said I would and anyhow, what I felt for Johnny was more like sisterly love. The way I feel about Peter is the real thing, so it would be nice if Johnny could accept defeat graciously, instead of trying to make me feel guilty.

'Penny for your thoughts?' Peter's voice held just a hint of impatience. Clearly, he had noticed her silence and did not think it appropriate.

Emmy wrenched her mind away from Johnny and

smiled, brilliantly, at Peter. 'I was wishing we'd been able to have just one dance,' she said wistfully, though untruthfully. 'It was a shame we had to leave before the musicians had even struck up.'

Peter leaned across and kissed her lightly, but lingeringly. 'Never mind, sweetheart,' he said gently. 'I promise you we'll have years and years ahead of us and we'll dance through all of them.'

Chapter Two

'Isn't she just the most beautiful thing?' Peter Wesley bent over the cot and gazed, lovingly, at its tiny occupant.

Emmy, propped up by lacy pillows and still pale from her ordeal, smiled mistily across at her husband. It was the end of March; she had experienced nine months of marriage and now she was the mother of the tiny, dark-haired girl who lay in the cradle at the foot of the bed, gazing up at the ceiling with round eyes whose intense blueness was already beginning to turn brown.

'She's a good baby, or has been so far, and naturally I think she's extremely beautiful,' Emmy murmured. She did not add, as she might have done, that she had been in labour for three days, had had a horrendous time, and had already decided that her first child would be her last. After all, Peter had insisted that she should give birth in one of the most expensive nursing homes in Liverpool. He had showered her with attention, buying the best of everything, and equipping the small bedroom at the house in Lancaster Avenue with all a child could desire. Unfortunately, he had been at sea when the baby had been born, but as soon as SS *Queen of the South* docked he had come hurrying to her side, his arms full of spring flowers, chocolates and a bottle of champagne, which he said she should drink to keep her strength up.

Her mother told her constantly that Peter was the best husband any girl could have and Emmy knew she was right. She lacked for nothing and nor would their child, though it had upset her when, a few days after their return from their honeymoon, he had told her he did not wish her to revisit Nightingale Court. 'Your mother won't be there very much longer since she's moving in with us,' he had reminded her. 'And your friends, people like Susie and Beryl, will be welcome here at any time. But I think it best if you keep away from the court, my darling, because some of the people living there are very – very . . .'

'Common?' Emmy had suggested, with a rather sharp note in her voice. 'Is that what you're trying to say, Peter? Because if so, you might remember that Mam and myself . . .'

But Peter had denied it vehemently, assuring her that he had been going to say 'strange', and this, of course, Emmy could not deny. The Telfords, a large and feckless family who had just moved into the court, were already heartily disliked. The children were dirty and rude, and though one occasionally saw a man entering or leaving the house, it seldom seemed to be the same one. Then there were others, all of them pretty strange when you came to think about it: Mrs Evans, who sang, tunelessly, beneath her breath all the time; old Mr Perkins – Beryl's ancient grandfather – who never left his house; and Miss Cardew, who kept ten scrawny cats, seven budgerigars, and a large, grey parrot whose vocabulary consisted of evil words learned, his owner claimed, from 'those nasty sailors'.

So instead of being angry with him, Emmy had been forced to admit that he was right, though she had not liked his prohibition. 'There are strange people everywhere,' she had declared. 'Captain Marriott up the road is pretty strange. He's got a telescope set up in his front bedroom and watches us all through it. And Mrs Ingham's maid, Mollie, says he wolf-whistles when she's hanging out the washing, because she shows a bit of petticoat and rather a lot of leg, reaching up, you know.'

Peter had guffawed but said that this was simply typical of an old sea-dog and not strange at all and Emmy had decided that the argument was not worth pursuing. After all, she had no real desire to revisit the court, and much preferred that her friends should come to Lancaster Avenue, where they would be impressed by the house and would enjoy her generous hospitality, for Peter gave her a great deal of housekeeping money and instructed her to buy nothing but the best and to apply to him at once should she ever find herself short.

'She's awake, you know; is it all right if I pick her up? Only I don't want some nurse rushing in and telling me off,' Peter said, breaking into Emmy's reverie. 'I say, isn't she tiny?'

Emmy felt affronted. She remembered the struggle of giving birth to a child who had seemed the size of a prize-fighter and shook her head violently. 'No she is not tiny,' she said firmly. 'She weighed over eight pounds when she was born, Peter, and since she guzzles and guzzles every four hours – sometimes more often – I should think she probably weighs a stone by now.'

Peter laughed indulgently and scooped the child's tiny form up in his arms. 'I say you're perfect, little Diana Sophia,' he said adoringly. 'Who's Daddy's precious girl, then?'

Emmy had been lying back on her pillows,

dreamily contemplating father and child, delighted to realise that Peter was going to be a marvellous father, but at his words she shot upright. 'Diana Sophia?' she squeaked. 'But – but I've been calling her Gertrude – Gertie for short – after my mam. I thought you said I could choose any name I liked. You said if it were a boy, it would be different.'

Peter bent and placed the baby in the curve of his wife's arm. 'Does she look like a Gertrude?' he demanded. 'Or like a Gertie, for that matter? No, no, my love, she's far too beautiful to be called after anyone other than a goddess.'

Emmy leaned back on her pillows again. Secretly, she thought he was right. Diana was a lovely name and she had already more or less decided that Gertrude was both too long and too old-fashioned to suit her little daughter. She had toyed with giving the child a short, modern name – Sarah, or Julia – followed by Gertrude, knowing how this would please her mother. Now, however, she looked suspiciously up at Peter. 'Well, all right, if you're really keen on the name Diana we'll call her that, but just tell me where you found the goddess Sophia? Because I'm sure I've never heard of one.'

Peter laughed again, though a trifle uneasily. 'Actually, it's my mama's name,' he admitted. 'I thought it would do no harm to keep in with my parents because, in the nature of things, they aren't going to see much of their grandchild.'

'Their only grandchild!' Emmy corrected, looking fondly down at her daughter's mossy head.

There was a short silence, then Peter spoke. 'Well, actually, no, she isn't their only grandchild,' he said, half apologetically. 'I've a younger brother, Ralph. He and his wife Josephine have a little boy who will be a year old any time now. They live with my parents; the house has been properly divided so that the two families don't have to share any of the amenities. Have I never mentioned Ralph before?'

Emmy stared very hard at him, noting the flush which stained his cheekbones and his unwillingness to meet her eyes. 'You know very well you haven't,' she said accusingly. 'Why didn't they come to the wedding? And your mam . . . I mean your mama . . . never said a word, either.'

'No. Well, I suppose she wouldn't,' Peter said. 'Ralph and I fell out badly years ago; we've not seen one another since then. I didn't send him an invitation to the wedding because I knew very well he wouldn't come; in fact, I did wonder whether Mama and Papa would turn up – they took Ralph's side, the same as they always have – so you can imagine, I was jolly pleased when they came after all, and even more pleased that they approved of you.'

Emmy thought for a few minutes, then spoke carefully. 'Is – is that why you don't go home any more, Peter? I've been hoping that you would take the baby and me down to Southampton the next time you get some leave, though you've never suggested it. I suppose it's awkward with your brother and his wife sharing the house, but if it's been properly divided . . . well, it would be nice to see where you were brought up.'

Peter smiled at her, the anxious look clearing for a moment. 'Oh, I'm sure that can be arranged, my darling,' he said easily. 'After all, Ralph and I are both married now and we both have children. I'm sure we'll get along fine, the way we used to when we were boys, once we all meet up again.'

'Lovely,' Emmy said contentedly. The baby in her

arms began to whimper and thresh about. 'Oh dear, she's hungry; I'd best feed her.' She pulled her nightie aside as she spoke and guided the child's eager mouth to the nipple, continuing to talk, though she had to raise her voice above the enthusiastic sucking sounds. 'What exactly did you row over, Peter? It must have been a pretty dreadful quarrel to have kept you away from home for so long.'

'Oh, it's easy to see you don't have brothers, my love. Brothers can quarrel over almost anything, like a couple of young stags, locking horns over who will get to eat the best grass. Ralph has a jealous nature, always has had, and resented everything my parents did for me. He works in the family business, you see, but I chose to follow my Uncle Reg, who went to sea as a young man, and rose to be captain of an ocean liner. Seeing that I was getting nothing from the business, the parents gave me a pretty handsome lump sum and Ralph . . . well, he showed his resentment, accused me of battening on Mama and Papa . . . I'm afraid I hit him, he hit me back, and from that moment on we kept away from each other.'

'Aren't boys and girls different?' Emmy said wonderingly, holding her little daughter even closer. 'I know I'm an only child, but Beryl has been like a sister to me all my life. Oh, we fell out sometimes, and in school I had a fight or two with my pal Peggy, but it never turned nasty, if you get my meaning.'

'Yes, but as you've already pointed out, neither Beryl nor Peggy is your sister,' Peter said sharply. 'Ralph is four years younger than me and spoilt rotten, if you want the truth. Mama always says that she nearly lost him when he was two years old and got a bad attack of croup, but whatever the reason,

Ralph has *always* got his own way; not usually, or sometimes, but always.'

'That's very hard, certainly,' Emmy said slowly. 'But you will take me to visit them, won't you, darling? And then I'm sure you and Ralph will find all the old resentment and jealousies have disappeared. Why, it will be lovely for me to have a brother and sister, and even lovelier for Diana to have a boy cousin.'

Peter was beginning to assure her that they would visit the family home as soon as Diana was old enough to take the long journey south, when a nurse popped her head round the door. 'Did you change Baby's nappy before you started to feed her, Mrs Wesley?' she asked, rather accusingly. 'Baby should be dry and comfortable before she is offered a feed.'

Flushing guiltily, Emmy admitted that she had not yet changed Baby's nappy, and when this task was done and the nurse had left them, Peter began to talk about fetching Mrs Dickens in a taxi, so that she could spend an hour or so with her daughter. 'And then I'll take her out somewhere really nice for lunch,' he said expansively. 'You'd like me to do that, wouldn't you, my dear?'

Emmy agreed, realising that the moment for questioning Peter about his brother and their quarrel had passed. But what did it matter, after all? It had taken him a long time to unburden himself to her, but now that it had happened she was sure there would be no more secrets. She said as much to Peter just as he was preparing to leave her and he stopped, with his hand on the doorknob, to say laughingly: 'My darling, I would never keep a secret from you. We must share everything, always.'

After he had been gone ten minutes, it occurred

to Emmy that his last remark was meaningless. He *had* kept a secret from her, doing so quite deliberately, though she was still not sure exactly why he had let her believe him to be an only child. But I'll find out, she told herself, snuggling down the bed again. When he takes me to Southampton, I shall jolly well ask Peter's mama, or perhaps his sister-in-law Josephine, what's really behind the rift between the brothers. She let her mind play with several conjectures but then slid, easily, into sleep and did not wake until the nurse came in with her lunch tray.

When Emmy answered the front door, she was delighted to find Beryl and her two small sons on the doorstep, whilst the baby, Beryl's little daughter, slumbered in the big, old-fashioned pram. She had dropped Beryl a note a week ago, suggesting that her friend should call, and now she ushered them inside, then sent the older children to play with the two-year-old Diana in the garden, and parked the pram under an apple tree. It was a lovely day in early May and Diana was delighted to see the visitors. She thought Charlie, who was five, almost grown up, and joined in the boys' games with great gusto whenever they came to call.

'I'll put the kettle on,' Emmy said eagerly, pulling Beryl into the kitchen, where they could sit on the tall stools and watch the children as they played. 'I'm so glad you could come, Bee, because I've got a bit of a problem. It's more than two years since Peter told me he had a brother, and almost three since he last saw his parents, but every time I suggest we might visit his relatives, he comes up with another scheme – a week in Llandudno, or Southport, a trip to Blackpool Zoo, even a week in the Lake District. What do you think I should do?'

'I think you should dig your heels in,' Beryl said frankly. 'He's a grand feller, your Peter. I weren't too sure at first if you were doin' the right thing, queen, 'cos you and young Johnny Frost seemed made for each other, just about. But I soon saw I were wrong. In a way, Johnny and you were more like brother and sister; I reckon you knew each other too well for a marriage to succeed. By the way, did you know Johnny were courtin'? He met some girl when he were on his holidays and brought her back to introduce her to his folks. I think her name's Rhian. She's really nice. She's norra bit like you, queen, she's dark an' rather dumpy, but she's very lively, always laughing; just right for Johnny, in fact.'

'That's wonderful; I hope they'll be very happy, just like Peter and me,' Emmy said. She found, to her slight surprise, that she meant every word. Johnny had been a good friend, but she realised now that she had never really loved him, whereas she loved Peter with all her heart. Everything she did, she did to please him, and best of all was the way he treated Diana. He was a marvellous father, always ready to play games or tell stories, yet he was also firm. When he denied Diana something, it was for the right reasons, and unlike Emmy herself, who could be relied upon to change her mind, any decision he made would be final. Emmy admired this in Peter, knowing how he idolised the child, and how comparatively brief was his time with her. She herself hated saying no to their daughter, even when she knew it was the correct thing to do.

So now she was able to say gaily: 'If you see Johnny

do pass on my best wishes, Bee. Is he still working at the brewery?'

Beryl shook her head. 'No, he took a white-collar job in the shipping offices some while ago, but I believe they're going to move away from Liverpool. Old Mrs Frost told me that Rhian's first language is Welsh, so they'll mebbe move over the border if they get married. But what on earth are we doing, talking about Johnny Frost, when you wanted to know whether you should press Peter to visit his mam and dad? I say you should, and the sooner the better.' She gave her friend an affectionate hug. 'You're too soft, young Emmy – you always were. Say you want to visit your mama and papa-in-law and stick to your guns. He loves you ever so much, queen; you've only got to look at him to realise that. He'll not deny you when he sees you're in earnest.'

The trip to visit her in-laws was actually arranged, when tragedy intervened. Mrs Dickens had moved into the house in Lancaster Avenue, as planned. Peter had had one of the bedrooms converted into a bed-sitting room so his mother-in-law could make her meals in her own room should she wish to do so, although in actual fact both Emmy and her mother were far happier sharing the kitchen and chattering away as they worked. When Peter was at home, Mrs Dickens tried to spend more time in her own room, or went and visited old friends in Nightingale Court, but for the most part she and Emmy shared both the work and the fun of looking after Diana.

It was a pleasant, October day, with the leaves on the apple tree outside the window beginning to change colour. Emmy, gazing absently out as she washed up the porridge saucepan, thought that she ought to begin to pick the fruit. She would store it on trays, so that they could have their own apples when Christmas came. Mam will give an eye to Diana whilst I work, she told herself, but if I don't do it now the apples will all have fallen by the time we get back from Epsley Manor.

It was only then that she realised that she had not heard a sound from her mother's room. Mrs Dickens was usually an early riser, but she had visited old friends the previous day and had come in late. She's having a lie-in, Emmy told herself. Diana was two and a half now, old enough to be left, securely strapped in her high chair, whilst she polished off a plateful of porridge, liberally sprinkled with brown sugar, so Emmy set off for the stairs. At the head of them, she tapped lightly on Mrs Dicken's door, then opened it. She was smiling as she entered the room, thinking that she had caught her mother out. The older woman always claimed that she was a light sleeper who took little pleasure in her bed and much preferred to be up and about. Now, however, it seemed that she had given way to temptation and was actually enjoying an extra hour between the sheets.

However, if anyone had earned a rest, Emmy knew it was her mother, who had worked hard all her life. Indeed, it was only since she had moved into Lancaster Avenue that things had been easier for her, so Emmy decided not to tease her but went straight to the window and pulled back the curtains, turning to say cheerfully, but softly: 'You must have been tired, Mam, because you've actually overslept! I couldn't believe it when I found myself first down until I remembered how late you came in last night. If it were me, you'd say I was burning the candle at both ends, but—'

She stopped speaking abruptly. The small figure in the bed had not moved, and all in a moment Emmy knew, with dreadful certainty, that her mother would never move again.

It was at the funeral tea that Emmy met Johnny Frost's young lady for the first time. The other girl was much as Beryl had described her, but she was also extremely pretty. She had large brown eyes fringed with very long lashes, a small, straight little nose, and the whitest teeth Emmy had ever seen. She clung to Johnny's arm when he brought her over to introduce her to Emmy, but she soon lost her shyness and chatted away as though they had known one another all their lives.

'Your mam was ever so nice,' she confided. 'Johnny and me is savin' up and won't be able to get married until we can afford a place of our own, so when I come to visit him I stay with Mrs Jones in Nightingale Court. Your mam was really good to Mrs J.; she'd come in at least once a week to do any marketin' that the old lady wanted an' she'd always tidy round and cook up a big batch of scones or fruit loaf so Mrs J. had something to offer folk who popped in. But I expect you know all this, Mrs Wesley.'

'Yes, my mother had a good many friends in the court. It's odd, really. She longed and longed to move out because it's such a dark and dismal place, but I think she missed her friends dreadfully.'

Rhian laughed. 'Aye, she used to say that all you got in the court was two penn'orth of sky,' she said. 'And isn't it true? I made Johnny promise we'd never live in such a place, no matter what. I'm a country girl, used to fresh air and a bit of space around me, and I do like to feel the sun on my face. But I suppose you have to take what you can get in a great big city like this. And you and Mr Wesley have got a beautiful house.'

Despite the fact that she had always despised Nightingale Court, Emmy felt she should ruffle up in its defence. But before she could open her mouth, Johnny had joined them. He took Emmy's hand, giving it a gentle squeeze before letting it go. 'Em, I'm that sorry,' he said earnestly. 'Your mam were a lovely lady, always thinking of others. And she wasn't so very old, either. She'll be greatly missed.'

'She was sixty-three,' Emmy said. 'She and my father had given up hope of having a child when I was born. But you're right, Johnny. Everyone who knew her loved her and – and I don't know how I'll go on without her.'

Later that day, when everyone had left, Peter asked Emmy if he should try for a shore job. 'The money won't be so good, or the prospects, but if you'd prefer it, my love . . .'

'I wouldn't dream of being so selfish,' Emmy said quickly, 'but it's awfully generous of you to suggest it, darling Peter. Of course I'm going to miss Mam horribly, but it's something I have to face.'

Peter said no more, but next day he went out on some mysterious errand and came back to proudly announce that he had secured the services of a maidservant. 'Her name's Lucy Waters and she'll live in,' he told Emmy. 'She's sixteen years old and she struck me as being a bit old-fashioned but very dependable. She's moving in the day after tomorrow, so you won't be on your own for long, my darling.'

'Oh, Peter, you're so good to me,' Emmy gasped, though she was not at all sure that she wanted a live-in maidservant. But, on the other hand, Peter was leaving next day and without her mother's constant companionship and support, she knew she would find it very hard to manage. She looked shyly up at him. 'When will we go to see your parents now? I know you must have written to tell them what had happened and why we had had to delay our visit, but did you make any plans for your next leave?'

'I telephoned them,' Peter said briefly. 'It may well be some while before I get sufficient leave to take you into Hampshire, my love, but as soon as it can be arranged, I'll see to it.'

All Emmy could do was acquiesce, but she was beginning to wonder whether she would ever visit Epsley Manor and the rest of the Wesley family. And if he's really reluctant, I suppose I shouldn't insist, she told herself. This time, I won't ask again. I'll simply wait to be told, and hope that it won't take too long to arrange.

As soon as Lucy Waters walked into the house, Emmy knew that Peter had been right, as usual. Lucy might be young, but she was everything that Emmy could have asked. Being young meant that she was happy to play with Diana, to take her to the park and to spend time with her, yet she never neglected her household duties. She told Emmy, frankly, that she had done very little cooking, but she was a quick learner and had soon taken most of the kitchen work into her small, capable hands. Emmy had not realised how much her mother had done. All the baking, for a start, a great deal of the cleaning, and more than her share of cooking, bottling fruit and making jam. Now, Lucy took on such tasks easily. This was particularly helpful when Peter was home because it freed Emmy to spend more time with him and of course it also meant that Lucy could keep an eye on Diana whilst her parents took a taxi into the city centre to visit the theatre, cinema, or some other place of entertainment.

'She's a treasure,' Emmy murmured on the first night of Peter's next leave as they lay, entwined, in their bed. 'I know she's young, but she doesn't seem it, somehow. She's very responsible. Is that why you chose her?'

'Yes, I suppose it must have been,' Peter said dreamily. 'It certainly wasn't for her looks!'

Emmy thought of Lucy up to her elbows in suds, her small, freckled face streaked with perspiration, her mousy hair damp with it. When she had first joined them, Emmy had marvelled at the girl's strength, for she was thin and stringy, weighing a good stone less than Emmy herself, though they were the same height; but now she realised that the girl was still growing and would probably get both taller and heavier before she reached maturity. She said as much to Peter, reminding him, rather sharply, that since one should not judge a book by its cover, one should not condemn a girl simply because she did not happen to be pretty. But Peter made no reply, and Emmy realised that he was fast asleep.

Chapter Three
July 1925

It was a brilliant day. Emmy had woken Diana early so that they could be in Nightingale Court in good time to pick up the Fisher family for their trip to New Brighton, as it was a fairly long journey. What was more, they would be taking a picnic lunch with them – though they would buy a teapot, and some lemonade for the kids, when they reached the resort – so she needed time to pack everything into her wicker basket and then to get the bathing things and any other seaside equipment organised before they left. It was Lucy's day off, which was why Emmy had chosen it. Normally, Lucy would have accompanied them, but today she and a friend were taking the overhead railway as far as it would go, and then tramping into the countryside. Lucy was looking forward to her day out enormously so it had seemed only sensible to Emmy that the suggested visit to New Brighton, with the Fishers, should be on the same day.

Emmy sang to herself as she moved around her sunny, well-equipped kitchen, preparing for the day ahead. She was in a happy mood, not only because she and Beryl were taking their children for a day at the seaside, but because in two days' time her dearest Peter would be home once more.

Emmy's thoughts were interrupted by the sound of the back door being thrust open and Diana's small body appearing in the aperture. 'I got the stuff you asked me to buy from Cubbon's, Mammy,' the child said breathlessly. She was lugging a shopping basket, using both hands, but a triumphant smile lit up her face. 'You said to get a dozen currant buns and a box of iced fancies. And I went to Mr Mayor's and bought the Smith's Crisps, the ones with little blue screws of salt in them, and half a pound of humbugs. And here's your change.' She had dumped the bag on the kitchen floor, and now produced a small purse from the pocket of her little pink dress and spread the money out carefully on the kitchen table. 'There you are! I went to Mr Wetherby's and you always say he's an honest man, but he writ down the prices anyway, so's you can see I wasn't cheated.'

'Thank you, sweetheart,' Emmy said gaily, giving her little daughter a hug. Diana's thick, shining brown hair was fashionably bobbed, and her pink gingham dress was stylishly low-waisted. She wore neat white socks and patent leather strap shoes, and Emmy loved her to bits. She and Peter wanted more children but it was a side of their marriage which they seldom discussed. Emmy knew Peter 'took precautions' because he did not want her exhausted by childbearing, but he had said, last time he was home on leave, that once Diana was in school, it might be time to think about providing her with a brother or sister. Emmy was none too keen to repeat the experience of giving birth, but she always went along with Peter's suggestions and agreed with him that it would be nice for their daughter to have a brother or sister.

'Mammy! If you stand there dreaming, we'll never get to Nightingale Court, let alone New Brighton! Gerra move on!'

Emmy jumped and hastily continued wrapping sandwiches in greaseproof paper and packing them into the large wicker basket. Diana was very like Peter; both father and daughter tended to give orders and expected instant obedience. However, Emmy did not mean to be ordered about by a five-year-old and said dampingly: 'Don't you let me hear you talk like that, my girl, or you'll get a slap you won't forget in a hurry. It's "get a move on", not "gerra move on". What do you think your Daddy would say if he heard you talking like that?'

Diana put a thin little hand over her mouth but her round, tawny eyes gleamed with mischief and she clearly did not fear the threatened smack. 'He'd say, "That's Nightingale Court talk,"' she said brightly. 'So since we're going to Nightingale Court just as soon as you finish packing those sandwiches, I don't see as it matters.'

Despite herself, Emmy smiled back. She thought Diana had a point. When in Nightingale Court Diana, like herself, used the other language and since Peter was never around to disapprove, for he never accompanied them to the court, she supposed that the pair of them would continue to do so. However, she had no intention of being beaten, if only verbally, by her daughter. 'That's all very well, but at this moment you're in Lancaster Avenue, so just you behave accordingly,' she said severely. 'Now run upstairs, there's a dear, and fetch me down your bathing costume and the big blue and white striped towel. And if you want to take a bucket and spade, you'd better fetch them too.'

'Right, Mammy,' Diana said, trotting towards the door. 'Shall I fetch your cozzie as well?'

Emmy laughed, but shook her head, though a trifle regretfully. She could do a splashy and rather ineffective breast stroke which Peter had taught her, thinking it shocking that any girl living alongside the Mersey with the Leeds and Liverpool Canal close by should be unable to swim, but she was no expert, and was only prepared to enter the water when Peter was close at hand to prevent a catastrophe. 'No thanks, darling. Your Aunty Beryl can't swim, so the pair of us will hire nice comfy deckchairs and watch you kids splashing in and out of the waves. Hurry now!'

Beryl Fisher gazed around at the golden sand and the happy crowds, searching idly for Charlie, Lenny, Becky and baby Bobby. All her children were bright except for Becky who, Beryl had had to accept sadly, was not quite the same as other four-year-olds. She could not eat with a spoon and her speech was poor, her vocabulary small. The older boys were aware of this and always kept an eye out for Becky, willingly helping her when she needed it, although they themselves were as self-willed and independent as they could possibly be, having decided to take after their father, Beryl concluded. Wally Fisher was nothing if not independent, and took it for granted that his kids could look after themselves, but he was the kindest man Beryl knew; it was the reason she had married him. Like Emmy's husband, Wally had been at sea, but on his marriage to Beryl he had managed to get a job in Higson's brewery in Stanhope Street. He did not earn the sort of money which would have enabled him to rent anything more expensive than No. 4 Nightingale Court, nor did it allow his wife to remain at home all day, looking after the children. Beryl cleaned in a big store three nights a week and took in washing for several establishments – restaurants, boarding houses and small cafés – who wanted linen cheaply laundered. At twenty-nine she knew, without rancour, that she looked at least ten years older than Emmy, possibly even a little more. She loved and understood Wally, though marriage to him had had its difficult moments. Sober, he was a decent enough feller, but when he had a few bevvies inside him he could do a lot of damage, though always without meaning to do so. He had never touched a hair of her head in anger, would have been shocked at the mere thought of hurting a child. Even their scruffy mongrel, Bones, had never fled the house when Wally was drunk, though he did hide under the table as Wally lurched around, breaking anything he tripped over and setting fire to his own eyebrows in his attempts to light up a Woodbine. On one occasion, he had put his foot clean through the coke hod when trying to make up the fire, and had clumped round looking like a man in one iron boot, apparently oblivious of the strange appendage attached to his right leg. However, it had been several years since Wally had come home drunk. No man with four children could afford to drink more than a pint or two if he meant to see them decently fed.

Wally and Beryl were both large but Wally was a good six inches taller than she, and at least five stone heavier, so it was a real blessing, Beryl often thought, that he was not a violent man. It was also a blessing, though Wally did not always agree, that Granny Pritchard, Beryl's seventy-five-year-old mother, lived with them. She contributed her tiny pension to household expenses, only keeping back a few pennies for her own use, and without her to look after the children, Beryl did not know how the Fisher family would have managed. Neighbours were always kind but there was no doubt that the young Fishers were a bit of a handful. Even Granny Pritchard sometimes complained that they were more inventive than the devil himself, and they minded her more than they minded most since she had been a part of their lives for as long as any of them, even Charlie, could remember.

Still, Granny Pritchard was having a rest today, Beryl thought, gazing dreamily to where her four and little Diana were building what they boastfully announced would be the biggest sandcastle in the world. And she and Emmy were having a rest too, leaning back in their comfortable deckchairs with nothing whatsoever to do until it was time to eat their carry-out, and even that had cost her no trouble today, since Emmy had provided all the food and intended to pay for the drinks they would fetch later.

Beryl glanced sideways at her friend and saw that Emmy's lids were drooping. Apparently, doing nothing all day could be almost as tiring as working every hour God sent, Beryl thought, without bitterness. Right from the moment that Mrs Dickens had asked the young Beryl to keep an eye on Emmy – had actually paid her a few coppers to do so – she had loved the younger girl, admiring her pretty looks, her beautiful clothing and her sweet, affectionate nature. Even now, when they were both married women with children, she felt no envy of her friend and understood why Peter did not wish his wife to visit Nightingale Court. One glance at Emmy's frail beauty and one wanted to protect her, and though the majority of those living in Nightingale Court were simply the victims of poverty, doing their best to rear families and feed themselves on hopelessly inadequate wages, there were others whose fights and physical violence often disturbed the night-time peace.

Emmy stretched, yawned, and turned towards her friend. The sun had brought the faintest flush of rose to her cheeks and she looked even prettier than usual, Beryl thought affectionately. And of course, she would be getting excited because Peter's ship, SS *Queen of the South*, would be docking in a couple of days. But right now, Emmy's large blue eyes turned towards her friend and she spoke dreamily, as though she really had been almost asleep. 'Beryl? D'you fancy a cup of tea? It's a bit early to start on our picnic but there's a café on the prom where we could watch the kids and get ourselves a drink at the same time. Charlie's a real good little feller; he'll keep an eye on the others for twenty minutes or so.'

Beryl realised that she'd been feeling thirsty for some time and sat up straighter. 'That's a bleedin' good idea, Em,' she said, beginning to struggle out of her deckchair. 'I'll tell Charlie not to let the others mess around while you an' me have a cuppa. Not that much harm can come to 'em now, not with the tide out.'

The two women gathered their belongings into a neat pile and pulled the deckchairs close, then went and spoke to the children. The younger ones scarcely looked up, but Charlie said at once that the construction of the castle would keep them occupied whilst his mam and Aunt Emmy were gone. 'An' we won't start a-fillin' of the moat until you're back, 'specially as there's only me can carry a full bucket – an' there's only one bucket – so it'll be a long job,' he said cheerfully. 'When we've ate our carry-out and drunk the lemonade, we can use the bottles to fetch water as well as the bucket, but until then I'll keep 'em out o' the sea, don't you worrit yourselves.'

Emmy and Beryl smiled at one another as they

made their way across the golden sand towards the prom. 'He's a good lad, our Charlie,' Beryl said contentedly, as they took their places at a rickety table outside the small café. 'He'll keep them out of mischief until we're back.'

By mid-afternoon, the tide had come in and the wonderful castle, which had taken them all morning to complete, was disappearing fast beneath the little, white-topped waves. Diana watched it go gleefully. It had been an enormous task just to finish it in time; they had watched the moat fill and had danced a war dance round it, though by then little Bobby had gone to sleep in his mother's arms, so it had been herself, Charlie, Lenny and Becky who had watched the moat fill, had known that all their efforts had been worthwhile. Becky was a year younger than Diana, and this was fortunate because Diana's clothes, when outgrown, fitted Becky nicely. At this moment, she was clad in a blue cotton dress patterned with white daisies, and Diana had to keep reminding herself not to say, wistfully, that it had been her very favourite dress, because Mammy said it was rude to remind someone that their dress was second-hand.

Diana did not see the sense of this and was sure that Becky wouldn't mind at all if the dress was as old as the hills or just purchased from Lewis's, so long as it was pretty and comfortable. But Mammy was strict about such things so Diana never said a word about the blue dress, though she had not been able to resist spreading out her pink gingham skirt and remarking that she would probably have outgrown it by the following summer. Her mammy had given her a very sharp glance indeed, but Aunty

Beryl had merely remarked, placidly, that she wished Becky would take more care of her clothes, as Diana did, and the talk had changed to other things.

'Well, that's the last of our castle.' It was Charlie's voice, near Diana's ear, and she turned to grin at him, then tucked her pink skirt inside her white knickers and waded into the water, kicking at the remains of the castle until there was nothing left for the little waves to gobble up.

'Yes, it's all gone now,' she admitted. 'What'll we do next, Charlie?'

Charlie considered this, his head tilted a little. Secretly, Diana rather admired him. He had a straight brown fringe of hair which fell almost to his eyes and a cheeky grin, and his body was compact and strong. He could do lots of things that she could not, but then he was three years older than her, almost a grown-up, so she waited for his decision. He might suggest they should build another castle further up the beach, or they could draw out a hopscotch game on the wet sand. Or they could skim stones – except Charlie was very good at it and she was not – or simply paddle, only that would mean she ought to put on her bathing costume again because if one ran into the sea and kicked up spray, which was the best way of paddling, one's knickers and dress would be bound to get drenched and she had no desire to have her lovely day spoiled by a telling-off, or even a slap.

So Diana turned to Charlie, waiting for his next bright idea, and was disappointed.

'You and Becky can play round the deckchairs; I'm going to climb out to Perch Castle,' he said loftily. 'It ain't no place for kids. It's real dangerous, 'specially when the tide's in, 'cos there's deep pools and slippery seaweed and all sorts. I can do it, 'cos I'm older and 'cos boys is stronger an' better'n girls any day o' the week. Just amuse yourselves for half an hour. I've got work to attend to.'

Diana's mouth opened in an O of horror. No one was allowed to climb up Perch Rock to reach the castle at high tide. Everyone knew it was dangerous. She did hope Charlie wouldn't really ruin the day by getting himself drowned. She started to say as much, threatening to tell Aunty Beryl, but the only result was to make Charlie laugh scornfully and give her a push towards the small group on and around the deckchairs. 'Go on, baby tale-clat,' he said nastily. 'By the time you reach 'em, I'll be on Perch Rock. See ya later, kid.'

He set off, whistling jauntily, slowing down when he reached the first ridge of rock. Diana thought, vengefully, that he was pretending to plot his climb, and looking past him she thought that, in fact, it would not be so difficult. Why, I believe I could do it, she thought, surprised. It's a bit of a scramble but I bet I could reach the Rock, if I really wanted to. I'll go a little way, just to show him.

Cautiously, she glanced towards the grown-ups. They were not even looking in her direction; their attention was fixed on something happening on the prom. She remembered, with a little stab of excitement, that Mammy had said they might all have one go on the funfair before catching the ferry home, and hesitated; would it be wiser not to clamber on the rocks? It had been such a lovely day . . . but she would not go far. It would not take her more than a few seconds to reach the first big outcrop.

She turned back towards the sea and saw that Charlie was already more than halfway to the castle. Hastily, she hurried after him.

She was only a few yards from him when the disaster occurred. Hurrying, not taking proper care, she did exactly what Charlie had foretold. Her foot met a patch of slippery weed and she slid sideways, grabbed at the empty air, and plunged, head first, into a deep pool.

For a moment, there was nothing but confusion and gradually dawning fear. Salt water invaded her mouth, her eyes were full of it, her flailing hands hit sharp rock; she tried to cling to the rock, to pull herself out, but the swirling water loosened her grip and seemed to be deliberately dragging her down. She opened her mouth to scream and swallowed more water, saw bubbles racing up past her, making their way to the surface she could not even see. She wanted to scream for her mammy, to say she was sorry, that it was her own naughtiness in following Charlie which had got her in such a pickle. Pictures swept through her mind, pictures of Mammy crying, of Daddy wanting his little girl, of the garden at home, the apple tree, the happy family party somewhere above her on the golden sands. But the pictures were darkening, her strength was ebbing, as the darkness gathered. She could no longer breathe, there was a tight band of steel round her chest, her head was bursting . . .

And then there was a hand gripping the nape of her neck and she was being hauled upward. Her head broke the surface and she took a desperate gasp and felt air, blessed air, invade her burning lungs. Charlie's voice above her said furiously: 'You stupid . . . why'd yer foller me? You could of . . . well, you was nearly drownded, d'yer know that?' He heaved her up in his arms and carried her off the rocks and on to dry sand, then dumped her, unceremoniously.

Diana tried to take a breath to thank him, to say she was sorry, and instead found herself vomiting – mostly sea water – on to the sand, whilst tears ran down her cheeks.

There was a thud as someone sat on the sand beside her and a hard young arm went reassuringly round her shoulders. ''S awright, Di. You're gonna be awright,' Charlie said comfortingly. He must have glanced up the beach for he added: 'We won't tell your mammy what happened. We'll say you slipped when you was paddling, else they won't let us go on the funfair. Are you game to say nothin'? Only it's been a grand day and we don't want to spoil it, does we?'

Diana was still at the wheezing, gasping stage. Her lungs felt as if someone had lit a fire in them; her throat ached and her eyes burned. She had not the slightest desire to go on the funfair, but longed, urgently, for a cup of hot, sweet tea and a cuddle from her mammy. However, there was no doubt in her mind that Charlie had saved her life and the only way she could truly thank him was to take his advice and pretend nothing untoward had happened. Aunty Beryl and Mammy were waking the baby and spreading out the picnic cloth. She might not get the hot tea for which she craved – children were thought to prefer lemonade – but at least Mammy would give her a cuddle when she saw the pitiful state her daughter was in. And . . . and Charlie had been wonderful.

Diana braced herself; she would *not* let him down! She fished a tiny, soaking hanky out of her knicker leg, wiped it briskly round her face and then blew her nose on it. A great deal of sea water had managed to secrete itself up her nostrils, and now that it was out she felt a good deal better. She pushed her dripping hair off her forehead, anchored some loose strands behind her ears, and scrambled to her feet. 'Right you are, Charlie,' she said huskily, in a voice which scarcely resembled her own. 'They haven't seen a thing. They're wakin' Bobby and gettin' our tea out of the basket. C'mon!'

Keeping the incident quiet proved impossible, since the moment Emmy looked round and saw her daughter, soaked to the skin and liberally bespattered with sand, she knew that something dreadful had happened. She jumped to her feet, wrapped Diana in the striped towel, and began to rub energetically at her daughter's hair. She did not ask Diana what had happened, for the child's teeth were chattering so hard that she doubted if she would get a coherent reply, but she cast an enquiring look at Charlie. 'She fell in,' Charlie said briefly. 'I hooked her out just as soon as I could, Aunty Em, but she'd swallowed sea water by then. She's awright though, honest to God she is.' He glanced from Emmy's face to the towel-wrapped and shivering child. 'Well, mebbe she's still a bit shook up, but she'll be fine, won't you, Di?'

'Y-y-y-yes,' Diana said shakily. She turned to her mother. 'I – I – I'll be awright, only . . . oh, Mammy, can I have tea instead of lemonade?'

Emmy laughed and hugged her little daughter closer, then set her down on the deckchair she herself had just vacated. 'All right. I suppose a ducking isn't going to kill you,' she observed. She fished in the pocket of her jacket and handed Charlie some loose change. 'Run up to the café, there's a good lad, and get a teapot big enough for four. When you come back, the young lady diver here and the rest of us can have a cuppa, and then we'll eat our carry-out.' For the first time, she noticed that Charlie was almost as wet as Diana, and his knuckles and one knee were bruised and bleeding. Guiltily, she realised she had not spared a thought for the boy who had very likely rescued her daughter from a watery grave, though he was now making light of it. 'Oh, Charlie, you're hurt! Look, you stay here and let your mam clean up your cuts and bruises. Diana will be fine just while I fetch the teapot.'

Beryl, who had been seeing to the younger children, turned to examine her son. She grinned at Charlie, then turned to grin at Emmy, too. 'If you think them scratches will worry our lad, you've gorra nother think coming,' she said roundly. 'Go on, Charlie, an' gerra move on; me tongue's hangin' out like a Jacob's carpet an' me stomach thinks me throat's been cut.' She turned her shrewd eyes on Diana. The child was beginning to rub her own hair with the towel and was looking a good deal perkier. 'You awright, queen? I can see you're feelin' better. Fancy a corned beef and pickle sandwich?'

Diana scrambled off her chair and Emmy realised, not for the first time, that Beryl's matter-of-fact attitude did Diana more good than all the fussing in the world. As for Charlie, he had already almost reached the prom and now Beryl was pouring lemonade into Bakelite mugs and handing round sandwiches to the rest of her family, and Diana had sat herself down beside Becky, and the two small girls were discussing the ability of a piece of seaweed hung outside one's bedroom window to forecast next day's weather. 'If it's goin' to rain next day, the seaweed feels wet, but if it's goin' to be sunny, it's nice and dry,' Diana told the younger girl. 'My daddy told me that an' my daddy knows *everything*.'

Lenny sniffed. 'If the seaweed's wet, I reckon it's 'cos it's already rainin',' he said gruffly, helping himself to a sandwich. 'That's what *my* dad says.'

Emmy turned away to hide a smile. The Fishers might be perennially hard up and the kids might go to a poorly provided and overcrowded school, but they were sharp as needles. Emmy found herself thinking, not for the first time, that it was a pity Peter was so set against his family's visiting Nightingale Court. It would do Diana nothing but good to mix with children like Beryl Fisher's brood.

'Here's the tea, Aunty Em.' Charlie, bearing a large enamel teapot, placed it in front of Emmy with a triumphant flourish. 'Will you pour out?'

It was dark by the time the two families climbed wearily off the ferry and went their separate ways. Beryl gave Emmy a hug before they parted, thanking her for a wonderful day out, a real treat.

'I don't see why you're thanking me,' Emmy said, flushed and excited herself, for the two young women had forgotten the weight of their years and had gone on all the funfair rides they could afford, had eaten popcorn and candyfloss, and had behaved like two girls again. 'Spending time with you is always fun, Beryl. You never let anything get you down.'

Beryl smiled a trifle grimly. 'I wish that were true, queen, but I'm only human. There's days when I snap at the kids and shout at poor Wally, and think that if I have another bleedin' sheet or tablecloth to launder, I'll go mad. But I get through somehow, and it's a help to have kids what's good-hearted and a feller who can turn his hand to anything.'

'Yes, I know what you mean. When Peter's home, it's as if someone has lifted a heavy weight off my shoulders,' Emmy agreed. 'Well, it's been a grand day, Beryl, and I hope we'll have many more of them. Cheerio, kids; take care of your mam, she's precious.'

She and Diana walked to their tram stop. The basket was a good deal lighter than it had been on going out that morning, even with the damp and sandy towel folded across the empty mugs and bottles within. Emmy reflected, ruefully, that she might be the wife of a man who could afford all sorts of luxuries, but old habits die hard. The lemonade bottles could be handed in at any public house in exchange for a penny, and she would reuse the grease-proof paper many times. Peter, she knew, would have tossed such remnants into the nearest rubbish bin, because he had been brought up the son of rich parents who had never had to scrimp and save in their lives. His uncle had been captain of a Cunarder and Peter had lacked for nothing at Epsley Manor, either as a child or as a young man. He had told her that there were greenhouses and a walled kitchen garden behind the house and that his parents had employed a gardener and two assistants, and that there had been an indoor staff of three maids and a cook. Emmy still had not visited her parents-in-law's house though she was hoping to do so during Peter's next proper leave; he had promised her that they would do so and her husband was a man of his word. She was looking forward to the visit though she was secretly sure she would be overawed by the servants and might well feel out of place, but Peter would protect her as he had always done.

The rattle of the arriving tram brought Emmy's mind back to the present. She and Diana scrambled aboard and got a seat near the door. Emmy sank on to the hard, slatted seat with a sigh of pleasure and pulled Diana on to her knee, for despite the lateness of the hour the tram was quite crowded, and seats were scarce. Diana leaned against Emmy's shoulder and Emmy rested her chin on top of her daughter's dishevelled hair. 'If you weren't so tired, I'd get you into a nice, hot bath, but I think we'd best leave that till morning,' she murmured. 'What a blessing your bathing suit was dry enough for you to change into so that Aunty Beryl and meself could spread your wet clothes out on the deckchair. By the time we'd ate our tea and you kids had played a few running and jumping about games, they were dry as tinder. You're a lucky girl, you know, Di. You might've drowned, only Charlie saved you from that, and you might have contracted pneumonia wearing wet clothing, only the sun was as hot as your daddy says it is in that Africa place he goes to.'

She gave her daughter another squeeze. 'Only two more days and your daddy will be picking you up and giving a great shout and telling me how much you've grown while he's been away. Oh, Di, I do love it when your daddy's home.'

'So does I,' Diana murmured sleepily. 'What'll he say when I tell him I were nearly drownded, Mammy? I 'spects he'll buy me something lovely to make up. Or he might take us to the pictures . . . I do love the pictures, Mammy.'

Emmy laughed but tilted her daughter's face until they were looking straight at one another. 'I don't think we'll say anything about going to New Brighton, or falling in the water,' she said. 'You see, it would only worry Daddy and make him think I wasn't taking proper care of you. He – he doesn't understand that a boy of Charlie's age is – is really very responsible and sensible. He'll say I should have stayed with you, stopped you playing on the rocks.' She paused; she had not asked Diana just how the accident had occurred, but now realised she should do so. 'What exactly *did* happen, queen?' she asked, rather apprehensively. 'I know it were an accident, but I don't quite know how you fell in.'

'Oh, I were followin' Charlie out along the rocks,' Diana said readily. 'He telled me not to, Mammy, but I like to go where he goes, so I followed. The sea was up round the rocks an' I trod on a patch of weed and went straight in where there were a deep pool. Charlie must've seen me go, 'cos he grabbed the neck o' me dress an' pulled me out an' said as we shouldn't worry you. Only as soon as you saw me, you knew I'd fell in, didn't you? But it weren't Charlie's fault,' she ended hastily. 'He's the best boy I know, is Charlie, and the bravest one too.'

'I see,' Emmy said, nodding slowly. She did see. Her small daughter had always admired Charlie, wanting to do everything that Charlie did, so perhaps the near drowning would be a lesson to her. She said impressively: 'But it's time you got some sense, sweetheart. Little girls of five can't possibly do as much as big boys of eight, and boys were made by God to be stronger than girls, because when they grow up they have to do hard, difficult things, like your daddy does. When girls grow up, they do gentle things, like your mammy does. So you see, if you try to imitate Charlie, you'll end up getting hurt again, and I wouldn't want that.'

There was a long moment of silence whilst Diana obviously considered her mother's remarks, and when she spoke, it was thoughtfully. 'But Aunty Beryl does hard things, an' she's a lady like you,' she observed. 'And Lucy does hard things, too. They scrub floors and black grates, and light fires, and cook meals . . .'

Emmy sighed. Reasoning with Diana was clearly not going to be easy. In fact, perhaps it was a mistake to try. Instead, she said firmly, 'Never mind all that. Just don't try to do what Charlie does and don't tell your daddy you fell in the sea. Is that clear?'

'Why not?' Diana's voice had the dreamy note of one who is almost asleep, but Emmy found she was tired of answering questions and trying to be tactful.

'Because I say not,' she snapped. 'And what I say goes, understand?'

Diana giggled. 'I weren't goin' to tell Daddy anything, anyway,' she murmured.

Emmy could see that the tram was nearing the stop. She slid Diana off her lap, picked up her basket, and, holding the child's hand in a firm grasp, joined the line of people about to descend. 'Good girl,' she said, as the two of them descended from the tram at the corner of Arundel Avenue and began to walk towards Lancaster Avenue. She realised there was little point in discussing the matter further tonight but decided that she would go over it again in the morning.

Later, when Diana was tucked up in bed and fast asleep, Emmy ran herself a warm bath and climbed, thankfully, into the tub. A proper bathroom was an undreamed-of luxury for people who lived in Nightingale Court, but after more than five years of living in the Avenue, Emmy took it for granted. Yet now, as she soaked in the warm water, letting her aches and pains dissolve along the way, Emmy realised all over again how very fortunate she was. She had a wonderful husband who gave her everything she could want, a beautiful home and a delightful daughter. It was a pity that she could not talk freely to Peter about her friends in Nightingale Court, but that was probably her own fault. She should have insisted that he go with her to her old home. Because his times ashore were usually short, he avoided such meetings, but on this occasion she would tell him that he really must accompany her to Nightingale Court to meet the Fishers. He would both like and approve of them, would admire their sturdily independent children, and then she need no longer feel guilty when she visited at No. 4.

Satisfied on this score, she climbed out of the bath, reached for a towel and was very soon in bed.

Chapter Four

Diana was on the back lawn, picking daisies, when the doorbell rang. For a moment, she stopped in her task, wondering who could be calling in the middle of the morning – and coming to the front door, furthermore. If Mammy had ordered something from a shop, then the tradesman would come whistling round the side of the house, basket on arm, to deliver at the back door, and have a chat with Lucy at the same time.

This was obviously not a tradesman and morning callers held no interest for Diana. None of the neighbours had children her age, and though her mammy sometimes took her to the local park where she met other children, they were not in the habit of coming to the house – probably did not even know where she lived.

She wished that the caller could have been Charlie, or even Becky, but she knew it would be neither. Charlie and Becky would not undertake the long journey from Nightingale Court to Lancaster Avenue just to see her, for she knew, without bitterness, that her affection for Charlie was one-sided indeed. He had told her the other day that girls were a bloomin' nuisance. 'But you saved me life, Charlie, so I've got to love you,' she had wailed, dismayed by the thought of her affection's being spurned. But Charlie had only snorted and repeated his assertion that girls were a bloomin' nuisance, adding that she was not to foller him around or else she'd get a thick ear.

Diana did not know what a thick ear was but she gathered that it was a sign of disapproval and resigned herself to worshipping Charlie from afar. Becky, of course, was a very different kettle of fish; being younger than Diana it was she who tended to follow the other girl around when the two families were together. Diana approved of Becky and would have been delighted had she come round to play, but she knew Becky was too young to leave the court, and anyway, why should she? There were dozens of children there; Becky would never lack a playfellow in the way that Diana did. Oh, there were no lovely gardens, no daisy-starred lawns, no trips to the park to feed the ducks, but there was companionship in plenty.

Having settled in her own mind that the caller could be of no possible interest to her, Diana sat back, spread out the skirt of her yellow cotton dress, and regarded her daisy harvest. She meant to make the longest daisy chain in the world so that when Daddy came home he would be able to admire it. She knew that daisy chains, if put in the cool of the big scullery, could last for as long as three days, so there was no fear that this one would fade and die before Daddy's arrival. Frowning with concentration, Diana began her task.

A few moments later, whilst she was still working, she heard a most peculiar noise emanating from the house. It sounded a bit as though someone had shut a dog's tail in the door. Diana distinctly remembered the long, pained wail which Bones had given when Aunty Beryl had slammed the back door on his nether regions by mistake. She stopped what she was doing and half rose to her feet, but then she realised that if she stood up, the daisies would go everywhere, and sat down again. Since they didn't have a dog, she supposed that poor Lucy must have cut herself, or shut her finger in the door. I could go and see what's happened, only Mammy is there and she's much better than me over cut fingers, she told herself, picking up the next daisy and beginning to thread it through the slit she had already made in the previous stalk. I wish *we* had a dog, her thoughts continued, as her fingers sorted and selected daisies from the mound in her lap. If we had a dog, it could chase a ball, or just sit beside me on the grass and be company. Daddy would like a dog but Mammy's afraid of big dirty paw marks all over her shiny floors and carpets, and she says dogs need exercising even when the snow's a foot thick, or the rain's belting on your head and flattening the flowers in the garden. She says we'll have a dog when Daddy retires from sea and then they both laugh and Daddy says when I'm six . . .

Thinking about a dog brought Diana's mind full circle, so to speak. To the best of her knowledge, no one ever exercised Bones. Sometimes he accompanied Aunty Beryl when she went to the shops, sometimes he trailed in Charlie's wake, or gambolled ahead, keeping an eye out for anything of interest. At other times, he disappeared on his own mysterious errands, but Diana was jolly sure that no member of the Fisher family ever tried to attach a lead to Bones's collar – indeed, she realised, belatedly, that she had never seen a collar on the Fishers' unkempt mongrel.

She was still pondering over why her mammy should deny her a dog on account of having to take it for walks when Bones took care of himself, when Lucy opened the back door. She emerged, somewhat timidly, bearing a tray upon which stood a mug of milk and a plate of sugar biscuits. She kept glancing over her shoulder, as though frightened that she was being followed, but set the tray down beside Diana, saying cheerfully: 'There's your elevenses, Miss Di.' Usually, she chatted for a moment and then went back indoors, but now, with another almost conspiratorial glance around her, she sat down on the grass beside Diana. 'There's a gentleman – two gentlemen – in the front room, come to see your mammy,' she said, lowering her voice until it was scarcely above a whisper. 'Did you hear that noise? Like – like as if someone were hurt? I ran into the hallway and one of the fellers come out and telled me, ever so sharp like, to make a pot of strong tea and to tap on the door when it were ready. I just took it to 'em, and – and your mam's sitting in a chair, all scrumpled up like, wi' her face in her hands. I tried to go across to her but the fellers – gentlemen, I mean – pushed me out of the room and telled me to go back to me work. Oh, Miss Di, I'm that worried – I dunno what best to do.'

Diana got to her feet and shook the daisies, rather regretfully, from her skirt and into Lucy's. The maid usually knew exactly what to do in every situation. It was not like her to appeal to Diana and Mammy often remarked that they were lucky to have found a servant as sensible and practical as young Lucy. However, this was clearly an occasion when Diana would have to take matters into her own hands. 'Look after my daisy chain, Lucy, while I go in and see what's happened,' Diana said firmly. 'No one isn't going to push *me* out of the room.' She turned serious eyes on the older girl. 'Should I take the sticking plaster, do you think? If Mammy shut her fingers in the door . . .'

Lucy gave a watery smile. 'Yes, you do that,' she said encouragingly. 'You're a good kid, Miss Di. I'll wait here . . . no, I'll come into the kitchen, then if you or your mam need me, you can either give a shout or tug the bell. Awright?'

The two of them made their way back into the kitchen, Lucy with her apron full of daisies which she tipped carefully on to the draining board in the scullery. She reached down the First Aid box, which contained sticking plaster, bandages, lint and various other similar items, and handed it to Diana, who took it and trotted confidently across the hallway. She threw open the sitting room door and was halfway across the room when she saw her mother's face. Emmy was white as a ghost, save for her eyes which were swollen and red. Clearly, she had been crying for some time, and Diana dumped the First Aid box in the arms of a tall man in uniform before rushing across and casting herself into her mother's arms. She realised that whatever had happened could not be put right with lint or sticking plaster. All in a moment, she found that she was afraid, that she really did not want to know why her mother had been crying so bitterly, because when she knew . . .

'Oh, darling, these gentlemen are – are from the *Queen of the South*. They've come to tell me . . . to tell me . . .'

But it was some time before Diana managed to sort out, from her mother's garbled words, spoken between sobs, that her father would not be coming home that day, would never come home again.

*

For many weeks, life had been a nightmare for Emmy. At first, she had hardly been able to take in that Peter was dead, though one of the officers who had come to tell her the sad news had been careful to explain what had happened.

'The men were disembarking from the ship when a scuffle broke out on the dockside. Mr Wesley hurried down the gangway to break up the fight, but he must have caught his foot in a coil of rope, because before he even reached the men, he went down. I myself was present, and was the first person to reach him.' He had looked earnestly at Emmy, his own face pale. 'It seemed such a slight fall, but his head had hit one of the metal bollards to which the ship was moored, and he had broken his neck. Death was instantaneous . . . I assure you, Mrs Wesley, that he could not have suffered; it was all so quick.'

'Then . . . then it was an accident? No one attacked him, or anything like that?' Emmy had said dully.

'Oh yes, it was an accident,' the captain had agreed. 'Mr Wesley was a very popular member of the crew. Both his fellow officers and the men are devastated, and anxious to do anything they can to help you at this time.'

Emmy had thanked them but all she had really wanted, at that moment, was to be left alone to come to terms with a tragedy greater than she had ever experienced before.

In a way, it had helped that there was so much to do, so many problems to sort out. The funeral had had to be delayed because of the inquest, which Emmy had attended, hearing the coroner's verdict of accidental death with considerable relief. Despite the captain's assurance, she had been worried that people might assume her husband had been killed in a dockside brawl, and she knew how this would have distressed Peter and, of course, his family. Even Diana might have been touched by it, but as it was, the child could still think of her father as a wonderful person, a hero figure.

When Emmy began to plan the funeral, she was told that the ship's owners would hire a church hall and a firm of caterers and would undertake to pay all expenses. Emmy was doubly grateful since she was already beginning to realise that her financial position was precarious. Peter had had a good job and a good salary but, naturally, this ceased upon his death and the pension she would receive would not even pay the rent of the house in Lancaster Avenue, let alone such things as Lucy's wages, or bills for coal, gas and food.

Because the ship's company was in port, however, the funeral would be well attended and, of course, Emmy knew she would have the support of old friends and neighbours. She had notified the Wesleys and invited them to stay in Lancaster Avenue, but, as they had done for her wedding, they booked themselves into the Adelphi Hotel, saying briefly that this would be less trouble for everyone.

The day of the funeral arrived and, as they had promised, the whole ship's company attended and virtually everyone from Nightingale Court – Beryl had seen to that. Her neighbours in Lancaster Avenue had sent flowers and expressed their condolences but the young Wesleys had not mixed much with their elderly neighbours and only Captain Marriott, the retired naval officer from the end house, attended the funeral.

Mr and Mrs Wesley came up though, to Emmy's distress, neither Ralph nor his wife attended. Peter's parents showed no outward sign of grief. They kept very much to themselves, and when she asked them to come back to the house, they refused to do so.

'We want to be back in Southampton before nightfall,' Mr Wesley said gruffly, when Emmy approached them outside the church. 'We shall return to the hotel, pick up our suitcases, and leave at once.'

Emmy must have looked shocked, as well as stricken, for her mother-in-law patted her arm and drew her aside. 'My dear, I know you must think us strange parents because I'm sure Peter never explained the deep rift between himself and the rest of the family,' she said. 'I can't explain now, it's too long a story; I'll write, when I get home. But I must tell you that I was pleased with Peter's marriage and thought it might well be the making of him.'

Emmy's eyes flashed. 'Peter didn't need marriage to make him a wonderful person; he was that before I met him,' she said. 'But surely you could stay on for another day or two? I – I don't need to tell you that I'm in desperate straits, with no one to help or advise me. My mother died three years ago, and—'

Mr Wesley had been standing back, appearing not to listen to the conversation, but at these words he stepped forward, his face reddening angrily. 'If you're expecting financial help from us, then you'll be disappointed,' he said thickly. 'My younger son and his wife have cost us a fortune and almost bankrupted the business. Twelve months ago we had to sell Epsley Manor. We wrote to Peter, asking him to come back into the business so that we might try to turn things round. He replied, eventually, saying that such a move would be fatal to his career and that he was sure we would sort things out. We've not done so. Besides, we gave Peter a large sum when he joined the Merchant Navy and a pretty handsome wedding present. You've not done badly out of us, young lady.'

'We – we spent the money on furniture, Mr Wesley, we didn't fritter it away,' Emmy said numbly. 'I wrote and told you at the time, I know I did.'

Her mother-in-law patted her arm. 'Yes, I know,' she said quietly. 'But I'm afraid Peter's brother and his wife are continuing to spend as though we were still rich; they will be the ruin of us all, which is why we can't help you. But you're a very beautiful young woman; you will doubtless marry again, and if I may venture to advise you . . .'

But Emmy had heard enough. The very thought of marrying again was dreadful to her, and that his mother should suggest it, with Peter's funeral service scarcely over, was like a slap in the face. She could feel tears brimming in her eyes and turned away to hide them. 'It doesn't matter,' she muttered. 'We'll manage, Diana and me. We'll be all right.'

Behind her, she heard Mrs Wesley start to speak, heard Mr Wesley's harsh voice cut the words off short, but she did not turn back towards them. Instead, she went over to where the Fishers stood, with Diana, very tiny and pale in her blacks, standing beside them. It would take a good deal of Beryl's kindness and common sense to wipe out the nastiness of her recent conversation with the Wesleys, but she knew that Beryl would give whatever comfort she could.

And presently, climbing into the funeral car, she saw the Wesleys driving off in their long black limousine and was conscious of considerable relief. After what had occurred, meeting them again would have been painful, to say the least.

*

Beryl was a tower of strength. She came round to Lancaster Avenue to help Emmy try to sort out her financial position, assuming that her friend would at least be able to manage, and was shocked to discover that, apart from the pension, there was no money. 'Because Peter was so young – only thirty-six – the widow's pension I shall receive will be very small,' Emmy told her, as the two of them sat thankfully down to share a pot of tea in the kitchen. 'And neither Peter nor myself ever thought about saving for a rainy day, because there always seemed to be money. But there's hardly any, Beryl. He – he talked about his family being rich and I always assumed he had some sort of private income, but I was wrong. If I'd known we had nothing behind us, I could easily have put away a bit of money every month towards Diana's schooling, if nothing else. Peter was always generous; he never asked me to go careful this month, or anything like that, and now, of course, it's all down to me. I can't stay in this house, Diana will have to go to a council school and I suppose I'll have to start looking for a job, because we certainly couldn't live on the pension.' She turned to her friend, unable to keep the sudden anxiety out of her voice. 'Oh, Beryl, I wish to God I was still living in the court; at least I'd have friends round me instead of strangers.'

Beryl smiled at her. 'There are worse places than Nightingale Court,' she agreed, 'so why not come back, queen? The Vaughans moved out of your mum's old house months back an' no one's took it since. It's in a pretty bad state, but nothin' you an' me an' Wally couldn't put right with a big bucket of whitewash, a tin of scouring powder and a bottle of Jeyes fluid.'

Emmy stared at her friend, almost unable to believe

her ears. 'And – and d'you think Mr Freeman would let me rent it?' she asked incredulously. 'Oh, Beryl, if I were back in Nightingale Court, I'd manage somehow, I know I would.'

'You'll manage, wherever you're livin',' Beryl said bluntly. 'You'd have to, queen, but as you say, you'll be much better off in the court. Either meself or one of the other women will keep an eye on Diana for you, so's you can get a decent job, and you know how we stick together when times is hard, so you needn't fear you'd not have support. The fact is, when they know you're lookin' for work, everyone will keep an eye open and let you know when jobs are comin' vacant. As for Mr Freeman, he'll be so glad to see No. 2 bringin' in money again that he'd let it to Sweeney Todd if he came knockin'.'

Emmy jumped to her feet. For the first time since the dreadful news of Peter's death, she felt a surge of hope. 'I'll go round there at once, if you don't mind, queen,' she said excitedly. 'Oh, Beryl, just to know I had somewhere to go to would be good, but to go back to Nightingale Court is best of all! And wait till Diana hears. She'll be thrilled to bits.'

'I'm glad you feel like that, though mebbe Peter would have been happier if you tried somewhere else first,' Beryl was beginning, but Emmy cut her short.

'Peter didn't know you at all,' she said, taking her coat down from its peg by the back door. 'If he had, he'd be glad I was going back.' She glanced across at the clock above the kitchen mantel. 'If we hurry, we can get to Mr Freeman's house and back here well before Lucy and Diana are home from the park.'

By the time Emmy entered the house again that afternoon, it was all arranged. She had paid Mr

Freeman a month's rent in advance and would move out of the Lancaster Avenue house just as soon as No. 2 Nightingale Court had been cleaned up. As Beryl had warned her, the old place was in a disgraceful state and would need a good deal more than whitewash and Jeyes fluid to put it to rights, but even the prospect of the hard work ahead of her did not damp Emmy's spirits. Besides, she had had a rare piece of luck as she had emerged from Raymond Street on to Vauxhall Road. A tall young officer, whose face seemed vaguely familiar, had given her a charming smile, taken off his cap, and reminded her of his name.

'Carl Johansson, Mrs Wesley, Second Officer from SS *Queen of the South* – I was best man at your wedding.' The young man spoke with a slight foreign accent.

At the first sight of the uniform, Emmy's heart had missed a beat, before recollection flooded in. She tried to smile but guessed it was a poor effort. 'Oh . . . Mr Johansson, yes, of course I remember you. You . . . you were wonderfully helpful over my husband's funeral. So . . . so you're in port again?'

'That's right. In fact, I've just come from Lancaster Avenue. The maid told me I might find you in Nightingale Court. We were wondering, the other fellows and myself, if there was anything we could do.' A flush mounted to his cheeks, but he went doggedly on. 'We realise you'll be all right for money, because Mr Wesley came from a rich family and no doubt his private income will be paid to you, but if there's anything—'

Emmy had interrupted quickly. She could not let this young man believe her to be comfortably off when the opposite was true. 'I'm afraid Peter didn't have a private income and we both spent rather lavishly.' Pride was all very well but if Peter's shipmates were keen to help her and Diana, then they had better know the truth. 'Peter's family had pretty well cast him off and have made it plain they're not interested in Diana or myself. All I shall have will be a very small widow's pension and whatever money I can get when I sell up the contents of the house in Lancaster Avenue.'

The young man's fair brows had shot up. He looked astonished and also shocked. 'Sell up the contents of your beautiful house?' he echoed. 'But why on earth . . . surely there must be *some* money . . . have you actually spoken to his parents? I know they quarrelled with Peter some years back but surely they would help you now?'

'Yes, I did speak to them, after the funeral, and they made it painfully clear that they were not interested. Peter's mama advised me to marry again,' Emmy had said, rather bitterly. 'From what Mrs Wesley told me, I think Peter's younger brother is proving expensive; he has an extravagant wife, I gather. I thought they might have helped us for Diana's sake, but it seems I was wrong.' She watched as a deep crease appeared on Carl Johansson's brow.

'I see. I am sorry,' he had replied. 'I had no right to jump to conclusions but – but the offer of help still stands, Mrs Wesley, if there's anything we can do . . . anything at all.'

Emmy had looked up into his concerned face and made up her mind. She was going to need all the help she could get. 'We're moving out of Lancaster Avenue, Mr Johansson, because we can't afford the rent, and I'm selling the furniture, because I've taken a very much smaller house in Nightingale Court. It's

– it's in an awful state; the last tenants ripped a good few of the floorboards up, the walls need replastering and the stairs are a death trap, but if you fellers from the old *Queen* really would help . . . oh, I can't tell you what a weight off my mind that would be.'

'We're in port for a week while essential repairs are carried out, so I'll get a working party together when I go back to the ship. We'll meet you in Nightingale Court in a couple of days and you can tell us what you want done. We can help with the move itself once we've done whatever is necessary in your new home. And don't worry about the cost of materials,' he added hastily, as Emmy opened her mouth to protest. 'We'll have a whip-round, and there's always timber, paint, and stuff like that in the ship's stores, which no one will miss.'

'It's awfully kind of you, Mr Johansson; I'd be right glad of some help,' Emmy had said, despising the tremor in her voice, but unable to prevent it. 'I don't want you to think badly of Peter – he was a good husband, the best in the world – but, well, we neither of us expected . . . that I'd be widowed, so young, so there wasn't any provision made. I don't want you to think that Peter was irresponsible, or anything like that?'

'Good God, no!' Mr Johansson had said, looking horrified. 'Why, if I were to die tomorrow, there wouldn't be much in my bank account! I'll just tell the chaps that things are still not resolved. In any case, the working party who'll come to clean up your new home will be members of the ship's crew, not the officers. They won't ask questions; they'll just get on with the job.'

So when Emmy entered the kitchen of her home, on that bright and sunny afternoon, it was with a lighter step and a more cheerful countenance than she had shown since hearing of Peter's death, and Diana and Lucy, sitting at the table eating bread and jam, looked up and beamed.

'Hello, Mammy,' Diana said. 'We had a grand time in the park, so we did. We fed the ducks, and Lucy pushed me on the swings till my toes nearly touched the oak tree, and we met Sarah – she's in my class at school – and played hide and seek, and then Sarah's nanny bought us both ice creams.' She looked curiously across at her mother. 'Did you have a nice afternoon, Mammy? When we went to the park, you never said you were goin' out too, so when we came home and the house were empty, we thought mebbe you'd gone round to Aunty Beryl's. Did you?'

'Yes, I did in a way,' Emmy said, sitting down at the table and helping herself to a slice of bread and butter. She suddenly realised she was ravenously hungry – thirsty, too – and accepted the cup of tea Lucy handed her gratefully. 'Aunty Beryl was here when you left, wasn't she? Well, I told her we – we wouldn't be able to continue to live here and she said that Grandma Dickens's old house in Nightingale Court was up for rent. I know you've always liked the court, sweetheart, and it would help me enormously to be near Aunty Beryl, so I went round there to see the landlord and now it's all arranged. We're to move in just as soon as the place has been made ready.'

'I do 'member you showed me the house,' Diana said doubtfully, 'but it were a long time ago, Mammy. It's – it's quite a little house, isn't it? And there's no garden, nor any back door.'

'Yes, it is small, and no one in the courts has a garden,' Emmy said, 'because they're all what we call back to backs. But it's right next door to Aunty Beryl and Uncle Wally, and you'll be able to play with Becky and Charlie, and all the others, to your heart's content,' she finished craftily.

Diana beamed and helped herself to more bread and jam. 'Yes, I'd forgotten that,' she said joyfully. 'Ooh, and I'll go to school with the Fishers, won't I? Lucy can take us all each morning and pick us up each afternoon.'

It was weird, but Emmy had simply never thought about that, never realised that she should have told Lucy that they would not be able to continue to employ her as soon as she knew the financial straits into which she had been plunged. She opened her mouth to speak, but was forestalled by Lucy herself.

'I'm awful sorry, Miss Di, but I won't be able to come with you to the court. I'm going to work for old Captain Marriott, at the end house, when you and your mammy move out of here,' she said, shooting Emmy a friendly, conspiratorial glance. 'But just as soon as you're settled in I'll come a-calling, never fret.'

Diana had shed tears when she had first been told that her father was dead, but since then she had not cried once. She had accepted that she would have to leave her nice school and the friends she had made there, that they would lose their beautiful house, which they had all taken for granted, but at the mention of losing Lucy her whole face changed. Tears welled up in her eyes and trickled down her cheeks and she flung herself at the maid, burying her face in Lucy's bosom and mumbling that she did not care where they lived but she could not bear to be parted from Lucy.

'Oh, darling, don't cry,' Emmy said, greatly

distressed. It was her own stupid selfishness which had brought this about. She should have realised that the child regarded Lucy as a second mother, or at least an elder sister, and would bitterly regret parting from her. 'I should not have broken it to you so suddenly, but the fact is, Diana, we can't afford to pay anyone to help us in the future. That's why you and I are moving to a small house, because it's so much cheaper to rent, and so much easier to keep clean. Because it's so much smaller, we shall be able to sell most of the carpets, curtains, furniture and fittings which we shan't need.' Since her daughter did not answer, Emmy decided it might be best to make a clean breast of things. Lucy would not gossip to the neighbours and besides, what did it matter if she did? All too soon now, the people in Lancaster Avenue would be neighbours no longer. She and Diana – and Lucy, too – were about to start a new life. 'Look, darling, I am going to have to get a job, can you understand that? Whilst your daddy was alive, we had his salary to keep household – salary is the name we give to the money someone earns – and it was a good salary, so we could afford to buy whatever we needed. But when someone dies, that money stops.'

Diana looked at her soberly. 'Yes, because the company has to pay someone else to do Daddy's job,' she said. 'Lucy told me that days ago, didn't you, Lucy?'

'I did, Miss Diana,' Lucy said gravely. 'But now just you listen to what your mammy is saying because it's important that you understand, so it is.'

Emmy felt more ashamed than ever; she had not realised what a jewel Lucy was. The girl was only twenty, yet she had done more to prepare Diana for what lay ahead than her own mother had done. No wonder Diana had wept so bitterly at the thought of losing such a companion. But right now, she must continue her explanation, make sure Diana understood that they had no choice. They must begin to live by an entirely new set of rules which would be largely governed by what she herself could earn, and she knew she was a poor proposition as an employee.

'Well, women don't earn as much as men, so money will be a bit short for a while, at least. Whilst I'm working, either you'll be in school or else someone in the court will be keeping an eye on you.'

Diana sat back in her chair and rubbed her eyes briskly. 'I like Nightingale Court,' she said, picking up the bread and jam she had abandoned and eyeing it thoughtfully. 'I like Aunty Beryl and Uncle Wally and I like the kids – Charlie's me favourite – but what'll happen at teatime, Mammy? When you're not here, Lucy gets the tea, but if you're going to work . . .'

'Don't worry, someone will get your tea,' Emmy said, trying not to smile. Diana was not a greedy child but she did enjoy her food. 'Or I could leave you some tea on the kitchen table, only that would mean you'd have to go into an empty house to eat it, and you might not like that.'

'I wouldn't mind,' Diana said airily, beginning to eat her bread and jam once more. 'Becky telled me that when her mammy's out, she leaves the door key dangling through the letter box, on a piece of string, so any of the kids can get in if they want to. Why, when I'm six, I could make *your* tea, Mammy, as well as my own. I often help Lucy to cook, don't I, Lu?'

Lucy laughed and winked at Emmy, then said gravely: 'Indeed you do, and I'm sure you'll be a great help to your mammy, but you won't be six for a long while yet. Now how about getting into practice and tidying your room? Last time I looked in, there were toys all over the floor, books all over the bed and a half-eaten apple gathering dust on the window sill.'

Diana giggled, gobbled down the last piece of bread and jam and skipped out of the room, saying that all the toys would be in their places and the apple thrown out for the blackbirds to enjoy in no time at all. She had reached the stairs when something seemed to occur to her for she turned back. 'Mammy, what about my toys?' she asked anxiously. 'Will we have to sell *all* of them or just the newest ones? Only, Raggedy Jen and Barnacle Bill always come to bed with me, and I'd miss them terrible bad if we had to sell them.'

Emmy felt the tears come to her eyes but blinked them resolutely away. 'We aren't going to sell *any* of your toys, queen, and certainly not either Barnacle Bill or Raggedy Jen. Why, Daddy bought Raggedy Jen the day you were born and Barnacle Bill not long afterwards. I wouldn't dream of letting either of them go. And then there's Big Teddy and Little Teddy, the ginger dragon and the beautiful clockwork train set, and all your Meccano . . .'

'Well, I would like to keep the Meccano and the jigsaws and some of the other games,' Diana called over her shoulder, beginning to mount the stairs. 'But so long as Jen and Bill come too . . .' She stopped talking and began to give a spirited rendering of her favourite song. '*"Who's that knocking at my door, who's that knocking at my door, who's that knocking at my door," said the fair young maiden. "It's only me from over the sea," said Barnacle Bill, the sailor.*'

As soon as they were alone, Emmy and Lucy gave a simultaneous sigh of relief. 'I'm awful sorry, Mrs Wesley; perhaps I should have left it to you to tell Miss Diana what were goin' on, but I could see you'd got your hands full and she's bright as a button is Miss Di. She began asking questions . . .'

'Lucy, you are wonderful,' Emmy said sincerely. 'You did what I should have done, which has made things much easier all round. But anyway, I'm truly sorry I didn't tell you earlier how things stood with us.' She glanced curiously at the younger girl. 'Are you really going to work for Captain Marriott?'

Lucy giggled. 'He doesn't know it yet, but yes, I think I am. His housekeeper is a real old dear, but she's finding the work too much. She approached me months back, said if I ever wanted to change me place of employment, then there'd be a snug billet at the Captain's house. She knows I'm from an orphanage an' don't have no parents an' she knows I don't go out with fellers much, so I reckon she guessed I'd quite like a place which might lead to greater things. She said she'd train me up as a sort of assistant housekeeper, so that when she wants to retire, I'd be able to take over.'

Poor Emmy felt worse than ever. She had never bothered to enquire into Lucy's background; had not asked one single question about her parents or her home.

Now, she said, guiltily: 'Lucy, I feel thoroughly ashamed. I – I didn't realise you were an orphan. Where do you go on your days off? I suppose you only applied for this job because it was live-in . . . oh dear, why do I never *think*?'

Lucy was a small, skinny girl, with soft fawn-coloured hair cut in a Dutch bob, a snub nose and a large, generous mouth. She had rather watery blue eyes but now these smiled at Emmy, her glance frank. 'It's all right, Mrs Wesley. Folk don't take much notice of servants but you've been a grand person to work for, so you have, an' I'll be real sorry to leave you – and Diana, of course. As for where I go on my days off, I go back to the orphanage; I've got a heap o' pals there still and I'm fond of the old place.'

'But I expect you'll live in again at Captain Marriott's, won't you?' Emmy said shrewdly. 'It's a big house and with only him and the housekeeper, there'll be plenty of room for you.'

'Yes, I will, because it's easier for everyone if I do, but Captain Marriott's got other servants, you know. There's a starchy old parlour maid called Edith, a manservant – he's a sort of valet really – who looks after the Captain, a gardener and a gardener's boy. So I don't think I'll be lonely, particularly as I can still visit the orphanage to see me old friends whenever I want.' She had been sitting at the table opposite Emmy as they talked, but now she got briskly to her feet. 'Well, if you've a mind to move fairly soon, you'd best start deciding what you're goin' to take and what you're goin' to leave. Would you like me to have a word with Bailey & Neep, the auctioneers on Lord Street? They'll come and collect, I believe.'

'Yes please, Lucy,' Emmy said humbly. 'I'll start making lists at once.'

A couple of days later, Emmy answered a tap at the door and found young Mr Johansson, accompanied by four grinning seamen, on the doorstep. He pulled off his cap, revealing rumpled fair hair, then gestured to the men behind him. 'Here we are, Mrs Wesley, ready to give a hand in any way we can. If you'll show us to your new house, we can take a look around, see what's needed and start work at once. D'you have a key yet?'

'Oh . . . yes, I've got a key,' Emmy said. She had paid a whole month's rent in advance in order to get the key immediately and was glad now that she had done so, though at the time she had been doubtful. In all the years that she had lived in Nightingale Court, she had never come across their landlord, and when she had met him she had not taken to him at all. He was a skinny, weaselly-faced man with thinning, raggedly cut hair, a long pink nose which seemed to have a perpetual dewdrop on the end, and small, over-bright eyes. When he had smiled, ingratiatingly, at her, he showed a mouth over-full of dirty, rotten-looking teeth, and she soon discovered that when he spoke he tended to spray saliva over anyone who stood too close.

He had pretended that he already had a tenant waiting to go into No. 2, but as soon as Emmy turned away, saying that she was sorry to have bothered him, he had broken into hurried speech, assuring her that he would far rather she occupied the house since her mother had always paid her rent promptly and had kept the house in good condition.

'Unlike them bleedin' Vaughans,' he had added viciously. 'They did a moonlight on me, else I'd ha' made 'em pay up for the damage what they'd done.' He eyed her cunningly. 'They should've handed the place over decent, but as it is, you'll have to clean up for yourself. It ain't no duty of a landlord's to mek good what others ha' ruined else I'd be penniless in no time.'

'I'll get it nice, Mr Freeman,' Emmy had promised

eagerly. Later, Beryl had told her that it was a landlord's duty to supply the materials for such repairs as were needed at the house, or to lower the rent. Mr Freeman, of course, had done neither. In fact, he had charged an extra sixpence, saying, rather obscurely, that this was the rent he charged new tenants.

'Then, if you've got the keys, all we need is directions . . . only it might be better if you came with us this first time, Mrs Wesley, in case anyone queries our right to be in the house,' Carl Johansson said, interrupting her thoughts. 'Or you could send the maid with us, if you're busy.'

But Emmy decided at once to go herself. She was ashamed of the state of the house, ashamed that it was such a poor place, but the men were here to put that right. So she went with them, unlocking the door of No. 2 and ushering them inside. 'It's in an awful state,' she said, trying to make her voice matter-of-fact and not apologetic, which is what she felt. 'But you knew it was pretty bad, I dare say.'

'We'll see to it, missus,' one of the ratings said. 'Gawd, some people ruin everything they touch, don't they? But it's a decent enough little place, an' in a couple o' days it'll be a palace, compared to what it is now.' He smiled reassuringly at Emmy. 'So just you take yourself back 'ome an' start packin' up, an' let us get on here.'

Thanking him, Emmy looked at him properly for the first time. He was small, grey-haired and fatherly-looking and he had not been at all shocked by the size and state of the property; probably, she realised, because he lived somewhere very similar himself.

Emmy turned towards the door, bidding Mr Johansson farewell as she did so. 'It's most awfully good of you,' she said, in her best Lancaster Avenue manner. 'I'm moving in, all being well, a week today. Do you really think . . . ?'

This time, Emmy did not miss the quick glance from Mr Johansson to the elderly rating, nor did she fail to note the rating's emphatic nod. Mr Johansson was nice, and an officer, but it was this small, elderly man who would oversee the work and make sure it was done properly. However, it was Mr Johansson who answered. 'Why, with a whole week to go, you've no fears that the place won't be ready, Mrs Wesley. In fact, if you've linoleum which wants laying or curtains which want hanging, get them here in, say, three days, and we'll put them up for you.'

'Wharrabout shelves, missus?' one of the other ratings asked. 'I'm a chippy an' I could put a row of shelves in the parlour, and there's room in the kitchen for a load of shelving – unless you're bringin' cupboards an' dressers an' that wi' you?'

Emmy looked rather helplessly from the carpenter to Mr Johansson. She realised she had not given any thought to the practicalities of living in a house without a servant. Oh, she had chosen the furniture she would bring with her, but she had assumed – wrongly, obviously – that a kitchen would have such things as cookers, sinks and cupboards provided. Now, looking around her, she realised that apart from the closed stove and the low stone sink and wooden draining boards, the room was empty. There had been shelves – she could see the nails still protruding from the wall in places and guessed that the Vaughans had either used the shelving to fuel the fire or taken the wooden boards when they did their moonlight flit. Conscience-stricken, she recalled the room as it had been in her childhood. What a fool she was! Her mother had had a big old Welsh dresser on one wall, several cupboards containing crockery, pots and pans and the like, rows of hooks from which she had hung strings of onions and bunches of herbs, and, of course, the big kitchen table upon which she had done her baking. Then there had been the rag rug in front of the fire, the battered easy chairs, with their homemade cushions, the clock on the mantelpiece . . .

But the men were staring at her; hastily, Emmy burst into speech. 'My present kitchen is a fitted one so I can scarcely bring it with me! But there is a dresser and a table, of course, and – and something called a maid-saver, which is a cupboard with glass doors so you can see what's in it. I'll bring all those things but I'd be very grateful for shelving and – and some hooks. I'll pay for the materials, of course,' she added.

'Don't you worry your head about it, missus; it's all to be provided,' the carpenter said. 'Mr Johansson here says we're a-goin' to help you move your stuff over, so I'll know where to put the shelves once the dresser an' that arrive.'

Very pink-faced and mumbling more thanks, Emmy headed for the door. As she made her way back to Lancaster Avenue, she thought that she would really have to take herself in hand. I lived in Nightingale Court for the first nineteen years of my life, she reminded herself savagely, as she joined the queue at the tram stop. The trouble is that Mam did everything for me. For all of those nineteen years, I hardly lifted a finger in the house; why, I actually let my mam do my ironing, and she even darned my silk stockings when one got laddered. Then there was Peter, who saw to it that I never lifted a finger in my own house either. I had Mam to clean and cook for me when I was first married, and when Diana came along Mam did things like nappy washing and making up bottles as well. Then, when she died, dear little Lucy did just about everything. She looked after Diana and managed the house and ran all my messages and treated me like a perishin' queen, but now I've got to forget all that and start managing for myself. After all, Beryl's coped for years and she's a good friend. She'll put me in the way of things, teach me how to keep house. Oh, thank goodness for Beryl!

Chapter Five

'Oh, Mammy, I love my bedroom, so I do! And isn't Mr Reynolds kind? He's put up all those lovely shelves along one wall of my room and he says next time the old *Queen* is in port, he'll come back an' put doors on so my toys won't get dusty. Becky and me's been ever so busy unpacking the boxes and putting my stuff on the shelves, but we've come down for elevenses, 'cos you get really hungry and thirsty when you're working hard, don't you, Mammy?'

Emmy had been washing china at the sink but swung round and smiled at Diana and Becky as they burst into the room. 'I know what you mean and I could do with a cuppa myself,' she admitted. 'Just let me finish these cups and I'll cut you some bread and you can butter it. I'm afraid there's no milk, but if I give you sixpence, perhaps you could go down to the shop on the corner and buy yourselves lemonade.'

Even as she made the offer, Emmy felt guilty. She had always impressed upon Peter the importance of milk in a child's diet, yet here she was, on her very first day in her new home, letting Diana and Becky drink lemonade because it was easier. She had asked about milk delivery – in Lancaster Avenue, the milkman had left three pints on the doorstep each day – but this had only caused Beryl to give a short laugh. 'Milk delivery, chuck?' she had said incredulously. 'In the court? No one delivers here . . . don't you remember? That's why most of us has conny-onny in our tea.'

Emmy had pretended to remember – she certainly did remember the conny-onny – but in fact, the delivery or non-delivery of milk had been her mother's business. When she was in her teens, her mother had occasionally sent her to Jane McCann's on Silvester Street to buy fresh milk, or butter, eggs or cheese. At the time, the young Emmy had not known about milk delivery, so had never thought to question it. Now, she thought crossly, she was having to learn things which she felt she should have known. But at least Diana and I are learning together, she consoled herself, handing the child a sixpenny bit. 'Now don't go further than the corner,' she told her daughter. 'You're too little to go wandering the streets. It isn't as if you had an older brother or sister who could go with you, see you across roads and so on.'

Diana, on her way to the kitchen door, turned back. 'Charlie would go with us if we gave him a penny for his trouble, like Aunty Beryl does,' she said persuasively. 'He and Lenny do Aunty Beryl's messages as soon as they've had breakfast. He'd do ours as well, Mammy, if we asked him.'

'No, Diana. It's only a bottle of lemonade, not a whole lot of shopping, and you and Becky won't really even have to leave the courts, not if you go to the shop on the corner,' she said. 'Another day perhaps we'll ask Charlie to get our shopping when he gets Aunty Beryl's, but for today you and Becky can either go, or drink water.'

At this harsh remark, Diana's eyes flew wide open in pained surprise, but she raised no more objections and the small girls clattered down the hallway and out through the front door. Emmy finished washing the last of the china and turned to survey her new domain. The men had made an excellent job of it. The walls were snowy with whitewash and the shelving which Mr Reynolds had erected had been painted sunshine yellow, giving the room a far brighter appearance than most of the other kitchens in the court. They had done wonders in the parlour, too. They had distempered the walls in a pleasant shade which, one of the men had told her, was called deep cream. The carpet with roses on it from Lancaster Avenue had been reverently laid on the floor, after the boards had been sanded and then waxed until they shone pale gold. Emmy's beloved chintz-upholstered chairs and sofa just about fitted in, and the china cabinet, which contained all the pieces Emmy most valued, stood by the fireplace, the empty grate hidden by a fire screen embroidered with roses.

Upstairs, the two bedrooms on the first floor were practical rather than pretty, though Mr Reynolds had done his best. Emmy's double bed was flanked by a wardrobe and a washstand, which had been bought cheap from Paddy's Market on the Scotland Road – there had been no room for Emmy's bedroom suite – and Diana's little room held her bed, another cheap washstand and the shelving which Mr Reynolds had put up for her toys. Because the houses were terraced and back to back, all the windows overlooked the court itself, and there was no denying that it was a pretty dreary outlook. Once, when the houses had first been built, they must have been a cheery red brick with whitewashed steps and, no doubt, sparkling windows, but now, getting on for a century later, the bricks were blackened, the windows usually dirty and the steps – or the steps opposite No. 2, at least – more grey than white. It wasn't that no one cared, it was the grime from factory chimneys, warehouses and the railway, which had blackened the bricks and made it impossible for whitened steps to remain so.

Emmy glanced once more round her kitchen, then decided she simply had to get out of here, if only for a few minutes. It was probably because there was no back door, no means of entering or leaving except through the court itself, which suddenly made her feel as if she was boxed up and someone was hammering the last nail into the lid of the box, but, whatever it was, Emmy grabbed her short jacket from its hook on the back of the door, jingled a few coins into her pocket and set off in pursuit of Diana and Becky. I'll buy a few biscuits so we can have something to eat with our elevenses, she thought wildly, and then remembered that, though she had brought her tea caddy with her, she had not got any milk. Irritatingly, she felt tears rise to her eyes and despised herself for such weakness. She was determined to be independent, yet she suddenly felt she would die if she didn't have a cup of tea. She was about to turn back, to borrow some milk off someone, when she remembered Beryl's remark about condensed milk. Of course, she could buy conny-onny at any corner shop, and once the tin was in her possession she would be able to have tea as long as the tea leaves in the caddy lasted. Briskly, Emmy dashed her hand across her eyes, straightened her drooping shoulders, and made for the corner shop. Over the last few years, she had stopped taking sugar in her tea because she wanted to keep her slim figure, but what did that matter now? Peter had been proud of her looks, of her eighteen-inch waist and long, slim legs, but who was there to care, now, if she drank tea with conny-onny in it and got as fat as a balloon? Come to that, the thought of a cup of hot, sweet tea was downright comforting and Emmy knew she needed comfort almost more than anything else.

'Mammy! We've got the lemonade but why's you out here? Did you want some more messages? Shall we go back to Mr Hedges' shop? He's a funny man, Mammy; he axed us if we wanted to put it on the slate and then he laughed and gave Becky and me an iced gem each.' It was Diana, one cheek distended by the iced gem, both arms cradling the bottle of lemonade as though it were her dearest child. 'If you take the lemonade, Mammy, we'll go back to Mr Hedges for you.'

Emmy, however, refused this offer. 'We'll all go back together,' she said, with a gaiety she did not really feel. 'I'm going to buy a tin of milk so I can have a cup of tea and I thought I'd get some biscuits. You like biscuits, don't you?'

Both children agreed enthusiastically and turned back towards the shop, rather to Emmy's relief. She had just remembered that she had not locked her door behind her, and though she was sure no intruder would enter the place she had impressed upon Diana, three times already this morning, that they must never, never leave the house unlocked unless, of course, they were at home. It would clearly be best if her daughter did not discover that her responsible mother had ignored her own warnings and left the door on the latch. When they got back to No. 2, therefore, she made a pretence of unlocking and then herded the children before her into the kitchen. Once there, she made herself a cup of tea, poured the children's lemonade into two mugs, tipped the biscuits from their bag on to a plate, and looked around for her handbag. For an awful, heart-stopping moment, she could not see it and wondered, desperately, whether she had been wrong, whether someone had entered the house in her absence. But it was all right; her handbag had been partially hidden by the teapot and she pounced on it, drawing out one of the two keys to the house which she now possessed. 'I'm going to put this key on a piece of string, darling,' she told Diana. 'It isn't so important right now, because I haven't got a job yet, but when I do you may want to let yourself into the house after school, so you'll need a key of your own.' She had been knotting the string into a loop as she spoke and now she held it out to Diana, expecting the child to be pleased at this sign of trust, but Diana was putting both hands behind her back and shaking her head violently.

'No, Mammy. Everyone else in the court puts the key through the letter box, I told you they did, and that's what we should do.'

Emmy was about to expostulate, to say that a key dangling through the letter box was an open invitation to a thief, but then she checked herself. In all the years that she had lived in the court, she had never heard of a break-in, though there had been cases of people robbing their own gas meters, or popping next door to borrow a cup of sugar and never returning it. Besides, she realised that Diana, even if she did not know it, was trying to fit in. What other children did, she would do, and other children pulled the latch key up through the letter box, they did not have their own key on a piece of string round their necks. Indeed, for a big family, this would have been impossibly expensive, as well as risky, for, children being children, the younger ones would probably have lost their latch keys the first time the weather was warm and someone suggested a game of alley football or a dip in the Scaldy.

But Diana was still shaking her head, still staring. Emmy said, placatingly: 'Yes of course, I was forgetting. Now you may have two biscuits with your lemonade, and then you can play outside for a bit, whilst I get us some luncheon.'

'Dinner,' Diana said quickly. 'It's dinner in the middle of the day, Mammy, and tea when your daddy gets home. Or supper; some famblies call it supper.'

'Yes, of course. I'm sorry,' Emmy said humbly, as the two children left the kitchen. A pang had gone through her when Diana had mentioned the returning fathers, but Diana herself had clearly not been affected by her remark. This daughter of hers was going to fit in far better and more easily than she herself would, yet Emmy had been born and bred in this very house. But it will be all right when I get a job, Emmy reminded herself, finishing her cup of tea and going over to the cupboard where her vegetables were kept. Mr Reynolds had drilled holes in it, explaining that this would allow air to circulate, which would help the vegetables to remain fresh for longer. 'Though you'll be wantin' to buy spuds an' that each day at this time of year,' he had warned her. 'If you don't, you'll find the spuds wi' shoots six inches long and little green leaves at the top afore you know it. An' cabbage . . . well, they shoot like Jack's beanstalk, if you know what I mean.'

But the vegetables had only been in the cupboard since Emmy had brought them from Lancaster Avenue the previous day, so now she opened the door and began to count potatoes into the colander.

She decided half a dozen would be sufficient and was about to close the cupboard again when she heard a little scraping noise and caught a flicker of movement. She drew back just as a small, grey form emerged from behind some carrots. Emmy was almost sure it was munching. She was not frightened of mice but did not much fancy the thought of sharing her kitchen, let alone her vegetables, with the creatures, and began to try to evict it. She got it out of the vegetable cupboard but lost it under the sink, and was wondering how the working party had managed to miss its entry hole when there was a brisk bang on the front door followed by footsteps along the hallway, and then the kitchen door burst open and Beryl appeared.

'Hello, queen, how are you doing?' she said breezily. 'Most of us have our main meal in the evenin' when the fellers come home so I thought I'd come over and bring a loaf and a heel of cheese; if you'll provide the tea, I'll do the rest. I sent young Diana back to my place wi' Becky. I've left 'em bread an' cheese an' home-made lemonade – Charlie will see everyone gets a share – and I thought you an' me might have a bit of a chat while we eat.'

Emmy felt a huge wave of relief engulf her. There was so much she did not know, so much she needed to ask Beryl! Now that she came to think of it, she and Diana never had a main meal at lunchtime but saved it for the evening, even when Peter was not home. Of course, she had never had to prepare lunch, but Lucy had done so, and it was usually sandwiches and an apple, or a sausage roll each, followed by a piece of cake. What had she been thinking of, about to prepare potatoes and cabbage and carrots this early in the day? But Beryl was looking at her so kindly, with so much understanding, that she suddenly found her eyes were filling with tears and she flung herself on the other woman, weeping unrestrainedly. 'Oh, Beryl, whatever is the matter with me?' she sobbed. 'I *know* most folk have their main meal at night – we did ourselves in Lancaster Avenue – yet I started getting a proper dinner in the middle of the day! Oh, Beryl, am I going mad?'

Beryl gave her a hearty hug and then a shake. She was laughing but her eyes were still full of sympathy and understanding. 'No, you aren't goin' mad, queen,' she said gently. 'But you're in a rare old muddle, ain't you? Diana telled me you were goin' to cook a dinner so I thought I'd come over and sort you out a bit. Besides, I've got something important to tell you. Remember that big dining rooms on the Scottie? Well, it were more of a chop house really . . . heaps of businessmen go there for their grub. You were pally wi' one o' the girls what worked there – Iris, wasn't it? – afore you wed.'

'McCullough's,' Emmy said, triumphantly, after a moment's thought. 'Yes, I remember it. They paid all right and Iris used to get a lot of tips. She was ever so pretty and had a way of looking at the fellers through her lashes which brought the money tumbling out of their pockets.'

'Yes, that's right, McCullough's,' Beryl agreed. 'Well, they've got a vacancy for a waitress. I believe it's shift work because they open at seven in the morning for breakfasts and close around ten to half past, at night. But as you say, the money's good and I dare say they'll be able to arrange the hours to suit.'

Emmy could not help herself. She spoke before she had thought, the words tumbling off her tongue. 'Oh, but Beryl, I've never been a waitress. I mean to look for an office job, either on reception or as a secretary. I worked in an office before, and I thought . . . I thought . . .'

Beryl heaved a sigh. 'The sort of secretarial work you'd get wouldn't earn you enough to pay your rent and feed yourself and Diana,' she said bluntly. 'If I remember rightly, chuck, I earned more working on a factory assembly line than you got for being in the typing pool at the Royal. You can't afford to ignore the money for the sake of being able to say you work in an office, norrany more.'

Emmy felt her cheeks grow hot. Beryl was right, of course. She did not fancy telling folk that she was a waitress, but saying she had an office job would have been acceptable enough. Come to that, she remembered, guiltily, that she had never actually told Peter what her job at the Royal entailed. She had said she was the secretary for the Head of Claims, and since Peter hadn't visited her at work he had never discovered that, in fact, her position was rather more lowly. However, Emmy had never kept a secret from Beryl in her whole life and she remembered, now, how Beryl had laughed at her, telling her that she was lucky she did not have to take her wages home and hand over a weekly sum to her mother. 'If you did, you wouldn't have enough to buy yourself an ice cream in the interval at the flicks,' she had teased. 'I like me brothers and sisters and wouldn't be without them, but you've shown me the advantages of being an only child, young Emmy.'

Right now, however, Beryl was looking at her quizzically, and once more Emmy hurried into speech. 'You're right, of course, you always are – oh, how I wish I were sensible like you! But . . . but I don't know anything about being a waitress, so why should they employ me? I don't want to lie and pretend I've had experience at waiting on because they'll soon realise that it's not true.'

'They'll employ you 'cos you're so perishin' pretty,' Beryl told her frankly. 'As for waitin' on, I don't know as you'd need much experience, they just like you to be quick and neat, I think.' She eyed her friend consideringly. 'To tell the truth, Em, I think it'll be good for you. You'll meet lots of people – ordinary people, not smart ones earning big salaries – and you'll make pals. I know you had one or two friends at the Royal, but these girls will be more . . . more down to earth, I s'pose you could call it. The girl who told me about the job – Freda, her name is – said that McCullough's employs a huge staff and that everyone's real friendly an' helpful towards each other.'

'It sounds lovely,' Emmy said quickly, and was glad she had done so when she saw Beryl's face clear. 'Can I apply at once? Does it have to be in writing or do I just go round there?'

Beryl laughed. 'Freda's a pal of mine from way back, when we both worked on the assembly line. I axed her to let me know when a job were comin' up, 'cos the best thing out is to gerrin when the boss first hears he's goin' to be a member of staff short. Gettin' someone means advertisin' an' interviewin', 'cos McCullough's is too big just to put a card in the window, like. But if a pretty girl comes along the same day his waitress gives in her notice, then the chances are he'll give her the job an' save himself trouble, see?'

'Yes, I see,' Emmy said doubtfully. 'But you haven't answered my question, Beryl. Do I go round there or what?'

'The waitress who's goin' to give in her notice is

havin' a baby,' Beryl said. 'She's been waitin' until she begins to show but she's decided to leave at the end of this coming week because she's havin' what they call a sick pregnancy. She says it's all right when she's on the afternoon shift but she can't go on throwin' up out the back when she's on earlies without someone noticin'. So if you go round to McCullough's – Mac's, the girls call it – around eleven o'clock on Friday, you may be lucky.'

'Right, I'll do that,' Emmy said eagerly. Suddenly, she felt full of hope and enthusiasm. She realised she had been allowing the new little house – which was not really new to her at all – to depress her. She had not known how much she would miss the beautiful garden in Lancaster Avenue, nor the spacious airy rooms, not to mention the constant companionship of young Lucy. She guessed that Diana would not spend as much time with her as she had done in Lancaster Avenue, because here the child only had to step out of her front door to find a great many companions. All the courts swarmed with children and though Emmy might tell herself that this was a good thing and would make life very much easier for her daughter, she now had to acknowledge that it would mean that she herself would not be as important to Diana as she had been in Lancaster Avenue.

So, clearly, the sooner she could get work the better and what did it matter, after all, whether she worked in an office or a restaurant? What really counted was earning enough money to keep herself and Diana and being able to cope with the work. Thinking about it, she realised that, though she had not forgotten her shorthand, it would undoubtedly be extremely rusty, whilst her typewriting, which had once been fast, would have slowed down a lot. It was horrid having to remind herself that she might not be able to hold down an office job, but with Beryl's eye upon her she had to acknowledge the truth, if only to herself. If she went back into an office, she would have to start at the bottom of the ladder, and it might be many months – years, even – before the young Mrs Wesley earned as much as the even younger Miss Dickens had once done.

'What about clothes though, Beryl?' she said. If she had been applying for an office job, she would have worn her best and most expensive outfit, but she realised she had no idea what a prospective waitress should wear. 'Does it matter? Only they wear a sort of uniform, don't they?'

'Wear something plain, preferably dark,' Beryl said. 'They'll tell you what they want you to wear if you get the job, but for the interview . . .' Her eyes flickered over Emmy's figure and Emmy glanced down at herself. She was wearing a black skirt and a dark grey cardigan beneath the pink gingham wrap-around apron which she always wore when she was doing some small task in the house. 'What you're wearing now is fine, Em. Oh, and you'll need flat shoes, black ones. D'you have any?'

Emmy mentally reviewed the many pairs of shoes in her wardrobe upstairs, then shook her head sadly. 'I've got plenty of brown walking shoes but no black ones,' she admitted. 'I'd best buy some before Friday, then.'

Beryl cast her eyes at the ceiling and heaved a dramatic sigh. 'You will do nothing of the sort,' she remarked. 'We'll get some black shoe dye from Clarkson's on the Scottie; it'll only cost but a few pennies. Now, how about makin' me a cup of tea?'

*

'Becky, where's Charlie gone?' Diana's voice was shrill and aggrieved. 'He telled me to go into his house and fetch a piece of rope off the dresser, which I done, only now I can't find him *anywhere*!'

Becky was crouching on the paving stones trying to balance five small pebbles on the back of her hand, but she glanced up as Diana spoke and the pebbles clattered to the ground. Becky scowled. 'Him and Lenny's gone off. They's done Mammy's messages, took in water, chopped kindlin' an' that, an' now they's gone to earn some dosh, Charlie said. It's for the penny rush at the pictures, come Sat'day,' she added in a kindly tone, seeing Diana's look of puzzlement. 'That's the children's cinema show,' she finished.

'Oh,' Diana said vaguely. She had never heard of a children's cinema show – certainly never attended one – and could not imagine why Charlie should need to earn money. Surely, dear Aunty Beryl would give him his Saturday sixpence each week, as her own mammy did? But she was beginning to realise that life was very different here in Nightingale Court from the life she had lived in Lancaster Avenue. Today was Friday and it was the most different day of all, since Mammy had gone off all by herself, refusing to let Diana accompany her. When Diana reminded her mammy that she loved shopping and could help carry the parcels, Mammy had replied, quite sharply, that she was going after a job and that Aunty Beryl and Charlie would give an eye to her. 'Then what am I to do? What's you playin', Becky?'

Becky sighed and stood up. 'Nothin' much,' she said. 'Did you get the rope? If so, I'll show you how to skip.'

It was humiliating, having to let a girl a whole

year younger than herself teach her so many things, particularly as Becky was slow for her age, but Diana was getting used to it. Becky had shown her how to mark out a hopscotch pitch and how to choose a flat piece of slate, how to throw it into the square and how to retrieve it afterwards. She had taught her how to play cherry-wobs and marbles and instructed her in the art of collecting broken bits of china to use as currency when playing shop, and now, it seemed, she would teach Diana to skip rope. Diana sighed. She would much rather have been with Charlie, earning pennies for this Saturday rush, but she had promised Mammy not to go out of the court unless she was accompanied by a grown-up, so she had better knuckle down and learn to skip rope – until Charlie returned, that was. Once he was back, she would take up her usual admiring position, some six feet behind him, and would tag him for the rest of the day. She knew this sometimes irritated him, but could not help herself. He was her hero, he had saved her life at New Brighton, and anyway, he liked having someone to cheer him on when he played football, or to sit and chat to him whilst he chopped up orange boxes for kindling, or trekked to and fro carrying Aunty Beryl's water supply into the house, morning and evening.

'You holds the rope in both hands . . .'

It did not take Diana long to realise that Becky was trying to teach her an art which she could not do herself, and when an older girl, clad in a filthy grey wisp of a dress, her mop of tangled curls held back from her face with a bootlace, came and snatched the rope off Becky, Diana felt almost relieved. She would not have minded had the girl merely appropriated the rope for her own use, but apparently this was not her intention. 'You hold one end, littl'un, while your pal holds the other,' she instructed Becky. 'Turn it at the same time an' I'll run in an' you can watch what I does. Then we'll swap round and you can both have a go.'

'Thanks, Wendy,' Becky said gratefully. 'I's norra very good skipper but Di wants to learn, don't you, Di?'

Diana agreed that she did, and by the time Aunty Beryl called them in for bread and cheese and weak tea she had got the hang of it and thanked Wendy sincerely for her help. She thought she had never seen a girl as dirty as her new friend, and noticed Aunty Beryl's eyebrows almost disappearing into her hair when she saw with whom they were playing. But she made no comment, and since Charlie entered the house hot on her heels, Diana soon forgot the whole incident.

'I wonder how your mammy's gettin' on,' Aunty Beryl said idly, as she cut slices from the long loaf and handed each child a very small square of cheese. 'Did you have a nice game, you two? I take it, Charlie,' she added, addressing her son as she pushed a mug towards him, 'that you and Lenny were earning yourself a few pennies, lugging lino back home from Paddy's Market?'

'I can skip,' Diana said proudly. 'I'm better'n Becky, ain't I, Becks?'

'That's grand,' Aunty Beryl said. 'Charlie?'

'Lenny an' me carried bags, mostly,' Charlie admitted through a mouth crammed with bread and cheese. 'We've got twopence each now, so that's all right. Where's Aunty Emmy, Mam? Only we's off to St Martin's rec this afternoon for a game o' footie an' we can't take no kids.'

'I'll keep an eye on Diana,' his mother said. 'Aunty Emmy's off on – on business, but she'll be home for tea.'

Diana opened her mouth to say that her mother had gone after a job, then caught Aunty Beryl's eye and said nothing. She saw no reason why she should not tell the assembled Fishers where her mother was, but Aunty Beryl must have had a reason for that glance. So Diana continued placidly to eat her bread and cheese and to plan how she might persuade the older woman to take her down to the rec to watch the boys' game.

Emmy arrived at the dining rooms promptly at eleven o'clock and, after a moment's hesitation, went inside. She was immediately glad she had taken Beryl's advice to go when it was quiet since the enormous room was only half full of women, having coffee or tea, little cakes or biscuits, and chattering away like a cage full of birds. Emmy looked round, a trifle self-consciously, then took her place at one of the tables. A waitress approached her to ask for her order and Emmy said, in a shy whisper, that she would like a pot of tea, please, and some biscuits and that she was Emmy Wesley, who knew Freda. The girl smiled immediately, gave a brisk little nod, and went off to get her order, and Emmy thought thankfully that Beryl, as usual, had known exactly what she was doing when she had insisted that Emmy and Freda must meet. 'Freda will see you right,' Beryl had assured her young friend. 'As soon as she knows you're in the place, she'll tell you if the boss is about, an' if he ain't, she'll tell you where to wait till he is.' She had instructed Emmy to behave as any other customer would until Freda came over and told her what she should do. Emmy intended to follow these instructions to the letter, and just hoped that the boss was on the premises.

She had drunk two cups of tea and finished the ginger biscuits before Freda came over to the table. Emmy had met her the previous day; she was in her early forties, with a broad, placid face, neatly shingled grey-streaked hair, and a sturdy figure. Emmy had taken to her at once and now, watching her covertly, saw that she was light on her feet and quite as quick and agile as some of the girls half her age. She swooped upon Emmy's table, saying chattily: 'The boss is in the office, miss, if you was wantin' a word. I telled him you were enquiring about work an' he said to ask you to step through. I'll show you the way.'

Emmy murmured her thanks, picked up her handbag and followed the older woman. They crossed the enormous room and Freda tapped briskly on a door which said 'Private, No Admittance' then flung it open. She ushered Emmy inside, gave her arm a quick and encouraging squeeze, and said: 'Here's Mrs Wesley, Mr McCullough. If you'll give me a shout when you've finished with her . . .' She did not complete the sentence but whisked out of the room, closing the door firmly behind her.

For a moment, Emmy felt downright terrified, but then she remembered everything Beryl had told her. She straightened her shoulders and gave the middle-aged man behind the desk her brightest smile. She judged him to be in his forties and, possibly, to have some foreign blood in him since his hair and eyes were very dark and his skin was swarthy. He had a square face with broad cheekbones and a strongly cleft chin and she thought, apprehensively, that he looked stern and wondered whether she was wise to want to work for him. He must have sensed her doubts, however, for he gave her a smile of extraordinary sweetness which completely changed his face.

Emmy took a deep breath and returned the smile. 'Good morning, Mr McCullough,' she said. 'I was wondering if you have any vacancies? I – I would like to get work since my daughter will be going back to school in a fortnight and, to be frank, I need the money.'

'And you've heard on the grapevine that one of my staff's leaving me,' Mr McCullough said. He sighed. 'Don't trouble to deny it, young woman, 'cos I don't believe in fairy tales. However, you're presentable and you've got a nice big smile. Ever waited on before?'

'No, I'm afraid not,' Emmy said regretfully. 'But I'm a quick learner, Mr McCullough.'

'Oh aye, that's what they all say. It's hard work, d'you know that? The money's good but there'll be times when your feet are killing you and your back's aching and someone doesn't turn up for their shift, so you'll be asked to work double. What about that, eh? You say you've got a child. What'll happen when you're on earlies, or lates for that matter? And there's school holidays.'

'That's all arranged. I live next door to my best friend and she'll have Diana when I'm working,' Emmy said quickly. She had known that these questions were going to come and she and Beryl had prepared for them. Mr McCullough preferred his waitresses to be what he called 'steady' which often meant married and with children, though he also employed very much younger girls. 'And in case you're wondering, I'm – I'm a widow. My husband died in a dockside accident last month, which is why I need to find work.'

Mr McCullough nodded. 'I'm sorry for your loss, Mrs Wesley,' he said gravely. 'Now, as you may know, it is our usual practice to give our waitresses a trial run. Are you willing to do that? I can put you on from twelve till two with Harriet and keep an eye on you, see if you're up to the work. How would that be?'

Once again, Emmy had been prepared for this. 'He won't never take on anyone without his seein' 'em doin' the work,' Freda had told her the previous day. 'It's a job what needs someone who can smile at the grumpiest customer an' make 'em feel . . . well, as if they care, if you know what I mean.'

But right now, Mr McCullough was still staring at her, waiting for a reply, his dark eyes, fringed with thick black lashes, very bright.

'Yes, that will be grand, Mr McCullough,' Emmy said. She added, with a flash of humour: 'I'm as keen as you are to see whether I can do the work, to tell you the truth!'

Mr McCullough laughed. 'Good for you, Mrs Wesley,' he said approvingly. Getting quickly to his feet, he crossed the room and opened the door, then beckoned to her. 'Come along with me.'

It was a good thing, Emmy reflected, that she had worn a dark cardigan and skirt, for she was provided with a frilly white apron, a stiff white collar and cuffs and a rather becoming little cap which she wore perched on her smooth blonde hair. She did not look exactly like the other waitresses, but she doubted that any but a very observant customer would know that she was not a member of staff. Harriet proved to be a long, thin girl with bright ginger hair, pale blue eyes and an enchanting smile. She took Emmy round with her for the first hour, explaining in an undervoice how the ordering system worked and what one should say to customers to make them feel at ease. 'They'll ask you what's on, even though there's that bloody great chalkboard right in front of their eyes, and menu cards on every table,' she told her helper. 'What they mean is, "What'll I like best?" which is a hard one, believe me. I usually say, "The roast beef is prime today and the veggies are peas an' carrots," or else I say, "We're gettin' a bit low on treacle pud, but I dare say I could squeeze out one more helpin'," anything to make 'em feel you've got their interests at heart, see? An' once you get to know 'em, you'll remember that this feller always goes for a roast, or prefers a nice lamb chop, or can't abide gooseberry tart, and you act according. See wharr I mean?'

When the second hour started, Harriet told Emmy to start taking orders on her own account. 'But write each order out in full. Don't use abbreviations until you've gorr'em all by heart,' she told her. 'If the kitchen don't understand and send out the wrong grub, tempers get frayed.'

Emmy had already been provided with a pad and pencil attached to her waist by a long silver chain, and now she approached her first table. The four men seated there gave her only the most cursory of glances before demanding to know, in thick Lancashire accents, whether the steak and kidney pud was still on and if it came with boiled potatoes or mash.

'Which would you prefer, sir?' Emmy asked politely, knowing that was what Harriet would have said. Two of the men wanted boiled potatoes and two wanted mash and they all demanded extra gravy, which Emmy only pretended to write down, since she had seen for herself that the plates of steak and kidney were all swimming in the stuff. 'And to drink?' Emmy asked hopefully. Harriet had told her that if a customer ordered a bottle of wine, the waitress got a percentage of the money, but these men said they would have tea – a large pot – and would not order their puddings until they had finished their main course. Emmy nodded intelligently, swept the table with a smiling glance, and hurried off to spike her order. She tore the page with the order on it off her pad and thrust it on to the long metal spike which stood by the kitchen hatch, then remembered that she had not put the table number on it, remedied the fault, and turned back into the restaurant. When the cooks had made up the order, they would shout her name and she would go into the kitchen, find the order and return to the restaurant.

Time sped by and it was well past two o'clock before Emmy realised that the room was starting to empty. She was suddenly aware of aching feet, perspiration patches beneath both arms and a mixture of tiredness and excitement, for though it had been incredibly hard work she found she had enjoyed every minute.

She had noticed Mr McCullough seated at a corner table, apparently working on some books, for she did not once see him glance up at her. By the time Harriet told her that she had done all right and should seek out Mr McCullough, he had left the table, so she tapped on the office door and went in.

He was seated behind the desk and gestured her

to a chair, saying as he did so: 'Well? How did you find it?'

Emmy was surprised, having assumed that he would tell her how she had done, but answered readily enough. 'I liked it, sir. The customers are ever so friendly – at least, they're all polite – and though the work is hard and my feet do ache, people are so nice about the food and how they've enjoyed it . . . it's difficult to explain, but I feel . . . well, useful I suppose.' She stared across the desk, trying to read Mr McCullough's expression, and found herself hoping, fervently, that he would tell her she had got the job and begin to discuss terms.

Instead, he surprised her once more. 'Get many tips, did you?'

For answer, Emmy dug into the capacious pocket of her frilly apron and carefully laid the coins therein on the desk. Mr McCullough bent forward and counted, then leaned back and smiled at her. 'Three and sevenpence! Well, Mrs Wesley, the job's yours if you want it.' Emmy opened her mouth to speak but he shushed her with a wave of the hand. 'You've not heard the terms and conditions yet, so let's get down to business. You liked waiting on, all right, and you were good at it, but I must make it clear that it won't be your only job. The waitresses are responsible for the cleanliness of the whole dining room; that means windows and floors as well as the tables and chairs, of course. And if the place is quiet, I expect my girls to muck in with the kitchen staff, performing tasks such as peeling potatoes, cleaning cabbage, making a suet crust for a pudding . . . in short, doing anything that is needed. Again, if someone's ill or away, you may be asked to take over their job for a few days. And then there's the washing-up. We've got special staff for that, but sometimes they need a helping hand. Well, Mrs Wesley, how do you feel about the job now?'

'The same. I'd still love to work here,' Emmy said frankly. 'The only trouble is, Mr McCullough, I – I've never really learned to cook and I wouldn't want to spoil good ingredients by doing it all wrong.'

Mr McCullough laughed. 'Don't worry about that. We've a reputation for excellent food so you won't find yourself thrown into the deep end, as far as cooking is concerned. You'll be taught how to make simple things – under an expert's eye, of course – and before you know it, you'll be doing all sorts. Oh, perhaps I should mention that your wages won't vary whatever task you're carrying out, and I expect the girls told you that your tips are your own. At Christmas, all tips go into a pool and are divided up amongst the entire staff on Christmas Eve, but that's the only exception. And now to uniform. We provide aprons, caps, collars and cuffs, so all you will need to buy is a black dress, or a black skirt and blouse, and some flat black shoes. Can you manage that, do you think?' Emmy assured him that she already possessed a couple of plain black dresses, and Mr McCullough nodded approvingly. 'Good, good. I am Mr Mac to my staff – McCullough is such a mouthful – and you, of course, will be Mrs Wesley, though I dare say the staff will use your first name when you're not in the dining room. And now we had best discuss wages . . .'

'Mammy!' Diana flew across Beryl's kitchen and cast herself into her mother's arms. 'Oh, you've been gone ages. I would have been upset only Aunty Beryl said that were a good sign. What happened, Mammy? Did you get the job?'

Beryl, peeling potatoes at the sink, turned and grinned. 'One look at your mammy's face tells me she's now a waitress,' she announced. 'I tek it he were pleased with you, chuck? And by the grin on your face, I reckon you took to it like a duck to water. Am I right?'

'You are,' Emmy said, sinking on to a kitchen chair and arching her back, rubbing vigorously at it as she did so. 'It's awful hard work, you were right there, but I really enjoyed it, and the money's good, especially when you think of the tips. Why, I only waited on for a couple of hours – actually, it were only an hour by myself – and I took three and seven in tips, can you believe it?'

Beryl nodded. 'I can. You're a pretty girl, chuck, and you've got nice ways. I thought you'd do well, waiting on. So long as it ain't too much for you, of course. Fancy a cuppa?'

'I'd love one,' Emmy said eagerly. 'I had a cup before I left Mac's, but that seems a long time ago now.'

'When do you start? An' wharrabout uniform?' Beryl asked, dropping the peeled potatoes into a large pan of water and carrying it over to the stove. 'D'you have to provide your own?'

'I start first thing Monday morning, on the early shift, so I have to be up at the crack of dawn,' Emmy told her. 'But mornings are a lot quieter, so Mr McCullough – I mean Mr Mac, he said to call him that – likes to start new staff on earlies to get them used to it gradually, like. As for uniform, I have to provide two plain black dresses and they give me white collars and cuffs, a frilly white apron and a cap. I hand in my whites, as they call them, when I finish my shift and get clean ones next day.'

'Do you have two black dresses?' Beryl asked curiously. 'If not, we'll go down to Paddy's Market tomorrow and get you a couple o' second-hand ones. You can rinse them out on Sunday and they'll be fine for work on Monday.'

'It's all right. I've got several black dresses which will do,' Emmy said hastily; she did not fancy wearing a second-hand dress, no matter how carefully it had been rinsed. She indicated the bag on the floor. 'I've bought fish and chips for Di and me to celebrate, but I'll shove 'em in the oven when I get home and warm them through. To tell the truth, I'm far too tired and excited to turn round and start cooking.'

Diana, who had been diligently drawing pictures on a piece of old brown wrapping paper, looked up. 'Oh, Mammy, fish 'n' chips is me favourite food! Will we have it always when you're workin' at – at that place?'

Emmy laughed but shook her head. 'No, darling, not every night. When I'm on earlies, I'll be home well before you come out of school, so I'll have time to cook you something nice.' She turned back to Beryl. 'My mam never did teach me to cook, and when she died I always had Lucy to do it,' she admitted ruefully. 'But Mr Mac explained that part of the job would be helping the kitchen staff when they're busy and the restaurant isn't. And he says they'll teach me to cook.'

She beamed at Beryl, who laughed and shook her head. 'Some folk land on their feet every time, like cats,' she observed. 'But I'm real glad you got the job, queen, because it'll solve a good few of your problems, see if it don't.'

Later that evening, when Emmy was putting Diana

to bed, it occurred to her to wonder out loud why Beryl had not applied for such a job herself. After all, at the moment, Beryl worked extremely hard and did not get particularly well paid for her labours. Diana, pulling on her white cotton nightgown, eyed her parent with astonishment. 'Who'd look after the kids if Aunty Beryl went to be a waitress in a smart dining rooms?' she asked incredulously. 'Granny Pritchard can't help, now that she's bedridden. In fact she needs looking after herself. And anyway, Mammy, Aunty Beryl's fat and . . . well, she isn't like you, is she?'

'She's a lot more efficient than I am,' Emmy said severely, but even as she spoke, a picture of Beryl rose before her mind's eye and she was forced to acknowledge that her small daughter had hit the nail on the head. It wasn't that Beryl was fat so much as, well, sort of saggy, Emmy concluded. Once, her friend's thick brown curls had been fashionably cut and regularly brushed. Now it looked as though Beryl cut them herself with blunt scissors. After the birth of her youngest child, Beryl had developed bad varicose veins and now she walked with a limp, trying to spare her left leg where the veins were worst. Although she was always clean and as neat as possible, all her clothing was old and darned, and her down-at-heel shoes, the only pair she possessed, Emmy thought, were cracked and broken.

Emmy said goodnight to Diana and went downstairs. She remembered Beryl on her wedding day, looking so happy and pretty. She remembered her after Charlie's birth, showing her baby off, wearing a floral print and white sandals. But now, with four children and a multitude of small jobs, she was beginning to resemble a good many of the other women in the court. If she pulled herself together, Emmy began to think, then remembered Bobby. It was no use Beryl's pulling herself together, not until Bobby was old enough to be left with the other children. And then she remembered something else Diana had said. She had said that Beryl was fat. Emmy's hands flew to her mouth as realisation dawned. Beryl wasn't fat, she was expecting again!

For a moment, Emmy was tempted to rush round to her friend, to ask if it were true, but what good would that do? She remembered Peter saying, when they first got married, that too many children made women old before their time and forced men to work for miserably small wages because they dared not leave a job and try for a better one in case they found themselves without work, struggling to bring up a family on the dole. She had been lucky that Peter had known all about birth control and had 'taken precautions', but he was an intelligent man. Beryl's Wally was kind-hearted and sweet-tempered, but Beryl would be the first to admit that he was not at all clever. It probably never occurred to him that life would be easier if babies didn't arrive with such appalling regularity. And Beryl, of course, would not dream of discussing such intimate things, not even with her best friend.

But I'm not so squeamish, Emmy told herself, sitting down before the kitchen fire. I'll go over there first thing tomorrow and get her to come out with me, and we'll have a good talk. It's about time I did something for Beryl instead of the other way round.

Chapter Six

Diana came out of school at a run so that no one should see she was crying. It was mid-October, but the sun was still warm on her back and Diana, though still upset, was glad that at least it was not raining. She knew her mother would have told her to wait for Lenny and Charlie, but Diana, sniffing dolefully, did not intend to let anyone see her with her eyes all tear-blubbered and a runny nose. However, she was well ahead of the rest of the school, so she set off at a trot in the direction of the court. With a bit of luck she would get home, wash her face and tidy herself before anyone saw her.

Hurrying along, she fished in her knicker leg for a handkerchief and then remembered, crossly, that she had been in such a hurry this morning that she had neglected to take one out of her drawer. And if it hadn't been for that hateful Hilda Bridges and her pal Maureen she wouldn't have needed a handkerchief, she reminded herself. Hilda and Maureen, both more than a year older and a good deal stronger than Diana, took sadistic pleasure in making her life a misery – and for why? Because Diana, who was only five and a new girl, had been put up a whole year as she was streets ahead of the other five-year-olds in the school. So now she was in Standard II with big girls of six, or even seven, being taught reading, writing and sums by Miss Lovett, and being bullied by Hilda and Maureen.

They were far too clever to try to ill-treat her when anyone else was about, but this afternoon she had been sent to fetch a couple of new dusters from another classroom. As she passed the cloakroom on her way back to Miss Lovett's, the two girls had pounced on her, wrestled her to the floor, and smacked and kicked her, tearing her new grey tunic in the process, before hurrying off, sniggering, to get back to their classroom whilst Miss Lovett was still absent, for it appeared she had been called away only minutes after despatching Diana on her errand.

So now, reaching the court, Diana rushed towards her own front door, still with her head down and tears blurring her vision, which was how she came to run into someone. The someone caught at her shoulders and a laughing voice said chidingly: 'Where's you off to in such a hurry, kiddo? You damned near knocked me over. Hey, youse crying! Wharrever is the matter? Here, is your mam at home? I'll fetch her if you like.'

Diana cleared her eyes of tears with both fists and stared at the other girl. It was Wendy, the girl who had taught her to skip, the girl of whom Mammy disapproved. 'She's the dirtiest ragamuffin in the whole of Liverpool, I should think,' her mother had said disparagingly. 'She's a real menace, that one. All the respectable people in the court avoid Mrs Telford. *Missus!* Don't make me laugh. That one never saw a wedding ring, let alone a wedding.'

'But I like Wendy; she's kind,' Diana had said, bewildered by her mother's animosity. 'It isn't her fault that she don't have nice clothes; it isn't her fault that she's dirty, either.'

Her mother had pounced on this. 'Yes it is, because soap and water's free,' she had said. 'What's more, her hair's full of nits and if there's one thing I can do without, it's having to comb nits out of your hair every single blessed night. Look, darling, there are heaps of children living in Nightingale Court who want to be friends. Pick one of them.'

But now here was Wendy, offering to fetch her mother, clearly realising that something was wrong and doing her best to help. Diana pushed the hair out of her eyes and turned to face the older girl. 'Me mam isn't in,' she said huskily. 'But I want to get cleaned up afore the Fishers see me. I – I don't want 'em to know I've been cryin'.'

'Right. I'll come in wi' you an' whiles you tidy up you can tell me what's been goin' on,' Wendy said. She led the way to Diana's front door, pulling the key up on its string and unlocking, as though she did it every day of her life. 'Come on in then,' she said, as hospitably as if it had been her home and not Diana's. 'You needn't tell me you're being bullied by older girls; I can guess what happened. I used to get it myself afore I learned a trick or two worth more than anything they could come up with.' The two children had entered the kitchen and Wendy looked curiously about her. 'Ain't it nice, though?' she said in a wondering tone. 'Coo, you'd never think it were the same as our kitchen – same size an' shape, I mean. What's that?'

She was pointing to the gas stove which Emmy had had installed as soon as she was able to afford it. Diana told her, then trotted over to the sink and began to fill the big black kettle on the draining board from the bucket which her mother had filled earlier. She said, conversationally, as she did so, 'I'm not allowed to boil the kettle when I'm here by meself but I dare say it's all right when you're with me. Are you allowed to use matches, Wendy? I'm not, 'cos Mammy says I'll burn the house down, but if you light the gas I can wash in warm water.'

She looked enquiringly at her guest and saw the older girl's cheeks turn pink. 'Course I can use matches, but I ain't a-goin' to,' Wendy said. 'You wash in cold, queen, like the rest of us do. Now, if you'd asked me to boil the kettle for a cuppa, that would have been different . . . an' where's your 'airbrush?'

Diana, obediently slopping cold water into a basin and beginning to wash, thought that Wendy was probably right. Her mammy did not approve of Wendy, so she would not want the other girl using her stove or making tea in her teapot. In fact, Diana realised belatedly, her mother would not approve of Wendy's presence in the kitchen in the first place, let alone anything else. 'The hairbrush is in the top drawer of the dresser,' she said.

Wendy fished it out, and as soon as Diana had dried her face and hands she plied the brush vigorously on the younger girl's tousled locks. Then she stepped back to admire her work. 'There you are, Di; you look good as new, just about,' she said approvingly. 'It's a shame your skirt got tore, but apart from that, no one 'ud ever know you'd been in the wars. Now tell me how it happened.'

Diana took a deep breath. She had told no one how she had been suffering in her new class, but now she realised what a relief it would be to do so. After all, there was no point in pretending that everything was fine because Wendy had seen her crying fit to bust and knew, from her own experience, that she had been knocked about by someone. She stared across at Wendy, then spoke with decision. 'All right, I will tell you, but do you promise not to mention it to anyone else? Only I don't want them to know because they'll think I'm a real ninny. Lots of the kids at this school don't like it 'cos Mammy keeps me so neat 'n'clean – they call me goody two shoes – an' now I've been put up into the big girls' class, they say I'm teacher's pet.'

'See this wet, see this dry, cut my throat if I dare to lie,' Wendy said promptly, drawing a dirty finger across an even dirtier neck. 'Whose class you in? I bet it's Luvvy Duvvy's – she's ever so nice but she can't keep order, an' she's old, so the kids in her class gerraway wi' murder. Go on then, tell me how it is. And begin at the beginnin', not jus wi' what went on this afternoon.'

Diana began, and, as she talked, found it easier and easier to explain. She even saw, in a way, why Hilda and Maureen picked on her. Neither girl was bright – Hilda was almost eight and still in Standard II – and neither was popular with the other girls in the class, nor with the teacher. To have Diana thrust amongst them, more than two years younger than they, yet able to gain the teacher's approval without effort, must have been a horrid experience for them both. The fact that they took it out on her at every opportunity was almost understandable – almost, but not quite.

When she had finished telling her story, Wendy looked at her shrewdly. 'You're not fittin' in, that's the trouble,' she said. 'For a start off, I'll bet no one else in your class calls their mam Mammy; only posh kids 'n' babies do that. An' then there's your clothes. If you mussed 'em up a bit yourself before you went in each day, then they wouldn't have to do it for you, see? I don't know either of them girls what's pickin' on you but I guess it's the same reason some girls used to pick on me . . . well, not exactly the same, but sim'lar. They used to pick on me 'cos I were so filthy an' me clothes were rags; I were different from them, see? There weren't much I could do about it, 'cos me mam never has two pennies to rub together, an' anyway, if I gorra decent dress, it 'ud be in Uncle's before I could say knife. But it's different for you.'

'Yes, I know what you're saying and I know it's true,' Diana said. 'But I *like* being clean and neat, and I like getting all the answers right and being top of the class, and Mammy likes . . . oh dear, I mean me mam likes me to do well in school, too.' As she thought over the woes of this afternoon tears rose to her eyes, and when she spoke again her voice had a break in it. 'Mammy – I mean Mam – bought me a lovely new pencil box because I got all me spellings right, and two brand new pencils with little rubbers on the end – d'you know the sort? – only Hilda snapped the lid off and Maur-Maureen broke the pencils in two and ch-chucked them through the window.'

'Well, ain't that too bad?' Wendy said. 'But I'm tellin' you, queen, that if you can't fight 'em you've gorra join 'em. Tell you what, how about a bit o' saggin' off school? Luvvy Duvvy ain't the sort of teacher to gerrout the cane, and if you show her the pencil box . . . well, you know what teachers are. They don't seem to care if a kid gets bullied an' covered in bruises, but if property gets damaged they'll make a big fuss.'

'Saggin' off school? What does that mean?' Diana asked, her eyes rounded. 'If it means staying off, I can't. If Mammy's too busy to take me – she works now, you know – then I go with the Fishers, and if I didn't turn up there'd be a real rumpus, I'm tellin' you.'

'An' you don't want to sag off school, do you?' Wendy said shrewdly. 'Awright, queen, we'll try the other way first. Go in tomorrer, only kick up some dust off of the pavement so your socks ain't so perishin' white an' cobble up your skirt wi' a few pins; don't let your mam see it's been tore or she'll likely do such a good mendin' job that you'll be lickle goody two shoes again afore you know it. Ain't there nobody in your class what'll stand up for you against them bullies? I'd come in meself an' give 'em a good clack only I don't go to school no more.'

Diana thought her friend sounded almost wistful, and without thinking she repeated what her mother had once said. 'Oh, but Wendy, soap 'n' water's free. My mam often says so. You could have a real good wash – a bath, even – and then if you put your hair in a plait and wore the best thing you've got, I 'spect it would be all right.'

Wendy's eyes narrowed, and for a moment she looked so furious that Diana's heart began to beat overtime. She looked anxiously at her new friend but the annoyance had left Wendy's face and she was merely looking thoughtful. 'D'you reckon?' she said slowly. 'Only soap ain't free, queen. Still an' all, I wouldn't mind havin' a go in your sink if you think it would be all right wi' your mam.'

'I'll help wi' your hair,' Diana said eagerly. 'It won't take but a minute an' then we can sit outside on the front step while you dry off.'

Wendy was willing, and presently Diana dunked her friend's head in the bowl of water and began to rub, rather inexpertly, with a large chunk of carbolic soap, which her mother used when she scrubbed the kitchen floor.

An hour later, when Wendy's hair was not only

clean and shining, but also dry, the two girls returned to the kitchen where Diana brushed it out and then held the small mirror so that her friend could admire the result of so much scrubbing. Wendy's eyes rounded as she looked at her reflection. 'I wouldn't ha' believed it possible,' she said in an awed whisper. 'I never knew me hair was that colour. It's nice, ain't it? Cor, wait till me mam sees me!' She turned to Diana. 'Thanks, Di. You've done me a good turn, I reckon, and I done you one an' all. Tomorrer, just you tell Luvvy Duvvy what 'appened to your pencil box. She'll be that scared your mam will come up to school to mek a complaint that she'll do something about it, an' so she bleedin' should. A teacher what can't keep order ain't no perishin' good.'

'But the pencil case weren't broken in class,' Diana pointed out. 'An' they don't ever touch me when there's teachers about. It's usually in the breaks or when Miss sends me on an errand to another class because she says I'm trustworthy. They say they've got to go to the toilet and – and follow me and start on me before I can escape.'

'An' you go back into her classroom wi' your hair comin' down out of its ribbon an' bruises on your shins, an' she don't notice?' Wendy said incredulously. 'Of course she notices, but Luvvy Duvvy don't like trouble, an' two big girls like the ones you telled me about mean trouble, even for a teacher. So tomorrer, you're goin' to march into your classroom an' show her a broken pencil box, ain't you? You didn't chuck it away, did you? Is it in your satchel?'

'No, it's in my shoe bag, hanging on my peg,' Diana told her. 'I meant to bring it back with me to see if Charlie, or Uncle Wally, might be able to mend it. But then I realised they'd ask how it got bust, so I didn't.'

'Right you are, then. Tomorrer mornin', you an' me's goin' into that school an' you're goin' to tell Luvvy Duvvy what 'appened to the pencil box, an' I'll back you up,' Wendy said, a martial light in her eye. 'Only – only I'll have to go up to the police station an' get some clogs, 'cos they won't let you into school if you're bleedin' barefoot. I don't know why,' she added in an injured tone, 'because no one don't wear shoes in the summer hols, so why must you wear them in school?'

'The police station?' Diana said. 'Why the police station, Wendy?' A horrid suspicion seized her. 'You aren't goin' to tell 'em about me pencil box? I hate Hilda and Maureen all right, but I don't think they should go to *prison*.'

Wendy laughed, then shook her head sadly over Diana's ignorance. 'Nah, I ain't goin' to tale-clat, but the scuffers give kids wi'out shoes wooden clogs so's they can go to school. I – I never bothered before, but I'll do it now 'cos you're me pal.'

'Oh, thanks, Wendy; I won't be nearly so scared if you're with me,' Diana said. 'But you're a lot older'n me. Which class are you in?'

'Well, I don't go to school much. Haven't bin for more than a day or two for years,' Wendy said vaguely. 'But I'm nine, or thereabouts, so I'll probably be awright with Luvvy Duvvy.'

'Oh,' Diana said doubtfully. 'But will they let you be in my class, Wendy? I think girls of nine is usually in Standard III or IV.'

'Not when they can't read nor write,' Wendy said bluntly, and Diana saw a faint pink flush rise to her friend's cheeks. 'The thing is, queen, I don't know as I can stand school for more'n a day or so, but we'll see how I go on, shall us? Now that I'm real clean 'n' tidy, I reckon it's worth me while washin' out this here dress . . .' she fingered the hem of the grey and filthy garment she wore, 'an' givin' school a chance.'

'You mean you might *stay* in our class?' Diana gasped, happiness flooding her. To have a friend in the same school would have been good; to have one in the same class was downright wonderful. 'Oh, Wendy, please, *please* stay in school! I'll help you with your reading and writing . . . well, with everything . . . if only you'll stay.'

'I'll give it a go,' Wendy said cautiously. 'To tell you the truth, queen, that there schools inspector, wi' the big moustache, is gettin' a deal too close for my likin'. He don't know where I live yet – not the exact house – but he knows I'm in this area, so mebbe it's better to go to school of me own accord, rather'n wait till I'm took by the lug'ole and dragged there.'

Diana agreed, joyfully, that this was so. She found that she was actually looking forward to presenting Luvvy Duvvy with the pencil box – she would never think of her as Miss Lovett again – and knew that, if Wendy stuck to her resolution and stayed in school, her days of being a victim were over. As she prepared for bed that night, she decided that she must tell her mother all about Wendy, because if she were to help the older girl with her schoolwork, then Wendy must be allowed to come in and out of No. 2 whenever she was willing to receive instruction. Diana knew very well that her mother would be horrified if her daughter suggested going round to Wendy's home. Emmy had once remarked, wrinkling her nose with disgust, that she had walked past the Telfords' door and had got a whiff of what smelt like middens coming through it. No, she must make her mother see that Wendy was now her classmate and should be allowed to visit No. 2 whenever she wished.

Accordingly, when Emmy came up to her daughter's room with a cup of hot milk and a biscuit, Diana took a deep breath and told her mother everything that had happened that day. She ignored Emmy's horrified comments, but went steadily on with her account, finally ending up with, 'So you see, Mam, if Wendy doesn't stay in my class, I shall have to pretend I'm not clever, and go to school in dirty clothes, or they'll beat me up every time they get the chance.'

Rather to Diana's surprise, her mother raised no objection to having Wendy in the house. 'I'd a deal rather she came here than you went there,' she admitted, 'and if the kid wants to be clean, then clean she will be. Why, miss, what are you laughing at?'

'Oh, Mammy, you sound just like Mrs Do-As-You-Would-Be-Done-By in *The Water Babies*. She said that to Tom when he was a little chimney sweep, didn't she?' Diana said, still giggling. 'You read it to me when we lived in Lancaster Avenue, remember?'

Emmy laughed too. 'Yes, I remember,' she said. 'Or was it Mrs Be-Done-By-As-You-Did? Not that it matters. If Wendy is going to be your friend, then I suppose I should be grateful.'

To say that Miss Lovett was surprised when Wendy presented herself as a pupil the following day was an understatement, but she hid her astonishment as best she could. It was gratifying that the child insisted upon being in her class, reminding the teacher that, a year or so previously, she had attended over the course of the year as much as a fortnight in her class and thought she might have been beginning to get the hang of 'what all them letters and squiggles meant'. Miss Lovett did say, mildly, that she would have to speak to the headmaster, but both she and Wendy knew that this was mere lip-service. If Wendy really meant to come to school, but would only do so if she were in Miss Lovett's class, then they had best be philosophical about it. And the child was right, Miss Lovett mused as she added the extra name to the register. If she felt at ease here and had been beginning to learn her letters, then this was the best place for her.

Miss Lovett was an ingenuous soul and saw no reason to connect a broken pencil box with the arrival of her new pupil, but she did remember how extremely filthy Wendy had been the last time she had seen her and made the obvious connection. Diana was a pretty, lively little girl, though Miss Lovett had noticed that she had become very quiet of late. The teacher suspected bullying – the pencil box rather confirmed it – but she had no desire to interfere, nor to have trouble in her classroom, so she simply ignored the business as she had ignored it often before, hoping it would sort itself out in time. But a pretty, lively little girl might easily influence the child with whom she played, and since they lived in the same street – Miss Lovett had never entered a court – she supposed that the older girl had been encouraged to clean herself up by the younger one. Or possibly by her mother, Miss Lovett reflected, turning to the blackboard and beginning to write some simple words upon it. But it did not really matter why Wendy had decided to give education a chance. What mattered was that she was here, apparently eager to learn, and it was the attitude the children took up, in Miss

Lovett's experience, which determined their ability to absorb her teaching.

By the time the Christmas holidays arrived, Wendy was beginning to read most of the words in the infants' primer, though writing had so far eluded her. She was left-handed, and at first Miss Lovett had felt it her duty to constantly remove the pencil to Wendy's other hand, but this made the child so frustrated and cross that Miss Lovett had given in and the result was already beginning to be noticeable. Miss Lovett hoped that by summer Wendy would be able to write most of her letters, if not all, and told herself that she was a better teacher than she had dreamed, since Wendy had never remained in anyone's class for longer than a few days before, though the teacher did suspect that the help Diana gave her friend must be making a contribution too.

As for Diana, she was once more the bright, intelligent little girl she had been at the start of the autumn term. To be sure, she was no longer quite as immaculate, frequently coming to classes with dusty shoes and socks at half-mast, but Miss Lovett was shrewd enough to guess that Diana was trying to make the difference between herself and Wendy less immediately noticeable. The bullying – if there had been bullying – had stopped as soon as Miss Lovett had begun to make enquiries regarding the state of a brand new pencil box. Diana had refused to tell her who had snapped off the lid, simply staring Miss Lovett straight in the eye and saying that she did not know the culprit but suspected it was someone who had left the classroom whilst she, Diana, was running an errand for the teacher. Since Miss Lovett herself had been absent, though she should not have been, she could not immediately name the guilty one, but after much though she realised that Hilda Bridges and her crony Maureen were in the habit of slipping out of the class, with the weakest of excuses, rather more frequently than her other pupils. She had faced them with the battered pencil box and knew at once that she had guessed right. She hastened to tell them, severely, that no one had 'told on them' as they had clearly suspected.

'I came to you two first because I've noticed how often you absent yourself from my classroom on the flimsiest of excuses,' she told them. 'And one glance at your faces when I showed you the pencil box proved, beyond a doubt, that you were the guilty parties. Tell me, why did you destroy this very pretty and useful thing?'

'It were an accident,' Hilda whined, glancing shiftily at Maureen. 'I were tryin' to get the lid off – Maureen wanted to borrow a pencil – and the perishin' thing snapped off in me hand, honest to God it did, miss.'

'An accident?' Miss Lovett's eyebrows rose dramatically. 'And what about the pencils? I'm told they were found by the school caretaker, broken in half and with the points snapped off, lying outside the cloakroom window. How do you explain that?'

'Dunno, miss,' Hilda said, staring glumly at her feet. 'It weren't nothin' to do with us, miss. We wasn't in the cloakroom, was we, Maur?'

Maureen, very much a follower, muttered something beneath her breath, but turned pale when Miss Lovett said coldly: 'Very well, I won't question you further, but you must replace the pencil box and the pencils, which means you must go home this afternoon and tell your parents what has happened. I think a box like this one would probably cost as much as two shillings, though you can get quite nice pencils for a penny or two.' Both girls looked absolutely horrified, but at this point, to Miss Lovett's great surprise, Maureen spoke up.

'Please miss, me dad's a joiner, ever so clever wi' wood. If – if you'll give me the box, I could gerr'im to mek it good as new, honest to God I could. Please miss, let me take it. Me mam'll scalp me alive if she knows—'

Here, Hilda kicked her sharply on the ankle and Maureen subsided.

'Very well; but remember, the box must be as good as new,' Miss Lovett said coldly. 'And if you get the pencil box mended, Maureen, then I think it's only fair that Hilda should provide the pencils. New ones,' she added hastily. 'Is that clear?'

Both girls muttered that they would do as they had been told and left the room, with obvious relief, when Miss Lovett dismissed them.

Thankful to have got over heavy ground so lightly, Miss Lovett returned to her classroom and began to prepare the lessons for tomorrow. The fact was, this was her last year in school, since she would reach retirement age in March and meant to leave at the end of July. Already she was thinking, wistfully, of the small cottage her elder sister had bought on the Wirral, which the two women meant to share. Sarah had been a teacher, too, but she was five years older than Doris Lovett and had consequently retired earlier. Doris had rented a room in the village and had then searched diligently for a property to buy, finally settling on the cottage in its big, untidy garden the year before. It had needed a great deal of work, including retiling the roof, but because she had got it cheaply it had been possible to do all the necessary jobs in twelve months, and now Doris meant to start on the garden as soon as spring arrived.

Because she was looking forward to retirement, Doris Lovett did not want to muddy the waters by reporting that there had been bullying in her class. She supposed, vaguely, that it happened in every class and thought it best ignored, but she had dealt with it in this case because there had been material damage done, something definite to put right, instead of the 'she did, I didn't' scenario which had once caused her so much anguish, so many sleepless nights.

Looking back, she thought that perhaps she had never been the material from which good teachers are made; Sarah had become a headmistress before her retirement, but Doris knew herself to be unequal to such a task. In the early days, when she had taught the ten- to eleven-year-olds, there had been near riots in her class and she had shed many tears after school hours, but the headmistress at the time had decided she would be better off teaching the infants and she had settled down happily with the six- to seven-year-olds, who were, for the most part, eager to learn.

Of course, there were always exceptions; Hilda and Maureen had both remained with her for two years and looked like staying for a third, but at least that won't be my problem, the teacher thought thankfully, opening the large book in which she kept her lesson plans. Someone else, perhaps someone more forceful than myself, will have to deal with those rather unpleasant young people.

Christmas at Mac's was easily their busiest time of year, but it was also the jolliest, Emmy thought. For a start, the staff were presented with a large box containing paper chains, tinsel, cotton wool and baubles for the Christmas tree which Mr Mac would buy on 10th December, so that it could be set up and decorated by the 12th. Freda told Emmy that Mr Mac never allowed Christmas decorations to remain up after Boxing Day, so he liked to have the tree in place in good time. 'We water it each day, but even so, them little pine needles start to drop 'cos the place gets so hot,' Freda explained. 'It do have a lovely smell though, don't it? I never know whether I love Christmas or hate it, 'cos the work's enough to put you in 'ospital; I soaks me feet in mustard 'n' hot water every night from the first of December to New Year's Day, but even so I can scarce get me shoes on of a mornin'. Then, a' course, everyone's in a good mood, the food's a lot simpler 'cos most folk go for a turkey dinner, an' the tips just come pourin' in. We all buy each other presents – just little things – an' we gerra Christmas bonus off of Mr Mac. We buy 'is mother a big bunch o' flowers 'cos you can't give a feller a bouquet . . . well, you'll soon find out for yourself whether you love it or hate it.' She looked curiously into Emmy's face. 'You know that feller at the corner table . . . ?'

'There are several corner tables in the dining room,' Emmy said, then spoiled it by adding, 'What about him?'

Freda giggled. They were standing side by side at the enormous kitchen sink, diligently peeling a sack of potatoes since they were on earlies this week and, at Christmas, two waitresses could deal with the coffees whilst the rest of the staff threw themselves into preparations for the noonday rush. 'If you don't know which one I mean . . .' she began, then changed tack. 'But you do know, o' course. It's the chap what watches you all the time an' keeps givin' you the eye. I dunno 'is name but I reckon you do.'

'Oh, you mean Mr Spelman,' Emmy said, trying to look surprised. 'He's a neighbour of mine, or was, rather, in Lancaster Avenue. We usually have a word or two when he comes in but other than that I scarcely know him. To tell you the truth, I know his mam better than I know him; she's a nice woman.'

Freda nodded. 'Oh aye? But he likes you, don't he? I seen the tips he leaves, stickin' out from under his puddin' plate. He left you a bob last time, didn't he?'

'You nosy blighter!' Emmy said, with pretended indignation; everyone was interested in tips. 'I dunno what he left last time, but it might have been a bob.'

Freda narrowed her eyes. 'If he leaves you a bob every time he comes in for his dinner, an' he comes in every day, that's five bob a week,' she said, her voice reverent. 'Five bob! He must be rollin' in it, queen.'

Emmy laughed. 'If he left me a bob every day, it would be grand,' she agreed. 'But sometimes it's only twopence and sometimes, of course, it's nothing at all. And then there's other times, when he's at someone else's table. And there's times when I'm on earlies or lates . . .'

'Awright, awright, you've made your point,' Freda grumbled, 'but I bet he'll pay up handsome come Christmas. They all does.'

'And we share it out, so no one's any better off than anyone else,' Emmy reminded her. She fished in the bag for another potato and began to peel once more, thinking about Mr Spelman as she did so. He was, she supposed, in his mid-thirties, though he might be younger for he had a long, serious face, pale brown hair cut very short, and rather watery, nondescript eyes. His long, lean figure always seemed to be clad in jackets several inches too short in the arm and trousers several inches too short in the leg, yet his suits were clearly expensive and he was otherwise always immaculately turned out. Emmy knew he had a good job with a firm of insurance brokers; he had mentioned the name of his firm once, when he had come in earlier than usual and requested that his meal should be served immediately, since the staff of Huxtable & Bracket were holding a meeting early in the afternoon. Although Emmy had no interest whatsoever in Mr Spelman, she walked past the office of Huxtable & Bracket every day, on her way to catch her tram, and had noticed that they were insurance brokers.

'He's keen on you, ain't he?' Freda said bluntly, realising, apparently, that Emmy was not going to offer any other information. 'Has he asked you out yet?'

'No, of course he hasn't. Freda, you may have forgotten it but I certainly haven't. It's – it's not six months since my husband died. I wouldn't dream of accepting anyone's invitation to go out, not even if they were . . . well, a good deal nicer than Mr Spelman.'

Freda sniffed. 'Beggars can't be choosers, queen,' she pointed out. 'You're bringin' up that kid as well as you can an' doin' your best; Beryl often says you're doin' it well, an' all. But it's a big responsibility, an' one you ain't used to. If the right feller comes along, it don't matter if it's six months, six days or six years. It's your bleedin' duty to take him serious, that's what I say.'

Emmy finished peeling the last potato and turned the big brass tap so that water gushed. She knew Freda meant well and supposed, rather dismally, that the older woman was right. She was finding it incredibly difficult to manage her affairs without Peter's guiding hand, and though he had been away for long periods she found herself missing him every single day. There had always been letters, full of advice and comfort, and there had been Lucy. Now she had to cope with everything on her own. When the butcher sold her tough, stringy chops or half a pound of mince that was mostly fat, she had to do her own complaining and it never got her very far. Beryl always advised her to take the meat back, but it was usually too late. She and Diana had meat on a Sunday, and then again on a Wednesday, and by the time Emmy discovered it was of poor quality it was cooked and on their plates.

'Well, queen, if that Mr Spelman is real keen on you, you want to think serious about givin' him a bit of encouragement. His clothes are good, he's free wi' his money . . . you could do worse.'

'No I couldn't, or perhaps I could, but I'm not going to,' Emmy said, rather confusedly. She swung round to face Freda, looking the older woman straight in the eye. 'Could you bring yourself to go to bed with Mr Spelman, Freda? It 'ud be like climbing in beside a great knobbly skeleton. No, being on your own isn't so bad. Remember, my Peter was a seaman, sometimes away for months at a time, but marriage with him was fun. I couldn't possibly marry someone I didn't both love and respect – or someone who didn't make me laugh.'

Surprisingly, Freda gave her a great, broad grin. 'I dare say you're right,' she admitted cheerfully. 'Me old feller is fat and bald and boozy, but when I married 'im he'd got a great thatch of brown hair, a waist what I could get me arm round and a laugh you could hear right across to the Wirral. He's still gorra great laugh and though I *know* he's bald and fat and boozy, inside me head he's still the feller I married . . . if you know what I mean.' And then, for some inexplicable reason, Freda grabbed hold of Emmy and gave her an enormous hard hug. 'You were right an' I were wrong,' she declared. 'Just you wait, though. Mr Right will come along one of these days, you mark my words.'

Christmas, when it came, was as mad as Freda had warned Emmy it would be. Not being a great believer in mustard baths, Emmy simply staggered home each evening, flopped on to the sofa, and got Diana to put her little stool and a cushion under her feet. Mrs Lambert, a retired nurse living in the court, had advised Emmy to do this and it certainly seemed to help. At least when she left for work each day her feet felt comfortable and normal, even if by the time she returned home they were swollen and throbbing.

'But everyone's in such a good mood and so cheerful and happy,' she told Beryl. 'And the tips are absolutely marvellous. Oh, I know we share them at Christmas with the kitchen staff and all the temporary waitresses, but even so, we'll all do pretty well. I'm going to buy Diana a warm coat with my share, because she's grown out of the one we brought with us.'

'Go to Paddy's Market,' Beryl urged. Because of the pressure of work at Mac's, they scarcely saw each other at present, but this was Sunday, when the dining rooms were closed. The two women were planning to share their Christmas dinner on the day itself, with Beryl making the Christmas pudding, the mince pies and the Christmas cake, whilst Emmy had undertaken to roast the bird and the potatoes in her wonderful gas oven.

Despite Beryl's help, Emmy was still no cook, but she told herself – and anyone else who would listen – that she worked hard and was entitled to buy in bread, cakes, biscuits and pies, which a more provident housewife would bake herself. Diana never complained, though when Emmy was working a late shift the child usually had her tea at the Fishers' and sometimes commented, enthusiastically, on the delicious food which Beryl put before her family. Once, when Emmy had been rather scathing about Mrs Telford's housekeeping, Diana had looked at her sadly and had reminded her that they, too, ate bought cakes and pies. Poor Emmy knew she had flushed to the roots of her hair and had muttered, feebly, that she did not mean . . . had not meant . . .

Diana had smiled gently and Emmy had thought how her daughter was changing. The little girl who lived in Lancaster Avenue would never have made the connection which Diana had just made, nor would she have tagged along to the shops with either Wendy or Charlie, learning how to bargain, how to pick out the best items of fruit, the freshest bread. I suppose it's a good thing, Emmy had told herself, a little doubtfully. After all, unless my circumstances change, Di and I are going to need to manage for ourselves.

Diana awoke with that tingle of excitement which she had felt every Christmas, as long as she could remember. The room was still dark but there was light coming in round the edge of the curtains, and when she looked towards the foot of her bed, she saw the filled stocking. It *was* Christmas morning, then! Diana surged down to the bottom of the bed, heaved the stocking off the bedpost and took it back beneath the covers, for it was an extremely cold day. In other years, she had taken her stocking through to her parents' room before even glancing at the contents, but not today. Mam had had an exhausting Christmas Eve, not leaving work until seven in the evening, and she had begged Diana to let her lie in on Christmas morning. 'The staff are getting a longer holiday this year, because of Christmas Day being on a Friday,' she had explained. 'Saturday is Boxing Day and we're off anyway on the Sunday, so we'll get three days' holiday in a row and I mean to make the most of them. So if you don't mind, darling, you can open your own stocking when you wake and bring it through to me later. Much later,' she had added, after a moment's thought.

Naturally Diana had agreed, and now she delved eagerly into the old woollen seaman's sock which her mother had filled with small gifts every year. She knew it wouldn't be quite as good as it had been in other years because Daddy had usually contributed a number of small but interesting things he had picked up from abroad. One year, there had been a beautiful iridescent shell; another, a tiny porcelain baby doll with arms and legs that moved. Last year, it had been a beautiful necklace, made of polished nuts. So she must have no great expectations, though she knew Emmy would have done her best.

The stocking contained a blue hair ribbon and a red one, two pairs of white socks, rolled into a ball, a small book – *The Adventures of a Golliwog* – which

Diana thought somewhat childish for a person rising six, a bag of toffees, and an orange. Diana was pleased with everything – except the socks, which she felt were not really a Christmas present at all – but could not prevent a stab of disappointment because there was no toy. However, she had unwisely mentioned Christmas stockings at school and had speedily realised that such things were a phenomenon known only to a few members of her class. Other children were lucky to get one small gift, though most looked forward to a special dinner and perhaps even a fruit cake at teatime.

Diana carefully replaced everything in her stocking, trying to get the presents back in the right order, then snuggled down the bed again, but not to sleep. She was far too excited. She knew that Emmy had bought her a new winter coat and was looking forward to wearing it for the first time when they went to church. Mam had told her, apologetically, that it was not a brand new coat, but she had said it was clean and bright and the best they could afford. Diana had stared at her mam with surprise. Everyone in the court bought at Paddy's Market, rejoicing over bargains and boasting of how they had beaten the stallholders down from the original asking price. Now that they lived in the court, why should they be any different? She herself had gone with Charlie to the market and had pointed out the pretty pale blue scarf, made of some fine, silky material, which would exactly match her mam's best skirt. 'Only the lady said she wanted sixpence, and I've only managed to save four pennies,' she had hissed in Charlie's ear. 'So if I can't have that, can you ask her if there's anything else which we can buy for fourpence? There's a lovely pink rose which Mam could pin on her shoulder, or a string of blue beads . . . only she's got quite a lot of beads . . .'

It had been her intention to ask Wendy to go with her but she had decided against it because one of Wendy's more embarrassing habits was that of shoplifting. Diana appreciated that her friend almost never had any money, but she disapproved strongly of stealing and had no wish to find herself in possession of an article which had not been paid for. 'Be sure your sins will find you out,' her grandmother had been fond of saying, and Diana had horrid visions of waking on Christmas morning and finding a large policeman at the foot of her bed, having discovered by some means that she was the receiver of stolen goods. Worse, Mam might be wearing the present and be hauled off to prison by a scuffer who had noticed the item on a list of missing property.

So she and Charlie had ventured forth and he had purchased the silky blue scarf after knocking the price down to fourpence ha'penny, saying in a large-minded fashion that she might pay him back the odd ha'penny when she was in funds again.

Diana, gazing at him adoringly, had thought that there was no one like Charlie. She often accompanied him when he was doing messages for his mother or for hers, and since she was an extra pair of hands he usually let her tag along, but on this occasion he had come with her because she had asked him to, and because he had presents of his own to buy in Paddy's Market.

So now, cuddling down beneath her blankets, Diana anticipated the day ahead with real pleasure. First, when Mam got up, they would have a boiled egg each for breakfast, and then she would be given her new coat and in her turn she would give Mam the scarf, wrapped in pretty paper and accompanied by a home-made card announcing that the gift within was to Mammy from her loving Diana. Diana hugged herself. After that, they would go to church, where she would sing carols and exchange greetings with the rest of the congregation. And then, best of all, they would go round to the Fishers' and have their dinner all together at the big kitchen table. There would be the turkey, roast potatoes, bread sauce . . .

Diana sat up in bed with a small shriek. Her mam was supposed to be roasting the turkey, and instead she was still asleep. Halfway across the room, however, on tiptoe to save her heels from coming into contact with the cold lino, she saw the door creak open. Emmy stood there, smiling, with a mug of tea in each hand. 'Get back to bed, little goose,' she said when Diana explained her errand. 'I half cooked the bird yesterday, and since I woke at half past six, as usual, and couldn't get back to sleep, I've been preparing the potatoes and heating up the oven for a while already. Now if you'll snuggle down, you can open your stocking whilst I watch and we can both enjoy our tea.'

Diana took the mug with only moderate eagerness, though she was thirsty. A couple of weeks ago, Emmy had given up the unequal struggle to provide her child with fresh milk. At first, Diana had felt resentful because she enjoyed milk and considered tea in much the same light as her mother considered porter, or ale – as a drink for adults only. But Emmy put plenty of conny-onny into her daughter's cup and made the tea as weak as she could, and now Diana quite enjoyed it, though she had thought that Christmas Day might herald a return to fresh milk, albeit briefly.

'Put my dressing gown round your shoulders, Mammy . . . I mean Mam,' Diana said eagerly, beginning to pull the hair ribbons out of her stocking. 'Oh, Mam, beautiful satin ribbons! Can I wear one today, to church?'

'Of course you can,' Emmy said indulgently, but Diana saw, when she looked at her mother's face, that there were tears in her large blue eyes. 'I want you to have a lovely day, darling, and to be happy, although this is rather a sad day for me.'

'I know, Mam. It's our first Christmas without Daddy,' Diana said. 'I'm sad, too, deep inside, and I wish and wish that he were here, but he wouldn't want us crying, not on Christmas Day, would he, Mam?'

'No, he wouldn't,' Emmy said. Diana saw her turn her head away and pretended to be very busy with her presents and not to notice her mother delicately drying her eyes with a small white handkerchief.

'But Daddy wasn't always at home on Christmas Day, was he?' Diana said, when she could tell that her mother was in control of herself once more. 'Last year, we had two Christmas Days, didn't we? One exactly a year ago today, and one on the eleventh of January, when the old *Queen* docked.'

'That's right, darling. But last year we could afford . . . oh, don't let's think about last year, let's concentrate on this year. After all, we shan't be celebrating alone, which we would have been in Lancaster Avenue. We shall be with the Fishers, and Aunty Beryl and Uncle Wally will make sure we have a grand Christmas.'

'And Charlie,' Diana said eagerly. 'Charlie will make sure we have a grand Christmas, too.' She stood her empty mug down on the floor and jumped out of bed. 'I'm going to get dressed right now, this minute, because I can't wait to see my new coat and I'm dying to see if you like the present I've bought you.'

Charlie got slowly out of bed, sniffing at the wonderful smell of bacon which came floating up the stairs. He began to dress, hauling his shirt over his head without so much as a glance at the washstand. It was Christmas Day and a fellow was entitled to skip washing on such an auspicious occasion. Besides, Lenny's bed was already empty. Bobby still slumbered in his cot, so he might as well follow his younger brother's example and get down to the kitchen pronto. His mother always insisted that they had breakfast before unwrapping their presents, so the sooner he was downstairs the better.

He had greeted the news that Diana and her mother were to share their Christmas dinner with some dismay. It wasn't that he didn't like Diana, she was a nice enough kid in her way, but she would follow him around and his pals disapproved of all girls, as indeed he did himself. He had been desperately hoping to receive a pair of roller skates this year, and if he got them, he meant to be out on the pavements as soon as breakfast was over. Well, perhaps he would have to wait until after church, but then he meant to show off to his pals and it wouldn't do to have Diana tagging along. What was more, she was friendly with that awful Wendy Telford, and if there was one girl Charlie couldn't stand, it was she. Wendy was a year older than him, bossy and tough. He and she had once had a fight over a grand rubber ball. He had found the ball in the gutter just outside Mr Worrall's shop on the corner of Vesock Street and he and Wendy had pounced on it at the same moment, both shrieking, untruthfully: 'That's mine, hands orff!' Charlie's hand had been the quicker, so he had seized the ball first, but it had been no good. As he straightened up, Wendy had punched him hard on the nose, causing tears to bolt from his eyes. He had not let go of the ball then, but had been forced to do so when the fight had ended with Wendy sitting astride his prostrate body, grabbing him by the ears and banging his head on the cobbles until his grip on the ball weakened. Then she had grabbed it and run away, shrieking: 'Cry baby, cry baby!' as he rose, shakily, to his feet.

It had been the unfairness of that last remark which had crystallised Charlie's vague dislike of the girl into positive loathing. He had not cried – he never cried – but no one could prevent their eyes from watering when punched on the nose, or when one's head was being hammered on the cobbles. Naturally, he had retaliated in kind, and for some time had referred to her as 'Stinkin' Wendy no knickers', but it seemed that even this insult did not penetrate her armour, for she simply ignored him and went on her way.

Now, Charlie shoved his feet into his scuffed black plimsolls, pushed his hairbrush vaguely around his head and made for the stairs. At least Diana would not be bringing Wendy to share their dinner, and if she was tempted to follow him when he set off on his roller skates – if he's got roller skates – then he would beg a bit of cake, or a bun, or something from his mam, give it to Diana, and suggest that she might like to share it with her pal. He thought that there was little chance that the Telfords would have any sort of Christmas dinner, and though he felt no pity for Wendy – he could not forget her jeering cry, nor how his head had bounced on the cobbles – he was willing to sacrifice a bit of cake in order to bribe Diana to play with Wendy instead of himself.

He thudded down the stairs and burst into the kitchen, shouting 'Merry Christmas' at the top of his voice as he entered the room. His father looked up and grinned, revealing the fact that he was two front teeth short. 'Smell o' bacon must ha' drawn you down them stairs like a pin to a magnet,' he observed genially. 'C'mon, gerroutside o' this lot, then you can have your present.' Charlie grinned and slid on to the wooden bench next to Lenny, who was already devouring a bacon sandwich at great speed. His mother's arm reached over his shoulder and deposited a big, bulging sandwich before him. Charlie seized it and took a bite, then let his eyes wander to where the presents stood. There was a bulky-looking parcel, tied up with rather grimy string, which could easily be a pair of roller skates. O God, Charlie prayed, cramming more sandwich into his mouth and helping it down with a gulp of tea. O God, lerrit be skates!

Sitting quietly in her own kitchen, with Diana dreamily curled up in the other fireside chair, Emmy was able to go over Christmas Day in her mind.

She had really enjoyed it, despite a feeling of guilt because, though she missed Peter terribly, she had managed to forget her loss for most of the time. It had been so different from the Christmases she had shared with Peter. He had liked a quiet day, a day for just the two of them – three, once Diana was born – and had not wanted to play games or behave in the riotous fashion which the Fishers took for granted.

In the Fisher household, when dinner was finished,

old Mrs Pritchard, wrapped in blankets and beaming with excitement, had been ensconced in the best fireside chair and friends had come in to join in the merriment: Beryl's married cousin Ella and her kids, and a widow and her son, who were the Fishers' other next door neighbours. Consequences was succeeded by Chinese Whispers which was followed by charades and then Postman's Knock and Musical Chairs, though due to a lack of chairs it should have been called *Musical Cushions*. Wally played the mouth organ for Musical Chairs and Emmy was delighted to see how eagerly Diana joined in the fun, especially when Charlie returned from an outing with his skates. He had two skinned knees and grazes on the palms of his hands, but no one seemed worried by this, Charlie least of all, and Diana clearly admired her hero more than ever when speckled with blood and nursing a bruised elbow.

They had had a wonderful high tea, helping themselves from a table laden with good things, which Beryl had set up in the hallway, and then Emmy had thanked the Fishers with true gratitude for a grand day and brought Diana home.

A knock on the door brought Emmy's mind abruptly back to the present. It must be one of the Fishers, of course, come over to tell them they had left something behind. She looked round the kitchen and saw the crocheted collars and cuffs which had been Beryl's gift to her, and the scarlet woollen gloves which had been the Fishers' present to Diana. There was her big baking tin, but Beryl could scarcely return that with the turkey carcass still in place. Emmy glanced at Diana, who usually rushed to the door as soon as a knock sounded, and saw that the child was asleep. Never mind; whoever was knocking would be wanting her, and not her daughter. Emmy opened the kitchen door and shivered a little. The hallway was cold after the cosy kitchen, and dark, too. She was about to turn back into the room to fetch a candle when the knock sounded again. Emmy hurried along the short hallway and pulled open the door. It was full dark outside and she could see very little, apart from the shape of a man's head, dark against the dim light of the one and only street lamp in the court.

'Mrs Wesley? I don't suppose you remember me, but since I'm in Liverpool I thought I'd pop in and make sure you and the young 'un are all right. It's Carl Johansson – I helped with your move.'

Emmy gasped, then stood back, ushering the young man into the house. 'I'm so sorry, but I couldn't see your face with the lamplight behind you,' she explained, 'Come into the kitchen – it's warm in there.' He hesitated a moment, cap in hand, then passed her, heading for the light which he could see streaming through the open kitchen door.

Emmy shut the front door and followed him. In the warm, gaslit kitchen, they smiled at each other, both, Emmy suspected, a little uncertain of how they should behave. They were, after all, virtual strangers, but it was kind of him to call.

'Please take your coat off, Mr Johansson,' Emmy said, pointing to the chair she had just vacated, 'and sit down.' She lifted Diana up and sat down herself, arranging the still sleeping child comfortably on her lap. 'It's good of you to call, Mr Johansson,' she said. 'Actually, Diana and I have spent the day with a neighbour; we've only been home about half an hour. And how have you spent your Christmas?'

Carl Johansson smiled and Emmy thought how very nice-looking he was, with his crisply curling fair hair and his tanned face accentuating the blue of his eyes. 'I know you've been out,' he said. 'I have called twice already today. You see, although I popped in several times whilst the working team were here, I never did see the end result. The men told me you seemed pleased but . . . well, I thought I should have checked myself.' His blue glance slid, appreciatively, round the kitchen. 'It looks pretty good, I must say, but I guess that's a woman's touch. Still, it's better to have a nice clean canvas, so to speak, and I reckon the men did that.'

'They were all wonderful,' Emmy said warmly. 'They made all that shelving, and Mr Reynolds said that when he was able to spare some time he would come round and put doors on the front of the shelves, which would make them into proper cupboards.'

Mr Johansson nodded. 'Aye, he's a real craftsman, is the chippy.' He glanced at the sleeping Diana and Emmy saw what might have been a blush darkening his cheeks. 'I – I wondered if you and the little missie might do me the honour of – of coming to the pantomime at the Royal Court, tomorrow night . . . or we could go to the matinee performance, if you'd prefer it.'

Emmy hesitated. If he had invited her to go dancing, or to the cinema, she would have refused unhesitatingly. But a visit to the pantomime . . . well, that was the sort of treat an indulgent uncle, or an old family friend, might suggest. Because her job was so demanding, she had not been out once in an evening since Peter's death, had not really wanted to do so, and when Freda had teased her about Mr Spelman she had told herself that even if he had been charming, young and handsome, she would not have gone out with him. But she felt she owed Mr Johansson the courtesy of a considered reply, at least. 'A visit to the pantomime? I'm not sure . . .' she was beginning, when Diana suddenly sat bolt upright.

'A pantomime?' the child squeaked. 'Oh, Mammy, d'you 'member the pantomime last year, and the lovely fat lady – only you said it were a man – with the striped woollen stockings and a big red nose? Oh, and a giant's kitchen . . . and the hen that laid the golden eggs and they dropped on the fat man's boot . . . and the nice young man with the long green legs – only you said he were a lady – told all the children to shout when we saw the giant coming . . . oh, Mammy, *please* say we can go.'

Emmy looked helplessly across at Mr Johansson, who was smiling. 'And I thought she was fast asleep,' she said ruefully. 'Well, I think you've had your answer, Mr Johansson; thank you very much for your kind invitation to go to the matinee performance, which Diana and I are delighted to accept.' She hesitated only a moment before adding recklessly: 'And if you would like to come back here afterwards, for a meal, you'd be more than welcome.'

Mr Johansson coloured again and said that he would consider it an honour. Then, all of a sudden, it seemed that he felt at ease with them, because he began chatting, telling Emmy how he had spent Christmas Day and giving her little snippets of information about the ship and about his fellow officers. Before she knew it, Emmy found herself telling him about life as a waitress in McCullough's Dining Rooms, with Diana chipping in from time to time. In fact, it was only when Emmy happened to glance at the clock and see that it was past ten that she jumped to her feet, a hand flying to her mouth. 'Oh, how dreadful of me. It's well past Diana's bedtime, and since we are to have an outing tomorrow we shall both need a good night's sleep. I'm so sorry, Mr Johansson. And I haven't even offered you a cup of tea.'

The young man had got to his feet as Emmy did and was already struggling into his coat. 'It is I who should apologise, Mrs Wesley,' he said. 'It is too bad of me, to call so late and stay so long, but when one is a seaman and far from home, it is a real treat to find oneself in a cosy kitchen, feeling oneself amongst friends.'

As she followed him out of the kitchen and into the cold hallway Emmy said, 'Where is your home, Mr Johansson? You speak such excellent English, but with a name like Johansson . . .'

'Oh, I come from Sweden,' the young man said. 'But my connections with my own country are not so strong since I joined the British Merchant Navy. However, I have a sister, a brother-in-law, and three nieces living near my parents, and whenever I have a long leave I visit them.' He opened the door as he spoke and stepped out into the cold night. Turning up his coat collar against the bitter chill, he pulled his cap well down over his fair curls and saluted. 'Thank you for a delightful evening, Mrs Wesley,' he said formally, his breath coming out in puffs of white mist with every word. 'The performance starts at half past two tomorrow afternoon, so I shall pick you up at two o'clock, in a taxi cab. Is that all right?'

Emmy and Diana chorused that it would be fine, that they were already looking forward to it, and then Emmy ushered her daughter back indoors. 'It's high time you were in bed, young lady,' she said severely, guiding Diana towards the stairs. 'No, sweetheart, no excuses, and no hot milk either, it's far too late. Go straight up and start undressing, and I'll follow you in five minutes when I've damped down the fire and tidied round.'

Alone in the kitchen, she wondered whether she had done the right thing by accepting the young officer's invitation. She did hope that he realised she would probably have said no, had it not been for Diana. She thought, guiltily, that if Freda knew, she would purse her lips and nod, saying with satisfaction that it was high time her young friend began to socialise once more. But she won't know because I shan't tell her, Emmy thought grimly, damping the fire in the stove with coal dust and shutting the doors in the base of the grate so that it would not burn up brightly until next morning. As for the neighbours, they would think it sensible and provident of her to go to a pantomime at someone else's expense. It was not until she had climbed into bed and was settling herself to sleep that she remembered she had asked him back for a meal, and that he had accepted.

Oh dear, Emmy thought to herself, I wonder if it was wise to ask him back here? The trouble was, she was really appallingly ignorant about how one should behave with members of the opposite sex. Peter had been her first real boyfriend after Johnny and had behaved so beautifully that her mother had always encouraged her to spend time with him. But Peter had been a dozen years her senior, and would not have dreamed of placing her in a difficult position where folk might think badly of her behaviour. Mr Johansson was not only young, he was a foreigner, and could not be expected to know the correct thing to do.

Next morning, as always when she was perplexed or worried, Emmy flew next door and told Beryl everything. She found her washing up after the family's breakfast, and picking up a tea towel Emmy began to dry the crockery whilst she talked. At the end of her recital, Beryl turned away from the sink, gazing at her friend with mild astonishment. 'If you can get yourself in a state over a visit to the panto wi' your daughter and a young man, then it's high time you did begin to go about a bit more,' she said roundly. 'As for askin' him back for a meal, I should hope you would. When you think of all he's done for you – cleanin' an' decoratin' the house, just for starters – givin' the poor feller a cuppa and a slice o' cake is the least you can do.' She smiled at Emmy and patted her arm with a water-wrinkled hand. 'Don't *worry* so much, queen! I know you keep thinkin' that you only lost poor Peter six months ago, but you aren't one of them Indian women what commits harry-karry over the body of their dead husband, you know. You're young and pretty, an' you've gorra child to bring up, so get on wi' livin' life, 'cos that's what you were born for, same as the rest of us.'

Emmy choked on a giggle. 'Indian women don't commit harry-karry, as you call it – I think that's the Japanese. I think Indian women commit suttee . . . at least, I remember Peter telling me once that they're supposed to throw themselves on their husband's funeral pyre, only mostly they're drugged and thrown on by someone else.' She shuddered. 'Isn't that just dreadful, Beryl? Peter said often they're quite young girls . . . it doesn't bear thinking about.'

'No, it don't,' Beryl agreed. 'But there's other ways of endin' your life, queen, an' one of 'em's shuttin' yourself away in your house and refusin' to have any fun, because you're a widow. So just you enjoy this here pantomime . . . an' tell me all about it when you get home.'

Chapter Seven
September 1926

They were two weeks into the new term when Diana realised that she had not seen Wendy in school for at least three days. Wandering across the playground, she reminded herself that they were in different classes now, for Diana had gone into the next year and was being taught by Miss Williams, whilst Wendy had been kept down with Hilda, and one or two others, though Maureen had been allowed to go up with the rest of the class.

Wendy had been philosophical about it when they had first heard. 'I know I ain't caught up wi' the rest o' you yet,' she had said airily, 'but Luvvy Duvvy is a nice old bird. She'll see me right, an' you an' me can still play out at break time.'

Then Miss Lovett's retirement had been announced, and pupils and teachers alike had given towards a leaving present. Wendy's optimism had trembled a little, but everyone had assumed that Miss Lovett's place would be taken by a young woman, Miss Bourne, who did relief duties when a teacher was away. Instead, a Mr Withers had been appointed, a skinny, middle-aged man with a sharp tongue, who was always ready to crack a ruler across one's palm or a switch across the back of one's legs.

Wendy had hated him from the first, and it seemed he hated her since he taunted her with being so much older than the rest of the class, constantly criticised her personal appearance, and generally made her life miserable.

Diana had listened to Wendy's grumbles but had thought that her friend's desire to be able to read and write would outweigh her dislike of the new teacher. Now, however, it looked as though this was not the case. Diana searched the playground and then, with extreme reluctance, asked Hilda if she had seen Wendy Telford.

'No, I ain't, and for why? 'Cos she ain't been in school for three days,' Hilda said morosely. 'She's saggin' off, and I for one don't blame her. If it weren't that me dad would beat hell out o' me with his belt – and buckle end, most likely – I wouldn't be in school meself. That Withers is a pig. He picks on me, 'specially if Wendy ain't there.'

'Poor Wendy,' Diana said mournfully. 'And she needs to be in school, she keeps saying so. But I'll go round to her place when class is finished and try to get her to come back tomorrow.'

'Yeah, you do that,' Hilda said eagerly. 'Tell 'er we really miss 'er. Tell 'er if she comes back I'll be real nice to 'er. Tell 'er we'll gang up on old Withers and report 'im to the head if he starts beatin' people up.'

Diana nodded absently, knowing full well why Hilda was suddenly prepared to be nice to Wendy. She wanted the other girl to get all the nastiness poured on her head instead of on Hilda's; but there was one thing: Diana would be very surprised if there was any bullying in Mr Withers's class. Oh, sure, he was a bully himself, that went without saying, but he was also a disciplinarian and would not stand for his authority's being flouted.

Miss Williams, on the other hand, was neither a disciplinarian nor a good teacher. She had a flat, monotonous voice, which tended to sink to a whisper, and she was a great believer in repetition. She would write a poem or a times table on the board, or some rules of grammar, and the children would then sit in their places and repeat what was written in a sing-song chant. Diana was soon bored by these methods, and began to dislike Miss Williams more and more. After only a couple of weeks, she felt that if she did not escape from lessons occasionally, she would go stark, staring mad. She realised that, even without effort, she could be top of the class once more, but since her schoolfellows now accepted her she had no wish to rock the boat by becoming teacher's pet, and Miss Williams already showed a tendency to praise her in front of the others. Disliking the teacher as she did, Diana thought praise from such a source was nothing to value; in fact, it made her feel truly uncomfortable.

But right now, her main objective was to give Wendy a piece of her mind. What was the point, she would ask her, of all the hard work they had put in in the previous year? The pair of them had worked like slaves to get reading and writing into Wendy's thick head, but it would have been in vain if she was going to throw it all away. Sagging off wouldn't please Mr Withers either, and when she did return she would be in deep trouble, sure as eggs were eggs.

So as soon as school was finished for the day, Diana set off for the Telfords' house. Halfway across the court, however, she heard Mrs Telford screaming at Wendy that her daughter would do as she was told or she would knock her bleedin' head off her bleedin' shoulders. Wendy, apparently uncowed by this threat, screamed back that she would do as she bleedin' well pleased and would thank her mother to leave her alone. ''Cos you can take the rest of them, but you ain't takin' me,' Wendy shrieked. 'I'm stayin' here!'

Standing there listening, Diana realised she could not possibly say anything in front of Mrs Telford. Nevertheless, she was poised to knock on the door when she remembered her mother's prohibition. Wendy can come here, her mother had said, but you are never, under any circumstances, to visit the Telford house. 'Is that clear?'

Diana was still hovering, wondering what to do next, when the Telfords' door shot open and Wendy erupted into the court. She saw Diana and grinned at her friend, though tears were still running down her rather grimy face, but she did not stop in her onward rush and Diana had to turn and run after her. She caught her up as Wendy skidded round the corner into Raymond Street, and grabbed at her sleeve. 'Wendy! What's happened? And why weren't you in school today?'

For a moment, it seemed as though Wendy was going to refuse to answer. She tightened her lips and glared down at Diana, but then she seemed to change her mind. 'Is your mam in?' she asked. 'It's a long story, but we could go back to your place . . .'

'Mam's out,' Diana said briefly. She turned, still clutching her friend's sleeve, and the two of them crossed the court and went into the Wesley kitchen. 'My mam buys lemons and sugar and Aunty Beryl makes them into lemonade,' Diana said, pouring the drink into two tin mugs. 'And there's some biscuits . . . want one?'

Presently, seated opposite one another at the kitchen table, with a drink of lemonade before them and a plate with four biscuits on it conveniently close, Diana repeated her question. 'Wendy, why weren't you in school today? And Hilda said you'd missed yesterday, and the day before that as well. If you keep saggin' off, you'll forget how to read and write.'

'No, I shan't,' Wendy said defiantly. 'I pick up the old newspapers what the fellers chuck down when they've finished with 'em, and reads 'em out loud to meself. I reads 'em to the other kids an' all . . . only I leaves out the really long words and the foreign bits. Oh no, I shan't forget readin', don't you fret.'

'Well, that's better'n just not bothering,' Diana admitted grudgingly. 'But what about writing? And sums? And things like geography? You can't do that at home without the proper books an' that. Oh, Wendy, *do* come back! I'm ever so lonely without you.'

'I'm not goin' back into that place so's Mr Withers can clack me head as hard as ever me mam does,' Wendy said decidedly. 'Luvvy Duvvy was awright, but that old Withers . . . well, he hates me and I hate him, so I'll never learn nothing in his class. What's old Williams like?'

'Awful, just awful,' Diana said, rather thoughtlessly, as it turned out. 'She writes something on the board – something like the seven times table – and make us sit there for hours, just reading it over and over. I've never been so bored in my whole life.'

'Well, there you are then!' Wendy said triumphantly. 'Even if I could stick old Withers, which I can't, what have I got to look forward to, eh? A nice dose of bein' bored to death by old Williams for a whole miserable year. I tell you, queen, if that's their idea of learnin', then they can stick it.'

'We-ell, maybe Miss Williams will improve,' Diana said, realising that her criticism of the teacher had not been wise. 'Anyhow, Hilda says if you go back, everyone will stick by you and – and stop old Withers being horrible. How about that? I used to hate Hilda, but perhaps she's getting nicer as she gets older.'

'No she ain't. It's just that if old Withers don't have me to beat up, then he'll turn on Hilda,' Wendy said acutely. 'And anyway, me mam says she's movin' out o' the court. If you asks me, she's bein' thrown out for not payin' the rent, but anyway, she says she's movin' in with her pal Aunt Flora, what lives out Garston way, by the gasworks. I hates Flora and her husband Bert, an' I don't mean to live there. The house is crammed that full 'cos her mam and dad live with them, as well as eight kids. I tell you, queen, the only way to fix Mam where she is, is for me to earn some dosh so's I can pay the rent meself. An' that's another good reason for saggin' off school,' she finished.

Diana stared at her, open-mouthed. 'But you aren't big enough to have a job,' she said finally. 'How can you earn so much money, Wendy?'

Wendy leaned over and took another biscuit, then crammed half of it into her mouth. 'I can run messages, help carry heavy baskets back from the market, chop up orange boxes and sell kindling for fires, mind babies for their mams,' she said. 'I dunno as I could really earn five bob a week, which is the rent for that rat pit we live in, but I could earn enough to help wi' Mam's scrubbin' money.'

Diana thought this over for a moment, then brightened. 'But when you're real grown up, you'll earn much more money if you can read and write and do sums,' she said craftily. 'Don't you remember Luvvy Duvvy telling us that the future would be a brighter place if we learned our lessons well?'

'Oh aye, I remember that awright,' Wendy said scornfully. 'But it's now that matters, don't you see? By the time I'm old enough for a real job, anything could have happened. But if I'm carted off to Garston, I'll be out of this school anyway, so I might as well forget school and do anything I can to keep Mam 'n' the kids 'n' me in the court, ain't that right?'

Diana would have liked to refute this, but at the thought of Wendy's leaving the court her heart sank. Becky Fisher was the only other girl she really knew in the area, and Becky had her own friends. Diana still adored Charlie, but knew better now than to dog his footsteps since she had noticed he was much nicer to her when she spent most of her time playing with Wendy.

She stared thoughtfully across the table at her friend. They were more or less in the same boat, she realised suddenly. Time spent by Wendy in Mr Withers's class was time wasted, as was time spent by her in Miss Williams's class. Indeed, I could be away for the whole year and still keep up, the way Miss Williams teaches, Diana told herself. And if both of us earn some money . . .

It seemed to her, afterwards, that the idea was born in a moment. She leaned across the table and began to speak rapidly, seeing the change in her friend's face at her proposal, the way Wendy's eyes began to sparkle. 'You're a perishin' genius,' Wendy exclaimed fervently, as Diana revealed her great idea. 'Oh, Di, I'm sure it'll work – wharrever would I do wi'out you?'

'G'night, Freda, night Jen, night Mr Mac,' Emmy called, as she let herself out of the back door of the dining rooms. It was a cold, dreary November evening, but Emmy's step was light. It had been a quiet day, and besides, after over a year of waiting on, she had learned how to pace herself, and was finding the work a good deal easier than she had done at first. In addition, because they had had so few customers, she would not have to worry about getting a meal when she reached No. 2. Inside her basket was a large piece of steak and kidney pie, some cold potatoes and a dish of rice pudding, which would do very well for supper if she popped it into her oven for twenty minutes or so. In fact, there was enough steak and kidney pie for four, so she might well pop it round to Beryl's. Wally was always hungry, as were the boys, and though Beryl was an excellent cook, steak and kidney was expensive and did not often come their way.

Emmy made her way along the Scottie, smiling at people as she passed them. Because she worked such regular hours she had grown to know, by sight at least, a good many folk who were heading home at the same time as herself. Just ahead of her, a large woman in a black coat and scarlet headscarf turned and Emmy recognised Nellie Coggins, the Telfords' next door neighbour. Like Emmy, she was in the restaurant business, though she was only a washer-upper and general dogsbody in a rather seedy dining rooms further down the Scottie. She was a nice, friendly woman, whose docker husband did little to help her bring up their three kids, and, like Emmy, she carried a covered basket, no doubt laden with leftovers.

As Emmy fell into step beside her Nellie said breezily, 'Hello, chuck. Quiet day, weren't it? Mrs Brown, me boss, gave me the rest of the scouse an' a heap o' spuds, so me old man will have something besides porter in his belly when I gets home. How are you doin', eh? Heard from that feller o' yours?'

Emmy smiled, biting back an urge to tell Nellie that if she meant Mr Johansson, he was not her feller, but one of her late husband's oldest friends. After the pantomime trip, almost a year ago, she had told everyone who would listen that Mr Johansson was just a friend, but it had not stopped people nudging and winking, she thought crossly now. The trouble was, he always visited her whenever he was in port, and since she never knew when he would arrive she could scarcely suggest that they meet somewhere other than the court in order to stop tongues wagging. Indeed, when she had hesitantly suggested that it might not be wise for him to visit so often, his fair brows had risen and he had given her his most twisted, attractive grin. 'Why should people talk?' he had said quizzically. 'After all, we never go dancing, and rarely do I ask you to accompany me to a theatre or cinema without also asking Diana. I am happy to do small jobs for you around the house, but I understand completely that you are still in mourning for your husband. Don't let foolish gossip spoil our friendship.'

Emmy had known he was right; people would talk, nudge and wink so long as there was breath in their bodies, and her best course was to ignore such behaviour. But it was not always easy, especially since Diana had grown progressively less friendly towards their visitor and had several times suggested that Mr Johansson should be asked not to call.

'He uses up too much of your time, Mam,' she had said pettishly. 'And when he takes us to the pictures, it's to horrible films that bore me.'

'Oh, Diana!' Emmy had said, much shocked by

this tremendous untruth, for Diana adored the cinema and Mr Johansson was always careful to pick a film she would enjoy. 'But if you truly feel like that, if you truly don't want to come to the cinema, then I'll arrange for you to spend the evening with Aunty Beryl. How's that?'

Diana had flushed angrily. 'That would mean you and him would go alone,' she muttered. 'My daddy wouldn't like that.'

'Daddy would have understood completely that Mr Johansson is trying to give us a nice time, nothing more,' Emmy had said severely. 'Diana Wesley, don't be so selfish. *I* enjoy a visit to the cinema now and then, or a theatre trip. You've got the Saturday rush and your friend Wendy. Why should I be the only one who has to stay at home?'

Diana had been sorry then, had admitted that she enjoyed the cinema and would not wish to be left behind next time Mr Johansson asked them out. But Emmy knew, of course, that her daughter was jealous. Diana still talked constantly of her father, of his generosity, his jokes, the songs he sang and the stories he told. Emmy imagined that time would reconcile her daughter to her mother's new friend, or at least she hoped it would.

But now Nellie Coggins was looking at her, waiting for an answer to her question, and Emmy cast her mind hurriedly back. What had the older woman said? Oh yes, she had asked how Emmy was and whether she had heard from Mr Johansson lately. 'I'm fine, thank you, Mrs Coggins, and I've not heard from Mr Johansson recently. He doesn't write often, usually only to tell me roughly when he'll next be in the 'Pool. And how are you? And your family, of course?'

'We're doin' awright; been doin' awright ever since our Dicky started work down at the docks, steve-dorin',' Mrs Coggins said expansively. 'I see'd your young 'un down Paddy's Market t'other day. She were on one end of a roll of lino and the eldest Telford kid were on t'other. I reckon they was earning theirselves a copper or two towards Christmas.'

'Yes, they work very hard at weekends,' Emmy agreed. 'There was talk at one time of the family's moving out because money was short, but I gather Wendy wasn't keen so she's been earning extra cash to help her mother pay the rent, and Diana helps too. I think she quite enjoys it.'

'Oh, it weren't the weekend . . .' Mrs Coggins was beginning, when the noise of a tram drowned her voice for a moment. When she started speaking again it was to inform Emmy that her youngest, Freddie, had managed to get a job delivering Christmas wreaths. 'Of course, the work won't start until December and it'll be over by the New Year,' she admitted, 'but Freddie's made up.' Once they reached Tenterden Street they parted, and Emmy made her way along Raymond Street. She turned into Nightingale Court eagerly anticipating the hot cup of tea and the good sit-down which awaited her.

It was not until she was in bed that night that Emmy remembered Mrs Coggins's remark about seeing Diana and Wendy carrying a role of linoleum on a weekday.

Strange, Emmy thought drowsily, pulling the blankets up over her shoulders, for the night was extremely cold. If those two youngsters are making their way to Paddy's Market after school in order to earn money carting heavy rolls of linoleum, then I suppose I really ought to put a stop to it. I know that

Miss Williams doesn't hand out homework – I don't suppose the kids would do it if she did – but Diana does an awful lot in the house, and even when she's staying over with Beryl I believe she's quite useful. I don't want her wearing herself out for that young ragamuffin Wendy Telford, and I think it would be a good thing if the whole family did move away. They're a feckless lot, and if Wendy wasn't around, maybe Diana would become friends with a nicer sort of girl.

She would have a word with Diana next morning, tell her that she must not overdo it or she would become ill and then what would her poor mother do?

Having made up her mind how to deal with the situation, Emmy soon slept.

My brilliant idea really does seem to be working, Diana told herself next morning, when her mother advised her not to cart linoleum or any other heavy burdens after a day in school. It was easy to promise to do no such thing since neither Diana nor Wendy had attended school for some while. At first, they had followed Diana's original scheme which was to go into class in order to get ticked off on the register, and then to disappear. This plan, however, had had only moderate success. Miss Williams never seemed to notice, once she had called the register, whether her class contained thirty-nine or forty children, but the gimlet-eyed Mr Withers was a different kettle of fish. Wendy used various excuses – a sudden nosebleed, a pounding headache, a desperate plea from home for her to return there at once – but she soon realised that Mr Withers was not fooled, and when he announced his intention of calling on her mother she told Diana they would have to try Plan B.

Plan B was simple but it involved downright lies, so Diana had been keen to try Plan A first. However, in view of Mr Withers's attitude, Plan B would have to be put in hand at once. Accordingly, Diana got two sheets of her mother's best notepaper and wrote two identical notes, one addressed to Mr Withers and the other to Miss Williams. It was a well-known fact in the school that the two teachers disliked each other thoroughly and never spoke beyond the most cold and formal of greetings, so Diana felt she could send the same note without fear of either teacher's finding out.

The notes were simple, though she was careful to write one in a stumbling and illiterate hand and the other as neatly and beautifully as she could manage. Each note informed the teacher that the Telford/Wesley family was about to move away from central Liverpool to the Garston district, and Wendy/Diana would be attending one of the schools in that area. She thanked both teachers for their work with her daughter and signed off, first with a scrawled 'C. Telford', and next with a 'Yours faithfully, Mrs P. Wesley'.

She and Wendy had handed the notes in before school on a Monday morning, explaining that since they were moving that very week they would be unable to attend school anyway, until the move had been accomplished.

For some time, Diana had been in dread of a note's popping through the letter box, demanding of Mrs Wesley her new address and the name of whichever school her daughter meant to attend, but as the days and then the weeks passed she began to believe that they had got away with it. She had to be careful to steer well clear of the school, but that did not bother her, and whenever she thought how angry her mother would be if she knew that her daughter no longer attended classes, she told herself, righteously, that lessons with Miss Williams could never have done her much good. She also told herself that she would go back to school the following year and simply left it at that.

So when her mother said that she must not tout for pennies after school since overwork would make her ill, she simply smiled primly and promised to do no such thing. After all, since she was not attending school, she could scarcely overtire herself by carting parcels after a long day in the classroom.

However, there were certain rules that she and Wendy were forced to obey and one of them was that they had to leave the house each morning, in Diana's case tidily clad, as though going to school. Another was to swear Becky to secrecy, for a couple of times the younger girl had commented that she had not seen her friend in the playground for absolutely ages; Becky was slow, everyone knew it, but she could be very shrewd at times.

'No-o, 'cos sometimes I have something to do which is more important than school,' Diana had told her grandly. 'You wouldn't understand, Becky, you're too young, but don't you go telling anyone I'm not always in school. D'you promise me now?'

Becky had stared at her for a long moment and then nodded. 'I promise I won't tell anyone you're saggin' off school,' she said, in her flat little voice. 'But I thought you *liked* school, Di.'

'I did, in Miss Lovett's class,' Diana admitted. 'But Miss Williams is so *boring*, Becky, and she teaches us nothing. She just goes over and over things like times tables and rules of grammar, so if I miss a day or two here and there I'm no worse off. But you mustn't miss school, queen, because you really need the lessons. If you're ever going to learn to read and write, you've got to work hard in class. You don't want to be in Standard I for ever, until you're old and grey, do you?'

Diana was fond of Becky but she acknowledged that the child was nowhere near as bright as the rest of the Fisher family. She was a sweet little girl, both generous and loving, but she had no idea of her letters and did not seem to understand figures at all.

'It's possible that she is a late developer,' her teacher had told Aunty Beryl. 'Give her as much attention as you can, Mrs Fisher, and maybe she'll catch up with the rest of her age group one of these days.'

But in the end, it was not Becky who let the cat out of the bag, but Charlie, and Diana knew that it was done completely by accident, and Charlie had had no intention of upsetting their apple cart.

It was getting near Christmas and Wendy and Diana were revelling in their new-found freedom and, of course, in their earnings which, as Christmas drew closer, increased by leaps and bounds. People asked them to carry ever larger and more awkward burdens back to their homes from the market stalls in Byrom Street, from Paddy's Market – in fact, from anywhere which could be relied upon to sell as cheaply as possible. Charlie was no saint; Diana knew that he, too, sagged off school from time to time, but she would not have dreamed of telling on him and she knew that, had the positions been reversed, he would have felt exactly the same.

It was 21 December and schools were breaking up the next day so, though Diana had changed in the privy from her nice school clothes into an old and ugly dress which she had got for fivepence from one of the stalls, she felt that it scarcely mattered if she was seen by authority. With only one day to go, half the school would be sagging off, which meant she would be in good company. So when a large, red-faced man hailed them and asked them if they could carry a Christmas tree to his home on Brownlow Hill for sixpence, they agreed enthusiastically. But they had not seen the Christmas tree.

When they did so, Wendy's exclamation of horror found an echo in Diana's heart, though not on her lips. 'Bleedin' hell, it must be one of them forest giants what Luvvy Duvvy said growed in Canada,' Wendy said, eyes rounding. 'Oh, queen, we'll never manage it. It must weigh a couple of tons.'

Both girls looked wildly round for the red-faced man, but he had diplomatically disappeared. Wendy, being the stronger, went resignedly to the root end of the tree and Diana seized it round its midriff. 'We could ask someone else to give us a hand,' she was beginning, when a voice spoke in her ear, making her jump six inches.

'What in heaven's name is you doin', young Di? Don't say you're tryin' to move that perishin' tree back home to the courts, because you'll never do it. And what d'you want a huge tree like that for, anyroad? If you asks me, trees is nothin' but a waste of money.'

Diana turned her head sharply, then grinned at Charlie. 'We're carrying it home for a fat chap with a red face who's going to give us sixpence,' she explained. 'What are *you* doing, Charlie? You should be in school.'

'Been to the Mill Road Infirmary to see the dentist,' Charlie said briefly. 'The old devil tried to say he were goin' to take me tooth out, so I telled 'im there were nothin' wrong with it and I weren't havin' no tooth out unless me mam said so, and then I kicked him in the belly and cleared out,' he added with understandable pride.

'Oh, Charlie!' Diana breathed. 'Oh, you are brave! But I say, are you going straight back to school? Because if not, we'll give you twopence to help with carting this here forest giant up to Brownlow Hill.'

'OK, I don't mind,' Charlie said easily. 'Shunt up, the pair of you, so's I can take the heavy end.' He seized the trunk, then sagged at the knees. 'Gawd, did you say he were goin' to give you sixpence?' He heaved an exaggerated sigh, casting his eyes to the heavens. 'Girls don't have a ha'p'orth of sense; luggin' this thing to Brownlow Hill is worth a bob of anyone's money. By rights, the feller should have hired a hand cart, and they don't come cheap.'

'I don't think he's the sort of man you can bargain with,' Diana was beginning doubtfully, when Charlie suddenly cut in.

'Come to think of it, what are you two doin'? Your mam would have a fit if she could see you now, young Di. You haven't been to Mill Road, have you? I didn't see you there.'

'I'm earnin' some money for Christmas,' Diana said briefly. 'We could ask the man for more money but I bet he won't give it us. He had mean little eyes.'

Charlie laughed, rather breathlessly. 'Well, if you've made an agreement, I s'pose you've got to stick by it,' he said. 'C'mon on then, let's be goin'.'

Along Byrom Street and into the Old Haymarket the three children staggered with their enormous burden. Diana looked enviously at the trams parked up alongside the pavement, but even if they had been rich and could have afforded three tickets, the 'forest giant' would never have fitted on to a tram. On St John's Lane they stood the tree down for a moment, then veered to their right, pushing apologetically through the crowds outside Lime Street Station and continuing doggedly along Lime Street itself, though by now all three of them were perspiring freely.

At the Adelphi Hotel they turned left into Brownlow Hill, but their ordeal was by no means over for it was a steep hill, and the red-faced man lived some way up it. 'Keep goin',' Charlie said hoarsely when the girls would have put their burden down for a moment's rest. 'If we stop now we won't ever start again, not wi' the hill so steep an' all.'

By the time the children reached their destination they had made many enemies. The pointed end of the tree had inserted itself up ladies' skirts, got between men's legs and swept things off stalls. People had walked into it, barking their shins and, in one case at least, laddering their stockings. When Diana plunged into the road to cross to the other side, brakes screamed and vehicles juddered to a halt, as they suddenly realised that the tree covered a good half of the carriageway. Diana had never apologised so frequently – or so fervently – in her whole life. And she had never been so scratched and bruised, either. The little needles off the tree had even slipped inside her shoes and socks so that walking was a prickly business, and her hands and arms were covered in tiny cuts, spitefully delivered by both the bark and the branches.

They were all heartily relieved, therefore, when they reached the address they had been given, and bitterly disappointed when the woman who came to the door did not immediately take their now hated burden from them.

'It ain't to come here, you stupid brats,' she said rudely. 'Where d'you think I'd put a thing that size, eh? Why, it's too big to stand upright in an ordinary house.'

Diana was so dismayed that she simply goggled at the woman, but Charlie spoke up. 'We brung it to the address we were given, missus,' he said boldly. 'A big feller with a red face gave us this address. Would it be your husband, now?'

The woman did not reply but half turned, bawling over her shoulder as she did so: 'Reggie! There's three kids here tryin' to deliver a Christmas tree the size of a bleedin' oak. You'd best come and deal with it.'

There was the sound of heavy feet descending stairs and then the man who had employed them appeared in the doorway. 'Oh aye, that's right, only I forgot to tell you it were for the church hall on West Derby Street. It's locked, so I'll have to come wi' you to let you in, which is why I give you this address.' He leered ingratiatingly at them. 'Schools break up tomorrer and there's to be a party for policemen's kids tomorrer afternoon. Wait here while I get me coat.'

He disappeared back inside the house, closing the front door behind him, and the three children stared unbelievingly after him. They had put the tree down and Diana thought, with loathing, of all the horrors of taking it yet further. 'Where *is* West Derby Street?' she hissed desperately to Wendy. 'I'll die if it's much further, truly I will.'

Wendy shrugged but Charlie said: 'It's a fair way off and it'll feel miles luggin' this perishin' fir. What's more, he bleedin' well lied to you, so he can cough up a bob or move his own tree.'

This seemed fair to all three of them, though Diana baulked at being the spokeswoman. 'He won't take any notice of a kid like me,' she said desperately. 'Oh, please, Charlie, you tell 'im.'

Charlie was willing, so when the man rejoined them, warmly clad in a thick navy blue coat with shiny silver buttons, Charlie informed him of their decision. 'It's too far to carry a tree as big as this one for twopence each, mister,' he said, speaking politely but firmly. 'We think a bob between the three of us is more like it. Why, we're scratched to bits already and our arms an' legs is aching like billyo. If I hadn't been around to give 'em a hand, these kids 'ud never 'ave reached this far, not even if they'd dragged it.' He jerked his thumb at his companions.

'Sixpence I said, an' sixpence I meant . . .' the man was beginning, as the three children struggled to get the tree off the ground once more. He hastily retracted as all three let go and the tree crashed back on to the pavement. 'Awright, awright, I dare say a bob won't break me.'

'OK, but we want it up front, 'cos we've already done the best part of it,' Charlie said. 'You can't be afraid we'll run off wi' the bleedin' thing, mister, 'cos it's all we can do to walk, so you're goin' to get your tree an' I'd like to make certain we get our money.'

'You'll get your money,' the man growled. 'Oh, awright then.' He fumbled in his pocket, producing a handful of loose change. He was walking level with Diana. 'Don't let go of the tree,' he said hastily. 'I'll put it in your pocket, young shaver.'

Diana felt the coins slip into her pocket and was relieved. There was something about the man she had disliked from the start, but at least he had paid up, and presently they arrived at the church hall. The man fumbled once more in his pocket and produced a key. He unlocked the large door and swung it open, gesturing to the children to carry the tree inside. He's as lazy as he's hateful, Diana thought indignantly. He had not once put so much as a hand on the tree, yet he must have realised how heavy and awkward it was. She dumped her share of the burden, glanced around the hall, admiring the paper chains and Chinese lanterns which were already in position, then followed her two fellow lumberjacks, heartily glad to be rid of their burden at last.

Outside, the man did not even have the decency to thank them or to say goodbye, but merely set off along West Derby Street, back towards Brownlow Hill. There was a low wall beside the church hall and all three of them collapsed on to it. 'Phew!' Charlie said. 'Wasn't he a horrible feller? And you'd think he might have shelled out a bit of extra without having to be blackmailed, like. Cor, what wouldn't I give for an ice cream or a long drink of lemonade, for all it's a cold day – I'm sweatin' like a dray horse.'

'We all are,' Wendy said mournfully, rubbing her skinny arms. 'I don't think me muscles will ever be quite the same again. What's more, we're miles an' miles away from the market, so there won't be no return load, like. Did he give you two tanners, Di, or were it all in coppers?'

Diana rooted in her pocket, feeling a sudden trepidation. There were three coins, about the size of a sixpence . . . her fingers closed round the money, and for a moment she actually believed that the man had handed over a bit extra. She was beginning to smile as her hand came out of her pocket, and then the smile was wiped clean off her face by the sight of the three coins nestling in her palm. Without saying anything, she handed the money to Wendy, then began to turn her pocket inside out, knowing as she did so that it was useless. The man had given her three farthings, had known what he was doing, and now he had made a complete fool of her. She felt tears rise to her eyes, blurring the three farthings until they looked like six; Charlie was going to be so cross with her – and rightly.

Charlie leaned across and stared, unbelievingly, at the three farthings. As Diana watched, a tide of crimson flooded his face. 'The wicked old blighter,' he said furiously. 'Well, we know where he lives.' He snatched the three coins from Wendy's hand, then jerked Diana to her feet. 'C'mon!'

They returned to the house on Brownlow Hill, indignation speeding their footsteps. Charlie hammered on the door – you could scarcely call it knocking – but there was a long wait before it was answered, and then it was crashed open impatiently, and a voice said: 'What d'you want?' The three children all stepped back, mouths dropping open in astonishment. A policemen stood there, his tall, domed helmet on his head, his long overcoat and regulation boots announcing that here, indeed, was a scuffer. For a moment, no one recognised him, then Diana saw his mean little eyes glittering in the shadow of his helmet and realised that their enemy had not merely turned into a policeman, but had been one all along.

'Well? I'm just off to work so don't you come botherin' my good lady while I'm away.'

'We want our money,' Charlie said, when the two girls did not so much as open their mouths. 'We agreed a bob and you said you'd put the money into Di's pocket, but it were three farthings, norreven a perishin' penny. If it were a joke, then it weren't a very funny one and you owe us elevenpence farthing.'

'If the kid's gone an' lost the bob I gave her, then you'd best go back to the hall, keepin' your eyes down,' the policeman said, beginning to close the door. 'Clear orff or I'll gi' you a whackin' you won't forget in a hurry.'

Charlie began to speak again but the policeman slammed the door and they could hear his boots stomping off down the hallway. In a frenzy of frustrated rage, Charlie hurled himself at the door once more and began to bang on it, but Diana caught at his jacket and tugged as hard as she could. 'Don't, Charlie, don't,' she said imploringly. 'I know he's a horrible old man and a cheat, but he's a scuffer! It will just be his word against ours and no one believes kids rather than a policeman. Oh, come away, do!'

'I'm going round to the police station and I'll tell 'em all that the feller what lives over on Brownlow Hill cheated us out of our money.' But Diana took one of his hands and Wendy the other, and they towed him away from the policeman's front door.

'It's no use, Charlie,' Wendy said. 'Di's right; no one would believe us, or even if they did, they couldn't make the feller give us our dosh. But we knows where he lives an' he don't know us from Adam. One day, when we ain't so busy savin' up for Christmas, we'll do something really horrible to him.' She tilted her head in a considering manner. 'Dead rats through his letter box? Or we could chuck a stone through his window if we come up in the middle of the night, so's we aren't caught.'

Charlie allowed himself to be led away, but when he saw that Diana was crying he put a brotherly arm round her shoulders and said, through gritted teeth, 'Never mind, it weren't your fault; he knew damn well you couldn't check the money what he'd put in your pocket, not with both arms round his perishin' Christmas tree. But he's a wicked old bugger and we'll get even with him one day, I promise you.'

'I'll do it,' Diana said tearfully, knuckling her eyes. 'I'll spread lard on his doorstep an' I hope he breaks his back! Oh, Charlie, I ache all over, honest to God I do. And I'm so scratched! And I did want some money so's I could buy some things for Christmas.'

'Well, tomorrow's the last day of school, and then there's two whole days before Christmas,' Charlie said comfortingly. He turned to Wendy. 'Tomorrow's out, of course, but do you have anything planned for the next day? If not, the pair of you can come with me. I've got a pair of old garden shears and I'm goin' to cut holly to sell on the market stalls, or from door to door. With three of us at it, we'll make a nice little sum an' there'll still be a day to go before Christmas.'

Wendy grinned gratefully at Charlie. 'That 'ud be just grand,' she said. 'We'll come along with you, won't we, Di?'

'Yes, of course we will,' Diana said joyfully. 'Wendy an' me can start in the morning, Charlie, 'cos we won't bother to go to school tomorrow, not on the last day.'

Charlie cocked a quizzical eye at her but said nothing, and when Diana's mam was making their tea that evening he came knocking at the door. He grinned at Diana and then held up a threepenny piece. 'I went round to that house on Brownlow Hill and spoke to the woman what answered the door when we first knocked,' he said. 'I told her what her old man had done and at first she just grinned, spiteful like. But then I got Tatum and Hector out of me pocket and pretended I were goin' to throw them at her. She give a scream like a train whistle and started gibberin', saying she'd call the scuffers, she'd clip my ear . . . an' all the time, she were edgin' backwards an' I were edgin' forwards. I told 'er if she'd just pay me the bob I'd go, an' I'd take me pals wi' me. An' I tell you, the money just flew out o' her purse. So here's your share, except for the other penny, which you can have in the mornin'.'

Diana began to ask for more details but Charlie, grinning, said he must go since he had another call to make, and disappeared out of their door once more. Diana smiled, rather doubtfully, at her mother. 'He's ever so kind, Charlie,' she said. 'I – I'm saving up for Christmas, so we've been earning a bit of money . . . I do like Charlie, Mam.'

'Yes, I'm sure he's very nice,' Emmy said distractedly. 'But who are Tatum and Hector? And why did Charlie threaten to throw them at someone? No, I want a proper explanation, Diana, so sit yourself down and start talking.'

Diana heaved an enormous sigh; she could see that her free and easy life was about to become public knowledge and guessed she had a difficult time ahead. 'Tatum and Hector are Charlie's mice,' she said. 'And – and there was this horrible lady . . . oh dear, I suppose I had better start right at the beginning . . .'

*

When the story was told Emmy sat for a long moment, elbows resting on the table, chin cupped in her hands. Things were beginning to fall into place at last and the letter she had received that morning was no longer quite such a mystery. The letter had been from the headmaster of Diana's school. He had stated that though Mrs Wesley had written to the school, informing them that the family had moved to Garston, he had been unable to find any member of staff, in any of the Garston schools, who had received Diana as a pupil. Puzzled by this, he had asked young Charlie Fisher whether he could supply the school with Mrs Wesley's new address and Charlie had told him that their address was still No. 2 Nightingale Court, and had asked the headmaster whether he was confusing it with Lancaster Avenue, where the Wesleys had lived the previous year.

Since Diana had not been in school for many weeks now, he had considered it his duty to contact her parent and to ask her to visit him at the earliest opportunity. *I do realise, Mrs Wesley, that you are now in full-time employment and may find it difficult to attend school between 9.00 a.m. and 4.00 p.m., but if you could visit on the last day of term, I am always in the building until 8.00 p.m. supervising the cleaners and making sure that all is well,* his letter had said. *Diana is a bright child and we have great hopes for her but constant – indeed prolonged – absence can do nothing but harm. However, if you have already entered her in a private school, please ignore this letter.*

Emmy had been flabbergasted, had believed that there must be two children named Diana in her daughter's class. Did she not see the child leaving for school each morning, neatly dressed and with her satchel on one shoulder? Did not Diana regale her with stories of her day in school when she, Emmy, returned from work? But, in telling her story just now, Diana had made it plain that she had not attended school today and had not meant to do so tomorrow. And Mr Ellis, the headmaster, had made it equally plain that Diana had not been in school for weeks. Emmy stared across the table at her daughter's bland little face. Diana was looking down at the table, her long dark lashes veiling her eyes. For a moment, Emmy wondered wildly what she should do or say. Diana was her beloved child; surely she would not lie? And she *liked* school, had always done so. Yet there was the letter . . .

Emmy got to her feet and walked over to the mantelpiece, where Mr Ellis's letter was propped up behind the clock. She took it down, removed the neatly written pages from the envelope and placed them before Diana. 'Read that,' she said, her voice even. 'And then tell me just what has been going on.'

Diana raised her eyes for a moment and Emmy could see the guilt and misery in them. Poor kid, she thought impulsively. If she had been truanting, it would be because wretched Wendy Telford had led her into bad ways. She had never approved of the friendship and now she knew she had been right. Diana would not have dreamed of missing even a day's schooling until she met Wendy. Wendy was a bad lot – the whole Telford family was a bad lot – so though Emmy was deeply disappointed over Diana's behaviour, she could not blame her completely. I should blame myself, she thought remorsefully. I should have put my foot down right at the start and told her to keep well away from Wendy and her family. I shouldn't have let Wendy visit us here . . .

She took a seat opposite Diana and watched closely as the child read the letter. She saw tears rise to Diana's eyes and begin to trickle down her cheeks; heard muffled sobs start as Diana finished reading the letter, pushed it aside, laid her head on her arms and began to cry in earnest. 'Oh, Mammy, I'm sorry, truly I am,' she mumbled. 'Only – only Miss Williams is the most boringest teacher in the whole world, and – and the other girls started calling me teacher's pet again, 'cos I couldn't help getting top marks. And Wendy was left behind in the lower class with a new teacher, and he's a beast, Mammy, honest he is. He whacks and kicks and says horrible things – he hates Wendy and she hates him. And Wendy was going to have to move in with her aunt 'cos her mam couldn't afford the rent and she's my friend, my only friend really. So when she said she wasn't coming into school again because she needed to earn money so the Telfords could stay in the court, I – I wrote letters to Miss Williams and Mr Withers telling them that neither Wendy nor me would be in school 'cos we were moving away. Oh, Mammy, I'm so, so sorry!'

Emmy longed to run to her daughter and give her a great big hug, and tell her that it was all right, that she had done a wrong thing but that she, Emmy, understood her reasons and would always stand by her. However, she knew that Peter would have been furious with her had she acted in such a manner. By her own admission, Diana had forged two letters, told a great many lies and caused a deal of trouble. It was all very well saying that Miss Williams was a bad teacher, but even Diana must realise that bad teachers came one's way occasionally and simply had to be endured. So Emmy remained sitting in her chair, though she did stretch a hand across the table to push the hair out of Diana's eyes, saying bracingly as she did so: 'Now it's pointless getting in a state, Diana, because what's done is done. You've been very naughty indeed; you've done a great many bad things, but I believe you did them because Wendy encouraged you. She's a good deal older than you and should definitely have known better. Now I shall have to see what I must do to put things right. First and foremost, you must come with me to your school tomorrow – fortunately, I'm on the late shift – and explain to Mr Ellis just what has been going on.'

Diana quailed. 'Oh, Mammy, I can't, I can't! How can I tell Mr Ellis that I sagged off school because Miss Williams was the boringest teacher in the world? He'll be ever so cross. He might even cane me – and it wasn't Wendy's fault because it was my idea to write the notes. Oh, please don't make me see Mr Ellis. I know what I did was wrong, but I'm only six. Children of six are – are irresponsible, isn't that true?'

Emmy hid a smile. 'It doesn't matter what age you are, darling, because you knew very well that what you were doing was wrong. The letters you wrote to the teachers were forgeries . . . do you understand what that means? And you've been telling me lies, haven't you? You've been telling me what happened to you in school on days when you've not been there at all. I'm just so glad that Daddy never knew his little girl was a liar and a cheat.'

This produced such a frenzied wail that Emmy was forced to take Diana on her lap and tell her that this must be a lesson to her. 'Always tell the truth, no matter what the consequences,' she said impressively. 'There's a saying which you might do well to learn – *Oh what a tangled web we weave, when first we practise to deceive*, and you can see how true it is. You started off with one little lie and you ended up having to tell more and more to keep your guilty secret. Now stop crying and go up and wash your face and brush your hair. Tomorrow morning, first thing, we'll go round to school and face Mr Ellis together.'

The interview next day was a painful one, though Mr Ellis did not wield his cane. What he did do was impress upon Diana the error of her ways and tell her that, as a result of not being in school, she might well have to spend an extra year in Miss Williams's class. This elicited such a groan from Diana that Emmy saw the headmaster's lips twitch, but it certainly added the final touch to her daughter's regrets over her behaviour. Clearly, the thought of two whole years under Miss Williams's sway was enough to make Diana promise earnestly never to play truant again.

'I am naturally distressed to see that Mrs Telford and Wendy have not yet come to school to explain Wendy's absence,' he added. 'It's possible that they may come along later, though I very much doubt it. I have contacted Mrs Telford before over the matter of her children's rarely attending school, and she has never accepted my invitations to visit me. So I must insist, Diana, that all contact with Wendy ceases from this moment on. After all, she's four years older than you, so you can scarcely call it an equal friendship.' He turned to Emmy. 'I think you should make it clear to Mrs Telford that Wendy is a bad influence on Diana and will no longer be welcome in your house.'

Emmy agreed meekly that she would see to it and Mr Ellis smiled at Diana for the first time. 'Now, Diana, I shall take you along to Miss Williams's class and you will take your place as though nothing has happened. I dare say you will have some explaining to do to your classmates but since this is the last day of term, and you've got the whole of the Christmas holidays before you, you will probably be luckier than you deserve. When school starts again in January, everyone will have forgotten your long absence.'

'Will – will Miss Williams be very c-cross?' Diana asked, her voice shaking. 'Oh, I wish I hadn't done it!'

Over her daughter's head, Emmy's eyes met Mr Ellis's and she saw that the headmaster was once more suppressing a smile. 'Naturally, Miss Williams will be very upset, but glad that you have come to your senses and returned to your class,' he said and Emmy smiled gratefully at him. He was not the ogre she had feared he would be, but a grey-haired, middle-aged man, in a well-worn flannel suit, who had not attempted to make Emmy herself feel guilty and had smoothed Diana's path back into education. A less sympathetic man might have terrified Diana into hating and fearing school, and Emmy was grateful to him for his forbearance.

She said as much when they had left Diana in her classroom and were retracing their steps along the echoing corridor. Mr Ellis ran a hand through his hair, making it stand up comically, then smoothed it down with both palms. 'When you think she's only six and managed to fool the lot of us, even you,' he said, 'I have to admit a sneaking admiration. Your daughter is worth cultivating, Mrs Wesley. I think we shall all be very proud of her one day.'

Emmy, flushed with gratification, made her way home to the court, thinking that things could have been a lot worse. Then she remembered the interview with Mrs Telford and Wendy which lay ahead of her and felt her mouth go dry with apprehension. She had always avoided any sort of contact with the Telfords, but this time a confrontation would have to be faced. She had heard Mrs Telford blinding and swearing at her children and guessed that she would be verbally abused the moment she opened her mouth.

There was no help for it, however. Not only had she promised Mr Ellis that she would speak to the woman, she had realised that she would simply have to do so, and since there's no time like the present Emmy squared her shoulders, crossed the court, and banged the knocker on the Telfords' door. She knew the colour was draining from her face, could feel her knees beginning to wobble, but she gritted her teeth and lifted her chin as the door was abruptly opened to reveal Mrs Telford's squat, untidy figure.

She eyed Emmy suspiciously. 'Yes? Whaddayer want?'

'Good morning, Mrs Telford,' Emmy said evenly, with a bumping heart. 'I'd like a word. May I come in?'

She half hoped that Mrs Telford would refuse to let her enter the house but, after a moment's hesitation, the older woman grudgingly opened the door a little wider and ushered Emmy inside. 'I s'pose there's trouble,' she muttered, as the two women entered the dirtiest kitchen Emmy had ever seen. 'You wouldn't come round here if there weren't trouble – you've never so much as given me the time of day afore.'

'Yes, I'm afraid it is trouble,' Emmy said bravely. 'I imagine you had a similar letter from the headmaster of the school to the one I received. In fact,

I've just returned from an interview with him . . .'

Mrs Telford muttered something; Emmy thought it sounded something like *stupid old fart*, but since she was not sure whether Mrs Telford was referring to Emmy herself or to Mr Ellis, she decided to ignore it and ploughed gamely on.

'It seems that Wendy and Diana have not been in school for several weeks . . .'

When she returned from work that evening, Emmy told herself that she had recovered from her meeting with Mrs Telford. It had been every bit as bad as she had feared. Mrs Telford had screamed at her and called her names. She had said it had been Diana who had led Wendy into evil ways, then that the two girls were as bad as one another, then that she would beat Wendy to a pulp when she caught her.

'An' you can keep that prissy little brat o' yours away from my girl,' she had shrieked belligerently, as Emmy began to cross the court, heading for her own door. 'An' don't you come here threatenin' me, 'cos our Wendy won't want to play wi' a kid half her age. You better not come near me again wi' your fancy ways, you stuck-up bitch, or you'll get a crack on the jaw what you won't forget in a hurry.'

So now Emmy advanced across the cobbles with some caution. Telling herself that Mrs Telford seldom emerged from her own house was all very well, but it was nine at night, and when Mrs Telford was in the money she visited the Jug and Bottle on the corner at about this time, and could be seen hurrying there and coming very slowly back with a tin jug of ale clasped to her breast, as one would usually carry a beloved child. Emmy told herself that Mrs Telford's drink-sodden brain would have forgotten the encounter an hour or so after it had happened, but she was still glad to enter her own kitchen without having seen so much as a glimpse of Wendy's mam.

Diana was sitting at the kitchen table, working her way through several sheets of sums and handwriting exercises which Emmy had left for her, but she looked up and smiled cheerfully at her mother. 'Aunty Beryl brung me home ten minutes ago, but said she wouldn't stay since she's not got the littl'uns to bed yet,' she said. 'Did you see Wendy's mam this morning? What did she say?'

'She said a great many rude things,' Emmy said repressively. 'And now the subject is closed, Diana. You've agreed not to see Wendy again and Mrs Telford agreed – more or less – that Wendy would not see you again, either. The pair of you are going to have to make friends of your own age; the sort of girls that I'll be happy to have visit us here. Now, off to bed with you, or you'll be fit for nothing in the morning.'

Chapter Eight
July 1927

'Oh, Mam, don't say that perishin' Diana has got to come with us. Can't you tell her she has to play with Becky, or one of the other girls? Ever since the big row last Christmas, she's dogged me perishin' footsteps. I don't see no harm in young Wendy meself, so why does Aunt Emmy have to cut up rough and say the kids can't play together? It ain't as if Di has missed so much as a day of school since Christmas, an' now it's the summer holidays. Can't you put in a word, persuade Aunt Emmy that there ain't no real harm in Wendy? It wouldn't be so bad, but Diana hangs round wi' me and the fellers, pretendin' to keep up, even when we know she's wore out.'

Beryl Fisher sighed. She understood Charlie's feelings but she knew it was useless to suggest to Emmy that Diana might be allowed to play with Wendy, now that the long summer holiday was upon them. The trouble was that Wendy had reverted to her old ways as soon as the split between the two families had come. She stole, she lied, she called names and, of course, she never attended school. She stopped taking care of herself and once again wore her filthy rags, seldom bothering to wash and going barefoot even in the coldest, wettest weather. Beryl did not blame Emmy for wanting the two girls to be kept apart, but she did sympathise with Charlie. It was usually the older girls in a family who got landed with the younger ones, but of course her eldest girl was Becky, and even at six she was not able to look after Bobby and the baby, Jimmy, when Beryl wanted a bit of peace. So naturally, when Charlie went off to get the messages, he took the younger children in the pram, piling bags of flour and sacks of spuds around their feet. At first, he had not minded Diana's accompanying him on such shopping trips, but when, as now, he, Lenny and their friends Phil and Steve were going fishing in the canal, then a neatly dressed little girl with white socks and brown sandals on her feet was nothing but an embarrassment.

Beryl tried to marshal her thoughts. It was useless to tell Charlie that Wendy was no fit companion for the daintily dressed Diana, because he would promptly reply that he was no fit companion for her either. Beryl had tried telling Emmy that dressing Diana up like a little princess was no way to go on, especially when school was out and everyone else wore their oldest things, but Emmy had said firmly that keeping up appearances was important. 'It stops Diana indulging in dangerous or messy games,' she had said severely, 'and it stops her seeking out the – the lower elements in the courts for playfellows.'

'I take it by lower elements you mean Wendy . . . but you might bear in mind, Em, that my kids play in the oldest clothes I can find them,' Beryl had told her friend. 'I remember a time when you realised yourself that life would be easier for Diana if she behaved like everyone else and didn't stand out like a sore thumb. You seem to have forgotten that lately.'

Emmy had blushed, but remained firm. 'I'm sorry, Beryl. I didn't mean to be rude or upset you,' she had said humbly. 'But the truth is, I'm desperate to keep her away from that Wendy and one way to do it is to keep her looking smart all the time. Wendy won't want to play with her if she's always clean and neat, I'm sure.'

Thinking it over now, Beryl was not at all certain that her friend was right. Wendy would not care how Diana looked; it was her friendship that the older girl missed. Beryl had noticed her hanging wistfully around any group of children which contained Diana, but the younger girl would only give her a quick, diffident glance and a shy smile. Her mother's prohibition was not to be easily forgotten.

However, Diana was now refusing to play with Becky and her pals, saying that they were babies and played baby games, and adding that she preferred to be with Charlie. Once or twice, Beryl had decided to help Charlie out and had said, bluntly, that the boys did not want her. This had caused Diana to blush to the roots of her hair, and had given Charlie a day or two of freedom from his small admirer. But Diana had soon reverted to her favourite pastime, which seemed to be tagging along behind Charlie and his pals.

'Well, Mam? Please will you have a go at Diana today? Think, if she ends up in the canal, drowned dead, everyone'll say it's my fault. I'm tellin' you, I can't fish with the lads and watch out for a kid what's got no more sense than to wear decent clothing in the holidays.'

Beryl sighed again. Her mam, Granny Pritchard, had died four months previously. In a way, this should have made life easier for Beryl, since it was one less person to look out for, one less mouth to feed. Yet even though she had been bed-bound and no longer able to help with the children, Beryl missed her sorely. Her tiny pension had been a help, but what Beryl missed most was sharing her problems and worries with another woman whose experience and wisdom had always been on hand. Her mam would have told her how to break it gently, both to Diana and to Emmy, that a boy of Charlie's age needed a bit of time to himself . . . a bit of space, like.

Since Emmy paid her a small weekly sum to keep an eye on Diana, however, Beryl knew she would be quite within her rights to tell the child that she needed her in the house to give a hand with young Bobby and to keep an eye on the baby. The trouble was, as she herself was not working during the day – unless you counted laundering tablecloths, napkins, pinafores and overalls for half the cafés and canny houses in the district – she would be hard put to it to find Diana anything to do. Bobby liked to play out in the court with other children his age if it was fine, in which case there were always older children, including Becky, who would dash in to inform a parent of any disaster which might have befallen their child. If it was wet, he and a couple of pals would be quite content to play on the kitchen floor, preferably under the big, square kitchen table, where Beryl herself could keep an eye on them. But the problem would have to be faced. Charlie was quite right: Emmy did not like it when Diana returned home with dirty socks and stains down her dress. It was time she tackled the younger woman again, explained that she was creating real difficulties for Charlie and Lenny.

'Mam?' Charlie's tone was impatient, yet hopeful. 'Couldn't you dash over now and have a word wi' Aunt Emmy? We've been off school for two weeks an' I've not had a moment's peace in all that time.'

Beryl couldn't help laughing; she had heard those

very words on the lips of a number of people, but they had all been women with large families, not young boys. 'Well, I don't know about dashing,' she said. 'But if you'll give an eye to the porridge, I'll have a word with Emmy before she goes off to work.'

'Thanks, Mam,' Charlie said fervently. 'It ain't that I don't like Di; she's norra bad kid, but no one wants a girl taggin' them all day – no feller does, I mean.'

Becky was still upstairs, helping Bobby to dress, and Lenny had disappeared some time earlier, taking bread and jam and saying he didn't want breakfast since it was his turn to dig for bait. Beryl knew that the boys collected worms from parks and gardens in the area, knew also that they had to be out early to avoid the park keepers, so had let Lenny go without comment. Now, she scooped Jimmy up from where he squatted on the hearthrug, nuzzling his neck as he squawked a protest and telling him that he was a grand boy and that Aunt Emmy would very likely give him a bicky if he was good.

Jimmy cooed agreeably and Beryl headed next door, with the comfortable weight of him in her arms and his rather sticky cheek pressed to hers. She did not bother to knock, but opened the door and let herself into the kitchen with the air of one sure of a welcome, which she certainly was.

Emmy looked up as she entered. She was alone in the room, which was fortunate, and smiled at Beryl and Jimmy, going immediately to the biscuit tin and handing Jimmy a finger of shortbread. 'Hello, Beryl, you're early,' she said. 'Anything wrong? Only I start work at eight this morning, so I shall have to be off in ten minutes or so.'

'No, nothing's wrong exactly,' Beryl said, sitting down at the table and settling Jimmy comfortably on her knee. 'Look, Em, I've told you before that it ain't fair to dress Diana up so neat and clean for a day's play in the court. What I haven't told you is that she's driving Charlie mad because she won't leave him alone. She follows him everywhere, even when he's with his mates and they go places which aren't suitable for a little girl, let alone one dressed so fancy. Today they're going fishing in the canal an' I'm tellin' you they'll come back covered in muck and dog tired. Probably they'll go along to the Scaldy for a swim and that 'ud be downright dangerous for Diana.'

Em sat down at the table opposite her friend, her eyes rounding. 'But – but I thought she played with Becky when Charlie left the court,' she said. 'Why, she often tells me that Becky and she have been playing shop, or hopscotch, or that they've gone down to the park to play Relievio. Is – isn't it *true*, Beryl?'

'Of course she does play with the other girls sometimes,' Beryl said, not wanting to get Diana into more trouble. 'But for the most part she simply follows Charlie around, and when they're playing out, which they do whenever the weather's fine, I don't always know exactly where she is.'

'Well you should,' Emmy said, her face flushing pink. 'I thought you always knew exactly where she was! Oh, Beryl, I trusted you to take care of her, not to let her go wandering off.'

Beryl felt the first stirrings of annoyance with her friend. She would have liked to reply, hotly, that for half a crown a week Emmy was getting more than her money's worth without expecting Beryl to spend her time following Diana about. Instead, she took a deep breath and counted to ten before she spoke. 'Diana is seven, quite old enough to know that she must either stay in the court, or leave it with someone both you and I trust. I trust Charlie completely, and thought you did too . . .'

'I do, I do,' Emmy said quickly. Tears filled her big blue eyes and she began to cough. She smothered the spasm in her handkerchief, waited a moment, then spoke again. 'But the canal! I shall never forget her falling into that deep pool when we took the children to New Brighton . . .'

'And I hope you'll never forget that if it hadn't been for Charlie, you probably wouldn't have a daughter at all,' Beryl said crossly.

'If Diana hadn't been following Charlie then, she would never have fallen into the pool,' Emmy said tearfully. 'Oh, I'm not *blaming* Charlie . . .'

'I should hope not!' Beryl said harshly. 'But don't you see, Em, that's just what I'm trying to talk to you about? Charlie goes places and does things which are safe for him but which just aren't safe for Diana. My boy's a good boy. He helps in the house, gets my messages and looks after the young ones, but he has to have some time for his own friends.'

'Well, since I'm not there, it's got to be up to you, Beryl, to see that she's happily occupied,' Emmy said obstinately. 'If you tell her she must play with Becky, I'm sure she'll do so. She's a good girl, Diana, whatever you may think. Or she could help you in the house, I suppose.'

'She wouldn't think much of that,' Beryl said ruefully. 'Half the time I'm down at the Burroughs Garden washhouse, laundering the tablecloths and that. Or else I'm at home ironing the stuff. Oh, I know she likes to help when I'm baking, but I only do that once a week, and she seems to think Becky and her pals are still babies.'

'Well . . . suppose you told Charlie not to go to the canal? If I gave him sixpence perhaps he could go to the cinema, or take Diana to the park and buy them both ice creams,' Emmy said distractedly. 'I can't think what else to do, if you aren't going to put your foot down and make her play with Becky.'

Beryl stared at her friend. The time for some plain speaking had clearly arrived. 'I can tell Diana to play with Becky until I'm blue in the face and she'll agree to do so as meek as you please, but the moment my back's turned she'll be off after Charlie. I didn't want to say anything because it seemed like tale-clatting, but the truth is Diana's no plaster saint. When she comes home again and I try to tell her off, she looks as if butter wouldn't melt in her mouth and says you told her she would be safe with Charlie, and she's been with Charlie all day.'

Emmy bristled, there was no other word for it. 'You're saying that Diana disobeys you, and I don't believe it. She's a good girl. Why, she's never missed a day's school since that row last Christmas and she's moving up a class in September, so she won't have to put up with Miss Williams any more. She wouldn't lie, I know she wouldn't.'

'I didn't say she lied, because no doubt she has been with Charlie. What I'm saying is she won't do as I tell her, but goes her own way and then justifies it by saying you told her it was all right,' Beryl said, with all the patience she could muster. 'The truth is, Diana needs a pal of her own. She's real fond of Wendy but you've put a stop to that friendship, so she's turning to Charlie. Remember, because of the way she's been brought up – being an only child and all – she's old for her age and don't get on with younger kids. Charlie suggested you might let her play with Wendy again because they used to get on so well before . . .'

Emmy jumped to her feet, the bright colour rushing into her cheeks once more. 'I'm going to work!' she snapped. 'And I'll thank you to mind your own business, Beryl Fisher! You know full well that Wendy's a bad influence and I'm beginning to wonder whether Charlie isn't a bad influence too. Taking a young girl like my Diana fishing in the canal! If you can't control a kid of seven, then mebbe I ought to make other arrangements.'

She snatched her hat off the peg and was struggling into her light coat when Diana came heavily down the stairs. The child opened the kitchen door, looking anxious. 'Hello, Aunty Beryl. Mammy, why were you shouting? Surely you aren't going to leave before I've had my breakfast? Oh, Mammy, you've been crying. Whatever is the matter?'

Emmy hesitated. 'You'd best have your breakfast with Aunty Beryl today,' she said brusquely. 'I dare say she won't mind having you for one more day, nuisance though you are to her.'

'One more day will be fine,' Beryl said, her voice icy. 'But from tomorrow, Emmy, you can find someone else to take on your responsibilities.' She turned to Diana. 'I'll put you a plate of porridge out; come round to No. 4 when your mam leaves.'

Beryl let herself out of the front door, literally shaking with temper and hugging the baby to her, for he was beginning to grizzle, upset by the raised voices. She had done her best for Emmy and for Diana, but apparently her best was not good enough. She thought, wryly, that Emmy was about to get one hell of a shock if she meant to offer some other poor woman half a crown to take all the responsibility for a precocious kid like Diana. And she was not only precocious but also slippery as an eel. Still, she would be somebody else's responsibility soon, and Beryl realised that not having to keep an eye on Diana would be a great weight off her mind.

Yet her heart was heavy as she opened her own front door. She had managed to remain friendly with Emmy for at least twenty years, though there had been many times when the younger girl's attitude had infuriated her. Now she had allowed their relationship to break down completely. She could have been more tactful, more generous, knowing that Emmy had only herself on whom to rely. Her friend adored Diana and was clearly unwilling to admit that no child is ever perfect, but Beryl felt Emmy had been downright ungrateful, blaming both her old friend and Charlie for everything that had gone wrong, and refusing to allow that any faults could be attributed to Diana.

Re-entering her kitchen, she set the baby down on the hearthrug and smiled across at Charlie. 'Well, chuck, I've done me best and you can go off on your fishing trip without no one tagging you. In fact, Emmy's going to look for someone else to look after Diana in the future. She – she understands that you need time to yourself and I told her Diana doesn't want to play with Becky. So you see, old feller, it's all for the best.'

Charlie stared at her, his expression troubled. 'Oh, Mam, you haven't fallen out with Aunty Em, have you?' he asked anxiously. 'And who'll she find to look after Di, apart from us? There's no one else in the court who'd take it on; they think she's an awkward little madam. But there's a house what childmind up Hornby Street; I suppose Aunty Em could try there.'

Beryl was tempted to reply that Emmy would find no one willing to look after Diana and give her her meals as cheaply as she had done, but realised that she must not do so. She hoped that Emmy would come round later and apologise, try to put things right, so she had no intention of allowing any member of her family to know what had transpired. Wally was a good husband and a patient man, but if he knew how Emmy had insulted her he would have seen red. He would probably have gone next door to give Emmy a piece of his mind, which would have helped no one, least of all Beryl herself. At the moment, I do believe I'm in the right, but if Wally or Charlie began on poor Em I would be very much in the wrong, she told herself.

Charlie had dished up the porridge and the children were now filling the gaps with bread and marge and weak tea. Beryl smiled reassuringly at her eldest. 'No, we haven't fallen out. We've agreed to differ,' she said diplomatically. 'I dare say in a couple of days I'll be keeping an eye on Diana again, but I've made it clear that I don't want you pestered. And now, how about you pouring me a nice cup of tea?'

'I hate Mrs Lucas, and I hate her dirty, whining kids,' Diana said furiously, two weeks later. 'I were going to try and stick it, but today was the last straw, so I've given her the go-by and come to Mac's to tell you I won't, I *won't* stay in her horrible house any more.'

Emmy had been serving a table of four with coffee and scones when she had spotted her daughter's small figure hovering just outside the door of the dining rooms. Despite the fact that it was August, it was raining in a steady and relentless sort of way and Diana was not wearing her mackintosh and looked half frozen. Emmy had served the customers and had then hurried over to the big glass-plated door and pulled her daughter inside. She had looked wildly round for a vacant table but almost every one was occupied, so she had ushered her bedraggled child through into the office, which, fortunately, was empty. She had begun to remonstrate, but Diana had forestalled her, airing her grievances immediately and at the top of her voice. Emmy looked round nervously; it would not do if one of the other waitresses came in to discover what the noise was about.

'Hush,' she said urgently, therefore. 'Keep your voice down, Diana! Do you want me to lose my job? Mr Mac is very understanding, but the customers come first – he's always telling us that. Now, take a deep breath and tell me exactly what poor Mrs Lucas has done to put you in such a flame.'

Diana pushed the wet hair out of her eyes and tried to wipe her rain-soaked face with the backs of her hands, and Emmy immediately felt remorseful. The poor child was drenched and in obvious distress. It was no use expecting her to explain what had happened when she was in such a state.

'Look, Diana, I'm just going to nip into the kitchen for a moment and get a towel, and I'll have to explain to Mrs Ridley – she's the cook – that I'll be off the floor for ten minutes or so. Sit down and wait for me.'

She left the room at a trot and went through to the kitchen. Mrs Ridley was extremely kind, hooking down a clean roller towel from the drying rack and telling Emmy, comfortably, that when the elevenses rush was over she might put her daughter at a corner table with a book and a plate of biscuits until they were quiet enough to allow her to return Diana to the childminder's place.

'If you're going to send her back, that is,' she added shrewdly. 'Because some of these women give the kids a hard time, I'm told. And you wouldn't want that for your littl'un. Mebbe it would be better to let her stay with a friend until you get things sorted.'

Emmy thanked her and hurried back to the office. Diana looked up and smiled rather guiltily as her mother re-entered the room and Emmy thought, hopefully, that the child might have had second thoughts. Truth to tell, she had worried at first over how Diana would get on with Mrs Lucas after having been treated as a member of the Fisher family for so long. She had asked her daughter to give Mrs Lucas a fair trial, but now it seemed things had come to a head. Emmy began to wield the towel, rubbing Diana briskly until she was pink all over and beginning to smile. Then she produced one of the spare overalls which the waitresses used when doing the kitchen work, stripped Diana down to her bare skin, and put her into the overall. It could have contained at least three Dianas but Emmy belted it firmly round the waist and then surveyed her handiwork. Diana's teeth no longer chattered and though there was still a mutinous glint in her eye, she looked a good deal happier than the child who had entered the premises some ten minutes earlier. 'Well? Just what happened this morning to send you flying off without your coat or your hat?'

'She hit me!' Diana said baldly. 'She often hits the other kids but she's known better than to try and hit *me*, because she must have known I wouldn't stand for it. But today she was really cross and lashed out. She hit me across the face so hard that she knocked me over.' Diana touched her left cheek gingerly, and for the first time Emmy realised that her daughter's left ear was scarlet and that there were what looked like reddened finger marks on her cheek. 'You can't see my shoulder because of the overall but I bet there'll be a huge bruise there in an hour or two,' Diana finished, with a certain satisfaction.

'But – but why did she hit you?' Emmy asked anxiously. 'Of course, she shouldn't have hit you at all and I shall tell her she is never to do such a thing again, but she must have had a reason.'

'She came into the room with her coat on and told me that I were the oldest there, so she were leaving me in charge. She said I'd been with her for two whole weeks so I ought to know the drill by now. I said that she was supposed to be looking after me and I wasn't there to do her job for her and she said I was to do as I was told and that meant I was to give the kids their dinner, prompt at noon, and then I was to peel a big bag of spuds and carrots and chop up some stewing steak, and get it over the fire so's it would be ready when she came back about five. I told her I wasn't a servant and didn't mean to act like one, so she might as well take her coat and scarf off, and start doing what she was paid to do. She began to shout at me – she called me awful names, Mam – and then she made for the back door and I grabbed hold of her coat. That was when she hit me. I picked myself up from the floor and ran into the yard. She tried to stop me, but I ducked under her arm and shot out of the back gate and ran up the jigger as fast as I could.' She chuckled suddenly. 'I could hear her yelling after me right down to the main road, but I don't think she left the house because the next oldest to me isn't quite five, and nowhere near tall enough to put the dinner on the fire, let alone get it off again.'

'Dear God,' Emmy said faintly. 'Does Mrs Lucas often go out and leave the children? No – this must be the first time or you'd have told me before.'

'No, I wouldn't, Mam, because you asked me to give Mrs Lucas a fortnight's trial . . . well, you didn't say that exactly, but that is what you meant . . . so I've put up with everything and kept my mouth shut, but in fact she often goes out, only usually she leaves Amelia in charge. Amelia's ten. Or sometimes an older girl comes in. Her name's Sheila and I suppose she's twelve or thirteen, and ever so strict. If someone's been naughty, she makes everyone sit down on the floor with their hands on their heads. They have to stay there till she says they can move, and the little ones cry 'cos their arms ache so.'

Emmy stared at her daughter; this was dreadful! She had not liked Mrs Lucas, had thought her sly and probably lazy, but she had never dreamed that the woman would ill-treat the children in her charge, let alone abandon them. She put a hand to her head, feeling the niggling pain at her temples which began whenever she became worried or over-stressed. 'Well, you can't go back to Mrs Lucas, that's plain, even if she'd have you, which she probably wouldn't. Oh dear, and I paid a month in advance . . . she's most awfully expensive. Oh, Di, darling, whatever are we to do?'

'I could go back to Aunty Beryl . . .' Diana began, but Emmy immediately shook her head.

'No, that's out of the question. If only there was someone in the courts whom I could trust! But I suppose that wouldn't be fair to Beryl, because as it is no one knows . . . well, I don't think they know I've moved you to Hornby Street. And there's another month of the school holidays to go . . . oh, whatever am I to do?'

Diana stared at her mother. 'What will happen when I'm back at school then?' she asked. 'You didn't mean me to go to Mrs Lucas after school, did you?'

'I thought you would be able to look after yourself after school,' Emmy said thoughtlessly. 'After all, you and Wendy used to trot in and out of the house last year until I got home, and you were only six then.'

Diana beamed at her mother. 'There you are then!' she said triumphantly. 'Why shouldn't Wendy look after me? We needn't use the fire, 'cos it's summer and we can have sandwiches and cold drinks for our dinners, and I'd be perfectly happy and safe. And you know, Mam, Wendy's good, she really is. She'd never dream of hitting me, not like that wicked old Lucas.'

For a moment, Emmy was genuinely tempted. Then she remembered Wendy's horribly unkempt appearance, her dreadful broad accent, interlaced with swear words, and the grime on her skin. She could imagine, all too clearly, what Peter would have thought had he ever come face to face with Wendy Telford: *Keep that little slattern away from my Diana,* he would have said. *I know you have to live in the court because there's no money for anywhere better. But that doesn't mean you have to let Diana mix with the worst elements. Go back and swallow your pride and apologise to Beryl. It says in the bible, 'He that toucheth pitch shall be defiled therewith.' That's what folk will think if you let our Diana spend time with that dirty brat.*

'Mam?' Diana's voice was hopeful. 'If you'd let me and Wendy be pals again, I'd be ever so ever so good! We'd keep the house lovely and tidy and we'd get your dinner for you every night, and do all the messages. And Wendy would clean up again, you know, and start going to school, honest to God she would.'

Emmy put her head in her hands. There was no doubt it would be the easiest solution, but how could she possibly do such a thing? She knew Peter would have disapproved and realised that Beryl would be cock-a-hoop because she had suggested it herself. Anyhow, Wendy was only eleven herself, and her awful mother would undoubtedly take advantage and seek Emmy out. The very thought of such a thing's happening made Emmy's head start to thump.

'Look, Diana, I'll try to arrange something when I get back from work this afternoon,' she said. 'Fortunately, I'm on earlies, so I can ask around and hopefully—'

The opening of the office door stopped her in mid-sentence. She was actually sitting in Mr Mac's chair, whilst Diana sat opposite her, and she suddenly realised that she was taking liberties. She jumped to her feet as Mr Mac entered the room and stopped short, staring from mother to daughter. He looked perplexed. 'Mrs Wesley? What's happened?'

Emmy could feel the hot colour flooding her face as she began to stammer an explanation, and was glad to realise that Mr Mac was not annoyed with her, but merely puzzled over Diana's presence. As she finished speaking she was relieved to see her boss eyeing Diana with a decided twinkle. 'I thought you were a bit young to work as a kitchen maid, miss,' he said jovially. 'I came straight to the office, so haven't seen Mrs Ridley, but I think her suggestion that this young lady should have some biscuits at one of the corner tables is a good one.' Mr Mac smiled at Diana. 'Off with you then, young lady. You'll find a pile of newspapers in the Welsh dresser and I'm pretty sure there are some comics there as well.'

Diana got up obediently and trotted out of the room, holding up her overall with one hand and closing the door carefully behind her.

As soon as her daughter had left, Emmy stood up, walked round the desk, and sat down in the visitor's chair, whilst Mr Mac took his own place. 'I thought it would be easier to talk without the child listening to every word,' he said. 'I've been thinking whilst you were explaining Diana's presence, and I believe we can work something out. I've been talking to Miss Symons recently and, odd though it may seem, she is in a position similar to your own. If the two of you got together, you might be able to kill two birds with one stone.'

Emmy looked bewildered. She sometimes walked part of the way home with Miss Symons, who was a spinster of forty-five, much given to knitting, crocheting and embroidery, and fond of talking of her hobbies. 'I know Miss Symons well, but I can't imagine she would have much experience with children,' she said. 'She lives with her old mother on Raymond Street, though I don't know exactly where. But if you think she could help . . .'

'I think you might help each other,' Mr Mac said gently. 'Miss Symons is becoming increasingly worried over leaving her mother alone for long periods, and you aren't too happy with your present childminder. Anyway, have a word with her.'

He nodded dismissal as he spoke, and Emmy thanked him and left the office. As she entered the dining room, she found herself wondering why Mr Mac had never married. She thought he would have made a good husband – reliable and understanding, the sort of man who would enjoy a quiet family life, trips out, perhaps holidays, children, even. Of course he was neither handsome nor young, but he must, she thought, have been both once . . . why, then, had he not married? His mother probably made him so comfortable that he had never needed a wife, she supposed, and then put Mr Mac out of her mind. She had other worries, including, at this moment, what to do with Diana. She glanced towards her daughter on the thought but the child was engrossed with her comic papers and did not look up, so Emmy went on into the kitchen. No doubt Mr Mac meant well, but she did not think his idea could possibly work; Miss Symons kept herself to herself and the old woman was housebound. Emmy doubted if either of them had ever heard of a childminder. However, Mr Mac was the boss, and clearly meant well by her, so she would have to mention the matter. In fact, she would find out the Symonses' address from Mr Mac's mother, who came down from the flat above each day to do the books, go round as soon as her shift had finished, and get the whole business out of the way.

She said as much to Mrs Ridley, who beamed at her. 'What a good idea. Trust Mr Mac to use his brain. Oh aye, he takes care of his staff, does Mr Mac. Why, when young Maggie were took bad with an appendicitis, he went with her to hospital hisself and stayed with the gal until her mam and dad turned up. And though he don't like it to be known, it's him what pays old Ivy's rent, so's to eke out her pension. She were the washing up woman afore Mrs Robson,' she finished.

'Yes, he's very kind, and I suppose his suggestion might work,' Emmy said, trying not to sound as doubtful as she felt. 'Well, I'd best get back on with the job. Diana seems happy enough with her comics. Only, when the midday rush starts, her table will be wanted. I don't know quite . . .'

'Oh, don't you worry your head about that; she can come in here and give a hand with peeling spuds or clearing plates, or some such thing,' Mrs Ridley said comfortably. 'Now, off you go, young Emmy. Suzanne's been doin' your tables, but the place is beginning to fill up. Best give her a hand.'

Later in the day, Emmy and Diana walked down Raymond Street and found the Symonses' neat little house. Emmy knocked on the door and was invited in by Miss Symons, who ushered them into a front parlour so crammed with furniture and ornaments that they had difficulty in reaching the chairs to which she waved them.

'Mother is in the back room, which is where we live, most of the time,' she explained. 'She might be snoozing, so we'd best talk in here.' She smiled kindly down at Diana. 'So this is your little daughter! How do you do, my dear? I expect your mother has told you that I'm Miss Symons and work at Mr Mac's.'

'Yes, she often speaks of you,' Diana said politely. 'When my mother is working on the evening shift, you and she walk back home together. I do like this beautiful room, and I love your china kittens,' she added, gazing wide-eyed at a small side table on which at least a dozen china kittens disported themselves.

Emmy saw Miss Symons flush with pleasure and was gratified to think that Diana still remembered her company manners. But she decided to go straight to the point and cleared her throat. 'I expect you're wondering why I'm here, Miss Symons. The truth is, Diana has been spending the hours that I work with a childminder on Hornby Street, but this has proved very unsatisfactory. She's a sensible little girl but not old enough to be left in charge of a dozen younger children, which is what happened this morning – or would have, had Diana not come to the restaurant to tell me what was going on.'

Miss Symons tutted, looking distressed. 'How dreadful, Mrs Wesley.'

'Yes. So I have to find somewhere else for Diana to spend her time. Mr Mac suggested that you and I might help one another, but I don't know . . .'

Emmy was watching Miss Symons as she spoke and saw a delighted smile cross the older woman's face as the light dawned. 'Of *course*,' she breathed. 'My mother, though past eighty, is a lively and intelligent woman, but she is unable to leave the house and spends most of her day writing notices for local shops in her beautiful, clear script, addressing envelopes, or doing any other small tasks of which she is capable. What she cannot do is things like shopping, and delivering her work when it is completed. Also, she loves company and must get very tired of seeing no one but myself. As you know, Mrs Wesley, I usually work the evening shift, but if your little girl could come in during the day for a few weeks, then I should be able to earn a little more money by doing extra shifts. It would be mutually convenient, so no money need change hands.'

Emmy looked doubtfully at her daughter. She could not imagine that Diana would relish being shut up in a small house for hours together with only a very old lady for company, for it seemed unlikely that the two ladies would need a great deal of shopping done. She looked questioningly at her daughter and received a beaming smile before Diana turned to Miss Symons, vigorously nodding her head. 'I think it sounds very nice indeed, Miss Symons. Could I go and see Mrs Symons, though? She might not want me under her feet for most of the day.'

'Yes, of course, my dear,' Miss Symons said, standing up. 'Come along; I'll introduce you and then show you over the rest of the house.'

Chapter Nine

After Diana had been staying with Mrs Symons for three weeks, Emmy realised that they had definitely made the right decision. The child was happier than she had believed possible, enjoying both the company and the work involved. Diana had always been mature for her age, Emmy reflected, and this suited Mrs Symons ideally. Together, the old lady and the little girl read books, played cards, and addressed envelopes when the weather was inclement. When it was fine, they embraced a number of pursuits which both enjoyed to the full. Diana grew in confidence daily and Mrs Symons made no secret of her affection for the child or of how she delighted in having a companion who shared her own interests.

So, what had seemed an insolubly knotty problem had disappeared in a trice when Diana and old Mrs Symons had met. It was immediately apparent that they had taken to one another on sight and it had been they who had made all the arrangements, leaving Emmy and Miss Symons to acquiesce in their suggestions. They had agreed that Diana should go every day to the Symonses' house in Raymond Street as soon as she had finished her breakfast. She would then give Mrs Symons her porridge, which Miss Symons would have left ready for her. After that, she would do any messages, and then she and the elderly lady would employ themselves in any way they saw fit. Mrs Symons had a bath chair, and though Diana did not feel herself capable of negotiating kerb work and busy road junctions, she suggested that it might be pleasant to visit St Martin's Recreation Ground, which was only a short distance away.

'And I do a great deal of work in our little back yard,' Mrs Symons had told Emmy and the child, when they had first met. 'Come and see how I employ my spare time.'

To Emmy's astonishment, the tiny back yard was crammed with half beer barrels filled with earth, in which flourished a great many flowers and vegetables. Emmy saw peas, runner beans, lettuces and even tomatoes, carefully staked and already reddening. Round the outside, the barrels held masses of nasturtiums, yellow daisies and other flowers which she was unable to name. She stared admiringly at old Mrs Symons and saw that Diana was doing the same.

'It's incredible,' she had said slowly. 'Why, you've brought a country garden into the middle of the city! And how you've managed to do it, all by yourself, is astonishing – or do you have some help?'

'Once the barrels were filled with earth, I've not needed help,' the old lady had said proudly. 'I save my own seed from year to year, so that costs me nothing. But I do pay the young boys a few pennies when they bring me . . . well, fertiliser.'

'What's fertiliser?' Diana had asked curiously. 'Oh, I know. It's something that makes flowers grow, isn't that right?'

'It's horse droppings,' the old lady had said frankly, with a twinkle. 'When I was younger, I would nip out whenever a horse and cart passed by, with my bucket and spade at the ready, but now I have to pay the lads to fetch it for me.'

'I could do it,' Diana had said eagerly. 'I'd like to do it.'

But though Mrs Symons had laughed, she had also shaken her head. 'No, no, my dear, you mustn't do the boys out of their pocket money. I shall find you plenty to do, don't you worry about that.'

Emmy had been astonished at how free from worry she felt when Diana was with Mrs Symons. Of course, she had had complete confidence in Beryl, but she had also known that her old friend had five children of her own to keep her eye on, as well as several jobs. She had been happy enough to trust Diana to Charlie, but realised that the boy would not always be present. Poor little Becky was slow and Diana, though she was quite fond of the younger girl, was the one who had to take responsibility when they played together. No, Emmy had no doubt now that the quarrel with Beryl had not been without its benefits. Diana was safe with Mrs Symons and Emmy never had to wonder where her daughter was or what she was doing; Mrs Symons saw to all that. It meant that Emmy was able to take on much longer shifts than those she had worked whilst Diana was with the Fishers.

Against this was the fact that Emmy was often very, very tired and sometimes lonely. At work, one's chances of idle chat were few, and anyway most of the staff at Mac's had known one another for years; Emmy was the newcomer, the one who was a bit different, and though the others were always friendly enough in the restaurant, they did not invite her to join them outside it.

Before, Emmy had not minded because she had had Beryl in whom to confide. When she was worried or depressed, or simply worn out from a long day's work, she had gone next door, knowing that Beryl would both understand and sympathise – give advice, too, if she asked for it. Now she had to rely upon her own company, for Diana was happy to stay in Raymond Street, sharing the Symonses' evening meal, until her mother arrived on the doorstep to take her back to Nightingale Court.

Subconsciously almost, Emmy had begun to look forward to the ending of the summer holidays and the beginning of the autumn term. Then, she had imagined, she would have her daughter back again and would have to finish her last shift at around four o'clock. Of course, she would miss the money, which had been a great blessing, but, as Mrs Ridley had once said, Mr Mac cared about his staff and tried to do his best to see that they were all happy in their work. He knew Emmy was desperately short of money and had arranged extra shifts for her accordingly.

However, the previous day, Diana had produced her bombshell. 'When I start school again, Mrs Symons says I can go straight round to Raymond Street and we'll have our tea and then I'll stay with her, doing bits and bobs about the house, until Miss Symons gets home round nine or ten. Miss Symons will bring me home so you needn't worry, and Mrs Symons is going to *pay* me! Yes, truly, she's going to pay me half a crown a week out of her envelope money, and you'll be able to work the evening shift, which will be grand, won't it, Mam, because I remember you saying you get more money and better tips then than at other times.'

Emmy had been dismayed, but had felt unable to protest. Of course the lunchtime shift in the restaurant was busy, but at least it was preceded and followed by periods of relative calm. In the evening, when the staff had finished serving teas, they began on main meals straight away and the restaurant filled first with workers having their dinner before returning home, then with young folk off to the cinema or the theatre, and afterwards with cinema- and theatregoers who had not had a chance to eat before the performance. This meant that the waitresses on the last shift were constantly on the go from five o'clock until ten or eleven at night. Thanks to Mr Mac's thoughtfulness, Emmy's evening shift ended at nine rather than ten or eleven, and she was truly grateful for the respite, though she was still so tired when she did arrive home that she frequently could not sleep but lay wide-eyed, staring into the dark, whilst every muscle twitched and ached and her poor feet curled into spasms of cramp, which forced her to jump out of bed and pace the floor until the pain eased.

Emmy, however, told herself that she must be prepared to put up with the weariness because the extra money she was earning was such a help. Mr Mac had told her that despite her initial lack of experience she was one of his most efficient workers and had given her a rise in pay, as well as making sure that she got a generous share of any leftovers and never quibbling when she asked for a Saturday off to take Diana somewhere, though it was the restaurant's busiest day. His mother, old Mrs Mac, often worked on the cash desk in the evenings, and she, too, seemed well disposed towards Emmy. Despite having lived in the city for many years, she still had a strong Greek accent, and when there was a lull, or when they were clearing up after the customers had left, she would talk wistfully to Emmy of the little

Greek island where she had lived until her marriage. She was a shrewd old lady, too, and had told Emmy several times that she was working too hard and should try to put her feet up as soon as she reached home. 'My son takes good care of his employees. He knows you badly need extra money so he gives you extra work. Because he is a man he does not realise that work does not stop for you when you reach home. You must rest more,' the old lady had said.

But now Diana's plans – and those of Mrs Symons – made it difficult, if not impossible, for her to get out of doing the evening shift. Of course, she could explain to Mr Mac that she needed time in her own home, but suppose he then decided to cut the daytime hours he gave her? He had proved to be a real friend, a grand person to work for, understanding and generous, but she knew he valued his experienced waitresses and wanted all of them to do at least three late shifts a week. He had been delighted when his scheme of helping both herself and Miss Symons had worked out so well. She could not find it in her heart to tell him that the work was too hard, and she wanted to go back to day work only.

The kitchen door's bursting open broke into her thoughts. It was Sunday morning and she looked up, unable to suppress the hope that it was Beryl, come to make up, but it was only Diana, one cheek bulging and a very large apple in her hand. 'Mammy, I know you don't want me going round to Aunty Beryl's and I know you don't like me playin' wi' the Fisher kids any more, but they're off to New Brighton for the day! Uncle Wally's gone to visit his sister Ellen, and Charlie says his mam and his aunt don't get on, so Aunty's taking the kids to the seaside. Oh, Mam, couldn't we go as well? Not with them, not if you don't want to, but just at the same time? Then – then I could play with Charlie, if he'd let me.'

Emmy had been making a pan of scouse, chopping scrag end of mutton into small squares, rolling them in flour and browning them before tipping them into her large stew pan. Now she stopped and stared across at her daughter. 'Did Charlie tell you he was going?' she said incredulously. 'I thought you said he never talked to you now.'

'He don't,' Diana said, ungrammatically but truthfully. 'I heard him shouting the youngsters in, and telling Beck she'd best find herself a clean dress, 'cos his mam wouldn't take her anywhere in the old rags she's wearing. But oh, Mam, it would be so nice, so comfortable, if you and Aunty Beryl were friends again.'

Emmy knew that this was true but, unfortunately, only a week before she had made things worse. She and Beryl had found themselves on the same tram and, having climbed down at the same stop, began to walk towards the court together. Emmy had said nothing, but presently Beryl had turned to her. 'I hear you've managed to get a childminder for Diana,' she had said, rather stiffly. 'I dare say it costs you a few bob, but so long as the woman's reliable . . .'

'Oh, it doesn't cost me a penny,' Emmy had said at once. 'She's – she's an old friend and enjoys Diana's company. She and her daughter give Diana her meals and she does little jobs for them – runs messages and so on – as well as reading to the old lady from her favourite books and magazines. Her sight isn't too good, you see, so Diana is really useful.'

Beryl had nodded thoughtfully. 'That's good,' she said, and then, as if impelled: 'You've always fallen on your feet, haven't you, Em? You've always been dead lucky . . . first you got me for a measly half a crown, and now you've got a poor old woman for nothing!'

Emmy had felt herself bristling with rage and disappointment. She had hoped that Beryl was about to offer some conciliatory remark which would make it possible for them to become friends once more, but instead she had twitted Emmy about the half a crown. As soon as she had visited Mrs Lucas, Emmy had felt ashamed that she had only paid her friend such a small sum, but she did not intend to let Beryl know this. She stuck her nose in the air and said haughtily: 'It's been arranged to suit both parties, not just me; and as for being dead lucky, I think you might remember that there's nothing lucky about being a widow. If Wally turned up his toes tomorrow, you'd be glad enough to find someone willing to take on your kids whilst you did a full-time job. Not that anyone would take on your kids,' she had added, before she could stop herself, 'not with Becky as backward as she is.'

Emmy thought she would never forget the look which Beryl turned on her before she whipped round abruptly, without so much as a word, and disappeared into the nearest shop. Continuing on her way alone, Emmy had told herself that Beryl had started the unpleasantness, but she still felt a niggle of guilt. If it hadn't been true that Becky was slow, it would not have mattered so much, but the older Becky grew, the more obvious it became that there was something very wrong. Emmy knew that Becky had had a very severe attack of measles when she was two. Before then, she had been as bright and lively as any other Fisher child, but afterwards her speech had become slow and her understanding poor.

I shouldn't have said what I did, Emmy had told herself, making her way back to the court. I should stop and apologise, tell Beryl it was a nasty remark made in the heat of the moment and that I didn't mean a word of it. However, she had continued on her way, and realised, now that Diana had mentioned it, that she herself had made the situation impossible. Beryl might forgive many things, but not a spiteful dig at her poor little daughter.

'Mam? Can we go? Oh please, please, please! I hardly ever see Charlie these days and I do love him so much! If we were all on the beach, I'm sure we could make up easier than here in the court. I'd even play with stupid Becky if it would please Aunty Beryl.'

'Becky isn't stupid, she's just very unfortunate,' Emmy said sharply. 'And no, we can *not* go to the seaside. I work all the hours God sends so I can make ends meet and give you a decent life, and as far as I'm concerned Sunday's the only day I get for housework, cooking and that. If you're at a loose end, you can fetch me down the dress and cardigan you wear for school. I reckon they'll fit you for a few weeks, but you're growing all the time, so it'll be new ones by half term, I dare say.'

'Oh, but Mam, I don't ever get to play out now I'm in Raymond Street most of the time,' Diana said, in a voice periously close to a whine. 'And you're always either working or too tired to do anything nice. Why, the last time Mr Johansson was in port, he only took us out once and then you fell asleep halfway through the big picture.'

'Well, don't pretend you weren't pleased, because I know very well you don't like Mr Johansson,' Emmy snapped. 'And it's not my fault that you spend all your time in Raymond Street. Now do as you're told, please, or I shall get really angry.'

'But Mam, in three days' time I'll be back in schoo-ool,' wailed Diana. This time she was definitely whining, Emmy thought crossly. 'It's the last chance we'll have for an outing because you'll be working Monday and Tuesday, I know you will, and I'll be at Raymond Street. It's – it's not natural for a child of seven to spend all her time cooped up with old folk. I heard Aunty Beryl telling Mrs Davies so the other day. Oh please, Mam!'

For a moment, Emmy was so furious that her hand itched to slap Diana's defiant face, but she had never struck the child in her life and knew she must not do so in the midst of a quarrel. 'Get up to your room and stay there, Diana,' she said in a trembling voice. 'How dare you defy me? You're not to come down until I call that the meal is on the table.'

Diana gave her one blazing glance and then turned and shot out of the kitchen, slamming the door behind her. Emmy expected to hear footsteps thundering up the stairs, but instead Diana's feet pattered briskly along the hall, the front door opened and slammed shut, and Emmy caught a glimpse of the top of her daughter's head through the window as the child fairly hurtled across the court. Emmy dumped her kitchen knife on the table and hurried in her daughter's wake. But when she emerged from the front door there was no sign of Diana. Children, small and large, played and argued on the dirty flagstones. A group of girls skipped rope, chanting 'Salt, mustard, vinegar, pepper' as they did so, and another group – of boys this time – were playing a game of what must be cricket, with a small plank of orange-box wood and a bundle of rags, but of Diana there was no sign.

Emmy stood on the top step for a moment, trying to pretend that she was merely taking the air, reluctant to admit that the child had actually run away from her. She spent a moment longer glancing casually round, and wondered whether she ought to ask the nearest child, a filthy, tow-headed girl of ten or eleven, in which direction Diana had fled. Instead, strolling idly, as though with no particular purpose in mind, Emmy crossed the court and went under the arch on to Raymond Street. Once more she looked to right and left, but could see no sign of her daughter. I suppose she's gone to visit Mrs Symons, Emmy told herself, retracing her footsteps and returning to her domestic task. I've never known her so naughty and defiant and I don't really know how best to deal with her. Once I would have run straight to Beryl and she would have told me exactly what to do, but old Mrs Symons is different. She's only ever had the one child and she treats Diana like an adult, I've often noticed it. Well, when she does come home, she'll find herself on bread and water until she apologises for her behaviour. I really can't cope with a disobedient child.

She finished chopping the last of the vegetables and flopped into the nearest easy chair. Her breath was coming fast and shallow and there was a nasty, niggling little pain in her chest. She coughed and the little pain grew worse. She had noticed, lately, that when she was flying round the restaurant, carrying laden trays, she frequently had to pause to get her breath, and now it seemed that the quarrel with Diana was tightening her breathing just as much as running with a heavy tray did.

I'll have to start taking it a bit easier, Emmy thought dolefully. And I'll have to make Diana mind me because worrying doesn't do anyone any good. I thought I'd miss her when school starts and she spends the evenings in Raymond Street, but now I think I'll come home by myself and have a real rest. I won't tell Mr Mac that I can work the late shifts; I'll just come quietly back here and potter around and get my strength back. Once I'm all right again, then I'll start to do more hours, because the extra money will enable Diana and myself to enjoy a better standard of living.

This should have been a happy thought and it was not until she felt the tears trickling down her cheeks that Emmy realised she was crying. Crying for the life she had known, for Peter's steady companionship, for the child Diana who had adored her mummy and would have done anything to please her; and for her lost friendship, though she was now beginning to realise that this was not so much lost as thrown away.

When the knock came at the door, she considered pretending she had not heard, because she did not want anyone to see that she had been crying. She knew it would not be Diana, or Beryl, of course, but it could be Wendy, or one of the other children, asking whether Diana might come out to play. After a short pause, however, the knock came again, and Emmy dragged herself to her feet, a tiny bird of hope fluttering within her breast. Suppose, just suppose, that it was Beryl, come to ask her if she would like to go to New Brighton with the Fishers. Even if Beryl had only called to ask her why Diana had flown off in such a hurry, the question would break the ice, enabling Emmy to apologise for what she had said and beg Beryl to be her friend once more. So she opened the door without trying to hide her tear-blubbered face and was astonished to find Carl Johansson standing on the step, cap in hand and a big smile on his face.

'Good morning, Mrs Wesley,' he said formally. 'I have come to ask you . . . but whatever's the matter? Oh . . . oh, Mrs Wesley – Emmy – you've been crying.' And without more ado, he stepped into the hall, dropped both his cap and the bag he was carrying, and took Emmy in his arms. For a moment, she was so shocked and surprised that she did nothing. Then she made a feeble attempt to free herself, but when this failed she leaned her cheek against his uniform jacket and gave way to the luxury of a fit of weeping.

'D-D-D-Diana's run away,' she wailed between sobs. 'W-w-we had a quarrel and she's ru-ru-run away. Oh, Mr Johansson!'

Mr Johansson half led, half carried her into the kitchen and sat her down tenderly on the easy chair, taking the one opposite himself. He looked so boyishly handsome, with his fair curls rumpled and his eyes anxious, that Emmy began to cry all over again. She felt so helpless, so weak, and he looked so strong and capable. She wished that she could lay all her burdens on his broad shoulders, but that was impossible. However, when he got to his feet and began to pull the kettle over the fire, saying that he would make them both a cup of tea, that she would feel better with something hot inside her, she felt she owed him at least some sort of explanation. Besides, to share her troubles with someone else would be an enormous relief. They were, she decided, ships that passed in the night. He would listen to her woes, perhaps even advise her, but then he would go away again and by the time she saw him next everything would have changed.

So when he had placed the mug of tea in her hands, she started to tell him what had happened to her since they had last met. She began at the beginning with the split between herself and the Fishers. She did not pretend that it had been anyone's fault but hers, though for weeks now she had been telling herself that there were faults on both sides. She went on to tell him about Diana's brief stay with Mrs Lucas and how Mr Mac had had the brilliant idea that she and the Symonses might help one another. This led, naturally, to the increase in her working hours, the subsequent weariness, and the incredibly spiteful things she had said to Beryl. 'I don't know why I said what I did. It was as though my mouth opened of its own accord and spoke the wickedest words it could think of,' she said miserably. 'Of course I've been telling myself that Beryl started it by saying I'd always been dead lucky, always landed on my feet, but she only spoke the truth, Mr Johansson. Apart from Peter's death, which was a terrible thing, I *have* been lucky, and a lot of the luck was due to my friendship with Beryl. She brought me back to Nightingale Court, she found me the job, she looked after Diana for me, and advised me how to go on. She looked after me even when I was a kid. And now I don't know how to manage without her.'

Mr Johansson pulled his chair nearer her own, leaned forward and took both her hands in his. 'Mrs Wesley, what you've just said is true. You need your friend Beryl, because everyone needs a friend, but there are other friendships – other relationships – which are just as important. A woman bringing up a child on her own, trying to do a full-time job, trying to make ends meet, needs more than just a friend. Mrs Wesley . . . Emmy – may I call you Emmy? I wish you would call me Carl – I would give anything to share your burden, to be able to help in a more practical fashion. I've not spoken before . . .'

Emmy stared into the young man's grave but eloquent countenance. The words he was saying did not seem to make sense. He was clearly offering her friendship and some sort of help, but he must realise she would not dream of taking money from him and she did not see how else he could assist her when he was only in the port of Liverpool three or four times a year.

'Emmy? You aren't offended? I know it's only two years since Peter died . . .'

Light dawned with the abruptness of a struck match's flaring up. He was proposing marriage; this nice young man with his good prospects was actually asking her to marry him. But it was absurd. To be sure, they had been acquainted ever since her wedding . . . no, you could not even say that. They had not got to know each other until after Peter's death, when Carl had first offered to help her.

'Emmy? I've said nothing before because I thought it was too soon. Also, I was afraid that if I – if I proposed, and you refused me, then our friendship would no longer be possible. But, my dear girl, you are working far too hard. When I saw you five months ago, you looked tired and perhaps a little pale, but now! You are so thin, so frail! Emmy, if you don't begin to take it easy, you'll be really ill. Won't you – won't you let me help you?'

Emmy pulled her hands from his grasp and stood up. 'You're a good, kind man, Carl, but we really don't know one another very well, do we?' she said gently. 'I'm going upstairs to wash my face and brush my hair because crying always makes me look awful, and when I come down I think it best if we forget this conversation ever took place. Then, you see, we can remain good friends and I hope you will continue to call on me whenever you're in port.' She smiled down at him. 'I should like Diana to grow . . . more accustomed to you, as well,' she added. 'Because, at present, I'm afraid she's just a tiny bit jealous.'

At these words, he jumped to his feet, his eyes glowing with ardour. 'Then – then there is hope for me?' he said huskily. 'You will not say that you'll marry me, but you haven't said no either.' He tried to take her in his arms but Emmy fended him off, though she was smiling. 'Ah, if I know there is hope, I can wait . . . oh, I can wait for years!'

Emmy went slowly upstairs. The whole episode might have astonished her – well, it had – but she found she was not displeased. She knew she was still in love with Peter, had not even considered marrying anyone else, but the dragging pain in her chest told her that she should seriously consider such a course. If she became really ill, ill enough to be taken into hospital, perhaps for many weeks, then who would look after Diana? The thought of living with another man was still repugnant to her but she simply must be practical. Being able to trust Diana to the Symonses was a great help; if she could cut down her hours at the restaurant, then she was sure her health would improve even though her finances would not. With better health, she thought she might begin to grow closer to Mr Johansson – no, she must call him Carl – and now that she knew how he felt, she realised her attitude towards him would undoubtedly change. At the moment, she had no idea what sort of husband he might make, because she had only thought of him, really, as a friend of

Peter's, who took her out when he was in port, as a tribute to her husband, rather than herself. Now, she acknowledged that it was not so. He liked her for herself; wanted her for herself, in fact.

Emmy reached her bedroom, poured water from the ewer into the basin, and seized her face flannel and the soap. The cold water would reduce the swelling round her eyes. Then she took the pins out of her hair, brushed it until it was smooth and shining, then coiled it up once more, thrusting the pins into place and examining her reflection in the small mirror as she did so. The face that looked back at her was white and wan, though her eyes looked a good deal brighter than they had done an hour previously. Mr Johansson's – no, Carl's – proposal had cheered her up more than she would have thought possible. Without realising it, she had begun to think of herself as being far too burdened for any man to show an interest in her. There were a great many women who had children but no husbands – look at Mrs Telford – and she had begun to see herself as one of them. Now, Carl had given her back her self-esteem. Other men might be regarding her wistfully; might, in the fullness of time, be as keen as Carl was to share her life, and the task of bringing up Diana.

Emmy smiled at her reflection, then let herself out of the bedroom and began to descend the stairs, rubbing her cheeks to give herself some colour just before re-entering the kitchen. 'I feel a new woman, Carl,' she said cheerfully. 'I was about to chase after Diana when you arrived – she's run off, the naughty little minx – so I'll have to go round to the Symonses' to check that she's all right. After that, however, the day is our own.'

Carl had got to his feet as soon as she came back

into the room and now he took down her coat from the peg on the back of the door, and helped her into it. He was smiling. 'That is wonderful,' he said. 'If Diana wishes to come with us, of course, that would be wonderful too. But a day to ourselves . . .'

When they reached the Symonses' house, however, a surprise awaited them. Mother and daughter had just returned from church and assured Emmy that they had seen neither hide nor hair of Diana. Emmy's high spirits were considerably lowered by this news and she felt, once more, a touch of the dragging weariness which had attacked her earlier. She thanked the Symonses, however, pretending that all was well, but once outside on the pavement again she and Carl looked at one another with some anxiety. Emmy was about to suggest that they report Diana's absence at the nearest police station when an idea struck her. 'She'll have gone to the Fishers' house,' she said crossly. 'She knows very well she's forbidden to go there, but she was in a mood to defy me and one good sure way of upsetting me would be to go round to see Beryl. I'll have to go and get her, Carl.'

The two of them returned to the court and went straight to the house next door, but it was only after repeated knockings had failed to elicit an answer that Emmy suddenly clapped a hand to her mouth. 'They've gone to New Brighton!' she gasped. 'That was why we quarrelled, Diana and me, because I said she wasn't to go with them. Oh, the little madam! Well, at least I know Beryl wouldn't dream of letting her get into any sort of trouble. Oh, Carl, I'm so sorry, but I shall simply have to go to New Brighton and make sure she really is with the Fishers. Do you mind?'

Chapter Ten

Diana had shot out of the house with every intention of going round to the Fishers and begging to be allowed to join their family party in a day at the seaside. She was quite bright enough, however, to realise that her mother would pursue her and drag her back if she were given half the chance, so the sensible thing to do would be to pretend to go round to Raymond Street and stay there until the coast was clear.

As she always did, she went down the jigger and entered the yard through the back gate. In her blazing temper, she had forgotten that it was Sunday, and it was the Symonses' habit to go to church at this hour, but it did not worry her. After all, she only had to remain here for ten minutes or so, and then she could return to the court and hang about until the Fishers set off for the ferry. Whilst she waited, she picked up a small fork and began to weed some of the tubs, a task she enjoyed so much that a good deal longer than ten minutes elapsed before she remembered she had other fish to fry. She dug the little fork into the nearest barrel and set off again, though much less impetuously this time.

Arriving back at the court, she stared long and hard at her own house before deciding that the coast was probably clear. There was no sign of her mother at the kitchen window, nor the parlour one, and the door was firmly closed.

Diana trotted across the flagstones to the Fisher door, and tried the handle. She was truly dismayed to find it locked. So they had left already! For a moment she was totally daunted. She had no money, so no means of getting to New Brighton. Skipping a lecky was a popular sport amongst the boys in the court, but though she might reach the quayside by this method she had never heard of anyone skipping a ferry, and was afraid it could not be done. For a moment, she toyed with the idea of borrowing her fare from a neighbour, then dismissed it. There was no way anyone would lend her money without asking a number of extremely awkward questions. Diana had no particular objection to telling a lie but knew how one thing led to another. No, it would be safer to simply forgo the trip to New Brighton, amuse herself somehow for the rest of the day and return home when it grew dark. By then, her mother should be thoroughly worried and would, naturally, have repented of her unkindness to her little daughter.

Because it was holiday time, there were several children playing about in the court but Diana knew better than to join them. Her mother would be bound to spot her and haul her off to teach her a lesson. No, she had best keep well out of the way until daylight faded.

She set off across the court towards the archway and was just ducking under it when something made her glance back. Her door was opening! Quick as a flash, she shot into Raymond Street and down the nearest jigger. There were several dustbins clustered in the entrance, waiting to be emptied next day, and Diana crouched behind them, staring intently at the archway to the court. Mam will be looking for me, she thought gleefully, but she isn't going to find me.

She's been horrid to me and to Aunty Beryl. I know it was her who started the quarrel, whatever she may say. She's been cross as a cat for ages, always finding fault with me and moaning about how hard her work is, so if she worries that I'm lost, it's her own perishin' fault.

But to her astonishment, it was not just her mother who emerged from the court, but also the young officer, Mr Johansson, who had been Daddy's best friend on SS *Queen of the South*. For a moment, Diana was so furious that she quite literally saw red. How dared Mr Johansson visit her mother when she, Diana, was not around to queer his pitch? She was tempted to come out of hiding, picturing how the happy expression would fade from Mr Johansson's handsome – but horrible – face at the sight of her, then thought better of it. After all, they would not have much fun searching the whole of Liverpool for one small girl. They would not be able to visit theatres or cinemas or go to posh restaurants, and anyway it was Sunday, so most places would be closed. No, she would stay hidden until they had gone.

Accordingly, she crouched back behind the dustbins. They would already have tried the Fishers and found them gone, so next they would try the Symonses. Diana hugged herself. After that, they would get really worried; they would go to the park, the big one. They would walk along the canal bank, half expecting to see her body floating in the water. They might even have the canal dragged; she had seen it done once, though she had not been lucky enough to see the body when it had been brought to the surface. Charlie had, and had told her all about it. At the time, she had blamed her mother bitterly, because it wasn't every day a kid got to see a dead person, but that, of course, had been before the big quarrel.

Diana sat back on her haunches and wondered how long she should stay here. The bins were very smelly and she did not much care for the large blue-bottles which buzzed around them. She remained where she was, however, until a couple of wasps decided to join the throng. When one of them threatened to alight on her face, she decided that enough was enough, and emerged from her hiding place.

She was wondering what to do next when an absolutely brilliant thought occurred to her. Her mam had gone off with the horrible Mr Johansson so the house would be empty. The key would be on its string, as usual, and the teapot with the cracked lid and the pattern of pink roses would be on the mantel. She darted across the road and under the arch. Two minutes later, she was in the kitchen of No. 2, reaching up for the teapot and emptying the contents on to the kitchen table. She was not surprised to find that there was a good deal of money in it, both notes and coins. Mr Mac paid his staff on Saturdays, after their shifts were finished, and Mammy put away the rent money in the little chest which she kept in her bedroom. Anything other than that went into the teapot and was used to buy food, candles and so on. Diana knew her mother had a Post Office savings book and usually paid the pension, and her tip money, into the Post Office on her way home from work. So she reasoned that she might take money from the teapot without feeling guilty.

She sorted out ten shillings from the loose coins and slid it into the pocket of her dress, then hesitated. It was awfully heavy, but if she took a note her mother would be bound to notice. She had no idea how much money she would need, but reasoned that if a tram cost twopence, the ferry would probably cost no more. And she knew the price of fish and chips, ice creams and so on. Half reluctantly, she returned most of the money to the teapot, holding on to only three shillings in assorted coppers. Then, feeling very grown-up, she lugged a loaf out of the bread crock and some cheese from the lower shelf of the meat safe. She hacked rather than cut the loaf into four slices and made herself a great untidy cheese sandwich and another of jam – she didn't bother with margarine – which she wrapped together in greaseproof paper and tied with string. She meant to buy herself fish and chips and the biggest ice cream she could lay her hands on when she got to New Brighton, but if her journey cost her more than she anticipated, at least she would not starve. There was a cracked and stained American cloth bag in which she sometimes put the messages she had been sent to fetch. She shoved the untidy parcel of food into it, added a small bottle of water, a mug and a tin of conny-onny. She thought about adding cake or apples but decided against them on the grounds that they would make the bag far too heavy. In fact, she abandoned the water, remembering that there was a drinking fountain somewhere on the front. Outside, the court was in shadow, as always, but she knew it was a sunny day and decided it was too warm for a coat. Mam would say only ragamuffins went far from home without a coat, but Diana thought this was daft; who needed a coat when it was hot and sunny? Boys never wore coats and few of the girls she knew bothered with even a jacket when the weather was fine.

Presently, with the money knocking comfortably

against her knee as she walked and the bag slung over one shoulder, Diana set off, passing a group of girls playing rope. One of them looked up and grinned at her; it was Wendy. 'Where's you goin', young Di?' Wendy asked chattily. ''S orl right, your mam has gone off with her boyfriend so you can answer wi'out bein' telled off.'

Normally, Diana would have given a regretful smile and moved on without a word, but then, normally, Wendy would not have spoken to her. And anyway, Diana's mood was still defiant, so she slowed her pace for a moment, to say: 'He's not her boyfriend, he's off me daddy's old ship, and I'm going to New Brighton, on me own.'

Wendy's eyes rounded, then narrowed in disbelief. 'You ain't,' she said scornfully. 'You ain't got the nerve! Why, if your mam were here, you wouldn't dare speak to me in case you gorra belt round the ear.' She snorted inelegantly. 'My mam says your mam's a bleedin' snob an' I'm not sure she ain't right.'

Diana considered this. Though furiously angry with her mam, she did not like hearing Wendy saying such things, so she replied, rather haughtily: 'You mind your own business and shut your gob. Everyone knows that both you and your mam are a couple of perishin' liars.'

'A fight, a fight!' a girl called Anita shouted.

But Wendy did not seem to take offence. In fact she grinned, saying encouragingly, 'That's right, young 'un, you stand up for yourself now you've come out from under your old woman's wing. I likes a kid wi' spirit, so I does . . . but your mam *is* a snob, you know.'

'Well, I know; but your mam *is* a liar,' Diana said, having given the matter some thought. 'But you ain't,

Wendy, and I still like you, no matter what me mam says,' she added honestly.

Wendy's grin widened and she opened her mouth to reply but was interrupted. 'It's your turn to jump in, Wendy,' shrieked one of the girls steadily turning the rope. 'Stop gabbin' or you'll ruin the game.'

Diana had been about to invite Wendy to accompany her, for she had suddenly realised that making her way to New Brighton alone might be rather scary. Tram conductors wouldn't query a child with a shopping bag, but the people selling tickets for the ferry might easily do so. However, Wendy was absorbed in the game and so Diana continued on her way, telling herself that once she reached the seaside resort she would join up with the Fishers and everything would be fine.

Despite her fears, Diana's journey was uneventful. She bought her ferry ticket for a mere twopence and went straight up to the bows where, in common with a dozen other children, she leaned over to watch the water creaming past and then rushed along the deck to the stern, imagining the curly heads of mermaids in every tumble of water. When the boat docked, she was one of the last off, having stayed to watch every movement of the sailors as they threw ropes to one another, lowered the gangway and began to shepherd the passengers ashore. Once on dry land again, she suffered a moment's panic, being unable to remember how one reached the promenade from here, but before she could grow too alarmed common sense reasserted itself. Everyone who came to New Brighton on the ferry was heading for the seaside; all she had to do was follow the crowd. Accordingly, she soon found herself on the familiar promenade, but was a little dismayed by the sheer number of people on the beach. You could scarcely see the sand for the people, deckchairs and piles of equipment such as buckets and spades and shrimping nets. Adults lay in the striped chairs or sprawled on the sand in bathing suits, their arms and legs turning pink beneath the hot rays of the sun. Diana's heart sank; how could she possibly hope to find the Fisher family in such a huge crowd? Why, she did not know what Aunty Beryl had been wearing that morning; she might even have acquired a bathing suit and be totally unrecognisable, though Diana was sure she would know her darling Charlie, no matter how cunningly he was disguised.

For a while, she just strolled along the prom, eyeing the beach keenly, but presently the hot sunshine made her thirsty and she decided to find the drinking fountain, have a long, cool drink, and then take off her shoes and socks and go for a paddle. She had heard the kids in the court refer to 'goin' in me bur webs' and knew that this extraordinary expression meant going barefoot, and now she decided it would be a good deal more comfortable, both on the beach and on the prom, if she, too, had 'bur webs'. Sitting down on the paving, she removed her shoes and socks and shoved them into her bag, then set off in the direction of the drinking fountain.

When she reached it there was a queue, mostly of small and ragged children, many of whom were carrying bottles. This was a nuisance, since it meant that they would fill the bottles at the tap under the fountain as well as having a drink from the fountain itself, so she might well be waiting for ages. She was considering making her way to the head of the line and explaining that she had no bottle and only wanted a drink, when she remembered that she had money. She could go to the nearest café and buy a bottle of lemonade, or she could make straight for an ice cream salesman. There was an Italian vendor whose ice cream she particularly loved. It was yellow as custard, sweet as honey, and smelt deliciously of vanilla.

She was still hesitating when a small girl who had been filling a bottle extremely slowly, and spilling great quantities of water over her own 'bur webs' in the process, turned away from the queue and Diana realised, with a thrill of real joy, that she had found the Fishers at last. It was Becky!

After that, of course, there was no question of waiting for a drink at the fountain. Becky was not hurrying because the water bottle was evidently heavy. She strolled along, gazing from side to side as though she had not a care in the world, and still spilling a good deal of water as she walked. Diana caught up with her without difficulty and bent to take the water bottle, saying as she did so: 'Eh up there, Becks, let me carry the bottle for you. You're slopping no end over your feet, you know.'

Becky turned defensively towards her, trying to retain her hold on the bottle. She began to say, in a trembling voice, that she was 'awright, fanks – lemme alone or I'll call me big bruvver . . .' when she recognised Diana and immediately relinquished her hold. 'Thanks, Di,' she said breathlessly. 'I din't know it were you.' An uncertain look crossed her small, rosy face. 'Didjer come wiv' us? I don't 'member you on the big ship.'

Diana forbore to scoff at this ingenuous remark as she would once have done. Poor Becky was still in the infants' class at school, and for the first time Diana realised that the younger girl was tiny compared with herself. Once, they had been roughly the same height, but now Diana must be ten or eleven inches the taller. 'No, I wasn't with you on the ferry, Becky,' she said gently. 'I came over by myself. Where's your mammy sitting? Shall I come and play with you? We could build a huge sandcastle – if you've got a spade, that is. I – I forgot to bring mine.'

Becky came to a halt opposite the man selling Diana's favourite ice cream. 'I dunno where they is,' she said in her flat little voice. 'But Charlie brung me this far and went to buy Mammy a teapot. He said to stop here by the ice cream man, when I'd fetched water, and he'd take me back to Mammy.'

'Oh, I see,' Diana said slowly. Before the great row had wrenched the two families apart, Aunty Beryl and Uncle Wally had decided to take a hand in Becky's education. She was getting very little learning at school but someone had told Aunty Beryl – Diana thought it must be a doctor at the Stanley Hospital – that home influence was more help than anything for a backward child. Maybe she would never learn to read and write, and maybe she would never have as many words at her disposal as other children her age, but if they worked hard with her, she could learn the practicalities of everyday life. She could fill a water bottle and make her way back to an arranged spot, for instance, and now that she thought about it, Diana realised that she had seen Becky returning proudly from the shops with a small bag, containing a few messages. Usually, Aunty Beryl only asked her to fetch one object at a time – if she needed more, she would write a list for the shopkeeper – and the little girl was obviously learning, though Diana knew for a fact that Becky had no idea of the value of money, could only recognise a penny when she saw one. The previous week, she had met Becky in Miss Morris's shop on the corner of Tatlock and Evans Street, trustfully offering a handful of loose change. Diana had watched the old lady carefully taking the money from Becky's little paw and placing it, coin by coin, upon the wooden counter, until she had the correct amount. Then she had turned to the shelf behind her, carefully chosen a bright red sweetie from one of the big jars and handed it to Becky, reminding her to put away the rest of her money so none of it got dropped by mistake.

Diana's thoughts were interrupted by Charlie's coming up beside them, the teapot in his hand. He completely ignored Diana but spoke, bracingly, to his small sister. 'Well, ain't you a good girl, then? I see you've fetched water, like Mammy telled you, and I've got the lemonade and the teapot, so soon we'll all be able to have a nice drink.'

Diana had stood the water down whilst she and Becky waited, but now she bent and picked it up. 'I'll carry it for Becky, Charlie,' she said, giving him her very sweetest smile. 'It's too heavy for her; she was spillin' no end until I come along and gave her a hand.'

Charlie's eyes skimmed quickly over her, their glance cold. He said, not addressing her, but apparently speaking into thin air: 'We can manage. You'd best go back to your mammy; she wouldn't want you mixing with the likes of us.'

Diana felt a hot flush of colour invade her face. Why was Charlie acting so strangely? After all, it was not as though they were in the court with folk watching. They were at the seaside; surely everyone was equal at the seaside?

But before she could voice her feelings, Becky spoke up. 'She ain't wiv' her mammy, Charlie. She come by herself; she telled me so.'

By now, the three of them were on the sand, weaving their way amongst the crowds, but at his sister's words Charlie stopped short, turning and staring incredulously at Diana. 'What the devil . . . ?' he said slowly. 'Your mammy never said you could come wi' us, surely? Why, she's been treatin' my mam and dad like dirt ever since she took you away and put you with that Lucas woman. What's more, she never said nothing to our mam this morning, I'm bleedin' sure of that.'

His stare was so belligerent, so unfriendly, that Diana did not dare pretend that Aunty Beryl knew all about it, but she simply must convince Charlie that she had permission to follow them to the beach. She took a deep breath and assumed her most innocent, yet earnest, expression. 'No, we were too late, you see. I heard you telling someone that you were off to New Brighton for the day, so I asked Mam if we could go as well. Mam said she'd see what Aunty Beryl thought of the idea but just as we were about to set out for your house, Mr Johansson arrived. You know, he were Daddy's best friend and . . .'

'I know, Second Officer aboard the old *Queen of the South*,' Charlie said loftily. 'So where are they, then? Him and your mam?'

'Oh, he were all togged up in his best uniform and he didn't have a swim suit, nor even a handkerchief to tie over his head,' Diana said glibly. 'So Mam gave me some money and told me to run to the ferry and catch you up. She and Mr Johansson went off to – to see a man about a dog.'

Charlie sighed deeply. 'An' if I'll believe that, I'll

believe anything,' he said sarcastically. 'Still an' all, we'll see what me mam says. What's in the bag?'

'Me carry-out,' Diana said triumphantly. 'Mam made me a carry-out in case I got hungry before I got to the seaside. She wanted me to bring apples and a bottle of lemonade, but it were too heavy, so she give me money instead.'

This must have satisfied Charlie for he merely grunted and continued to lead the two girls along the beach. Presently Diana saw Aunty Beryl comfortably settled in a deckchair, with her skirt folded back above her knees, and the wind teasing strands of her curly brown hair free from its bun. She half raised her hand as if to wave to them, then let it drop back into her lap. She got clumsily to her feet, staring so hard at Diana that the child hesitated, suddenly unsure of her welcome. But as she drew closer, Aunty Beryl's smile broke out. Diana ran towards her and felt her hands enfolded in Beryl's warm grasp.

'What's all this, then?' she enquired. 'Where's your mam, chuck? I didn't know she was going to bring you to New Brighton today!'

Diana seized Aunty Beryl's hand and cuddled it against her cheek. To lie or not to lie? If she told Aunty Beryl that she was here under false pretences, she might be sent back to the court and, what was worse, Charlie would know she had lied to him and Charlie was still very much her hero. Since her mother and Aunty Beryl were still not talking, however, she realised that a good lie might well remain undetected for days or weeks – perhaps, for ever. So she repeated the story she had told Charlie, adding mendaciously that her mammy had something important to say to Aunty Beryl and had been disappointed to find she had missed them. She was watching Aunty Beryl's face as she spoke and saw the expression of pure delight which crossed it before Aunty Beryl gave her a big hug and a smacking kiss on the cheek. Then she turned to her own children, advising them that food and drinks would be ready in five minutes, so not to stray too far away.

Diana felt so happy that she began to believe her own story. Of *course* her mammy still loved Aunty Beryl and would make up the foolish quarrel at the first opportunity. Why, Mammy would be so grateful to Aunty Beryl for taking care of her little girl that she would be willing to do anything. Filled with the milk of human kindness, Diana removed her ill-wrapped sandwiches from the bag and laid them, reverentially, upon the cloth which Aunty Beryl had caused to be spread on the sand. 'Them's my dinner, what Mammy made me,' she said, both untruthfully and ungrammatically. She turned to Charlie. 'When we've finished our sandwiches, I'll buy us all ice creams. Mammy gave me the money; she said I were to mug you.'

Charlie's stare, to Diana's puzzlement, was growing belligerent once more. He looked from the great, lumpy, uneven chunks of bread to Diana's face, to his mother's, then back again to Diana's. 'Your mam never made them abnabs, nor she never said to mug anyone in her life,' he said scornfully. 'And I don't believe she knows you're in New Brighton, lerralone with us Fishers. I believe you cut 'n' run 'cos you're jealous as a cat of that young officer. Why, right now, the scuffers is probably combin' the back streets, searchin' for you.'

Aunty Beryl had been staring at the sandwiches, then at Diana, then at Charlie. She had not said a word, but now she knelt down on the sand beside

Diana. 'Eat up this here food,' she said, setting out the sandwiches she had brought on their neat squares of greaseproof paper. 'Charlie, pour the lemonade into the cups. I'll cope with the tea.' She looked sadly at Diana. 'As soon as we've eaten, we'll have to go home. Charlie's quite right, Diana, your mam would never cut bread like that in a million years. You've run off, haven't you? Charlie was right about that, too. Oh, my God. If Emmy has reported you as missing to the police, we're all going to have to do a lot of explaining.'

Diana, deeply ashamed, had been staring fixedly down at her sandwiches, whilst large tears rolled down her cheeks. Now Aunty Beryl caught hold of her chin and raised it so that their eyes met. 'And no more lies, young Diana, or you'll get yourself – and us – into really serious trouble with the scuffers – the police, that is. Understand me?'

Diana threw herself into Aunty Beryl's arms. 'I'm sorry, I'm sorry,' she wailed. 'But I've been *so* unhappy, Aunty Bee! Old Mrs Symons is ever so kind, but – but she's *old*! I – I help her in her little garden and do her messages and play whist, and pelmanism, and draughts . . . things like that, but there's never no children there, 'cos she's *old* and – and I did *so* want to come to the seaside and play *real* games with Charlie and Becky and Lenny. Oh, Aunty Bee, *must* we go home? I'm sure Mammy won't be worrying about me. She'll guess I'm with you and – and Becky and me were going to make the biggest sandcastle in the whole world, weren't we, Becks?'

But Becky, stuffing a sandwich into her mouth, was clearly not listening and Charlie, who was, said scornfully: 'You weren't so keen to play with our Becky before, Miss High and Mighty! You said she were babyish and stupid.'

Poor Diana coloured hotly and felt Aunty Beryl's instinctive withdrawal with very real dismay. It was tempting to lie again, to say that Charlie was mistaken, she had never thought Becky either childish or stupid. Then perhaps Aunty Bee's arms would go soft and warm and comfortable again and she, Diana, would know herself accepted once more.

But it was not to be. Aunty Bee set her gently aside and said, in a voice which brooked no argument: 'There's no question of staying on the beach, no matter what. We've got to get back to Nightingale Court before your mother starts the sort of fuss which not even the truth will calm down. For if there's one thing I do know about Emmy, it's her ability to turn a molehill into a mountain.'

Charlie sniggered but Diana had no idea what Aunty Beryl meant and continued to weep whilst cramming her sandwiches into her mouth and swallowing the great lumps of bread with considerable difficulty. Aunty Beryl had told them all to eat up and this was one order she could and would obey.

As soon as the food was finished and the drink consumed, Beryl shepherded her small flock back on to the ferry. The boys were hot, cross and furious with Diana, though Becky was her usual sweet and placid self. Sometimes, Beryl wondered what time meant to her small daughter. Charlie and Lenny were grumbling loudly about their ruined day. They would not speak to Diana, nor look at her if they could help it, but Becky held the older girl's hand and chirruped about the sea and the sandcastle as though nothing had happened to spoil her outing.

Diana, Beryl noticed, grew less and less rosy-cheeked as they neared the court. When they had first boarded the ferry she had tried to chat to Charlie, but in the end his complete lack of response had forced her to try her wiles on Lenny. Lenny, following his older brother's lead, had ignored her, and even little Bobby, seeing her now as a stranger after her long absence from their midst, had refused to allow himself to be cuddled or played with.

It was an unhappy little party which entered Nightingale Court in mid-afternoon. Diana was feeling tired and wondering, apprehensively, how her mother would greet her. She would be cross, naturally, but if she was still with Mr Johansson, she might feel it politic not to show too much anger. After all, she would have enjoyed a pleasant outing with her admirer, which Diana's presence might well have spoiled.

Lost in thought, Diana entered the court looking towards her own house and walked slap-bang into Charlie, who had stopped short in front of her. 'Well, I'm damned. Wharra carry-on,' he said softly, and Diana's heart lifted. He was actually speaking to her. He must have forgotten the grudge which had kept him silent ever since they left New Brighton.

Diana opened her mouth to speak, but no words came out. She had followed Charlie's gaze and realised that he had not been addressing her, but had merely voiced the emotions which the scene before them had provoked. For now that she looked across the gloom of the court, she saw a very unusual sight. A great deal of shabby, broken-down furniture was heaped up on the flagstones and three large men were carting more stuff out of the door of the Telfords' house. Mrs Telford, screaming and shouting, kept trying to barge her way back into the house, but the men prevented her with ease, laughing at her futile efforts and ignoring the threats and imprecations which she was hurling at their heads. The Telford children were clustered around their dilapidated possessions. The smaller ones were crying and clutching at the legs of the older ones, but Diana saw at once that Wendy seemed more resigned than angry or tearful. She looked, Diana thought sadly, like someone taking part in a scene which had been enacted many times before.

'Oh my Gawd,' Beryl said softly.

'What's happening, Aunty Beryl?' Diana asked wildly, clutching the older woman's arm. 'And who are those men? I don't understand; it's Mrs Telford's house, isn't it?'

'They're the bailiffs, queen, and I guess the Telfords are being evicted for non-payment of rent,' Beryl said grimly. 'Well, it were bound to happen; Annie Telford's too fond of a drop of the hard stuff to put the rent money aside, the way the rest of us do. Them poor kids, though. It happens over and over; she takes the cheapest accommodation she can find and then the landlord has to haunt the place for weeks, tryin' to get his money, whilst she crouches behind the door, pretendin' she's out. Then she'll pay for a bit and the landlord thinks he's found the answer. Only he hasn't, of course, and in the end there'll be norra landlord in the city what'll let her into their property.'

'Then what will they do?' Diana asked. She was trembling and felt sick. Wendy had been her friend – was her friend – yet they were both children and powerless to stop what was happening to the Telford family. 'Where will they go, Aunty Beryl? Oh, poor Wendy!'

'Don't worry, chuck. Mrs Telford's got a sister living over in Birkenhead, who's took them in in the past when this has happened. She's a good deal older than Annie – Mrs Telford, I mean – and the absolute opposite. She's a great chapelgoer and her house is like a new pin, I'm told. Whilst they stay there, there'll be no drinking, and whatever money comes in will be spent on food and perhaps even on some clothes for the kids. I'm not saying Mrs Telford will like it, but at least the kids will be fed for a while.' She looked down at Diana, then gave the child an encouraging smile. 'Look, why don't you nip over and tell Wendy how sorry you are? Your mam isn't here to worry that you'll take up with the Telfords again and I won't say a word. Only the fact is, queen, that if the Telfords do come back to Liverpool, it most certainly won't be to anywhere near here. The two of you were good friends once, so it 'ud be a kindness to tell Wendy you're sorry for her misfortune and to say goodbye, and good luck.'

Diana did not hesitate. She ran across the court and hugged Wendy convulsively, saying as she did so: 'I'm so, so sorry, Wendy! I wish there was something I could do to help, but Aunty Beryl says you'll go to your aunt in Birkenhead. I really have missed you and I wish you weren't going, but one day, when we're both grown up, we'll be proper friends again, I'm sure of it.'

She half expected a rebuff, feeling she deserved it, but Wendy returned her hug with enthusiasm. 'I've missed you, too, Di, ever so much,' she muttered. 'But there's no way your mam would ever have let us play together again, and anyway, we won't come back to Liverpool, not this time. Me Aunt Naomi said, last time we landed on her doorstep, that Mam and the rest of us would be best under her eye, over in Birkenhead. She said if it happened again, then Mam must get a job on the other side of the water and stay under her roof until she was fit to care for herself. We knew this were goin' to happen so Lily and meself went to Aunt Naomi a week ago and telled her how things stood. She said as she'd take her sister in one more time, to save us all from the workhouse, but our mam must toe the line an' do as she was told or she'd find herself chucked out of me aunt's house as well.'

'But will your mam take any notice?' Diana asked fearfully, remembering what Beryl had said. 'You've been ev— evicted before, haven't you? Won't she just bide her time and then do it all over again?'

She was looking up into Wendy's face as she spoke and saw a broad grin spread over her friend's dirty, tear-stained countenance. 'No, that she won't,' Wendy said cheerfully. 'Me Aunt Naomi is a woman of her word and me mam knows it. Mam's terrified of the workhouse because there's no drink allowed in there – no fags, neither – and they make the women work, a thing me mam hates, especially as they don't pay you. No, Mam won't risk going agin me aunt.'

'I'm glad,' Diana said thankfully. 'I don't feel nearly so bad knowing you've got somewhere to go. But do you *like* your aunt, Wendy? Do you get along with her?'

Wendy heaved a sigh. 'I just keeps me head low an' does as she says,' she admitted resignedly. 'She makes us go to chapel three times on a Sunday, but she cooks us a grand dinner, meat as well as spuds and veggies. Oh, she ain't bad, really, provided you do as she tells you.'

Diana was about to say that this rule applied to

most adults, but at that point Mrs Telford stopped trying to force her way back into the house past the bailiffs, and turned to yell at her daughter. 'Wendy! Get yourself round to Jimmy Satterthwaite an' tell 'im we wants a lend of 'is 'andcart. I ain't seein' all me decent furniture an' effects carried off by these thievin' bloody magpies. It's bad enough to be turned out o' me house just for the want of a week or two's rent, but I won't 'ave me good furniture stole.'

The bailiffs seemed to consider this a good joke. 'You're welcome to that pile o' rubbish, missus,' the largest of them said scornfully. 'We're entitled to take furniture an' goods to the value o' the money owed. But you ain't gorra stick we'd touch wi' a barge pole. I doubt it's even worth the hire of a handcart, but you'd best move it out o' the court, even if you only go an' tip it into the river.'

Mrs Telford gave a shriek of rage at this frank assessment of her worldly possessions but Wendy gave Diana one last hug and then set off across the court towards the archway. 'I'm goin', Mam; shan't be two ticks,' she shouted. Then, turning to Diana, she added in a whisper: 'Goodbye, Di. We'll meet up again when we've growed.'

Diana watched her friend until she was out of sight, then allowed herself to be steered towards No. 4; she found she did not wish to linger now that Wendy had gone.

Beryl told Charlie to take Becky, Bobby and the baby straight home, and told Lenny to fetch his dad from Aunty Ellen's. 'Tell him we had to leave New Brighton early and I'd be obliged if he'd come home now. I'll take Diana to No. 2. I shan't be gone long. But you might put the kettle on so's we can all have a cup of tea when I get back.' She was a little surprised that Emmy hadn't spotted them and come running out of the house to either upbraid her daughter or shed tears of relief but, in the event, it was soon clear that Emmy was not at home. 'I expect she's gone rushin' up to the police station,' Beryl said resignedly, as she and Diana turned away. 'Well, we'd best follow suit else there'll be trouble.'

They went to the police station where a fat and sweating desk sergeant obligingly consulted a large book, though since he had been on duty from nine that morning he was able to tell Beryl that he knew for a fact no one had lost a child that day. 'You know what these mams are; if she's got seven or eight kids, she won't miss one until it don't turn up for its supper,' he said, smiling across at Diana. 'Just you slip back into your house before teatime and she won't never know you've gone missing.'

Outside on the pavement once more, Beryl looked rather helplessly down at her small companion. Diana looked back, a little smile on her lips. 'I did tell you she'd guess I were with you, Aunty Bee, so she wouldn't worry,' she said, a trifle reproachfully. 'Besides, she's with that Mr Johansson, so they could have gone anywhere. He's like my daddy, he earns lots of money.'

Beryl sighed. 'What am I going to do with you? You're too knowing by half, that's your trouble. But if your mammy guessed you were with me, why didn't she come to New Brighton? If I were in the same situation—'

Diana must have heard the critical note in her voice for she interrupted at once. 'But Aunty Bee, it's quite, quite different! My mammy knows you're the most trustable person in the world and understands all about kids. If your Charlie ran off to be with my mam, then he'd be telling her how to go on, not the other way round.'

This frank acceptance of Emmy's shortcomings tickled Beryl's sense of humour and she laughed out loud, then gave Diana's hand a reassuring squeeze as they set off for Nightingale Court once more. 'You'd best have your tea with us; then you can play with Becky until your mam gets back,' she said resignedly. 'Though considering the way she's behaved towards me just lately . . .'

'She doesn't mean it,' Diana said anxiously, peering up into Beryl's face. 'I – I don't think she's very well, honest to God I don't. She came back from Mac's one night, after a late shift, and fell asleep in the chair. It was a Saturday; I thought I'd give her a surprise and take her a cup of tea in bed, but when I got downstairs, there she was, in all her clothes, even her coat, though she'd kicked off her shoes and chucked her hat on the floor. She were fast asleep and she looked awful. Her face was really white and there were purple shadows under her eyes, and when she breathed in, she purred, like a cat.'

This information worried Beryl, though she did not mean to let it show. She knew Diana to be a truthful child in general, but she had told an alarming number of whoppers that day; perhaps this was just another such. It was easy to see that the child was desperate for her mother and Beryl to get back on friendly terms. Perhaps she thought that pretending Emmy was ill would soften Beryl's attitude. Yet the story of Emmy's falling asleep in the chair was not the sort of thing a child of seven could dream up, Beryl thought, and decided that she would have a word with Emmy later, preferably when Diana was in bed and Mr Johansson had returned to his ship. Beryl had been fond of Mrs Dickens, and knew that the old lady had trusted her to cushion her daughter against the harsh realities of life. Yes, she would definitely speak to Emmy this very day.

'I thought you said you were going to play with our Becky. Well, why don't you go ahead and do it? Or if you can't do that, then you could make Bobby some bread and milk; you know how to do *that*, don't you?'

Aunty Beryl had brought Diana back to the Fisher house and had then taken baby Jimmy and gone off to try to find someone who could tell her where Emmy had gone. She had said she would not be long but Diana, rejoicing in the fact that Charlie had spoken to her for the first time since they had reached the court, did not mind her absence in the least and answered almost humbly: 'Yes, Charlie, I'll make Bobby some bread and milk. I would play with Becky if you wanted me to, but I think she'd rather be left alone.'

Becky was sitting on the hearthrug with a home-made rag doll in her arms. She was crooning tunelessly to it whilst rocking herself back and forth, and when Diana had spoken to her five minutes before she had seemed oblivious, and had continued to croon and sway without giving Diana so much as a glance.

Charlie snorted and looked towards his sister, then nodded grudgingly. 'You're right there. She'll rock herself to sleep and fall over in a minute,' he admitted. 'That's why Mam puts cushions each side of her.' He walked across to the bread crock and got out the heel of a loaf, which he dumped down on the table beside an open tin of condensed milk. 'There you are. When you've made it, you'd best feed him an' all. Then we can get the little perisher to bed before Mam gets back.'

'Yes, Charlie,' Diana said meekly. She was still shaken by the encounter with Wendy. Whatever would she and her mother have done if something similar had happened to them? But it was no use worrying so. She began to crumble the bread into Bobby's plate, then poured some milk on to it. Just then Charlie turned away from the sink, where he was industriously scrubbing potatoes, and saw what she was doing. He clapped a wet hand to his head, giving a theatrical groan as he did so.

'Oh, Gawd, you've not got the sense you was born with! You've gorra half 'n' half the conny-onny wi' water afore you put it on the bread, else he'll be as sick as a dog.'

Diana knew that her own mother was sometimes forced to use conny-onny, when she ran out of fresh milk, and remembered that Emmy always diluted it with water. Cursing herself for her forgetfulness, she went and dipped some water out of the bucket, poured a small amount over the bread and conny-onny, then stirred vigorously. 'Is that better, Charlie?' she asked timidly. 'I know I put the water on last, but I don't think it'll matter, do you?'

Charlie did not deign to reply but jerked a grimy thumb to where Bobby sat amongst a pile of home-made wooden bricks. Diana went and knelt in front of the little boy, the bowl of bread and milk in one hand, a spoon in the other. She thought Bobby was eyeing the mixture without much enthusiasm, but pushed a spoonful into his mouth anyway, saying cheerfully as she did so: 'There you are, Bobby, lovely bread and milk! Eat it all up and your mammy—'

She stopped. Bobby had made a horrible gurgling noise before spitting the whole lot back at her. Instinctively, Diana gave the child a little push. 'You're a bad, naughty boy,' she said reproachfully, trying to wipe blobs of soggy bread and milk from her face and neck. 'If your mammy was here . . .' She filled the spoon again and was about to ram it into Bobby's now open and howling mouth when she was seized from behind. Charlie jerked her roughly to her feet and then gave her a shove which sent her staggering against the table.

'You're a wicked little bitch, Diana Wesley,' he said furiously. He grabbed at her and shook her hard. 'You've done something wrong with that bread and milk, you stupid girl, else our Bobby would have swallowed the first mouthful because he loves the horrible stuff. And as for shovin' more food in when the kid's screamin' his head off . . . well, you must be mad! And you pushed him, just for spittin' out a bit of food, so what'll you do if he sicks up all over you, eh? Chop his bleedin' little 'ead off?'

Diana was almost in tears. She would have liked to smack Bobby for getting her into Charlie's bad books again, but she knew this would be most unwise. Besides, she was really fond of the little boy and had missed him over the past weeks and months. 'I'm sorry, Charlie,' she mumbled. 'I really like Bobby and it was only a little push. But bread 'n' milk's easy. I couldn't have made it wrong.'

However, Charlie was examining the dish closely and now he gave a triumphant crow. 'Couldn't you? Oh, but you're wrong, Miss High and Mighty,' he jeered. 'You think you know every bloody thing, doncher? Well, you're wrong. You used far too much water – the stuff's swimmin' in it.'

'I'm sorry. But he shouldn't have spat it in my face like that, that was naughty,' Diana pointed out, trying to keep her temper.

Charlie did not reply. He took another slice of bread, crumbled it into the mixture and added some more conny-onny. Then he sat down on the nearest chair, pulled Bobby on to his lap, and presented the child with a spoonful of bread and milk.

Bobby ate it, and Charlie jerked a thumb at the sink. 'You'd best finish the spuds,' he said gruffly. 'An' I just hope that good-time gal you call your mam don't choose to stay out half the night and land us wi' you, 'cos I tell you to your head, we doesn't want you. Why don't you an' your mam go to the workhouse with that no-good Wendy Telford, which was such a *pal* of yours.'

Diana's heart swelled with indignation at these cruel and unfair words. 'How dare you say horrible things about my mother! And don't you jeer about Wendy, either, 'cos she's still my pal,' she said furiously. Without thinking twice, she grabbed a spud out of the sink and hurled it at Charlie with all her force. It hit him squarely on the head, making him drop the dish of bread and milk and causing him to give a bellow of pain. He set Bobby down on the hearthrug and jumped to his feet and in two seconds a royal battle was in progress, with everyone shouting and Diana using feet, fists and fingernails to do Charlie as much damage as she could.

They did not even hear the kitchen door opening, but Wally's bellow was so loud that it stopped them both in their tracks. Charlie's father stood framed in the doorway, round eyes expressing astonishment, mouth uttering condemnation of their behaviour. 'How dare you fight like a couple of bleedin' alley cats, with poor little Becky asleep on the floor and Bobby cryin' his heart out?' he demanded angrily. 'Charlie, you're the older, so you just explain and then you can go straight to bed – no supper for you.' Wally peered closely at Bobby. 'Why, he's covered in somethin' . . . what the devil's been goin' on, eh?'

Charlie began a muttered explanation, but Diana cut in. 'It was my fault, Mr Fisher,' she said humbly. 'I threw a potato at Charlie's head, really hard, and he dropped the bread and milk what he was feeding to Bobby.'

Charlie cleared his throat, then said gruffly: 'It weren't just that, Dad, it were my fault as well. I – I called names.' He walked over to Bobby and began to pick up the shards of broken china. 'I'll clear up the mess an' get the spuds on to boil, 'cos Mam asked me to do that. Then I'll go to bed if you want . . . or I could stay and put the fish in the fry pan when the spuds is cooked, and then go to bed.'

Diana saw Wally's mouth twitch, but he spoke gravely enough. 'Well, since it seems there was faults on both sides, we'll say no more,' he said. 'The pair of you, and Lenny, can gerron wi' cookin' a meal and laying the table, while I get Bobby an' Becky to bed. I see your mam is out and I suppose she's taken Jimmy with her, so the rest of us must bustle around and get this place cleaned up afore she gets back.' He plucked the sleeping Becky from amongst her cushions. 'Why did you come home so early, anyhow?'

'Little Miss – I mean Diana, here, followed us to New Brighton but she didn't tell her mam, so we had to come home,' Charlie said, a trifle bitterly.

Wally nodded slowly and turned reproachful eyes on their uninvited guest. 'I suppose your mam's goin' frantic an' Aunty Beryl's doin' her best to let her old pal know you're safe an' well,' he said heavily. 'If them gals can sink their differences, it'll be one good thing to come out of this mess, 'cos Beryl, she's that soft-hearted . . . oh well, we'll have to see.' He patted his daughter's back as she stirred in his arms. 'How Becky could sleep through the din you two were makin' is more'n I can understand, but I'll take her upstairs now an' tuck her in.' He addressed Charlie again. 'How much of that bread 'n' milk went inside young Bobby? There looks to be a fair bit on the floor.'

Bobby had been roaring a protest when his father had entered the room but he had been out-roared by Wally and now sat placidly on the floor, occasionally wiping a dribble of milk from his face. Charlie had prudently cleared both the broken china and the food from his little brother's vicinity and now said, resignedly: 'Norralot, Dad. I'll make some more, shall I?'

Wally grunted assent and left the room and the children began to do as he told them. Charlie started to make fresh bread and milk, this time in a tin plate. Diana went back to the sink and Lenny, glancing curiously from one to the other, started to lay the table. At one point, Diana sidled over to Charlie and whispered that she had not meant to get him into trouble, but Charlie only grunted and began to shovel bread and milk into his little brother's mouth, so Diana finished off the potatoes and then she and Lenny staggered across the kitchen with the heavy pot and pulled it over the fire.

By the time Wally came downstairs once more, the potatoes were beginning to steam and the kitchen looked clean, bright and welcoming. The table was laid for a meal, Bobby had had his face and hair washed by his eldest brother, and the other children were hovering helpfully around.

'That's better,' Wally said approvingly. 'I dare say Mam will be returning any moment with young Emmy in tow. Charlie, lay an extra place.'

Chapter Eleven

Beryl, with Jimmy tucked warmly inside her shawl, returned home after her fruitless search to find Wally presiding over what seemed like a happy, domestic scene. This should have pleased her, but it failed to do so. She was hot and cross. Her visits to the three nearest police stations had proved abortive; no one had heard of either Emmy or her missing child, so Beryl marched into the kitchen, laid the sleeping Jimmy in his cot, and then took her place at the table. She answered Diana's enquiring look with a shake of the head.

'No one's seen your mam, so she's not reported you missing,' she said briefly. She began to help herself to potatoes and fish. 'I reckon she guessed you'd have gone with us so it was safe for her to clear off with that young officer.' She sighed gustily. 'Well, I suppose I ought to be honoured that I'm trusted,' she finished, her tone so rich with sarcasm that even Diana noticed and looked at her doubtfully. Ashamed, Beryl leaned forward and patted Diana's cheek. It wasn't fair to take it out on the child just because Emmy was thoughtless and selfish. When she had first seen Diana on New Brighton beach, she had hoped it was a tacit sign that the feud was over, but now she knew better. She had always known Emmy was selfish but had never guessed the full extent of it, and she meant to give the younger woman a telling-off which would make her think twice before abandoning her daughter to Beryl's care again. Oh, Emmy might, probably would, say that the whole thing was a dreadful mistake but she, Beryl, knew better. The woman who looked after Diana during the week must have baulked at having her on a Sunday as well so Emmy had simply turned round and dumped the kid on her old friend. Even in her temper, Beryl did not believe for one moment that Emmy would have simply abandoned the child to her own devices. She would have sent her to the Fishers' home, not realising that they had already left for their day out.

Beryl began to eat her meal. She glanced across at Wally and raised her eyebrows, for it was clear that something had happened in her absence. Usually, mealtimes were accompanied by laughter and lively conversation but today no one spoke and they attacked their food with less than their usual gusto. Wally pulled a face and opened his mouth to speak, but before he could do so they all heard a loud and desperate knocking at the door and Beryl jumped to her feet. 'That'll be her, and since I've gorra word or two to say to her, I'll take her into the parlour,' she said grimly. 'The rest of you stay just where you are and finish your meal.'

She left the kitchen, shutting the door firmly behind her, and hurried to open the front door. As she had guessed, Emmy stood on the doorstep, but she was not alone. The young officer was with her, an arm about her waist, and as soon as the door was opened the two came into the house, staggering in a manner which made Beryl think that they must both be drunk. There was no light in the hallway, so Beryl could not see either of her visitors clearly, but she ushered them into the parlour. 'Sit down for a moment, both of you,' she said, and went to light the gas mantle, so that she could see her guests more clearly. When she turned back towards Emmy and the young man, she gasped with horror. During her quarrel with Emmy she had been at first so tense, and then so furious, that she had scarcely glanced at the younger girl. Now, seeing Emmy properly for the first time for many weeks, she was shocked both by her friend's extreme pallor and by the almost skeletal thinness of Emmy's body. The only thing which seemed to have remained unaltered was Emmy's great fall of shining, pale gold hair; without that, Beryl would scarcely have recognised the other woman.

She began to speak, but was interrupted. 'Diana?' Emmy asked, in a thin, hoarse little voice. 'Is she – is she with you, Beryl?'

All the anger and hurt had left Beryl as soon as she set eyes on Emmy in the light, leaving only loving concern. 'Aye, she's been with me all day and she's just fine,' she said robustly. 'But Em, you're ill.' She turned to the young officer. 'Lift her on to the couch, young feller, and prop her up with them cushions. What in God's name have you done to her?'

The young man looked hunted. 'I have done nothing,' he said defensively. 'She wanted to go to New Brighton, so we took the ferry and searched for you on the beach, but it was very crowded and we could not see you. I noticed she grew tired very quickly so I took her to a café place, but she could eat nothing. She said the food made her cough, though she had two cups of tea. Then I could see she was very unwell and must not wander about in the hot sun. We came back to the city and I took her to the Northern Hospital on Great Howard Street – it was the nearest – but when the doctor said she must stay, she grew very agitated. She kept saying she *must* go home, that she must find Diana.' He looked anxiously at Beryl, his eyes pleading for understanding. 'I did not know what to do. She says she won't stay in hospital and I am not a relative, so I cannot sign papers, cannot insist. I promised the doctor I would take her back when we had made arrangements for the child, but if she refuses' – he shrugged helplessly – 'there is nothing I can do. Do you understand?'

'Aye, I understand; our Em can be as obstinate as any mule when she chooses,' Beryl said. She plumped down on her knees beside her friend, taking the thin, blue-veined hands in her own strong and capable clasp. 'Em, my love, how long have you been ill like this? Why, you're as thin as a rail and pale as a ghost. This must have been coming on for some while. You didn't get like this just because you're anxious about Diana. What have you been doing?'

Emmy gave a wheezy little chuckle. 'I've been doing double shifts,' she whispered. 'Me and Peter, we never managed to save much, so I was determined to put a bit of money in the bank. Winter is coming, and—' Her words were cut short by a painful bout of coughing and the young man leaned forward and touched Beryl's arm.

'The doctor said she mustn't talk,' he said urgently. 'It tires her too much; she needs all her strength for breathing.' He gestured for Beryl to move away from the couch and she did so, seeing that Emmy's eyes had closed, as though she were too weary even to raise her lids. The officer pulled Beryl towards the window and then addressed her in an undertone. 'The doctor says it is consumption. He says she is very ill and must go to the chest hospital on Mount Pleasant and they will probably send her to a – to a

– I can't remember the name, but it is a hospital far from here, where air is clean and recovery more possible. She will say no, but he tell me it is that, or . . . pouf! She will get worse and be unable to work. Then she will die.'

Beryl stared at him, horrified. She had noticed how his English grew worse and his accent stronger as he became agitated but she was sure he was not mistaken. If Emmy had been driving herself too hard, worrying too much, probably not eating properly, then she was just the sort of person who would be most at risk of catching the illness. Emmy's father, after all, had died of it many years ago. Beryl thought back; Emmy had always appeared frail but there had been a healthy glow and a fluidity of movement which had given the lie to her apparent fragility. Now, this had disappeared. Brittle, terribly thin and wheezing like an old man, she was white as a sheet, save for two spots of burning colour in her cheeks, and her eyes were blue-shadowed, whilst the bones of her face could almost be seen through the translucent pallor of her skin.

'I see,' Beryl said slowly. 'It'll be a sanatorium you're meaning, Mr – Mr . . .'

'First Officer Johansson, of SS *Queen of the South*,' the young man said, belatedly pulling off his cap and bowing slightly. 'You, I know, are Mrs Fisher, her great friend. When the doctor made his pronouncement, she began to say at once that she must go to Beryl – I'm sorry, that is rude, but it is what she did say – so when I realised she was serious I put her in a taxi and brought her to Raymond Street, only he would not come into the court and by then she could hardly walk. Still, we are here now, and you will tell me what I must do.'

Despite herself, Beryl smiled. It seemed that this young man intended to take her advice over Emmy's welfare, and that suited her just fine. 'For a start, Mr Johansson, you may give me a hand in making up this sofa as a bed. Diana is in the kitchen, eating her supper; as soon as she is finished, she can pop in to say goodnight to her mam, and then she can share my daughter Becky's bed. When do you have to return to your ship?'

Once more, the hunted look appeared in Mr Johansson's face. 'That is the trouble; I tried to explain to the doctor but I was very upset and perhaps got many words wrong. I have to be back on board by midnight, since we sail at dawn, when the tide is right. I could apply for leave of absence but I do not know if my captain would permit. As I said before, Mrs Wesley is not my relative and I have no rights . . .'

'Don't you worry yourself, lad – Mr Johansson, I mean,' Beryl said quickly. 'I'll take her to the Mount Pleasant hospital myself, first thing in the morning. That will give us a chance to make arrangements about Diana and for Em to get a few things together.'

Mr Johansson could not hide the relief he felt, though he said: 'But will she go with you, Mrs Fisher? If she refuses . . .'

'Don't you fret yourself; she won't refuse,' Beryl said grimly. 'One glance at her face told me she were at the end of her tether. There's no alternative, Mr Johansson, not when it's live or die. Our Em loves life and she loves Diana . . . mebbe, she even loves me a bit. She's got plenty of sense, has Em, and when it comes right down to it she'll go into that sanatorium knowing full well I'd never let her down. Now you stay with her while I go and fetch some bedding, and next time your ship docks in the port of Liverpool you come straight round here, understand? And I'll tell you how she's keeping and where you can find her.'

Diana lay in bed beside Becky, completely exhausted. When Beryl had told her that her mother was really ill and might have to go to the sanatorium to be made well again, she had known that it was her fault. The eviction of the Telfords, which had seemed such a cruel and terrible thing, paled into insignificance beside her mother's illness and had, in fact, gone right out of Diana's head. It had haunted her that, for the first time in her whole life, she had ignored her mother's wishes and gone her own way. She had known she would be making Emmy unhappy and miserable and had hoped that she would make the hated Carl unhappy, too, but she had never meant to make Emmy ill. Since her father's death, she and Emmy had grown closer and closer and Diana realised that life without her mother would be unendurable, especially as she now blamed herself for the whole, horrible business.

Aunty Beryl had assured her that it was not her fault, that the consumption which was the cause of Emmy's illness must have been getting worse and worse for some time. To be sure, Diana's running away might have brought things to a head, but by and large this was a good thing, Beryl had said. It meant that Emmy now had a chance of recovery, whereas if she had gone on hiding her illness from everyone, she might have left it too late to get treatment.

It had taken a long time to convince Diana that it was not her own behaviour which had caused her mother's collapse, but when even Charlie joined in, saying gruffly that of course they all knew that she was real fond of her mother and wouldn't do nothing to hurt her, not for the whole world, she had begun to feel a little better. She had drunk a mug of hot milk, eaten two biscuits, and gone up to bed, squeezing in beside Becky. But since the last thing she had done before climbing the stairs had been to visit her mother, lying limp and pale on the sofa in the parlour, she had cried bitterly once she got into bed, soaking her pillow with frightened tears. She *did* love Emmy, she did, she did, and though Aunty Beryl had told her that she might live with the Fishers whilst her mother was in the sanatorium, she still dreaded Emmy's departure. Aunty Beryl had been certain that Emmy would recover but once she was alone, in the dark, Diana found that she was not so sure. After all, no one had ever thought that Daddy would be killed; he was young and strong, yet he had still died. Emmy, lying on the sofa with her eyes closed, had looked both old and weak to Diana.

But even tears cannot last for ever, and Diana gave a dry, hiccuping sob and slipped out of bed. She fell to her knees on the worn linoleum, clasped her hands together, and began to pray with more fervour than she had ever shown before. Please God, she thought, let my mammy get well again; you've got my daddy, so please, please leave me my mammy.

It was long past midnight when she stood up, rubbing her cramped and aching limbs, and climbed back into bed.

Emmy stared round the long, bare room as dusk crept over the town whose lights twinkled below her. She felt a lump rise to her throat, and tears flooded her eyes and trickled slowly down her cheeks. She thought that never, in her entire life, had she felt so alone. The sanatorium was perched on the side of the Great Orme, above the seaside town of Llandudno, and through the wide open windows which led on to a narrow balcony she could see the sea. The wind from the sea blew straight into the ward and since it was early September this was not too unpleasant, but the other occupants of the room – there were five of them – had warned Emmy that the windows were never closed.

'They say fresh air is good for us, though it's bleedin' cold in winter,' the thin, red-haired girl in the next bed had told her earlier that day. Her name was Violet and Emmy had warmed to her when she heard that she came from Coronation Court, off the Scotland Road. The other four girls were Suzy, Paula, Marj and Sian, and all had seemed quite friendly, but in this strange environment all that had really struck Emmy was the bareness of the room, the briskness of the staff and the strangeness of the little town, so different from the warmth and liveliness of home.

But it would do no good to cry; she had been told that crying was bad for her, as was too much talking, laughter and any sort of effort. There were medicines which could help her but what would do most good, at this stage, was complete rest. Emmy tried to pull herself a little higher in the bed and immediately felt a sharp, stabbing pain in her chest. She subsided once more on to her pillows, gritting her teeth and using the top sheet to mop up the useless, silly tears. She had promised Beryl – and a weeping Diana – that she would do everything in her power to get well again, and she meant to do just that. Beryl had promised, faithfully, to look after Diana as though she were her own child. Wally had taken her hand and said, gruffly, that he'd always admired her spunk and knew that she would be a sensible girl and follow doctor's orders, no matter how unpleasant. Even Charlie, hot and red with embarrassment, had mumbled that she needn't worry; he would see that Diana did not get into bad company, and would even let her tag along after him when he went out with the lads. This last may have been said grudgingly, but Emmy knew Charlie well enough to realise that he would keep his word.

As for Diana herself, once she had got over the first shock, she had been wonderful. When she had heard that the sanatorium was far away, she had said at once that she would work for pennies so that she might pay her fare to visit her mam every few weeks.

Mr Mac had blamed himself bitterly for not realising how ill Emmy had become. He had come to the hospital to offer any help he could and had promised Emmy that her job would be kept open. He had brought flowers and chocolates and as soon as he left Emmy had handed these to Beryl, kissing her friend fondly and assuring her that she'd do her best to get well.

'I'm so ashamed of having quarrelled with you, Bee,' she said remorsefully. 'But I was already beginning to feel ill and wondering how on earth I would cope. It's an awful thing to say, but I think I turned on the person I loved most and then I was too stupidly proud to back down and admit I'd made a horrible mistake.'

This conversation had taken place in the Mount Pleasant hospital whilst doctors came and went and nurses popped in to give her what they called a blanket bath, and arrangements were made for her transfer to the sanatorium, and for her tiny pension to be paid direct to Beryl to help with the expense of taking care of Diana.

The girls from the restaurant had visited her, bringing small presents and assuring Emmy that they would write so that she knew what was happening at work. Miss Symons had pushed her mother's wheelchair up to the hospital and the old lady, with tears in her eyes, had said she would be happy to continue to pay Diana half a crown a week to do her messages and keep her company whilst Miss Symons worked.

Emmy had been grateful, but told Mrs Symons that the decision as to what Diana could do after school must be left with Beryl and, as yet, Beryl was too concerned over Emmy herself to consider Diana's after-school activities. Emmy knew that half a crown a week was not to be sneezed at, but she was beginning to realise that Diana was no longer the meek and biddable little girl she had once been. It might be a good deal safer if Diana returned every evening to the Fisher household where Beryl could make sure she was behaving herself and not gadding off with some other lively child who might lead her into all sorts of mischief.

So it had been arranged that Beryl would accompany her in the ambulance on the long journey down to the coast. Diana would have liked to go, too, but there was the question of her train fare home and she had agreed, though reluctantly, that she had best delay her own visit until she had saved up the money for the fare.

A week ago, therefore, it had been Emmy and Beryl who had made their way along the echoing corridors to Wisteria Ward, where Emmy now lay. If Beryl had been shocked by the place, she had not let it show, but Emmy knew that her own dismay had not been hidden. The doctor had told her that for the first few weeks she must remain in her bed, though she might get out to eat her meals on the long balcony and use the bathroom, of course. The other girls were all better than she so had their meals in the dining room downstairs; Violet and Sian, indeed, were both allowed to visit the town, though because of the steepness of the road which led to the sanatorium on Hill Terrace they were conveyed both there and back by an ancient motor bus.

'Don't you worrit yourself,' Violet had said kindly, when the nurse had told Emmy, rather sharply, that there would be no outings for her for many months to come. 'That's old Stratton – Nurse Stratton, I should say – what works by clockwork and don't have no heart. She's never been married and she's plain as a boot, so she hates us young 'uns, an' hates us most of all if we're married. Anyroad, you ain't gonna feel like goin' nowhere for a bit, but that'll change as you gets your strength back.'

This information cheered Emmy, but she was promptly cast down when she opened the drawer of her locker to find a half-finished letter inside. Unwisely, perhaps, she handed it to Nurse Stratton, asking, timidly, whether the writer might realise the letter had been left and worry about it. Nurse Stratton took the sheet of paper from her and began to read what was written on it. Emmy knew that it was wrong to read another's correspondence, and before she could stop herself she had said so, in no uncertain terms. 'You mustn't read it – I haven't,' she had said accusingly. 'It's wrong to read other people's letters; the poor girl who wrote it will be really angry with me for giving it to you if she knows you've read it.'

Nurse Stratton was a large, cold-eyed woman, with sandy hair, tiny light blue eyes, and a mouth like a rat trap. She snorted at Emmy's words, though faint colour rose to her cheeks, and she stared angrily down at her patient. 'The girl who wrote this letter won't care one way or t'other, 'cos she's dead and buried,' she said brusquely. 'Anyroad, it were only to some feller.' And with that, she scrumpled the letter into a ball and shoved it into the pocket of her apron before marching out of the room, her rubber soles squeaking on the highly polished linoleum as she went.

'There goes a wicked old bitch,' Violet had said reflectively, but Emmy had seen that there were tears in her eyes. 'Denise were a good little girl; she didn't deserve . . . but they caught her too late.' She had eyed Emmy's troubled face. 'They knew right from the start that it were hopeless, queen, so don't go thinkin' about it. As for old Stratton, she's a bad lot, so tek no notice of anything she says. Now, tell me about your little gal. What was her name again?'

Emmy had tried to forget the letter and Nurse Stratton's cruel words, and during the daytime she usually managed it, but at night it came back to haunt her. She had barely glanced at the letter, but even so, the first lines seemed to be engraved on her mind in letters of fire: *My darling Sid, it seems an age since I saw you last, though it's really less than a week and I just can't wait to see you again. It won't be long, darling, before I'm home . . .*

Emmy turned restlessly in her bed, hearing the springs creak beneath her as she did so. Did everyone think that they were going to get better? Was Violet really as well as she claimed? She had heard the nurses discussing Sian, saying the other girl would be home again well before Christmas. Sian was going to get married in the spring. She was embroidering a set of pillowcases for her trousseau and her young man, whose name was Dewi, visited two or three times a week, since he lived in Rhos-on-Sea, which was scarcely three miles from the sanatorium. And I could be married again if I wanted, when I get out of here, Emmy reminded herself. Carl asked me to marry him and though I didn't say yes, I didn't say no either. If I married Carl, there would be no need for me to work, because he's First Officer on the *Queen* now, and earning the same as Peter got. We could rent a nice house, in a decent district, and Diana could go to a good private school. I could have a little maid to do all the hard work and a pretty garden to sit in when the sun shone. I could marry him right now, because there couldn't be any of that cuddling and bed business, not with me so ill. But I'd be secure, and so would Di, and Carl might not mind missing out on the bed bit because he'd know it would come later, when I was well again.

It was good to think about a future which did not contain the sanatorium, good to tell herself that she could marry from here, and be a wife once more, though without a wife's duties, but she knew it was all pretend. It would be cheating on Carl to marry him, not knowing if she would ever be able to be a proper wife again. Come to that, she was still very unsure that she would ever *want* to be a proper wife. Being married to Peter had been grand; being married to anyone else might be perfectly horrid. Though the responsibility of bringing up Diana alone had been too much for her at times, she realised, now that she no longer had it, that she had relished her independence. Would she willingly give it up for the sake of security?

Emmy was still wondering as she watched the stars begin to pale towards dawn; still wondering when at last she fell asleep.

By Christmas, Emmy was growing accustomed to life in Wisteria Ward. Though the days seemed long, the staff were beginning to let her take part in some, at least, of the activities around her. A brisk, fat little woman, with grey hair cut in an Eton crop, came in twice a week and supervised what she described as gentle exercise. At first, Emmy had just watched the others, but now, though she was still confined to her bed, she did the breathing exercises, hands on her ribs so that she could feel the movement drawing the icy air slowly and carefully into her lungs, and holding it for as much as three seconds before gently expelling it in a long sigh.

Then there was Miss Bolsover, who came in every other day with a supply of various materials, such as raffia, coarse linen, balls of wool and wicker. She taught them to make raffia place mats and bags, wicker waste paper baskets and footstools, tray cloths, shoe bags and aprons. With Christmas coming, Miss Bolsover did her best to persuade them to make presents for those at home, and Emmy was quite pleased to occupy her time by knitting a blue cardigan for Diana and crocheting a collar and cuff set for Beryl. She and the other girls enjoyed Miss Bolsover's sessions for though they were not encouraged to exert themselves, it was pleasant to chat quietly as they worked, knowing that Miss Bolsover never demanded silence and made it plain that she thought a joke or two, and a gentle smile, or even a laugh, did more good than harm.

Of all the girls in Wisteria Ward, Emmy and Violet

were the ones who received fewest visitors, for it was a considerable trek from Liverpool to Llandudno, and expensive, too. First there was the tram to reach the nearest underground station – or the ferry, if you were so inclined – then there was the train fare from the Wirral down to the coast, and then a bus fare to the sanatorium itself, for though one could walk it meant shortening one's visit by thirty or forty minutes.

Three days before Christmas, however, Emmy was sitting up in bed, putting the finishing touches to a cross-stitch kettle holder which she was making for old Mrs Symons, when someone came on to the ward, which was empty save for herself. She glanced up, beginning to say that the other girls were all in the dining room, for it was a weekday and her visitors almost always came on a Sunday. In fact, she had already said, 'If you are wanting . . .' when she recognised the visitor. Forgetting that she must never display excitement or emotion, she sat up so abruptly that the kettle holder flew from her hand. 'Johnny!' she shrieked. 'Well, if it isn't you! Whatever are you doing here?'

Johnny Frost gave her his shy, attractive grin, and the colour rushed into his face. He leaned over the bed and took her hands and then, as if impelled, dropped a light kiss on her forehead. 'Oh, Emmy, if only I'd known you were here, I'd have called before,' he said, his voice breaking a little. 'I've been living in Llandudno for the last six months and it weren't till I went home to visit me mam that they telled me you were here. I were that distressed, queen . . . well, as soon as I got back here, I made up me mind to come and see you the first chance I got. How *are* you, Em? Mam telled me you'd been working yourself into the ground . . . if only I'd known, I'd have stopped you . . . done something . . .'

'What could you have done, Johnny?' Emmy asked gently. 'You've commitments of your own, now, after all. You're a married man. You'll need all your spare time for your wife and your home.'

Johnny sighed. 'Oh, that,' he said, almost dismissively. 'We never did get married, me and Rhian. She were a nice girl, but the truth is, queen, I took up wi' her on the rebound and after a bit we both realised we'd made a mistake. When I heard about Peter's death – oh, Emmy, my heart bled for you, honest to God it did – I thought about trying my luck again, but I knew it were too soon. Now, I'm more organised and I might have tried again, but me mam telled me you'd took up wi' the officer who were best man at your wedding. Oh, but Emmy, I've missed you so much!'

Emmy felt quite guilty because she could not pretend to similar feelings. She had not thought about Johnny at all since losing Peter, but of course she could scarcely say so. Instead, she said rather feebly: 'Well . . . I thought you were married – out of the running, so to speak. And d'you mean to tell me you've not got another young lady?' She smiled up at him, suddenly feeling a surge of her old affection. 'Are all the young ladies of Llandudno blind, then?'

Johnny laughed with her. 'I told you I'd been busy, an' I meant it,' he said reprovingly. 'I've started a guest house, Em, specially for folk from Liverpool. Actually, it were me Aunt Carrie's idea. She's me dad's sister-in-law an' she come into some money when my uncle died. She knew I were at a bit of a loose end so she asked me to help her find a decent place, down on the coast. We chose Llandudno because it's lively and thriving, and property weren't that expensive, unless it overlooked the seafront, of course. Aunt put all her savings into buying the house, an' I put all mine into painting and decorating.' He grinned at Emmy. 'It were rare fun,' he admitted. 'We went to auctions – or rather, I did – and bought furniture, beds, linen, the lot. We started up last March, advertisin' in the *Echo*, always keepin' our prices a bob or two below what everyone else were chargin', and we've been full, just about, ever since we opened.'

His excitement was so evident that Emmy found herself excited too. She beamed at him. 'Who does the cooking? And the cleaning? I bet it's your poor Aunt Carrie,' she said. 'What do *you* do in this enterprise, my old pal?'

Johnny laughed delightedly. 'I cook, I clean, I serve at table and do the garden,' he announced gleefully. 'I'm a dab hand with a frying pan and I make a bed neat as you like, wash the sheets in the dolly tub, hang 'em on the line . . .'

Emmy knew her eyes had rounded with astonishment. Johnny had been like all the men in the court, thinking that domestic chores were for women, and cooking was no suitable occupation for a man. 'You've changed,' she said, almost accusingly. 'You never lifted a finger when you lived at home with your mam.'

'Well, I do now. It were part of the agreement Aunt and meself signed,' Johnny assured her. 'But we do have help in the house, now we're established. Bethan – she's the maid – does a lot of the housework and Mrs Crabb comes in each day to do scrubbin' an' that.'

Emmy was about to question Johnny further when the door opened and Sister Alma Evans came in. She was rather a favourite with Emmy, but now she was frowning and shaking her head. 'I told you no longer than fifteen minutes, Mr Frost,' she said reprovingly. 'We try to keep visiting down to the minimum for the first six months; it's really close relatives only, but since you said you'd come all the way from Liverpool I made an exception. Now say goodbye to Mrs Wesley and be off, or you'll miss your last train.'

Johnny looked a little sheepish but got up at once. 'If I promise to stick to fifteen minutes, can I come again, Sister? Emmy an' me – I mean, Mrs Wesley an' me – is old friends.'

'We'll see,' Sister Evans said, though she gave Emmy a little nod as Johnny turned to leave the ward. 'Mrs Wesley has a great many friends who want to visit, but they realise her welfare must come first, so they obey our rules. Her sister, Beryl, and daughter Diana have only been three times because when they come they stay a couple of hours, and though Mrs Wesley will not admit it, such visits exhaust her. Now run along, Mr Frost, do.'

As Johnny left the ward, closing the door softly behind him, Emmy sank back on her pillows, suddenly aware of the truth of Sister's words. It had been lovely seeing Johnny. For a moment, she had felt young again and almost well, but now she was totally exhausted. She put out a hand to pick up the kettle holder and let it drop. Breathing was difficult; she felt as though a tight band encircled her ribs and, for the first time, she realised that the staff were right when they said that laughter and excitement were not good for her. The truth was, she had tried to respond to Johnny in the light, flirtatious way she had always behaved with young men, and it had worn her out. She must be careful never to do such a thing again and found herself half hoping that next time Johnny called, he would be denied admittance.

Sister Evans had left the ward when Johnny did, but now she reappeared, carrying a bottle and glass. She smiled reassuringly at Emmy, then poured a dose of the bright pink medicine into the glass, and held it to her patient's lips. 'Drink it slowly but drink it all up,' she commanded. 'I imagine, from the look on your face, that you now realise there's method in our madness; quiet and calm are your best friends and emotion, even joy, is an enemy. That's why we try to keep visiting to a minimum; it's for your good, not because we are bitter old spoilsports.'

'Oh, I know *you* aren't, Sister,' Emmy said, rather breathlessly. 'But some of the staff seem to enjoy keeping us under.'

Sister Evans smiled. 'Maybe, maybe. And now, Mrs Wesley, I think it's time you had a rest. So I'll make you comfortable and then leave you. And don't forget, we are here to help you to get better, but for that we need your co-operation, so if the young man does call again, you must keep an eye on the clock at the end of the ward and turn him out after fifteen minutes.'

Snuggling down in the bed, Emmy agreed, drowsily, to do as Sister said. The ward was quiet now, and cold, the air blowing through the open windows distinctly nippy, though it was mid-afternoon and the sun was shining. Johnny can't possibly have tired me that much, Emmy was telling herself, as Sister Evans tiptoed from the room. I'll never sleep, and anyway the others will make a row when they come back in and that should be any moment now. No, I'll never slee—

She slept.

*

It was a wild March day. Diana and Becky were off to do the messages, pushing the rickety old pram with Bobby and Jimmy aboard and having to raise their voices to a shout just to be heard. Diana, however, was not talking much because she was thinking about her mother, and the letter she had received from her that morning. It had been a cheerful letter, though Emmy had complained that the gusting wind off the Irish Sea had kept her awake half the night, slamming against the long windows which were so rarely shut, and rattling the panes noisily.

Diana had last visited Emmy on Boxing Day and had been struck by the improvement in her mother's looks. Wisteria Ward had been decorated with holly and ivy and even some paper chains, made by the patients, and there had been a nice dinner, served in the dining room, to which Beryl and Diana had been invited. Diana had been thrilled because her mother, wrapped in the most beautiful pale blue dressing gown, and wearing the slippers which all the Fisher children, and Diana, had saved up to buy, had come down to the dining room, too. It had been her first meal not taken on the ward, and, though she had been warned not to get too excited, Diana could tell from her mother's bright eyes and pink cheeks that she was enjoying the occasion immensely. However, though she looked a little stronger, Diana did not think she was progressing as fast as she should, and had felt once more a rush of guilt. She knew now it was not her fault that Emmy had been struck down by consumption, so the guilt was not for that; it was because within days of her mother's going into the sanatorium she, Diana, had been suddenly conscious of a sort of lightness, as though a great burden had been lifted from her shoulders.

At first, this had not worried her, because she did not understand the reason for it; she simply rejoiced in the feeling that she was now a member of the much admired, much envied Fisher family. Then, one day, the truth had struck her. Ever since her father's death, she had felt responsible, not only for her own well-being, but for Emmy's too. She had thought of herself not as a child any more, but as a responsible person who must support her mother in all things and cast aside any desire to join in childish games or take part in juvenile pranks. Other kids might tie door knockers together, knock on doors and run away, or nick a few fades from the apple seller on the corner of Byrom Street and Alexander Pope Street, but she must do no such thing.

Being left in Mrs Symons's care had made things worse. The old lady was intelligent and lively but physically very disabled. She needed a great deal of help, and though Diana had been happy enough to give such help, the responsibility for the old lady had weighed heavier on her than she had realised. When Aunty Beryl had said, bluntly, that she needed Diana at home and could not spare her to the Symonses, Diana had been conscious of an enormous surge of relief – and that had made her feel guilty, too. She was truly fond of old Mrs Symons, had believed she enjoyed helping her, yet she knew that any regrets over the loss of the old lady's companionship would be more than outweighed by her increased sense of freedom.

So now she was a child again, a member of a large and happy family, and though there was little money to spare, and always another job to be done, she undertook such tasks willingly, knowing that once the messages were finished she was free to play out until Aunty Beryl called her in for her next meal.

Despite missing her mother, Diana was doing very nicely. Schoolwork had always come easily to her, so her marks were good. Charlie had unbent enough to promise that he would take her fishing in the canal when next he went, and she and Lenny had gone to the market and begged orange boxes from the stall-holders to be taken home and chopped into kindling, which they would sell from house to house at a farthing a bundle after school.

'Is we nearly there, Di?' Becky's voice was plaintive, for her legs were a good deal shorter than Diana's, and, because she had been thinking, Diana had been walking fast.

Contritely, she slowed her pace. 'Sorry, Becky; want a lift in the pram?' she asked. Becky shook her head and Diana smiled at her and smoothed the soft, mousy hair back from the younger child's forehead. 'You're a good girl, old Becky,' she said. 'You shall have first go on the swings and I'll push you high as the sky. Tell you what, when we've got the messages, we'll share a couple of sherbet dabs. How about that?'

Beryl, alone in her kitchen for once, was making bread. She pushed the dough into half a dozen large loaf tins, then stood them near the fire to prove. By the time they had risen, she trusted that either the boys or Diana and Becky would be back, so that they could take the tins along to Skillicorn's bakery on the corner of Blenheim Street. Beryl would have liked to bake her own bread, in her own oven, but it was too small to hold a week's supply and anyway she could not do with constantly having to turn the tins so that the bread continued to rise evenly. Instead, she would cook a large batch of sultana cakes. Well wrapped in greaseproof paper and put into sealed tins, these would last the family as long as a month, if she was careful and cut the slices thin.

And now I'd best start the washing, Beryl told herself, glancing towards the window. It was always difficult to guess what the weather was like in the court, but judging from the draught which hissed and whistled under the kitchen door there would be a good drying wind, and she had all McNab's tablecloths awaiting her attention. She always took her laundry along to the local washhouse, where she had plenty of room to wash, rinse and starch, and of course the place was criss-crossed with lines where it could be left to drip. But Beryl never took advantage of this last facility; she could not spare the time to sit on one of the long benches and gossip with the other women whilst the tablecloths dried. As for leaving them, that was out of the question; it was not unknown for one of the women, either accidentally or on purpose, to take a good item in place of a worn one, and Beryl shuddered at the thought of losing so much as a napkin, for old Mrs McNab was a real tartar and would probably take the work away from her, as well as charging her double the lost articles' value.

The tablecloths were tied up into a big fat bundle and Beryl was about to hoist it on to her head – easily the best way to carry such a burden – when the kitchen door burst open and the boys erupted into the room. 'Hey up, Ma,' Charlie said cheerfully. 'Gorrany messages? Or have them gals done the lot?'

Bones, entering the kitchen just ahead of Lenny, was carrying a large marrow bone in his jaws. He laid it carefully on the hearthrug and collapsed beside it, putting one proprietorial, hairy paw upon it when he saw Beryl watching him.

'The girls have gone to get my messages, but I was hoping you boys would come back in time to take the loaves to the baker,' Beryl admitted. She glanced, reproachfully, from the large marrow bone to Charlie's face. 'Why did you give that bone to him before I've boiled the stock out of it?'

Charlie laughed. 'I didn't give it to him; the butcher's boy from Granby's did, and old Bones fastened on to it like glue. But I dare say you could boil it anyway, 'cos he's hardly started it,' he added generously.

It was Beryl's turn to laugh. 'He's a good-natured old feller, but I won't deprive him of his meal,' she said. 'If you go round to the Todds, they'll lend you their handcart so you can take all the loaves at once, and by the time you get back I'll be home from the washhouse and have dinner on the go.'

'That's great, Mam,' Charlie said eagerly, whilst Lenny asked if they could have a bit of bread and jam to keep them going until dinner was ready. Beryl nodded and fetched the remains of the loaf from the cupboard, cutting two generous slices and smearing them, thinly, with plum jam. 'What *is* for dinner, anyroad?'

'Scrag end and dumplings,' Beryl said, and smiled at the boys' subdued cheer. All her family liked their food and she enjoyed their enjoyment. 'And a slice of sultana cake for afters, if they're cooked and cooled by then.'

The boys went off and presently returned with the handcart. 'Skinflint Harry tried to charge me twopence to borrow it,' Charlie informed his mother. 'But his da heard and gave him a right clack over the ear, and his mam asked us to take two trays o' buns, 'cos she's got company tomorrow and wants 'em baked by then.'

'That's grand,' Beryl said absently, balancing the washing on her head and making for the front door. 'See you in an hour or so, fellers.' Out in the court, she looked up at the 'two penn'orth of sky' and saw that it was blue, with small white clouds racing across it. The double lines which stretched between her house and that of Mrs Piggott, opposite, held no washing as yet, but were curved into bows by the wind. Good; it was an ideal drying day, then.

The boys had loaded the handcart and rattled along just behind her as she went under the arch and into Raymond Street. Here she turned right and the boys should have turned left, but Beryl felt a restraining hand on her coat sleeve. 'Mam,' Lenny said plaintively. 'Why's we havin' a cooked dinner on a Sat'day? Wharrabout Sunday?'

Sometimes, my kids are too sharp for me, Beryl thought resignedly. Aloud, she said: 'Tomorrow I'm taking young Diana to see her mam. It'll be the first time since Christmas, and it's to be a surprise. You see, the rules of the sanatorium have meant your Aunt Emmy hasn't been able to have many visitors so far, but now the time's up and they're willing for her to see folk a bit more often.'

Both her sons stared at her, dismay written large on their faces. 'More often?' Charlie said. 'But it costs a deal o' money, Mam, and Sunday's practically the only day we gets to see you, 'cept in the school holidays. How often's more often, anyhow?'

Beryl smiled reassuringly. 'I didn't mean meself, nor Diana, for that matter. I mean other people; Mr Mac, what Emmy used to work for, he's going to go and see her, and that young officer, when he's in port. Oh, an' one or two of the waitresses from Mac's thought they might have a day out there, now and then. Why, Mr Mac offered to take Diana with him when he goes, which would save me time and a few bob.'

Her sons' faces cleared. 'So long as you ain't intendin' to go every Sunday,' Charlie said. 'I'm goin' to take Di fishing in the canal this afternoon; she's norra bad kid and I did promise. D'you want us to take Becky along wi' us, Mam?'

Beryl smiled but shook her head. 'No, I'll keep her wi' me once the girls get back from doing my messages. This afternoon I want to go round to your Aunt Daphne and see the new baby. Becky will like that and she can play with young Alison while Daphne tells me how the baby's doin'. And you can keep the change from the baking money for a few sweets or an ice cream.'

'Thanks, Mam,' the boys chorused and made off, the handcart rattling before them. Beryl set off for the washhouse with an inward sigh. She loved Emmy as much as one person could love another, she reminded herself, but the trip to Llandudno took up the whole day and she always got home worn out. Diana was a good kid, but she chattered endlessly, demanding attention in a way which Beryl's boys never did, so that even the train journey, which should have been a relaxing time, was tiring.

And it was impossible not to worry about Emmy. She was better, Beryl was sure of it, but she was still so frail; her arms and legs like sticks, and her cheeks hollow. She said the food at the sanatorium was quite good, but the truth was that, because she was allowed to take no exercise, she had very little appetite. Her friend Violet had assured Beryl that they had all been the same at first, had all lost their appetites, and had promised that as soon as Emmy improved enough to take exercise she would begin to put on flesh. Violet herself was quite sturdy and the other girls in Wisteria Ward were a variety of shapes, but Beryl longed to see her friend's cheeks begin to fill out, and sometimes suffered from hideous doubts that Emmy would ever get well. In the six months or so that she had been in the sanatorium, there had been three deaths, and though the staff tried to make light of it, to say that the young women's illness had been discovered too late, Beryl knew that such sad events frightened her friend and probably put her recovery back.

But I'll see her tomorrow, and hopefully I'll be pleasantly surprised, Beryl told herself as she entered the long room, with its rows of sinks and wooden draining boards and the central table upon which one dumped first the washing to be done, and then that which had just been laundered. Women, busy at the sinks, turned and smiled as she entered, for everyone knew Beryl. 'Mornin' all,' Beryl said cheerfully, commandeering the nearest unoccupied sink. 'We've got a fine day for it; me tablecloths will be ready for ironin' in no time, which is as well, since I'm off to visit our Emmy tomorrow.'

Diana and Charlie hurried down the road towards the Houghton Bridge, carrying the shaved willow branches and lengths of line which they would presently employ. When they got to the path beside the canal, they would have a good walk before they reached the stretch where fishing was possible; closer to home, amongst the warehousing and factories,

Charlie was of the opinion that one was more likely to hook a dead boot than a moving fish. However, Diana was so thrilled to be actually asked to accompany her hero, that what he described as 'a good walk' seemed a small price to pay. She trotted alongside Charlie and when, at last, they stopped at what he considered a suitable spot, followed his instructions exactly, though baiting the hook caused her some anxious moments. They had purloined a chunk of rather stale bread and she helped to form this into a number of pellets, but she had great difficulty in persuading the pellets to stay on the hook, whereas Charlie's looked as if they had been glued on. It ended, of course, with Charlie baiting her hook as well as his own, and presently the two of them settled down to watch the brightly coloured floats which Charlie had constructed out of medicine bottle corks and painted with hard gloss filched from a neighbour's shed.

At first, Diana had been inclined to chat, but Charlie told her, severely, that any sort of noise frightened off the fish, so she had subsided and the two of them sat in companionable silence, watching the slow swirl of the water and the weed which swayed beneath the surface and the occasional glint as a fish turned to show, for a second, its silver underbelly.

After a couple of hours, during which the floats had not so much as dipped, Charlie heaved a sigh and said they might as well begin making their way homeward, since it seemed the fish were not in a biting mood. No sooner had he said this, of course, than Diana's float disappeared. Great excitement ensued whilst Diana screamed that she must have hooked a whale, it was tugging so hard, and Charlie shouted a great deal of contradictory advice. When there seemed to be a danger that the fish would win and Diana would be ignominiously hauled into the canal, he added his strength to hers, and with both of them pulling on the willow branch they managed to land a good-sized fish. When it emerged from the water it was bright-eyed and silver-scaled, but thrashing about on the dirt path did nothing to improve its appearance, and when Charlie despatched it with a sharp blow from his boot Diana felt quite sick. However, she realised that it would not do to say so, and when told to carry her catch home, so that Beryl might cook it for their tea, she obeyed without showing the reluctance she felt. She did remind Charlie that his mother had meant to visit his aunt and might not be home till late, but Charlie brushed this aside as unimportant. 'I've gutted and cooked many a fish, when I goes to Boy Scout camp,' he said grandly, and probably untruthfully, Diana thought. 'Here, wrap it in your skirt – it's slippery, ain't it?'

'It'll make an awful mess of my skirt,' Diana grumbled. 'Still, if you say so, Charlie . . .'

Charlie was firm and made her carry the fish all the way along the canal bank, but when they reached the road he relented and took over from her. The two of them trudged along, tired and dirty, but happy. But when they were almost at the entrance to the court, Diana jerked at Charlie's arm. 'Look, there's that Mr Johansson going into the court,' she said. 'I don't want to see him – I don't like him – but I expect he's come to ask Aunty Beryl . . . oh, damn and damn and damn! He's seen me.'

She was right, for the young man had stopped abruptly and turned towards them. Diana stiffened and made as if to change direction, but Charlie shook his head reprovingly. 'Don't be so bleedin' rude,' he hissed. 'Look, you have a word wi' the feller while I take the fish inside and gut it.'

Diana pulled a face, but obeyed, and presently she was smiling up at Mr Johansson as though he were her dearest friend. She was rather pleased when he jerked the cap off his head as if she were a real lady and not just a small girl, but his first words banished any softer feelings. 'Good afternoon, Diana. The last time we met was so long ago . . . it was the day that dreadful family got evicted from the court. Your mother mentioned it and said it was a blessing since she thought the eldest girl a bad influence on you.' He smiled down at her, but Diana thought his smile spiteful rather than friendly. 'Ah, well. I expect you've made many new friends since that day and do not miss the Telfords at all. But I must not digress. I have come to enquire after your mother. Mrs Fisher said I might go round to her house next time I was in port, but last time we only docked for a day; this is the first proper chance I've had. Can you tell me . . . I have written, of course, but it is not the same as seeing someone, and this time, I would very much like to visit her.'

Diana stared up at him, her mind seething with resentment. How dare he criticise the Telfords, whom he knew not at all? And what right did he have to ask questions about her mother, come to that? It was plain he wanted to start all that soppy business once more, but Diana told herself, righteously, that it was her duty to protect Emmy, who was not encouraged to have many visitors. She reminded herself how the staff at the sanatorium kept saying that quietness and calm were what her mother needed; reminded herself, also, that it had been during an outing with Mr Johansson that her mother had first been taken ill. But she did not let any of this show in her face; instead, she said guilelessly: 'My mam still isn't allowed visitors, Mr Johansson. She's been very ill, you know, and the doctors say she must not get excited. Why, I haven't been since Christmas and I'm *very* careful not to excite her when I do go. And, anyway, they've moved her, you know, because she's been so poorly. She's – she's in a sanatorium in – in Blackpool now, and that's quite a long way off. But I'll tell her you've been asking for her.'

The young man was staring down at her with a curious expression. 'Blackpool?' he said. 'And when will you yourself be visiting her next?'

'When will I . . . oh, not till June,' Diana said glibly, though she suspected that Aunty Beryl meant to take her the very next day. She had overheard a conversation between Wally and his wife in which he had given her a bag of Everton mints for 'poor old Em', so she guessed that a visit was imminent.

'Not till June?' Mr Johansson said slowly. 'Then I must be patient.' He returned the cap to his head and gave her a charming smile. 'I shall endeavour to visit Mrs Wesley next time I'm in port; I have a little present for her.'

He turned away on the words, leaving Diana to wonder, doubtfully, whether she had done the right thing. She did not know what the little present was, but it might have given her mother pleasure. She turned back into the court, telling herself stoutly that even if her mother might have liked his gift, she, Diana, just knew that a visit from Mr Johansson would have over-excited her, might quite probably have made her worse instead of better. It isn't as if he's a nice person, she told herself defensively. He's smarmy all right, always hanging over Mam and making pretty speeches, but I don't trust him. Besides, he's a foreigner and I don't want to live abroad, in some horrible country where they don't speak English. So it's better that he doesn't see Mam again.

At this point, she entered the Fisher kitchen to find Charlie at the sink, descaling the fish with Beryl's sharpest knife. He turned and grinned at her. 'Well, I guess he wants to visit your mam,' he said cheerfully. 'She'll be right glad to see 'im; I dare say she's bored out of her mind in that perishin' place. Will he go tomorrer?'

'He won't go at all,' Diana said airily. The words were out before she had thought and she hastily looked away from Charlie's penetrating gaze. 'It would only excite her and the nurses say she's best kept quiet. So – so I told him she'd been moved and was in Blackpool now. I don't think he really minded; he went off quite happily, anyway.'

Charlie stared at her, his eyes rounding with astonishment. 'You're jealous,' he said slowly. 'And you told him a lie, 'cos you know very well she's still in Llandudno an' likely to stay there for months, mebbe years. What's wrong with the feller, anyroad? Your mam would be a lot better off if she married again. She wouldn't have to worry about money.'

'You don't *know* him,' Diana said defensively, feeling the heat rush to her cheeks. 'He's horrible, really horrible and – and he comes from Sweden, or some foreign place, so if he did marry Mam, he'd take her far away. I – I don't want to live anywhere but here. He was awful rude about Wendy an' all, said it was a good thing the family had been evicted, because Wendy was a bad influence.' She saw, from the look on his face, that Charlie was about to agree with Mr Johansson's sentiments and hastily broke into speech once more. 'Charlie . . . oh, Charlie, don't be cross with me. I was only trying to protect Mammy from getting over-tired and making herself worse.'

Charlie shrugged and turned back to his work at the sink. 'The damage is done now, and you'll have to live with it,' he said brusquely. 'But liars always lose in the end; don't you forget that, Diana Lying Wesley.'

Next morning Diana woke early, full of delighted anticipation of the surprise ahead, but in fact the surprise was that there was no surprise. Nothing was said at breakfast, and by eleven o'clock Diana realised that she had been wrong; a trip to Llandudno was definitely in the pipeline, but it was clearly not to take place this Sunday, so she would have to possess her soul in patience for a week or so. Later in the day, she tried to question Charlie, but he was evasive, merely saying that he guessed his mam knew best what she was about and Diana shouldn't take things for granted. Baffled, Diana took Becky to the park in thoughtful silence, wondering precisely what had happened. She could, of course, ask Aunty Beryl outright, but did not quite like to do so. She had a feeling that Aunty Beryl was not best pleased with her and wondered, uneasily, whether Charlie had mentioned Mr Johansson's visit, then dismissed the idea. Charlie might be a good many things, but he was no tale-clat. No, it must be her imagination, she decided. Aunty Beryl was tired after washing and ironing all the McNab table linen; that must be it.

In fact, Beryl had met Mr Johansson as she returned to the court and had been horrified when he told her of his encounter with Diana, though she guessed from his expression that he had not believed a word of Diana's story.

'No, no, our Em is where she's always been, at the sanatorium in Llandudno,' she had assured him. 'And since Diana saw fit to lie to you, I won't tell her that I've put you right. But if you'd like to visit Emmy tomorrow – I were goin' myself, and taking Diana, but if you can go there's no need for us to do so – then I'm sure you'll be very welcome. I've not seen her meself since Christmas, but Mr Mac, the feller she used to work for, has been goin' down regularly, though he only stays for a short while. He's been awful good, going down almost every Sunday, because it's a devil of a journey when you only stay twenty minutes and then have to turn round and come all the way back. I believe he tells her all the restaurant gossip and then just comes away so as not to tire her. But he's said she's lookin' better.'

'He is an admirable employer,' Mr Johansson said gravely. 'If you're sure it's all right for me to go to visit, I won't stay for more than half an hour. But I do so long to see her again . . .' he added, looking worried.

'I'm sure it will do her a great deal of good,' Beryl said soothingly. 'I know she wants to see Diana but we can go in a week or two.'

'Diana does not like me, though I have done my best to be her friend,' Mr Johansson said. 'I wonder if, perhaps, there is some little jealousy . . .'

'You're right there. She's very possessive over her mam, but that shouldn't have made her tell you lies,' Beryl said. 'Fortunately, the visit tomorrow was to be a surprise, both for Em and Diana, so I'll simply put my plans off for a while.'

They talked for a little longer and then they parted.

Beryl returned home and sent Diana off on an unnecessary message so that she could tell Charlie that she would not be visiting Llandudno next day, after all.

Charlie glanced shrewdly at her, then grinned. 'You met that officer feller, didn't you?' he said. 'And I guess he told you all the whoppers Diana had told him. I said liars always lost in the end. But she's scared he'll marry her mam and take the pair of them abroad, you see, and she's happy here and don't fancy moving away.'

Beryl said she understood and began to get the evening meal, admiring the fish which Charlie had scraped and gutted. If Diana was afraid of her life's taking another violent change, then perhaps the lies were understandable, but if she caught the child out in more untruths, she would have to tackle the problem.

At this point, Diana returned and preparations for the meal began, and Beryl forgot her worries as the family surged into the kitchen.

Chapter Twelve
September 1930

Emmy sat on the veranda in front of Wisteria Ward, gazing out over a view which was as familiar to her as any she had ever known. It was one of those mild days which September sometimes brings, and the sea shone calm and silvery blue beneath a cloudless sky, whilst the leaves on the trees below her were touched with gold. Emmy stared at the scene, trying consciously for the first time to impress it upon her memory, for when she had last seen Dr Masters, he had had the results of the recent tests and X-rays, and had positively beamed at her.

'I'm happy to tell you that your tests show that you are now clear of the disease, Mrs Wesley,' he had said. 'We shall keep you with us for a further month – or perhaps a little longer – whilst you gradually increase your activity to what we might call a normal level. When that is achieved, provided there are no ill effects of course, you will be able to go home.'

Even now, Emmy could remember her initial delight and the attack of total dismay and panic which had almost immediately followed. How would she manage? Mr Freeman had re-let her house in Nightingale Court, for she had been unable to continue paying the rent when she and Diana had moved out. Beryl had sold all her furniture at Emmy's request, since no one had anywhere to store it, but she had kept small ornaments and similar knick-knacks, packed away in boxes, and stowed under beds and in cupboards at No. 4. Other things, such as clothing, had been kept, she knew, and there must be a little money in her Post Office savings book, for Beryl had refused to use the proceeds of the furniture sale towards Diana's keep, despite Emmy's urgings. She said that the pension was perfectly adequate, since a child like Diana scarcely ate enough to increase the amount of food she bought. If she needed to buy the child clothing as time passed and was unable to stretch the pension to cover this expense, she would dip into the Post Office account and tell Emmy what she had spent. She had never done so, always insisting that she could manage, so Emmy supposed that the furniture money would still be intact.

Emmy knew, of course, that Beryl would urge her to move into No. 4. Other families managed to cram a great many relatives into their homes, but Emmy was also aware that living in such circumstances was not at all advisable for someone who had recently recovered from consumption. When anyone left the sanatorium, they were lectured about the need for clean air, good food, exercise in moderation, and so on. She could get none of these things crammed into the Fishers' home; indeed, she did not think clean air was available anywhere in the courts. But sitting here on the balcony, gazing over the beautiful scene before her, it was difficult to envisage the court at all. She tried to conjure it up: the filthy flagstones, the brickwork, smoke-blackened by years of domestic fires and factory chimneys, the washing lines criss-crossing it, and the barefoot ragged children absorbed in their games, accustomed to the dinginess of their surroundings.

Emmy sighed. It was all very well telling herself

that something would turn up, but unless it did so quickly, she would have no alternative but to return to the court as Beryl's unpaying lodger, for she would be unable to work immediately and, in any case, Dr Masters had said she should not take up paid employment for at least six months, preferably a year.

Emmy had been forced to tell Beryl all this and knew that it had deeply worried her friend, but they had agreed to talk to the authorities once Emmy was back in Liverpool. Dr Masters was writing letters and thought that some money would be forthcoming, though he was not sure of the amount.

But that's charity, Emmy had thought to herself, shocked. Surely I don't need to accept charity? Before, I earned a decent living for Diana and myself; why shouldn't I do so again? Oh, waitressing is out, Dr Masters made that clear; when I work again it must be at what he calls a sedentary job – bookkeeping or typing, or something of that nature – but until then, I must try to accept Beryl's advice, and take each day as it comes.

And then she remembered what Violet had said, the last time she came visiting, for Violet had returned home almost a year before, though the two girls had kept in touch by letter. They had met by arrangement, at the entrance to Llandudno pier, and had enjoyed a wonderful afternoon together, for by then Emmy had graduated to thrice weekly trips to town as well as the days out organised by the staff, when all the patients who were sufficiently fit went off in a charabanc, sometimes as far afield as Holyhead, in Anglesey, where they would watch the ferries leaving for Ireland, and envy those aboard.

Violet had looked at her critically after their first, ecstatic greeting. 'You're looking grand, queen,' she had said. 'Mark my words, you'll be home before Christmas. Made any big decisions yet?'

'No,' Emmy had said, puzzled. 'What sort of decisions can any of us make in the sanatorium? Everything is decided for us – don't say you've forgotten *that*!'

'Puddin' 'ead!' Violet had said, laughing. 'Real life is about to knock the feet from under you, unless you sit up and take notice. Why, you were the only one of us in Wisteria with a choice of fellers visitin', payin' court, makin' their intentions clear. Which one of the three is you goin' to accept?'

'Three?' Emmy had said, mystified. 'Oh, I suppose you mean young Dr Morgan? You can't have meant Mr McCullough. He's my boss – or rather, he was – and anyway he's really old.'

Violet had laughed. 'No, I suppose you can't count your boss as a suitor, although he did come regular as clockwork for some time,' she said. 'I did notice Doc Morgan making sheep's eyes at you, though, whenever he come on to the ward. Is he still up there at the san? I thought he were only doing a six-month stint.'

'Yes, he was,' Emmy agreed. 'As for the other two . . .'

'I hopes as how you aren't goin' to tell me that Mr Johansson and Mr Frost haven't popped the question?' Violet said. ''Cos that would be too much for anyone to swaller, even me.'

Emmy, blushing, had admitted that both Carl and Johnny had asked her to marry them, adding, a trifle haughtily, that she had naturally refused. 'How can I marry anyone when I can't be a proper wife?' she had asked, rather petulantly. 'Dr Masters has gone on and on about getting plenty of rest, good food and gentle exercise, but he hasn't said who's going to do the housework, the scrubbing of floors and the heaving of wet sheets out of the boiler and over to the sink. Oh, Violet, however *shall* I manage?'

It was different for Violet, who was still living at home with her mam, though she was engaged to be married to a young man with a good job in Tate's. When she did leave home, Emmy reflected rather bitterly, her friend would go to a decent little house of her own, and would begin her new life knowing her husband's salary was secure.

At the time, she had passed off Violet's question by saying that she had no wish to marry again, but that had been before Dr Masters had told her, definitely, that she would soon be leaving the sanatorium. The question of marriage then had been something which could be pushed into the future. Now, it was imperative to seriously consider it.

Looking out over the calm sea, she reminded herself that Johnny and she might have married years ago, had not Peter come into her life. And no one could say Johnny had been inattentive since his first visit to the sanatorium. Despite constant warnings from the staff, he had persisted in visiting her three or four times a week, though he never tried to stay longer than fifteen or twenty minutes after she had told him, bluntly, that she tired easily.

She had visited him in his pleasant guest house on quiet, tree-lined Chapel Street a good many times, enjoying both his company and that of his practical, humorous Aunt Carrie. It was soon easy to see who was the more business-like of the two. Easy-going, gentle Johnny would never have found the courage to evict dirty, disreputable holiday-makers who came in drunk and spewed up on the hall floor. Nor would he have pursued, to the very railway station, the odd non-payer, or sat up half the night with a sick child, though it had been he who had fetched the doctor on the occasion when this had happened. He did the books – and did them extremely well – and dealt with plumbers, electricians, and other tradespeople who came to the house, but Mrs Carrie Frost had the energy and drive which Emmy was beginning to realise Johnny had always lacked. He was handsome, charming and easy-going. In many ways, he would make an ideal husband, but she did not believe she could ever love him as she had once loved Peter.

She reminded herself that she loved Beryl in one way and Diana in another so, naturally, she would love Johnny differently from the way she had loved Peter. She thought about Johnny, tried to imagine him taking her in his arms, sweeping her off her feet. She thought about waking to find his rumpled, dark head next to her own on the pillow . . . and found herself blushing. How imagination did run away with her, especially when you considered how she kept telling herself – and everyone else – that she did not mean to remarry.

But her obstinate mind continued to play with the idea. Carl came to visit her whenever he could and truth to tell he was a much more exciting visitor, a much more exciting person than Johnny had ever been. He was full of gaiety and charm and Emmy knew that all the staff and half the inhabitants of the sanatorium were a little in love with him. Including herself? Was it love that made her heart flutter when he put his arm round her or held her hand? It was nice to know that everyone envied her handsome Carl's affection . . . but then Johnny was good-looking, sweet-tempered, accommodating . . .

Sighing, she decided that she was trying to do things in the wrong order. First, she must grow accustomed to ordinary life. Only when she had done so could she consider marrying anyone, anyone at all.

'You awright now, Aunt Carrie? Only I thought I'd go up to the sanny for half an hour. Emmy were told a while back that she'd be home before the end of September, and – and . . .'

'And you still haven't plucked up the courage to tell her she's gorra marry you and bring the kid back here,' his aunt said cheerfully. She was a tall, raw-boned woman with thin grey hair curling closely about a narrow and bony face, whose only beauty was in the sweetness of her smile.

Johnny sighed. 'I can't seem to bring meself to risk it,' he said humbly. 'I asked her a year or so back, and she got real angry, said a fat lot of use she'd be to any man, the way she was. I told her I didn't care for such nonsense, wanted her on any terms, but that just made her angrier. She told me to gerrout and leave her alone and though I went back two days later, I were that scared she'd tell me to leave that I couldn't – dussen't – mention marriage again.'

His aunt smiled at him with real affection. 'I know what you mean, chuck, but you've gorra take your courage in both hands and ask her to wed you, else she'll be gone back to Liverpool, back to that wretched court and likely makin' herself ill all over again. Here, with you and meself to take care of her, and with clean air and good food . . . why, she'd go from strength to strength.'

'It ain't only her goin' back to Liverpool what bothers me; there's that Johansson feller,' Johnny said gloomily. They were in the kitchen where Johnny had just finished preparing vegetables for the evening meal, for though it was no longer summer several of the bedrooms were still let to guests. This was thanks to Aunt Carrie's business policy, for she always cut their prices as soon as August ended, and sometimes kept the rooms full until late October. 'I know for a fact he's proposed, and who's to say she won't accept? He's rare good-lookin', and as First Officer on a cruise liner he'll be a grand earner, as well.'

'All the more reason to pop the question,' his aunt said briskly. She was cleaning cutlery, rubbing between the tines of the forks with a rag dipped in a saucer of pink plate polish. 'Faint heart never won fair lady, Johnny, and besides, you're a good-looking young feller yourself.'

'I'm nothing special,' Johnny muttered. Any mention of his looks always embarrassed him, since he thought himself commonplace. 'I know you're right and I know if I don't chance me arm, I'll lose her for certain. So if there's nothing else for me to do here, I'll nip up to the sanny and see if I can get Em to meself for once.'

His aunt wished him luck and Johnny set off with a late rose in his buttonhole and hope in his heart. But two hours later he was back. 'It weren't no use,' he told his aunt. 'Oh, I asked her, all right, and she were really sweet, said she was very fond of me but she couldn't rush into anything until she sees how she manages ordinary life again. Apparently, that old feller what visits her – you know, the one she used work for – has offered her the sort of job Dr Masters has agreed she could tackle. She's to be his cashier, the job his old mam used to do, only the old gal wants to retire – she must be well over seventy – and it's something Emmy thinks she'd enjoy.'

His aunt pursed her lips. 'In a way, I understand just exactly how she feels,' she said thoughtfully. 'If she jumped at your offer, like a trout at a fly, you might both regret it in twelve months. She might end up feeling that she'd accepted you for all the wrong reasons. You don't want a wife who marries you for security and not for love, do you?'

'Yes, I do, so long as it's Emmy,' Johnny said obstinately. 'But I see what you mean. And she agreed I could visit her just as often as I liked. She even said that she'll be coming back to the sanny every three months for the first year at least, and when she does she'll visit us here.'

'Well, there you are then,' his aunt said, bestowing her sweetest smile on him. 'I've made a big pot of leek and potato soup, so we might as well have a bowl now.'

Johnny beamed at her. He loved her leek and potato soup. 'You're on, Aunty,' he said. 'Leek and potato, eh? That's me favourite.'

Now that Emmy was so much better, Mr Mac came nearly every Sunday, sometimes bringing Diana with him, and if the weather was fine the three of them would sample the delights of the pier and the front, though Mr Mac was always careful to see that Emmy did not get over-tired.

On this occasion, however, he came alone because, he said, he wanted to discuss the work-plan which he thought Emmy should follow. He took her into town by taxi, straight to the Queen's Hotel, and the two of them sat in the window table whilst Mr Mac went over his proposals for her employment.

'I should like you to work mornings only, and only three mornings at that, for a month,' he told her.

'Then, perhaps, if you find you can cope with three mornings, we might make it five mornings for a further month. That will bring us up to December which, as you will remember, is easily our busiest time of year. Even then I think you should still do mornings only, but perhaps you might include Saturdays, if you feel able to do so. My mother has agreed to work with you for as long as you need her and to take over as soon as you feel tired. As you know, our flat is above the restaurant, so it will be no hardship for her to come down whenever necessary.'

Emmy eyed him surreptitiously across the gleaming white tablecloth. When he had first started visiting her, she had been in awe of him and had not really enjoyed their time together, but this feeling had soon passed. The truth was, Mr Mac was a man full of good sense and humour. He was the only one of her visitors who regularly made her laugh, and she found herself telling him stories about life in the sanatorium which she could confide in no one else, save Beryl. Because he was visiting so regularly, he was able to keep her informed as to the doings of her fellow waitresses. Little things which were probably not particularly amusing at the time became funny when he recounted them. Soon Emmy began to look forward eagerly to his visits, and because he got to know both the other patients and the members of staff so well, she was able in her turn to amuse him with stories of various exploits. Six young women, cooped up in Wisteria Ward, got up to all sorts of mischief as their health improved. Several of the girls fell in love with young men who lived locally and it was by no means unknown for a girl to climb down from the balcony outside the ward, by means of the ancient wisteria which grew against the wall and offered excellent footholds, to have an evening out with some dashing young blade. Emmy herself had climbed down the wisteria three times, but only for the most innocent reasons, one of which had been to procure another two ounces of knitting wool, so that she might finish the cardigan she was knitting for Diana. It had not been as risky as one might suppose, descending in the grey of an overcast winter afternoon, but Emmy had barely escaped face to face encounters with no fewer than three members of staff. At the time, it had been hair-raising, but afterwards, the humour of the situation had struck her. In one instance, she had hidden behind the sanatorium's array of dustbins whilst Sister Griffiths had come by, and the sanatorium's fat ginger cat had spotted her and stalked towards her, tail erect and ears pricked, obviously hoping for a fuss. Poor Emmy had frantically shooed him away, afraid that the nurse would wonder why the cat was behaving with such obvious friendship towards a row of dustbins. But Ginger had persisted in his overtures and Emmy still considered that she had had a very narrow escape.

Now, she remembered with pleasure how Mr Mac had enjoyed the story, how he had chuckled and capped the tale with one of his own, for he had served with the Rifle Brigade in the War, rising to the dizzy heights of captain by 1918, and had travelled to Egypt, Mesopotamia and many other foreign places during his time in uniform.

'Well, Mrs Wesley? Do you think you could manage that? Naturally, as cashier you will be earning more than the waitresses . . .' Mr Mac named a sum which made Emmy blink, for it seemed a great deal for a part-time job. She was about to ask him if this was the full-time rate and, if so, what she would earn weekly for the first month, when he cleared up that problem, too. 'As you know, Mrs Wesley, I have always felt deeply ashamed that you became so ill in my employ. Usually, I am quickly aware of any problems, but for some reason your illness . . . well, I failed to notice it. You were always so lively, so quick-moving, and of course you hadn't been with us for long so I'm afraid I simply assumed that you had always been very thin and pale. When I realised you were ill, I made up my mind that, when you returned to work, I would make sure that it was to the right sort of job. I mean to pay you sufficient for the first three months, when you will be working part-time, to cover all your expenses. If you find yourself short, then you *must* let me know, if you please. I have the reputation of being a good employer and it's a reputation I don't wish to jeopardise.' He looked at her searchingly. 'Can you understand that, Mrs Wesley, and accept it as a – a reparation for what I feel was my neglect?'

'Oh, yes . . . it's most awfully kind of you . . . only it was all my own fault, really it was,' Emmy gabbled, thoroughly embarrassed to think that Mr Mac should blame himself for her illness. 'It's very good of you to trust me to do the work of a cashier when you know I've never done it before. But if I'm awful at it, I promise you I'll leave at once. Only I do think I'll enjoy it and it shouldn't present too much of a problem,' she added honestly, for though she could scarcely say so, she did not think old Mrs Mac was exactly a financial genius. If she can take the money, add bills up and so on, and balance the books at the end of the day, then I'm sure I can, she told herself.

Mr Mac beamed at her. 'Good, good,' he said

expansively. 'Ah, here comes the waitress; have you had long enough to decide between the pork and the beef? I think I shall have the beef, because of the Yorkshire pudding and the horseradish sauce. Are you going to join me, or do you fancy sage and onion stuffing and apple sauce instead?'

A few days after Mr Mac's visit, Carl Johansson came calling. Like Johnny Frost, he had proposed marriage but had not been unduly dismayed when Emmy had told him she needed time. When she told him the date for her return to Liverpool was fixed, he gave a boyish whoop of pleasure and grabbed her, lifting her off her feet and whirling her around. They were making their leisurely way down into the town, but he had stopped short at her news, his fair curls seeming to stand on end, and his blue eyes bright with excitement and pleasure. Emmy thought that he had never looked more handsome and found herself wondering what marriage to him would be like, then dismissed the thought, afraid that it might show in her face.

'It's nice of you to be so pleased, Carl, because it must be for my sake and not your own, since we can only meet when you are in port,' she said sedately, though with a gleam of amusement in her eyes.

Carl laughed boisterously. 'Ah, but I have news of my own to impart,' he said. 'I am now to be First Officer on a transatlantic liner, the *Cleopatra*. The money is pretty well the same as I got on the old *Queen*, but this is a newer, far more modern ship. And, of course, I shall be in port every three weeks or so. Ah, Emmy, if you were to marry me, how happy we could be! Although I know I asked you when I was still on the *Queen*, it was, perhaps, a little unfair. But being home more often . . .'

'I trust this isn't another proposal,' Emmy said severely, though with a twinkle in her eyes. 'I simply must have time to get back into ordinary living before I even consider changing my status again.'

Carl gave an exaggerated sigh, then linked his arm through hers. 'I understand you and I think perhaps you are right,' he said ruefully. 'But it worries me that when you return to your old life you may meet someone else, someone from your past, perhaps.'

Inwardly, Emmy could not help giving a slight chuckle. Johnny knew about Carl, but Carl had no idea that Johnny existed, far less that the other man visited her regularly and had already proposed marriage several times. She wondered whether she ought to tell Carl that he already had competition, but decided against it. It would only make him worry, and anyway, she really felt that it was no one's business but her own. There had been a young doctor at the hospital who had shown rather more interest in her than was usual between a patient and the medical staff, a policeman who had come with a local choir to sing carols at Christmas, and a brother of one of the other patients; all these young men had made it plain they admired her, had actually asked her out, yet she had felt no need to mention the fact to anyone. She remembered Beryl's wise words: 'You've got to learn to live your own life before you can start sharing someone else's,' her friend had said. 'Don't you go leaping into *anything*, young Emmy. Just tell yourself that the next twelve months or so are a time for you, and you'll do OK.'

'Emmy? What are you dreaming of?' Carl squeezed her arm. 'A nice little house in the country, with a few chickens and an orchard, and a pig in the sty at the bottom of the garden? If you were to say yes . . .'

Emmy scowled at him and pinched his arm, but she could tell from his expression that he was only teasing her. 'Save your breath to cool your porridge,' she advised him. 'Oh, look, there's a tram coming up behind us going to Rhos-on-Sea; shall we catch it? There's a lovely café there where we can get a cup of tea and they sell delicious cakes.'

Diana greeted the news that her mother was to leave the sanatorium with feelings almost as mixed as Emmy's own had been. Naturally, she was dizzy with delight and anticipation, unable to stop smiling and full of plans for the grand welcome she would give Emmy, yet at the same time she knew that with her mother's homecoming, her pleasant life with the Fishers would be bound to change. She was ten years old now, and had grown accustomed to thinking of herself almost as a Fisher. She, Charlie and Lenny took charge of the younger ones and she had grown used to giving Beryl as much help as she could. Little Jimmy, was three now, but the new baby, little Freddie, was Diana's special charge. He was seven months old and getting heavy for her to carry, but she adored him and had learned to feed him, to change his nappies, and even to bath him, when Aunty Beryl was busy. He was a good baby, fat and placid, and she knew that she would miss him almost as much as she would miss Charlie, if her mother took her away from the Fishers.

However, according to Aunty Beryl, this was not likely to happen for some time to come. 'Your mam will move in with us until she's settled,' Aunty Beryl had assured her. 'It ain't as if she could move into No. 2, even if she could afford it, because the Bellises don't show no sign of wanting to move on. Of course, other houses in the court do come up for rent from time to time, but I don't think your mam will want to take on a place of her own for a good while yet . . . mebbe as much as a year. She'll be under the sanatorium for that length of time and they're going to monitor her progress – that means doin' tests every three months, to make sure she's still OK – so, since she's gorra job, she won't be wanting a place of her own as well.'

This explanation had eased the anxiety which Diana had felt over her mother's return; things would not change that much, then. But she was still aware of changes in herself and dreaded that Emmy might try to treat her like a child, not realising that, in her three years' absence, her daughter had grown up.

She and Charlie were better friends now than they had ever been, so she decided to ask him whether he thought her mother would recognise that her daughter was no longer a kid to be ordered about. They were on Great Nelson Street, hovering between the stalls of the outdoor market, hoping that someone would buy a roll of linoleum, which the children might then offer to carry home for the customer. Their experience with the policeman had taught them that adults were not always to be trusted, so now it was half the money up front and the other half on arrival at the customer's home.

'Charlie, I've been wondering . . . it's about me mam coming home . . .'

Charlie listened attentively, as Diana carefully put her worry into words, then gave her a friendly punch on the shoulder. 'She may not realise, just at first, but she'll soon twig things is different, and you most of all,' he said reassuringly. 'Why, when you come to live with us, you couldn't knock the skin off a rice puddin', 'cos you'd never done no real work in your life. But now you're damned nearly as strong as our Lenny. You lug that fat baby about as though he weighed no more'n a kitten, and you can carry bags, when you're doin' the messages, which weigh a ton, or bleedin' nearly, anyway. And look how Bones does what you say! He didn't take no notice when you bawled at him three years ago, 'cos he thought you was just a kid, like Bobby is now. But now when you tell him to sit, his bum hits the ground just as fast as though it were me dad speakin'.'

Diana chuckled. It had not occurred to her before that Bones's obedience was a sign of her own maturity, but she realised, with a small glow of achievement, that Charlie was right. Bones often accompanied her and Charlie on expeditions into the countryside, and when they raided an orchard, or hunted for straying hens' eggs in hedgerows and ditches, she only had to hiss 'Down!' to the dog, and he would instantly obey her, lying still as stone until the danger, whatever it was, had passed.

'Thanks, Charlie; you've made me feel a whole lot better about me mam coming home,' she said humbly. 'I want her back, of course I do. Every night, when I say me prayers, the first thing I pray for is that Mam will get well and come home again. So – so it seems strange that I worry over whether she'll realise I've changed . . .'

'No it don't,' Charlie said bluntly. 'Just so long as you know that she'll have changed, too. After you'd gone to bed the other night, I heard Mam and Dad talkin'. Mam was saying that Aunty Em had lived a kind of unnatural life for three years, with no responsibilities, no work, and precious little fun, either. She said the nurses and that had told your mam when to sneeze, and it weren't goin' to be easy for Aunty Em to make her own choices, make her own decisions. Mam were sayin' we should all have to help Aunty Em as much as we could, and Dad said . . .' He hesitated, staring thoughtfully at his feet, and Diana realised that he was mentally editing what his father had said. She punched him on the arm and grinned.

'Go on, then; just what *did* your dad say?'

Charlie grinned, too. 'He said it were a good job Emmy was so pretty, because he didn't fancy she'd be a widow for very long,' he admitted. 'He didn't mean it nastily. It were a sort of joke.'

'Well, he were out there,' Diana said roundly, feeling a sort of bitter taste at the back of her throat. 'My mam's been locked away in that sanatorium seeing no one but old Mr Mac for the past three years, so it isn't likely she's thinking about marrying again.'

Charlie stared at her. 'Seeing no one?' he said slowly. 'Wharrabout that Carl Johansson, eh? And Johnny Frost? Or don't you count them?'

Diana frowned. 'But I told Mr Johansson she'd moved away, and Mam's never mentioned that he visits, when your mam and I go down to see her. And who's Johnny Frost?'

'Diana, I know you're supposed to be real clever an' I know you're top of your class, but sometimes I wonder about you,' Charlie said. 'You knew Mr Johansson wrote letters to your mam, you must have done! So you must have known that he'd find out you'd told him lies.'

Diana felt her face grow hot. 'If I told a bit of a – a fib, it was for my mother's sake, because having visitors, particularly visitors like that horrible Johansson man, was bad for her,' she said haughtily.

'But you haven't answered my question. Who's Johnny Frost?'

'Oh, he and your man were going to get married back in the old days, only then your mam met your dad and dumped Johnny,' Charlie said baldly. 'He left the 'Pool and started up a hotel or something in Llandudno. He's been visiting her for ages and ages.'

'I don't *believe* you!' Diana shrieked, suddenly losing her temper. 'You're the liar, not me, Charlie Fisher. You're making up stories to frighten me. And how would you know, anyway?'

'Don't you dare call me a liar, you nasty kid,' Charlie said wrathfully. 'You don't think twice about lyin' – look what you said to Mr Johansson – but I've been brought up different. As for how I know, it's because I stay up later'n you lot. And half the time Mam and Dad forget I'm there and talk pretty free, so put that in your pipe and smoke it!'

'Then your mam and dad are liars, if they think my mam would even dream of marrying again,' Diana yelled. 'Why, I've been visiting the sanatorium for three whole years and Mam's never said a word about either of those fellers. If they've been visiting her – *if*, I say – then it's just as friends, which is why she's not mentioned them to me. You're wicked, Charlie Fisher, to try to frighten me. I'll tell your mam of you.'

Charlie laughed scornfully. 'My mam believes in tellin' the truth, unlike some,' he said. 'And what's wrong with your mam marrying, anyroad? No one could be happier than my mam and dad . . . don't you *want* your mam to be happy?'

For a moment, Diana, quite literally, saw red. She told herself that of course she wanted her mother to be happy, but thought that Emmy should need no one but her daughter to achieve such a state. At the same time, self-knowledge insisted on creeping in. She, Diana, wanted all Emmy's attention and affection for herself – had she not been forced to do without it for three years? – and did not mean to share her mother now with anyone. And here was Charlie, looking smug and self-satisfied, accusing her of lying and ruining her mam's chance of happiness. Diana gave a growl of pure rage and flew across the short distance which separated them. She slapped Charlie's face hard and then went for him, a small tornado of fury intent upon doing as much harm as she could before he began to defend himself.

So far as Charlie was concerned, the attack must have been completely unexpected, for he staggered back, colliding with the corner support of the nearest stall. It rocked, tilted crazily, and then collapsed, partially burying Charlie under rolls of linoleum whilst Diana stood back, suddenly appalled by what she had done. Her wretched temper! She had been Charlie's pal for ages, and now what must he think? Charlie, red-faced, was struggling out from under, revenge in his expression. He would probably have thumped her despite his being so much older had not the stallholder's wife interfered. She was a fat, good-humoured woman, with apple cheeks and soft brown hair plaited into a coronet on top of her head. She grabbed Diana, lifted her off her feet and carried her behind the stall, where she sat her down on a tall stool and told her to stay where she was until she'd come to her senses.

'I dunno what your young friend said to annoy you, but there ain't never no excuse for behaving like a wildcat,' she said severely. 'It ain't as if he could really fight back, because he's a good bit older and bigger'n you and I 'spec his mam's telled him young fellers don't hit girls. Now what were the trouble about, eh? One minute you were chattin' away, friendly as you like, and the next you flew at him an' all hell broke loose. Well?'

Diana stared sulkily at her feet. She was deeply mortified, for she knew the woman had spoken nothing but the truth, but feeling thoroughly ashamed of the way she had behaved did not, unfortunately, let her off the hook. She looked at the woman through eyelashes still wet with tears of temper and said, sulkily: 'He called me a liar, and I'm not! And he said I'd been badly brought up – that's not true, either. He – he says my mam might marry again . . . oh, I hate him, I hate him!'

'It sounds to me as though you've got yourself in a right state for no real reason,' the woman said, looking very hard at Diana's hot and tear-swollen face. 'I seen you and that young feller here often and often, trying to earn a few pennies by carrying linoleum home for me customers. Now, are you going to apologise to your pal? 'Cos he's doin' his best to help Alfie – that's me husband – set things to rights and if there were any justice it ought to be you doin' it, because it were you started the whole row off, I see'd you.'

Diana slid off the stool, fished a hanky out of her knicker leg and rubbed her face dry with it. Then she said: 'I'm really very sorry I made such a mess of your stall, missus, because I didn't mean to. And I shouldn't have smacked Charlie's face; I know my mam would say it wasn't a ladylike thing to do. I'll give a hand with tidying up the mess – though most of the work's already been done – but I'll never forgive Charlie for the things he said. Not if I live to be a hundred.'

'You won't live to be twenty if you don't curb that temper,' the stallholder told her, though there was a twinkle in her eye. 'D'you realise the weight of some of those rolls of lino? Your pal might easily have been knocked unconscious . . . even killed. When I saw him go down, and the rolls crash on top of him, me heart were in me mouth. Ah, here comes your pal; what say you shake and make up?'

Under the woman's eagle eye, Diana grudgingly held out her hand and shook Charlie's, though she avoided his eye.

'I'm awful sorry, Charlie, only . . . only you upset me,' she said in a small, gruff voice. 'You're me pal, but – but you did say my mam hadn't brought me up right. Only I never meant . . . if you'll say sorry for that, I'll say sorry for hitting you.'

This seemed to her downright handsome, but Charlie was looking at her with narrowed eyes and she could tell that apologising was the last thing on his mind. But he said, grudgingly, that he was sorry if he'd upset her and then the two of them set off in the direction of the court, Charlie marching ahead and Diana dragging along behind him, head bowed.

When they were well clear of Great Nelson Street, Charlie spoke. 'I didn't mean to get your goat an' make you lose your temper,' he said gruffly. 'But it's no use pretendin' your mam hasn't been seein' fellers in the sanatorium because she has, so there is a chance she's thinkin' about marriage.'

Diana sighed heavily. 'You may be right, Charlie,' she admitted after a long pause. 'But I don't think you are. So don't let's talk about it. I'm sorry I hit you and I'm sorry I knocked you into the lino stall. I wonder what Aunty Beryl's got for our tea.'

Chapter Thirteen

Emmy came home on a wild autumn day, with a gale roaring up the Mersey and tearing the leaves off any trees in its path. She was supposed to be brought by ambulance, but Dr Masters had said, bluntly, that he did not think it was a good idea. 'The ambulance is old and the springs are worn,' he had told her. 'A long journey in that vehicle will shake your bones into splinters, very likely. No, you'll be best getting a friend or relative to come down on the train and accompany you back. What about your sister Beryl? She seems a sensible woman and won't let you overdo it, I'm sure. Write to her, Mrs Wesley, and tell her what I've said. I'm sure she'll be happy to oblige us both.'

Emmy had smiled to herself, remembering how she had lied to everyone at the sanatorium about her relationship with Beryl because, in the early days, patients were only supposed to be visited by relatives. The fiction, however, had stuck and everyone still believed that she and Beryl were sisters. So now she agreed to write to Beryl and was not at all surprised when her friend announced that she would catch the earliest train possible and then accompany her back to Liverpool.

After all, Beryl had written, *since you'll be staying with us in Nightingale Court, it makes sense for me to come and fetch you. If you have a great deal of luggage, I'd best bring Charlie to give a hand, but I won't keep*

Diana out of school, since she's planning a bit of a surprise for your first day back home (only don't tell her I said anything or she'll be as stiff with me as she is with Charlie)!

The last remark had surprised Emmy. Diana's letters were always full of Charlie, and when she visited the sanatorium his name seemed to be constantly on the tip of her tongue. However, children were always falling out and then falling in again; probably, by the time she got home, Diana and Charlie would be the best of friends once more.

Johnny Frost had offered to hire a car and take her all the way to Liverpool in it, and the last time Carl had visited he had made a similar offer, but she had turned them both down. She had told Mr Mac of both invitations and he had smiled, but then said that Dr Masters was a sensible man. 'Follow his advice and you won't go far wrong,' he had said. He had cocked an eyebrow at her, twinkling. 'You don't want to go giving anyone false hopes, do you?'

So now, here was Emmy outside Lime Street Station with Beryl lugging her large suitcase beside her, heading for the nearest tram stop. She found the traffic extremely daunting after spending three years in a sleepy seaside town and as an enormous lorry thundered past, making her flinch, she wondered whether she would ever get used to the noise and bustle again, for the pavements were teeming with people as the roads teemed with traffic.

The tram queue was a long one and the suitcase heavy. Beryl had placed it on the pavement and was beginning to say something to her friend when Emmy heard herself hailed by a familiar voice. She turned, startled, and saw Iris, one of the waitresses from Mac's, gesturing to her.

'I've been sent to fetch you back 'ome in a taxi,'

Iris shouted, raising her voice above the clatter of passing traffic. She ran towards them and began to heave at the case, giving Beryl a much needed hand with its weight. 'Come on!'

Thus it was that Emmy arrived back at the court in style. She climbed out of the taxi, with Iris's help, and stood for a moment, gazing under the arch and feeling her heart sink as she did so. She moved hesitantly forward, seeing the blackened walls going up, up and up to meet the 'two penn'orth of sky', as her mother had called it. She saw the filthy paving stones upon which dirty children played, and smelt the indefinable smell of poverty, combining, as it did, the stench from the lavatories at the far end of the court, the milder stink of the crude hen run and the odour of boiling potatoes and cabbage, as well as another, which was that of damp plaster and the crumbling brickwork of which the houses were constructed.

Emmy faltered, suddenly aware that she had travelled a long way from the court, in more than miles, and knowing a sort of dread at the thought of her return. She had struggled and worked to escape it, but it had been there all the time waiting for her, and now the archway loomed like an enormous black mouth, wanting to drag her down and gobble her up. She had the terrifying feeling that if she crossed the threshold now, she would be doomed to live there for ever, would never escape.

Then Beryl gave her a nudge and caught hold of her arm, pulling her forward and under the arch. And now she saw the other side of Nightingale Court as people came streaming out of their houses. Diana came tearing across the paving, in her best dress, her face rosy with excitement and her eyes bright with it. 'Oh, Mam, it's so wonderful to have you back,' she said rapturously. 'They let me off school early 'cos you were coming home today, and I've baked a cake . . . well, come in and you'll see.'

But Emmy was unable to go anywhere until she had been greeted by all the neighbours, many of whom pressed small presents into her hand. At the thought of such generosity from people who, she knew, had a struggle to keep their children fed and the rent paid, Emmy's eyes filled with tears. Her mother had always said it was the court itself which dragged people down, and not the other way round, and now she acknowledged the truth of it. She opened the little packages and knew each tiny ornament, or teaspoon, or little hairclip, had been lovingly chosen, and that its buying would represent a loss to the family involved. She stood on the dirty paving with tears streaming down her cheeks, telling them all that they were too good, too kind, and that they had made this homecoming something which she would never forget. Only then did she almost stumble into Beryl's house. There, the tears rose to her eyes again as she saw the laden table, with the younger Fishers already assembled and Wally beaming at her as he pulled out a chair and pressed her into it, telling her not to be a goose, for crying when you were happy had always seemed to him a daft way to behave, and shouldn't she be rejoicing now, because she was home and, by the look of her, fighting fit?

As soon as they saw Emmy seated, the whole family rushed to their places, the baby on Becky's lap. Beryl had been dragging the suitcase to the foot of the stairs, but now she joined them, smiling at Emmy with such love in her face that Emmy had to struggle not to start crying again. In the three years she had been away, Beryl had had another baby, had looked after her own family, had taken Diana in and treated her like a daughter, and had visited the sanatorium as often as she could, so that Emmy had known herself not forgotten. And now this woman who was better than a sister to her was taking her into her already crowded home without a word – or even a thought – of complaint. I don't deserve any of it, Emmy thought humbly, but oh, I'm so grateful to Beryl and Wally. Mam always said they were the salt of the earth and it's true. I mustn't let them down. I must never let them suspect that coming back to Nightingale Court is like re-entering a nightmare. After all, what was the alternative? The workhouse, I should think – or marriage to a man I didn't love.

The thought astonished her because she had never really allowed it to cross her mind before, but the truth was, she loved neither Johnny nor Carl. Oh, she might love one of them, one day, but not yet. Right now, she loved Diana and the Fishers – especially Beryl – but this was a very different sort of love from that which she and Peter had shared. She *might* love again, one day – she hoped she would – but though it had been five years since Peter had died, the time was not yet ripe.

'Well, Mam? Wharrabout the cake then? I made it all meself, honest to God I did, though Aunty borrowed the special tins off Taylor's and gave me a bit of a hand with the writing. D'you like it? Do you honestly?'

Diana's voice was shrill with excitement and Emmy looked properly at the cake for the first time. It was made to look like a castle, with four short, squat towers, one on each corner, a moat, which had been made with blue icing, and a candle in each tower. Between the towers, in rather wobbly writing, were the words, 'Welcome home, Emmy.'

'*Do* you like it, Mam?' Diana asked again. 'I couldn't put Mam because that would have meant that the cake was just from me, and it's from everyone, really. Uncle Wally bought the icing sugar and the candles and the boys carried it down to the baker's to have it cooked, because it was too heavy for me.'

'It's a wonderful cake; indeed, it's a wonderful tea,' Emmy said, trying to keep her voice steady. 'Oh, shrimps, and mustard and cress, my two favourites! Beryl, you've thought of everything.'

'Well, Diana shares your passion for shrimps so she went down to St John's Market and bought them before coming home after school,' Beryl said. 'Get stuck in, everyone!'

Despite a good many unspoken fears, Emmy settled easily into the Fisher household. She helped Beryl with gentle tasks such as darning socks, mending shirts and helping with food preparation, though Beryl kept an eagle eye on her, clearly determined that her friend should not overdo it. She was sharing a room with Diana and Becky, and after three years of Wisteria Ward she was not disturbed by the younger girls. They got up early, so that they could help Beryl before going off to school, but for the first week Emmy lay in until the house was quiet, and then joined Beryl in the kitchen. No matter how hectic the morning had been, Beryl always seemed calm and in control, pulling the kettle over the fire, giving the porridge a stir, preparing the baby's feed, or clearing away the family's breakfast things. Often, she settled Emmy in a chair near the fire and got her to feed Freddie whilst she moved quietly about her business, and Emmy was grateful for a peaceful start to each day, knowing that she was slipping back into normal life far more easily thanks to her friend's thoughtfulness.

Though she would never have said so aloud, Emmy was anxious about her return to work, and when she woke up on what was to be her first day back at the restaurant, she felt quite sick with apprehension. She dressed carefully, in a black pleated skirt and jersey, clipped on white collar and cuffs, and went downstairs. Beryl insisted that she swathed herself in a large apron before sitting her down at the table with a cup of hot, strong tea. 'Drink that slowly,' she commanded. 'Then eat the porridge.'

'I don't think I could eat a thing,' Emmy said uneasily. 'I never thought I'd be scared to go back to work, because I always enjoyed being there, but I'm scared now. Aren't I stupid?'

'Yes you are,' Beryl said, grinning at her. 'But I reckon anyone would be scared in your position. You've had three years away from it, remember, so it'd be a rum go if you *weren't* scared. But I'm comin' with you and I'll deliver you right to the door, so don't think you can cut and run, madam!'

Emmy was so grateful that she could have wept, but instead she began to eat the porridge. Very soon, she and Beryl were at the restaurant. 'There, you see, the place hasn't changed a bit, has it?' Beryl said robustly, giving her a push towards the door. 'I say, there's quite a reception committee waitin' to welcome you, so I won't come in. But I'll be here prompt at one o'clock to take you back home again.'

'Oh, Beryl, you can't . . . you mustn't . . . you're so busy!' Emmy gabbled. 'I'm not a child, you know.

Why, you're behaving as if this was my first day at school and I was about five years old!'

Beryl laughed and gave Emmy's shoulder a reassuring pat. 'I know, I know, but just for a couple of days I'd feel happier if I were with you. Some folk are awful pushy, and though you're much better, much stronger, you're not used to being shoved around. So I'll be here at one o'clock, an' mind you don't keep me waitin'.'

She turned away and made off along the pavement at a brisk pace. Emmy opened the door of the restaurant. Mr Mac was there and old Mrs Mac, their faces wreathed in smiles, and most of the staff Emmy remembered came hurrying over to greet her. Ena Symons gave her a hug and begged her to visit old Mrs Symons as soon as she felt well enough to do so. 'My mother has been really grateful to Diana for popping in from time to time,' she said. 'We realised that Mrs Fisher did not feel she could let Diana spend so much time in Raymond Street, but she raised no objection to the children doing our messages when they did hers, nor to Diana and Charlie keeping Mam company from time to time. They even took her out in her wheelchair to have a bit of an airing and see the shops; we both appreciated it.'

Emmy had heard all about this from Beryl, and promised to go and see old Mrs Symons as soon as she could. Then she was led to the cashier's cubicle, settled in one of the two chairs with a cup of tea, and bidden to watch old Mrs Mac until she was tired, when, Mr Mac said severely, she was to say she had had enough for the day.

Emmy declared that she was scarcely going to be tired out by watching other people work but, in fact, by one o'clock she felt as though she, and not the waitresses, had been running back and forth, attending to the customers. Mrs Mac looked at her shrewdly, a smile on her wrinkled face. 'You're wore out, because you ain't used to it,' she said kindly. 'What's more, I reckon you'll find it easier when you've got the cash desk to yourself. Now, off with you . . . I see your pal's hoverin'.'

After three days, Emmy realised that she did not need any more help or instruction from Mrs Mac. Mr Mac usually came over to speak to her once or twice during the day, so as soon as an opportunity occurred she told him that she would like to try the morning shift alone. He gave her a broad smile, his dark eyes twinkling. 'Mother thought you were ready,' he told her. 'She'll not be sorry; did you know she was a very skilful needlewoman? She's embroidering an altar cloth for the church and is keen to get on with the work. But if you need her, she'll be down in a trice.'

Next day, Emmy entered the cashier's cubicle almost shyly, wondering how she would get along, for old Mrs Mac knew most of the customers and chatted to everyone as she added up their bills, took their money and gave them their change. In fact, Emmy got on very well indeed, and at the end of her shift she handed over to the old lady feeling that she had done a good job. Naturally, she did not balance the books since that was done at the end of each working day, but she checked all her figures and the money in the till and they tallied correctly.

Beryl was no longer calling for her, so when Mr Mac strolled part of the way home with her chatting about the business it seemed a natural and pleasant conclusion to her shift and she arrived home positively glowing with achievement.

The days passed, some wet, some fine, some busy, some slow, with Emmy's confidence strengthening all the time. The job kept her mind active and her body rested and this was exactly what Dr Masters had wanted for her. She was not yet working on Saturdays since Mr Mac employed several Saturday girls and one of the waitresses, Liz, acted as cashier on that day, and Johnny Frost came home some weekends, ostensibly to visit his mother, but really to see Emmy.

Diana had not met him before and was a little wary when her mother introduced him. He announced that he had come to take Emmy out into the country for a day's relaxation and invited Diana to go along with them, if she had nothing better to do.

The invitation was lukewarm, but Diana turned it down so decisively that Emmy saw Beryl turn away to hide a smile. They were all in the Fisher kitchen, discussing their plans for the weekend, and Diana meant to go fishing with Lenny – she and Charlie were still scarcely speaking – taking a tram to Seaforth for a day's sport.

So life in the court began to fall into a pattern. Emmy saw Carl every three weeks or so and always enjoyed his time at home. He was good company, taking her dancing or out for a meal, and did not coddle her, as Johnny tended to do. Carl no longer bothered to invite Diana to accompany them and it was clear to Emmy that Diana's dislike of the young officer had not altered. Surprisingly, the child did not dislike Johnny Frost, seeming to accept him more as an old friend of her mother's than as a suitor, though Johnny's dog-like devotion was plain to everyone else.

Life under the Fisher roof continued comfortably, with Emmy able to undertake more and more small tasks. Only one thing made Emmy determined to find a place of her own, and that was the feud between Diana and Charlie. Either they were not speaking at all, or they were bickering, and Emmy realised that this caused tension and was unfair to the rest of the family. She tried speaking severely to Diana but got very little response. 'You don't know the things he said about you and me; if you'd heard them, you'd hate him an' all,' Diana informed her mother succinctly. 'I get along very well with everyone else – Lenny's me pal – so I don't need horrible Charlie.'

'He saved your life when you were a littl'un,' Emmy reminded her daughter. 'You used to follow him everywhere and were probably a real nuisance, but he put up with you. Please, Diana, try to be a bit more thoughtful. You're making Aunty Beryl unhappy.'

'I am not,' Diana said indignantly, but Emmy noticed that her cheeks flushed, even as she spoke. 'One person not speaking to another makes things quieter at teatime, I can tell you.'

Emmy sighed but said nothing more. It was useless arguing with Diana; she would just have to redouble her efforts to find somewhere affordable for rent.

'Emmy! It's wonderful to see you . . . come on, give us a hug.'

Emmy stepped off the train, virtually straight into Johnny Frost's arms. Laughing, pink-cheeked, she gave him a quick hug, but stepped back, shaking her head, when he tried to prolong the embrace. It was a fine day in late March and she was going to the sanatorium for a check-up. Johnny had been coming back to Liverpool to see her most weekends all through the winter, but Emmy knew he would be unable to do so once the holiday season started, and was secretly not displeased at the thought of having some time to herself. Johnny was very good, taking her out for days in the country, always anxious for her welfare and eager to please. At first, she had felt that her Sundays away from the court gave Beryl and Wally more time for their own family, but lately, Johnny's gentle persistence had made her feel a trifle hunted. He wanted to marry her, to take her away from the bustle of a big city, back to Llandudno where the fresh sea breeze was always with them.

'You loved me once,' he had said wistfully only the previous Sunday. 'Why can't you love me again?'

Emmy wondered this herself; wondered also if she did love him. She was certainly very fond of him, admiring his hard work in the guest house and the fact that he never lost his temper, but was always patient and kind towards herself. Even when she was rather abrupt with him, he never reproached her. Which was why she had agreed to spend a couple of days at the guest house after her next check-up. It would give her a chance to get at least some idea of what living with Johnny would be like.

So now, she tucked her arm in his and let him take her small case, and lead her towards the station entrance. He smiled down at her, his dark eyes liquid with affection. 'I did wonder whether you might turn up with Diana in tow. Of course, I'd welcome her because I think we ought to get to know one another better if—'

Emmy interrupted him hastily. 'Oh, it's term time, don't forget, and anyway, Diana is growing quite useful. Beryl relies on her to take care of Becky when they come out of school. Indeed, she says it's entirely due to Diana that Becky is learning to read. They never thought she would, you know, but Diana reads her stories very slowly, moving her finger along the lines so that Becky can see the written word and hear the spoken one simultaneously. Everyone is most awfully pleased . . .' She stopped speaking as Johnny shook her arm reprovingly, aware suddenly that she had been chattering in order to stop him completing his sentence with the words 'if we're going to get married'.

'It's all right,' he said quietly. 'I weren't going to propose again . . . well, not exactly, that is. I reckon you know how I feel, Emmy, and you've got to remember that with me, your health comes first. I know Carl takes you racketing round dance halls, theatres, music halls and the like, because that's the sort of life he enjoys. I'm not saying he's wrong, I'm just statin' a fact. But I've changed since I came to live here. I like long country walks, a quiet stroll along the pier of an evening to watch the sunset, a sea-bathing summer and a trip to the theatre at Christmas, when the panto's on.'

They had been walking down Madoc Street and were now crossing into Chapel Street, and Emmy looked at the neat, clean houses whose brickwork was unsullied by soot, at the gardens where already tulips were coming into bud and the daffodils and narcissi were in brilliant bloom. Even the trees which lined the street were big with bud, their branches swaying gently in the spring breeze. Johnny was quite right, Llandudno would be a good deal healthier, both for herself and for Diana. And she was fond of Johnny, but being fond did not mean you could live with a person.

And that's what these few days are about, she reminded herself, as Johnny swung open the gate of the guest house. They say you have to live with someone to know them; well, I'm a very lucky girl, because I shall be living in the same house as Johnny without having to go through a ceremony of marriage first!

Next morning, Emmy went up to the sanatorium. Johnny had wanted to go with her; however, Emmy had been polite but firm. 'You would be very much in the way, my dear old friend,' she said, and saw him wince, without feeling particularly guilty at the phrase. 'A good many girls who were in the sanatorium when I was attend this clinic. We talk amongst ourselves, about work, families and so on, which takes our minds off all the tests and X-rays we are there to undergo. I've arranged to meet Violet outside the station and we'll walk up together, so I shan't be on my own for one moment. Besides, I heard you telling your Aunt Carrie that you would put up some more shelves in the pantry; why not do that today?'

She had to admit that Johnny took his dismissal very well. He smiled, said he quite understood and agreed that he would go down to a local sawmill and purchase the shelving, and would probably actually erect it over the course of the day. Then he waved her off with a cheerful face and Emmy, who was greatly enjoying her stay in the guest house, strolled up to the station feeling at peace with the world. He was nice, was Johnny! Perhaps she would make him a happy man and marry him, live in this beautiful clean town, send her child to the local school. She would learn Welsh, become a member of the WI, bake bread as good as Beryl's and have half a dozen children.

Her thoughts broke off at this point, making her laugh aloud. How absurd she was being! If she wanted to bake bread as good as Beryl's, marriage to Johnny was not a necessity. But it might be fun . . . no, not fun precisely. It might be a satisfying sort of life and perhaps, if they were married, love might follow.

She reached the station and consulted the clock. She was ten minutes early, so she went on to the platform and sat down on a green-painted wooden seat to wait. She reminded herself that Johnny was not the only man eager to marry her. Carl now knew about Johnny since Diana, the little wretch, had seen fit to inform him that he had a rival. Carl had been at first incredulous, and then sulky, accusing her of deliberately deceiving him. But his ill-humour had passed and they had settled back into their old routine of having many outings and pleasure trips during his time in port, and writing to each other in between. Carl had met Johnny one Sunday, when they had both come visiting, and Emmy thought that this encounter, oddly enough, had calmed the fears of both parties. Johnny had said afterwards that Carl was a grand feller but not, he thought, ideal husband material. 'But mebbe I'm wrong,' he had added hastily, clearly reading the disagreement in her expression. 'Mebbe he'll settle down to quiet evenings at home and so on.'

Carl, for his part, said that Johnny was delightful, though obviously not an ambitious man. 'If you were to marry him, you would be in partnership with the aunt more than with him, because from what he was telling me, she's the one with drive and ambition,' he had said shrewdly. 'And my old mother used to say, "Two women into one kitchen doesn't go."' He had laughed at her expression. 'Don't be cross, my little cherry pie! I am only saying what you must have thought. Johnny is a grand fellow, but he isn't going to set the world on fire.'

Emmy had said, tartly, that she did not want a man likely to start a conflagration and Carl had laughed and given her a squeeze. 'Well, Carl Johansson is going places, going right to the top,' he had said exuberantly. 'And I'll take my wife and family with me, you mark my words.'

So now, waiting for the train, Emmy mulled over what Carl had said, and decided he was mistaken in one thing, at any rate; Johnny's Aunt Carrie was a delightful woman with whom Emmy would be glad to share not only a kitchen, but a life. She was generous and tolerant, and it was plain that the girls who worked in the guest house thought very highly of her. Mr Mac often said that he valued the good opinion of his staff. Most workers grumbled about their boss from time to time, but Emmy knew that everyone connected with Mac's liked and admired their employer, so that the restaurant was a pleasant place for both staff and customers.

Her reverie was interrupted by a train, steaming to a halt alongside the platform. The quiet vanished as doors opened and passengers erupted from the carriages, Violet amongst the foremost. Emmy jumped to her feet, thinking how well her friend looked. She had put on quite a lot of weight but it suited her, and her smile and the warmth of her embrace convinced Emmy that Violet felt as well as she looked.

'Emmy!' she squeaked. 'Wharra lovely coat . . . and I like the little hat 'n' all.' She drew back a little to display her own garments. 'I know all redheads go for green, but I thought I'd have a change. What d'you think?'

Violet was wearing a navy blue coat with an emerald green scarf tucked in the neck, and her navy blue hat was trimmed with green feathers. Emmy, in the blue which matched her eyes, admired her friend's outfit and received Violet's admiration in return. Then the two of them made their way out of the station and headed towards Hill Terrace and the sanatorium.

Diana and Charlie had made up their difference and were now hand-in-glove once more. Their coldness towards one another had lasted until Christmas, when Emmy had warned her daughter that she was going to receive a present from her small enemy.

'I don't want it; I hate him and I want to go on hating him,' Diana had said fiercely. 'He's a horrible boy. He said beastly things, and I like Lenny best, anyway.'

'You are making life difficult for everyone and Charlie's sensible enough to realise it,' Emmy had said quietly. 'If you continue with this absurd feud, then I shall have to move out, because it's not fair on Beryl. As you know, we have very little money, but I could afford a bedsit over one of the shops. If you persist in being enemies with Charlie, then that is what I shall have to do.'

It had brought Diana up with a jolt. She had stared at her mother, unable to believe that Emmy would do such a thing. Diana adored living with the Fishers and knew that Emmy did, too. She thought about moving out, living in a cramped, one room flat over a shop, toiling up and downstairs carrying water, a slop bucket, all their food. Her pride had kept the feud with Charlie going, but deep down inside her she still liked Charlie very much. And since he had bought her a Christmas present, he must still like her too. She looked up at her mother, wondering what was expected of her.

'Well, young lady? What's it to be? War or peace?'

Diana giggled. 'Peace, I suppose,' she had said, with assumed reluctance. 'Only I'm not telling him I'm sorry, because it's *him* that ought to say that.'

'All you have to do is buy him a Christmas present. I'll give you some money,' Emmy had said. Her voice had sounded lighter, almost gay, and Diana realised that the quarrel between herself and Charlie had seriously worried her mother, and felt guilty.

'Right, but I'll buy it with my own money, thanks very much,' Diana had said decisively. 'I'll get him something really nice. The only thing is . . . well, I want to buy presents for everyone and I don't have an awful lot of money saved, because me and Charlie used to earn together and you can't earn money with someone when you aren't speaking to them.'

Emmy had smiled. 'Very well, you buy Charlie's present from your money and I'll give you some money to buy the rest of your presents,' she had said. 'We'll start our shopping first thing tomorrow morning.'

Diana had agonised over the present and had ended up buying Charlie a proper fishing rod. It had cost her every penny she possessed, but his pleasure had been worth it. They had grinned sheepishly at one another as they exchanged presents on Christmas morning – Charlie had bought Diana a pink woolly hat and matching scarf – and ever since had reverted, with secret relief, to their old friendship.

The previous day, Charlie had accompanied Diana

and Emmy to the station, carrying Emmy's weekend bag, though why it should be called a weekend bag, he had said, when she was travelling mid-week, he had no idea.

But right now, school was over and supper was not yet ready, so Charlie and Diana decided to take a stroll along the Scottie. They intended to go to the Penny Rush at the Commodore – the Commy, as they called it – on Saturday, and this necessitated earning at least fivepence, and probably eightpence since they usually took care of the younger ones at weekends, so that Beryl might have a bit of peace and quiet about the house.

Scotland Road was a good place for a kid to earn a copper or two. As they walked, Diana looked rather doubtfully up at the sky above. 'There's an awful lot of cloud about,' she said dolefully. 'Oh, Charlie, I do hope Mam got on all right at the sanny this morning. But she won't know the results of the tests and things yet, of course. She said they'll tell her by letter. Only I do think she looks better, don't you? She's working pretty well full-time at Mac's now, but your mam sees that she comes straight home and rests until supper time, so she doesn't get over-tired.'

Charlie grunted. 'She's doing pretty well,' he agreed. 'Shall we try Ellen Turtle? She sometimes lets us have orange boxes.'

'Ye-es, I suppose we could,' Diana said reluctantly. 'But selling chips is such hard work, especially when the weather's fine, and folk aren't having fires in the parlour. I'd rather cart someone's shopping, or deliver parcels, or run messages for the shop ladies.'

'It's a bit late for running messages because the shop ladies mostly want us to fetch them in something for their dinners,' Charlie pointed out. 'Tell you what, we could try the ironmonger's. Old Mr Brown got me counting nails last time I went in. He don't pay much, but it's better'n a slap in the belly with a wet fish.'

'All right, we'll give it a go,' Diana conceded, after some thought. 'It's not a good time of year for earning money, is it, Charlie? There aren't many gardens round here, so we can't offer to weed flower beds, you can't sweep up leaves in March, because there aren't any, and it isn't Christmas, so folk don't need a hand with carrying huge marketing bags.'

Charlie agreed that this was so, and presently they reached the hardware store. They went inside cautiously, for Mr Brown was a man of uneven temper and was as likely to bawl them out as to offer them a job, but they were in luck. The old man was standing behind his counter, staring balefully at a huge tea chest. He looked up as they entered and his expression brightened. 'Ah, I remember you, young man,' he said, indicating Charlie with a pointing finger. 'Now how about you sorting this little lot out? I ordered three gross of two-inch nails and three gross of one-inch, and they've just copped the whole lot in together, so I don't know whether they've sent me the right amount. How about sortin' them out for me? I'll pay you twopence.'

'Twopence each,' Charlie said, immediately. 'Twopence each is fair, Mr Brown.'

Mr Brown was reluctant, or pretended to be, but gave way quite quickly when Charlie turned back towards the door. 'All right, all right, twopence each,' he agreed. 'I'll give you me little bags so you can sort 'em straight into 'em.'

For a long while, the children squatted round the packing case, counting nails into small brown bags.

It seemed to Diana as though the task would never end, and when they had finished she stood up carefully, glad to ease her cramped knees. She looked distastefully at her hands, which had come out clean and would go home grimy, pocketed the twopence which Mr Brown handed over, and left the shop at a trot, for she had lost the will to work and was secretly frightened that Mr Brown might come up with some other task.

Outside on the pavement, they grinned at one another. 'Only another fourpence to go and we can all go to the flicks and have something over for a bag of sweets,' Charlie said exultantly. 'We've missed supper but I told Mam we were trying to earn money for the Commy, so she'll keep some back for us. Now, what'll we try?'

Diana was tired and would have liked to go home, eat her supper and make for her bed, but she did not wish Charlie to despise her, so she said stoutly: 'Anything you like, Charlie. Only the shops are going to shut soon, and I don't know if we'll get much work now.'

'You're probably right,' Charlie said reluctantly. 'There's always tomorrow evenin', after school . . . oh, I've had an idea! There's a good film on at the Burlington Cinema on Vauxhall Road, so there's bound to be a queue. How are you on cartwheels and handstands?'

Diana snorted. She knew that some of the more agile kids – and the ones who didn't suffer from stage fright – entertained cinema queues, but she did not intend to join *that* band. 'I'm not showing off my knickers to half Liverpool, not for all the money in the world,' she said loftily. 'And don't you go suggesting that we go round the pubs, either, because your mam would kill us if she found out, and so would mine.'

'We needn't go round the pubs. We could just pop into one or two and see if anyone wanted anything doing. We could guide the drunken old wretches home, or – or hold their heads over the drain, whilst they was sick,' Charlie said, ducking as Diana aimed a blow at him. 'Only I do like to get the Penny Rush money sorted, and—'

'And what?' Diana asked, curiously, as Charlie stopped in mid-sentence. He promptly seized her by the arm and swung her round to face the nearest window. 'Look at them – them roses,' he said urgently. 'Who'd have thought anyone would be selling roses in March, eh?'

Diana stared, unbelievingly, into the florist's shop. Why on earth was Charlie suddenly interested in a display of glasshouse-reared roses? Then he made himself clear. 'There's bunches of flowers behind the roses, on the counter,' he said. 'And the shop's still open. Let's go in and see if they want deliverin'.'

Diana agreed but the shop assistant, though kind, was firm. She meant to deliver the flowers herself, on her way home, and needed no help from anyone.

The children emerged from the shop and walked straight into Lenny, who was whistling jauntily and listing heavily to starboard under the weight of a large marketing bag. Charlie seized his arm. 'You goin' home, Lenny?' he asked breathlessly, and when Lenny nodded, added: 'Can you take our Di home with you? Only there's something important I gorra do.'

Diana opened her mouth to protest, but Charlie shook his head reprovingly, gave her cheek a condescending pat and disappeared into the crowd.

Lenny grinned at her. 'Give us a hand with the basket then, queen,' he said. 'I dunno what Charlie's up to, but we'd best do as he says. C'mon.'

Charlie wove his way among the crowds, his eyes intent upon two figures ahead. He kept telling himself that he must have been mistaken, could not have seen what he had imagined. But he knew he would get no peace until he had found out for sure. So he wriggled through the crowds and presently crossed the road, dodging trams, buses and other traffic. Once on the further pavement, he speeded up, running with his head down until he felt it was safe to cross over once again. Then he turned and began to walk back the way he had come. He shoved his hands in his pockets and ducked his head because he had no wish to be seen and recognised, and soon he spotted what he was looking for: two figures, arms entwined, heads close, coming towards him.

It was Carl Johansson and a young woman; she was as blonde as he, with a sharply pretty face and a curvaceous figure, and she was clinging to Mr Johansson's arm and leaning towards him, whilst he looked down at her, laughing, his arm tight round her plump waist. Charlie knew his mother would have taken one look at the girl and pronounced her 'no better than she should be', and he thought she would have been right. Mr Johansson's companion wore a low-cut, off-the-shoulder white blouse. It was a frilly, silly garment and was tucked into the waist of a very short, very tight purple skirt. Her legs were clad in silk stockings and her very high heeled, patent leather shoes were cracked and dusty.

As soon as he had passed them, Charlie turned round again and fell in behind. He knew Mr Johansson had said he wanted to marry Aunt Emmy and pretended she was the only woman he had ever loved. If this was so, what was he doing cuddling a painted tart in the street? He must have known that Emmy was in Llandudno and thought himself, on this one occasion, safe to behave as he probably behaved when his ship docked in New York.

Charlie trotted along for some way, intent upon his quarry, but then a large, fat woman with an enormous marketing bag barged in front of him. He ran into her with such force that he was momentarily winded, and by the time he had recovered there was no sign of the young officer, or his companion.

Charlie made his way back to Nightingale Court in a pensive mood. He was not quite sure why he had decided to hide Mr Johansson's behaviour from Diana. After all, it was far more her business than his, when you came right down to it. But Diana was prejudiced already, regarding Mr Johansson with deep, and Charlie thought undeserved, dislike. If she knew about his yellow-headed companion, she would undoubtedly use such knowledge to make trouble between her mother and the officer and Charlie was not at all sure that this would be a good thing. His mother liked Mr Johansson and thought he would make Emmy an excellent husband. 'Emmy's always had an easy life, and she's always been fussed over and made much of,' Charlie had heard her say, more than once. 'She's not strong. She's gorra weak chest, so she needs someone who can take care of her, and give her all the things she needs. She had a grand life with young Peter; Carl Johansson is going places and he'll take our Em with him. If she marries him, he'll buy her a beautiful house somewhere and she'll never have to work again. Johnny Frost is a nice chap, but he weren't right for our Em years ago – not enough spunk – and to my way of thinking, he ain't right for her now. If she were to wed him and go to that guest house, likely the aunt would move on and Emmy would find herself managing the place, 'cos Johnny could never say boo to a goose. No, if I had the choosing, I'd see her married to a feller who'd take responsibilities off her shoulders, not pile more on.'

Charlie had never known Johnny Frost except as a visitor, and thought him a pleasant, friendly fellow, but he was shrewd enough to realise that his mam and dad, who had known Johnny for many years, were probably right. So, the less Diana knew about Carl's blonde companion, the better.

But Charlie felt that he would have to tell someone. After all, if Emmy decided to marry Carl and he ran out on her, Charlie knew he would blame himself bitterly for having kept his mouth shut. He wondered whether to confide in his mother and would probably have done so had he not, the very next evening, walked slap bang into his father as he returned from school.

Wally greeted his son cheerfully and would have walked on by – he was doing a late shift at the brewery – but on impulse Charlie turned and accompanied him, saying as he did so: 'Dad, I've gorra problem, an' I'd like to know what you think I should do. Can I walk along with you and have a bit of a talk, like?'

Wally smiled at Charlie, looking immensely pleased. 'Of course you can,' he said gruffly. 'Only don't you young fellers usually get your mam's advice? I'll do wharr I can but I don't know as I'm as sensible as your mam, when it comes down to it.'

To say that Charlie was astonished by this somewhat humble attitude was putting it mildly. A member of the superior sex actually admitting that a woman might give better advice than a man was something Charlie had never expected to hear. But he took the plunge anyway, explaining what had happened the previous evening and how he had lost track of the couple after a foolish old woman had impeded his progress with her bulk and her huge marketing bag.

Wally laughed. 'I dare say you walked into her, not lookin' where you were goin', an' never even apologised,' he said reprovingly. 'Still an' all, that ain't the question, is it? You're goin' to ask me whether you should tell your Aunty Em that you see'd her feller with another woman, ain't that right?'

Charlie frowned up at his father, sudden doubts plaguing him. He had thought Mr Johansson was doing the wrong thing; could he have been mistaken? Then he remembered the way Mr Johansson had looked down at the blonde and decided that if he ever saw his father looking at a woman other than his mother in that fashion, he would be disgusted and angry. He said as much and Wally cuffed him good-naturedly on the shoulder. 'Have you axed yourself just what Emmy is doin' in Llandudno?' he asked, with apparent irrelevance. 'Why, you young puddin' head, she's gone there to see Johnny Frost, what were her intended years ago. Then she'll come back to Liverpool and very likely take up wi' Carl – wi' Mr Johansson, I mean. Have you ever heared the expression that what's sauce for the goose is sauce for the gander, young feller?'

'I dunno as I have, but I get your meanin',' Charlie said, after a thoughtful pause. 'You're sayin' that if

Aunty Em can go around wi' Mr Frost one day and this Mr Johansson the next, then why shouldn't Mr Johansson do the same? Is that it?'

'Aye, that's it. You're not such a fool as you look,' Wally said genially. 'So you just keep your gob shut, Charlie, me lad, and let your Aunty Em work out her own salvation. OK?'

'Ye-es, I'll keep me gob shut, then,' Charlie said. 'Only – only I don't think she were a very nice lady, Dad. Not – not respectable, Mam would say.'

Wally sighed. 'No, I didn't think for one moment she'd be respectable,' he admitted. 'But fellers, particularly sailors, sometimes get lonely, and there's girls what'll spend an evening with them, wi'out – oh, hang it, Charlie, leave it up to me. I won't let Emmy get mixed up with a wrong 'un because it'd be us Fishers what'd pick up the pieces when the whole thing went to blazes. Awright?'

Charlie, with a sigh of real relief, said that it was all right indeed, and for the rest of the walk the two conversed happily on such subjects as school, football, and a projected trip into the country to rid a farmer's barn of rats by encouraging Bones to earn his keep, for once.

Wally was relieved that his son was prepared to back off from any sort of confrontation over Mr Johansson's behaviour but he did wish, devoutly, that his son had never set eyes on the officer's little tart. It was all very well to reassure the lad and promise to deal with the affair himself, but despite his words to Charlie, Wally Fisher was a man with a strong sense of right and wrong and he thought, now, that the last thing he wanted was to see young Emmy betrayed. He was also honest enough to admit that he was looking forward to the day when Emmy moved out of Nightingale Court. She was a nice enough girl and Diana, he knew, was a real help to Beryl, but the house was full enough without them and he knew that Beryl worried over her friend and wanted, desperately, to see the younger woman established in a place of her own, with a husband who truly cared for her. He supposed it was perfectly possible that marriage to Emmy would mean that Carl Johansson would never so much as look at another woman again, but in his heart he doubted it. He believed that highly sexed young seamen, who were away from home for long periods, often sought the company of young women and he supposed that there was little their wives could do about it.

Frowning heavily, he contemplated confiding in Beryl, then dismissed the thought. I'll have a word with young Johansson the next time he comes calling, he promised himself. It ain't fair to put any more on Beryl. Yes, I'll have a word wi' the lad. After all, the whole thing is probably completely innocent; she was mebbe the sister of a shipmate, or – or an old friend from before he met Emmy.

Aware that he was deliberately playing the incident down, Wally turned into the brewery.

Carl Johansson came whistling along Waterloo Road, his ditty-bag slung on one shoulder, heading for the great ship which towered above him. The dock was busy since the *Cleopatra* would be sailing next day and was taking on stores, and he had to shoulder his way amongst the dockers, sailors and others making for the gangway.

He had reached the foot of it when someone gripped his shoulder. 'Hang on a minute, young feller,' a rough, masculine voice said in his ear. 'I tried to catch you earlier – I saw you on Burlington Street – but you walk awful fast. Can I have a word?'

Carl swung round, feeling a considerable degree of irritation, which increased when he realised he did not know the person who had accosted him. He was clearly a working man, clad in faded dungarees and large boots, and Carl was about to brush him aside when he remembered having seen his face before, though he did not know where and could certainly not put a name to it. As always when he was vexed or anxious, his accent became stronger, so he was annoyed to hear his own voice saying crossly: 'Vhat do you vant? I do not zink I know you and I am about to board the *Cleo*. I have no time . . .' He had expected the man to step back, perhaps to apologise, but instead the stranger tightened his grip on Carl's shoulder. Carl realised the chap was very strong, and, though he seemed peaceable enough, no First Officer of a transatlantic liner wants to be caught up in a brawl within sight of his ship, especially if it is a brawl he is unlikely to win. Accordingly, Carl turned away from the *Cleopatra* and walked to where a tower of packing cases gave them a little privacy. As soon as the man released his shoulder, Carl said impatiently: 'Well? As I told you, I'm needed aboard. Who are you?'

To Carl's surprise, the man grinned, holding out a huge hand. 'I'm Wally Fisher of No. 4 Nightingale Court, and your young lady lives wi' me and my wife,' he said, shaking Carl's hand vigorously, his grip so hard that Carl almost winced. 'And you're Carl Johansson, First Officer on the *Cleo*, right?'

Carl returned the grin. 'I'm so sorry, Mr Fisher. I didn't recognise you,' he said politely. 'How can I help you? Only I really do have to get aboard fairly quickly . . . I take it Emmy's all right? You are not the bearer of bad news . . . oh, my God, she was spending some time in Llandudno, having tests at the sanatorium . . . don't tell me they think she's worse?'

It was the right thing to say. He had said it instinctively because he loved Emmy and would have been horrified to hear that her illness had returned, but it was still a fortunate remark, because the last traces of Wally's antagonism immediately disappeared. 'Don't worry, she's fine, just fine,' he said hastily. 'It ain't that. The fact is, Mr Johansson, that I feel kind o' responsible for young Emmy, 'cos she's under me roof and me wife treats her like a younger sister, and . . . and . . .'

'And you want to know if my intentions are honourable?' Carl said, annoyance and amusement fighting for first place in his voice. 'I assure you, Mr Fisher, that I mean to marry Emmy just as soon as she gives the word, and when she is my wife, she will have everything her heart could desire. A nice house, proper schooling for the child, a place in society, if that is what she wishes . . .'

'No, it ain't that, either,' Wally Fisher said, and Carl saw the other man's cheeks redden. 'And yet it is, in a manner o' speakin'. If you're so keen on our Em, what was you doin' four days ago, walkin' along the Scottie wi' your arm round some blonde who looked to be a bit of a goer?'

Carl felt his own face grow hot. What a bloody awful fool he had been! But he had known that Emmy had gone to the sanatorium in Llandudno and had thought himself safe to spend time with Cissie Malone. Long before he had met Emmy, he had often visited Cissie, because she was great fun, sweet as honey and – to him, at any rate – generous with her favours. She knew he was no longer interested in her as a companion when he was in port, for he had played fair by her, had told her that he had met the girl he meant to marry. She had taken it in good part, wishing him luck, though he had known there were tears in her large blue eyes, had heard the slightest of trembles in her voice.

He had felt bad about it, of course, but Cissie had always known that theirs was not a serious relationship. He had stayed in her snug little room, knowing that when he went back to sea someone else would take his place. But there had been genuine affection there, though never love; they were both far too sensible for that.

Then, on the first day of his leave, he had met up with Cissie by chance and because he knew he would not be able to see Emmy on this occasion it had seemed harmless enough to pick Cissie up in his arms, give her a smacking kiss, explain the situation and offer to take her out for a meal and then on to the theatre. They had both enjoyed their evening together, talking a little wistfully over old times, but he had refused her invitation to go back to her room and by midnight he had been in the small hotel he favoured and she, he imagined, had gone straight home, for he had given her a very nice present of money to make up for having taken up her evening and prevented her from selling her wares to anyone else – if such had been her intention, of course.

But right now, Wally was staring at him enquiringly, so Carl took a deep breath and decided that truth, in this particular instance, would probably serve him better than a mishmash of lies or protestations. The fellow had seen him with Cissie, had probably witnessed their fond embrace, and was clearly not to be fobbed off with a story of mistaken identity, or a long lost twin brother who resembled him exactly. Instead, he looked hard at Wally. 'Were you ever a seaman, Mr Fisher?' he asked bluntly. 'If so, you must know that one meets many women in many different ports as one's ship sails the world. I met Cissie Malone ten years ago, when I was green as – as the sea, and hungry for a woman – any woman. I didn't earn much money in those days and I was afraid of going with a dockside whore because of . . . how do you say it, catching a disease. But Cissie was young, younger even than myself, and very sweet. Also, she was very poor . . . and kind to a young sailor, far from home. I swear to you, Mr Fisher, that I stopped seeing her when I started courting Emmy. I told Cissie I was in love with someone else and we agreed not to meet again. That was almost five years ago and until the other night I'd not set eyes on Cissie, not even thought about her. Then I walked into her on the Scottie and the years rolled back. And she was my little friend once more. Oh, not in the way she had been; this time, I mean she was literally my friend. We went out for a meal, and we saw the show at the Empire, then we went our separate ways. It never occurred to me that I was doing wrong, but I see now that what I did was unwise, though not, I promise you, in any way sinful.'

He gazed anxiously at his companion and was infinitely relieved when Wally nodded slowly, then clapped him on the shoulder. 'I believe you,' the other man said simply. 'But if I were you, Mr Johansson, I'd make a clean breast of it to Emmy. I don't mean to open me gob 'cos I ain't one to tale-clat, but if you were seen by someone else . . . well, you know how gossip gets around.'

'I'll tell her,' Carl said humbly. As soon as the other man had said the words, he had realised he would have to tell Emmy. After all, he and Cissie had walked openly along the Scotland Road, at one of the busiest times of the day. A great many people must have seen them and he had no wish for Emmy to be hurt by some old shawly giving her the wrong impression. 'Thanks, Mr Fisher. You have been a good friend to me as you are to my Emmy. And I wish you would call me Carl, because I hope we shall be friends when Emmy and I tie – tie the knot.' He grinned deprecatingly. 'Have I got it right? Is that what you would say?'

Wally chuckled. 'Aye, only she's not agreed to tie any knot yet,' he observed. 'And now I'll walk back with you to the *Cleopatra* and then gerron me way. And I wish you luck; our Emmy's a grand lass and Diana's a nice kid.'

The two men shook hands and Carl climbed the gangway, vastly relieved that his new friend had been so honest and understanding. He decided he would tell Emmy all about Cissie – well, not all – the next time he was in port and then dismissed the matter from his mind as he hurried across the deck to report that he was aboard.

'Mam, it's wonderful! It's the most wonderful view I've ever seen! Oh, how I wish Charlie were here. He'd be bowled over.'

It was a beautiful August day, and Diana and Emmy were standing at the very top of the Great Orme, looking out over the Conway sands and the glinting Irish Sea to the dim blue bulk of the mountains beyond.

When Johnny had suggested that Diana might like to accompany Emmy and enjoy a weekend at the seaside, Diana had jumped at the chance. Truth to tell, she had only jumped at it because it had been in her mind to try to put her mother off the thought of marrying Johnny. She loved living with the Fishers, being one of a big family, and having Emmy in the house as well had proved to be a real bonus, but it just happened that this particular weekend Charlie and Lenny were both off to the Wirral, camping with the Boys' Brigade, and had she remained at home Diana knew she would have been expected to take care of the younger ones. She did not mind this in the usual way, but thought it would be rather fun to see the Frosts' guest house, particularly when her mother assured her that she would not be expected to help in any way. 'Johnny's Aunt Carrie – that's Mrs Frost to you – is a grand person; I'm most awfully fond of her and I know she'll see you have a good time,' Emmy had said. 'She never asks me to help when I'm staying there, only I rather enjoy it. Anyway, just you come along and you'll see why I like going to Llandudno so much.'

And standing on the sweet turf at the very top of the Great Orme, Diana thought how right her mother had been. Aunt Carrie had fussed over Diana as though they had been old friends, giving her money for ice creams and donkey rides, and coming down to the beach one afternoon with a wonderful picnic, so that when Diana had emerged from the sea she had been rubbed briskly dry and presented with a positive feast of tiny sandwiches and cakes, followed by strawberry jelly and a large, whipped ice cream. There had been delicious cherryade to drink and little iced biscuits to nibble. In fact, Aunt Carrie had made sure that Diana had a wonderful time and would want to return again and again.

And Johnny, too, had surpassed himself. He had accompanied them to the beach, had donned his own swimsuit and had gone into the water with her two or three times a day during her stay. He had told her that anyone living near water should be able to swim and had patiently instructed her in the art until she was able to stay afloat, and even move forward, in a thoroughly satisfactory manner. He had also helped in the construction of sandcastles and had spent an afternoon with her playing the penny machines on the pier, whilst Emmy watched indulgently.

But now, holding Emmy's hand tightly as she exclaimed over the view, it occurred to Diana that if her mother married Johnny, she, Diana, could live in this beautiful seaside town for ever, if she wanted to. After all, she liked Johnny a good deal better than Mr Johansson, and though Llandudno was a far cry from Liverpool, she was sure that Aunty Beryl would bring the kids down to visit as often as she could. Why, Charlie could actually come and stay! Why should he not? The guest house was huge by Nightingale Court standards, and though it was full to bursting in the summer, Aunt Carrie had told her that they were never full in winter, which was when she and Johnny did any redecorating or repairing that was necessary.

'Well, darling? Have you seen enough? The trams go up and down pretty frequently at this time of year but I'd like to be back in time to help Aunt Carrie get the tables set up for the evening meal . . . if you're ready to go, that is.'

Emmy's voice broke across Diana's thoughts. She smiled at her mother, then they both turned away from the breathtaking view and began to retrace their steps. 'You really like helping Aunt Carrie with the waitressing bit, don't you?' Diana said, as they approached the tram stop. 'I believe you miss being a waitress at Mac's, though you quite like being on the cash desk, don't you? If – if you did decide to marry Johnny, would you want to be the waitress at the guest house?'

Emmy laughed and squeezed her daughter's hand. 'If I married Johnny – and I'm not sure I want to marry anyone – then I certainly wouldn't be a waitress! I suppose I'd be the proprietress . . . and you wouldn't like it if I did Bronwen or Sian out of a job, would you?'

Diana was fond of both the elderly waitresses at Mountain View, who let her help them with small tasks and rewarded her with titbits from the kitchen, so she agreed that she would hate to see them lose their jobs. She frowned at the thought of her mother as proprietress, however, pointing out that this was Aunt Carrie's position. 'And you wouldn't want to do her out of a job either, would you, Mam?' she asked. 'Besides, she works awful hard and knows just how to manage things and who should do what. I don't think you could take over her job, even though you're clever as clever.'

Emmy laughed again but Diana, looking up into her mother's face, saw that Emmy was not really amused, but quite worried by what her daughter had said. However, she said lightly: 'No, no, I wouldn't do Aunt Carrie out of her job for the world. Only – only one day, I suppose she'll want to retire, and then Johnny's wife – whoever that may be – will have to take over. Oh look, here comes the tram! Let's see if we can bag a front seat.'

All the way down in the tram, with its navy blue and gold livery, Diana thought hard. It occurred to her that if she backed Johnny as a prospective suitor, at least she might put Mr Johansson out of the running. It was clear that Emmy liked the thought of living in Llandudno and being the boss of the guest house – Diana thought that proprietress was really just another name for boss – but was not so keen on the work and responsibility involved. And though Llandudno is lovely, and the guest house a beautiful place to live, I don't believe it would be nearly so nice without Aunt Carrie, Diana told herself. But Johnny would be all right as a stepfather because he never tells anyone to do anything. I'd get my own way all the time; I bet he wouldn't even make me go to school if I didn't want to. Yes, if Mam really *must* marry again, then I'd sooner she took easy-going Johnny rather than Mr Johansson, because I've got a feeling he would be a good deal more difficult to handle. I remember my own daddy; he used to tell everyone what they could and couldn't do. Mammy said it was because it was his job on board ship to order the sailors about, and though it was all right from Daddy, I don't want Mr Johansson bossing me.

'You're very quiet, love,' Emmy said, as the two of them descended from the tram and began to walk along Happy Valley Road and into North Parade. 'A penny for your thoughts.'

'Oh, I was just thinking that this would be a beautiful place to live,' Diana said dreamily. 'And I was thinking how nice Johnny and Aunt Carrie are. You do *like* Johnny, don't you, Mam? I bet you like him more than you like Mr Johansson, don't you?'

But on this point, it seemed that Emmy was not to be drawn. She laughed and said that both gentlemen were good company and good friends, and then firmly changed the subject. Diana wondered whether to reopen it, then decided to let sleeping dogs lie. She felt she had planted a seed and intended to nurture it, constantly making small remarks about liking Johnny and disliking Mr Johansson, because, obviously, life would be a good deal easier for Emmy if she married a man her daughter got along with. But I won't overdo it, Diana told herself, as they re-entered the Mountain View guest house. I know what it's like myself when someone keeps telling you to do one thing; you end up wanting to do the opposite. I remember when Mammy nagged me to play shop with Becky; I went off to play kick-the-can with Lenny, and got meself a bruised knee and a cut shin, when really I'd much rather have played shop.

And having decided what she wanted, she promptly became a delightful companion so that everyone thoroughly enjoyed the little holiday and when the time came to go home, both Johnny and Aunt Carrie implored Emmy to bring Diana with her whenever she came to Llandudno.

Chapter Fourteen

It was October and Emmy was sitting on the end of her bed in the tiny attic room she shared with Diana and Becky, painting her nails with shell-pink varnish and trying to concentrate on Carl's impending visit. She had fallen into the habit of spending every other weekend in Llandudno with the Frosts, though she was always careful not to be away when Carl's ship was due to dock. She was fond of both young men and had not been at all shocked when Carl had confessed to a previous girlfriend called Cissie Malone; nor had she minded that Carl had taken the girl to the theatre whilst she had been in Llandudno. However, she had realised it would be wiser to confine her weekends away to times when the *Cleopatra* was not in port. She did not do this because she was afraid of Carl's renewing his friendship with Cissie, but because she knew how eagerly he looked forward to their time together. At least, that was what she told herself. Beryl had chided her with having both young men on a string, but she had assured her friend that this was not the case. 'I've been ill and shut away in the sanatorium for three years, remember,' she had said reproachfully. 'I'm biding my time until I've decided what course the rest of my life is going to take. Is that so wrong? After all, it isn't as though either Johnny or Carl lives just around the corner; I don't see either of them that often.'

But now, sitting on her bed, and listening for Carl's knock at the door, she was beginning to believe that it was time she made up her mind. The fact that Diana was so very keen on her marrying Johnny naturally weighted the scales in his favour, for life would be much easier if Diana approved of her choice. On the other hand, Emmy had taken a good hard look at herself recently, and had been forced to face some home truths. Johnny was a thoroughly nice young man, full of good intentions and certainly very fond of her, but he was not assertive and had very little self-confidence.

However, she had grown to love the town of Llandudno, with its beautiful beach, wonderful views from the Great Orme, and entrancing countryside. She enjoyed helping in the guest house and being fussed over by Carrie Frost, but the more she visited, the more she realised that Johnny himself was quite a small part of the attraction the visits held for her. If I'm honest, she told herself now, am I considering marrying him simply in order to have the sort of life I enjoy? And how long would I go on enjoying it if I was sharing it with a man who sought my approval – and that of his aunt – before every move he made?

It was a pity that Diana didn't really like Carl very much and was so fond of Johnny, or appeared to be so, but the child would be twelve next birthday and one day, in the not too distant future, she would be considering marriage on her own account. If I deny myself a husband to suit Diana, it won't stop her going off when she meets a man of her own, Emmy reminded herself. Beryl always tells me to consult my heart and marry for love – as I did with Peter – and I should do just that. Carl reminds me of Peter, and yet . . . and yet . . . I know! I'll ask Mr Mac if I can have a word. He's far more experienced than I, even though he's never been married himself. Why, all the girls ask his advice when they're in any sort of trouble, and he's been a real friend to me. Though he doesn't know either Carl or Johnny personally, I've talked so much about both of them to him that his advice would be well worth taking.

And when, presently, she heard Carl's knock on the door, she felt a flutter of real excitement and a sort of glow which, she told herself, might be the first stirrings of a warmer feeling towards him, for she was vaguely aware that she did not actually love either Johnny or Carl; not yet, at any rate. However, she knew she had not truly loved Peter until they had been married for several months, so this did not worry her. Love came as a result of being together and getting to know the other person, she concluded. It was awfully romantic to think that love came first, but it was not her experience. Perhaps I'm cold, she thought rather dolefully, since most girls fall in love before marriage and not after. But if I am, men don't seem to notice. Cheered by the reflection, she ran lightly down the stairs.

She reached the front door just as Beryl emerged from the kitchen, dusting flour off her hands. 'It's all right, Beryl,' Emmy said breathlessly, tugging the door open. 'It'll be Carl; the *Cleopatra* is due to dock today, and—' She stopped short, rendered speechless by surprise. The man standing on the doorstep, smiling at her, was not Carl Johansson, nor was it Johnny Frost. It was Mr Mac.

To say that Emmy was taken aback was putting it mildly; she was truly astonished. Mr Mac had sent messengers round to Nightingale Court several times, asking if she could do an extra shift, or some such thing, but he had never actually visited No. 4 before. So now she stood and stared at him, then hastily remembered her manners. 'I'm so sorry, Mr Mac. I was expecting . . . but that doesn't matter. Won't you come in?'

She said the words without the slightest expectation of his accepting the invitation. She thought he would shake his head, deliver some message or other, and leave. Instead, he mounted the three steps, saying as he did so: 'I'm sorry to intrude, Mrs Wesley, but I rather wanted a word.'

'You aren't intruding, Mr Mac,' Emmy said warmly. He was her employer, her boss, yet insidiously, over the years they had known one another, he had become a good and reliable friend. She had no idea why he had come here – it was probably something to do with work – but as she led him into the parlour, she realised that this was the ideal opportunity to ask him for his advice about Johnny and Carl.

So she bade him sit down in one of the rather stiff parlour chairs, and asked him if he would like a cup of tea. Mr Mac shook his head, his eyes twinkling. 'No, thank you, Mrs Wesley. I mustn't take up too much of your time. I came along to tell you that Mrs Chamberlain will be leaving us next week to go and live with her married daughter at Great Sutton. I wondered if you would make a collection amongst the staff – and any customers who know her, of course – and then buy a suitable gift on our behalf. Normally, my mother would undertake this task, but, as you know, she hasn't been too well recently and we thought you would make a very good substitute. You have excellent taste and have known Mrs Chamberlain for some time, so you may be able to choose something to please her.'

Emmy had sat down opposite Mr Mac, and now she agreed readily to undertake the task, though she could not help wondering why Mr Mac had approached her at home rather than at work. Maggie Chamberlain was the charlady who cleaned and washed up in the kitchens and it would have been simple enough for Mr Mac to call Emmy into his office, rather than come all the way round to Nightingale Court.

Mr Mac must have had a shrewd idea of what she was thinking, for he smiled again, then leaned forward in his chair. 'Yes, Mrs Wesley, I could easily have asked you this tomorrow at work, but the fact is, I have another favour to ask. Mother and I have been talking for some time about the possibility of buying a small property in some pleasant suburb. Living over the shop is convenient in many ways, but it is not ideal. Mother is almost seventy-five and is finding the stairs increasingly difficult. What is more, she feels we are both too much "on call" whilst we're living in the flat, and she would love a little garden of her own. I don't intend to retire, but I would certainly hope to work perhaps a three- or four-day week, and to take proper holidays. If we lived in the suburbs, the countryside would not be as inaccessible as it is at present, so we should be able to enjoy days out without feeling that the business would suffer in our absence.'

'But it would – suffer, I mean,' Emmy said, rather wildly. She realised that she could not imagine Mac's without Mr Mac, so to speak. He was a quiet man; she had never known him shout at a member of staff or throw his weight about. He treated delivery boys and important customers with the same quiet friendliness, and even when things went wrong and everyone else was shouting or weeping or bewailing their fate, Mr Mac was cool, calm and collected, often even amused, pointing out that no one is perfect and that problems, if faced without fuss, usually disappeared. 'Even when you're only away for a day, Mr Mac, things seem to go wrong. Though your mother is awfully good, of course,' she added hastily.

Mr Mac smiled. 'Well, naturally, I could scarcely leave the business without appointing a deputy – a sort of manager – to keep the place running on an even keel,' he admitted. 'So I was thinking . . .'

But a ghastly thought had occurred to Emmy. 'Oh, Mr Mac, if you were thinking that I could act as manageress in your absence, then please don't ask me, because I just know I couldn't possibly do it,' she said breathlessly. 'The – the responsibility . . . telling the staff what to do . . . buying ingredients . . . talking to tradesmen . . . I *couldn't* do it; I think it would kill me!'

'Dear me, Mrs Wesley, how you leap to conclusions,' Mr Mac said mildly, but Emmy saw, to her relief, that he was smiling. 'I wouldn't dream of burdening you – or any other young person of your age – with such a job. I've already approached a cousin of mine. He's actually a bookkeeper, and a very good one, too, but the firm which employs him is moving its head office to Manchester and he has no desire to go with it. I haven't told anyone else at Mac's about my plans, nor shall I do so until everything is cut and dried, but I had to tell you because I'm hoping you will accompany me to look over some houses. Monday is a quiet day at Mac's, so I have no qualms about leaving Millie in charge. Young Ada is proving very reliable on the cash desk, and since it is your day off it seemed an ideal opportunity – unless you have some other pressing engagement? Mother says she will be perfectly satisfied with whatever I choose, but I'd feel very much happier to have a woman's opinion before committing myself.' He fished in his pocket and produced a sheaf of papers. 'There are five properties here which sound quite suitable, so if you feel you could give me the pleasure of your company, we will hire a taxi and take a look at them.'

Emmy was in a dilemma. Mr Mac was a true friend and one on whom she could rely, but Carl would be arriving at any moment, expecting her to spend the rest of the day with him. However, the lure of looking over five houses was strong, and to be honest, she suddenly realised that Mr Mac's proposed expedition would be a good deal more relaxing than the sort of outing which Carl enjoyed. Carl would be charming, amusing and energetic, whisking her from place to place, showing off a little, demanding her attention. Mr Mac, on the other hand, would be his usual quiet, companionable self, making no demands, not trying to impress her, simply asking her opinion on each of the houses they visited.

Emmy looked across at Mr Mac and made up her mind. 'What woman could resist the chance to examine another woman's house?' she said gaily. 'Of course I'll come, Mr Mac. If you'll just wait here a moment, I'll tell Beryl and then we can leave.'

She shot into the kitchen and explained, in a hasty gabble, what Mr Mac wanted. Beryl raised her eyebrows, giving a tight little smile as she did so. 'Well, well, well,' she said slowly. 'So what do I say to Mr Johansson when he calls? And suppose you walk slap bang into him as you turn into Raymond Street? I know he couldn't tell you what time he would arrive, but he did say he hoped to be with you today.'

'Oh, Beryl, I know it sounds awful but he *is* my boss and he's been most awfully good to me,' Emmy said, rather reproachfully. 'If you explain to Carl that I've been unexpectedly called away, I'm sure he'll understand. Tell him to come back around seven this evening and we can go to a flick, or a dance, or something. Only – only I wouldn't want to let Mr Mac down.'

'No, I see that,' Beryl acknowledged and Emmy saw, with relief, that her friend was smiling, so she could not disapprove entirely of her choice. 'Off you go then; we'll see you back here around six, I dare say?'

'Yes, I should think so,' Emmy said, heading for the kitchen door. Having explained her actions to Beryl, she felt almost light-headed with relief, though as she and Mr Mac left the house she scuttled across the court with her eyes on the ground, as if Carl might suddenly materialise before her, demanding to know what she was doing when she should have been awaiting his arrival.

Once on Raymond Street, Mr Mac approached a taxi cab standing by the kerb. He explained, as he handed Emmy in, that he had come by cab and had asked the man to wait, and Emmy, settling comfortably on the long leather seat, dismissed Carl from her mind. She would enjoy today, knowing that she was helping Mr Mac, who had so often helped her.

'Well, what a day we've had, Mrs Wesley,' Mr Mac said, as they emerged from the last house and crossed the pavement to the waiting taxi. 'I know you didn't want to stop for lunch but, quite frankly, if I don't have something to eat soon, I shall probably faint away. Tell you what, we'll get down to the serious business of which house – if any – we prefer over a nice high tea. What do you say to that, eh?'

Emmy beamed at him. She had had a marvellous day, though it had embarrassed her at first that every householder had assumed she was Mrs McCullough. But once the first lady had made the mistake, Mr Mac had taken matters firmly into his own hands, introducing Emmy as an old friend who was deputising for his mother, who was, unfortunately, rather poorly. In the third place they had visited, which was a very large house indeed, the owner had been full of questions and Mr Mac had told her, rather shortly, that he was hoping to get married some time in the near future and needed a larger house than the one he had at present. As soon as they were back on the pavement, Emmy had put the inevitable question, for she felt completely at ease with him and had seen the twinkle in his eye as the woman had stared from one to the other.

'And just who are you thinking of marrying, Mr Mac?' she asked roguishly. 'It's the first I've heard of it – my, that would give the girls something to talk about!'

Mr Mac laughed with her. 'Next, you'll be saying you didn't realise my flat was really a house,' he said. 'But why are you so surprised at the thought of my marrying? I'm not *that* old, you know, though I suppose forty-two sounds very ancient to a young girl like yourself, still in her twenties.'

'Not so young any more, alas,' Emmy said, mournfully. 'I'm thirty-two next year so I'm catching you up fast. But I don't know why I'm telling you. As my employer, you must be well aware how old I am.'

'Well, you don't look a day over twenty-nine,' Mr Mac said. 'Now where shall we go for this high tea, eh?'

'You choose. I'm sure you know all there is to know about cafés and restaurants, seeing as you're in the business yourself,' Emmy said, rather guardedly. She did hope that Mr Mac would not choose somewhere in the centre of town where they might bump into Carl. Of course, she had every right to go out with Mr Mac, particularly as Carl had been unable to tell her at what time of day he would visit her, but she still felt rather guilty; she had been happy enough in the past to wait for him, knowing that he would be along eventually. She supposed she should have refused the invitation to high tea, but she was very hungry and anyway she still wanted to consult Mr Mac about Johnny and Carl. What better time would there be to put her problem before him? It was difficult to talk personally at work, and anyway Emmy's problem had nothing to do with the restaurant. Accordingly, she agreed to let him take her to his favourite tea rooms, and explained that she had a problem which she wanted to discuss with him.

So when the taxi headed away from the city centre and out towards the Wirral, Emmy suffered only the slightest pang of conscience. She might be later back than she had anticipated but the brilliant autumn foliage on the trees, and the soft golden light as the sun sank in the sky, made the trip a memorable one. She and Mr Mac chatted quietly about the merits and demerits of the houses they had seen and, when asked for her opinion, Emmy gave it frankly. 'They say a girl has to kiss a lot of frogs before she finds her prince,' she remarked sagely. 'And by the same token, you'll have to see a lot more houses before you make up your mind. The first two places we saw were totally unsuitable, you said so yourself. They were cramped and overlooked, with back yards instead of gardens. And the third . . . well, it had been let go and the smell of damp in the bedrooms was enough to put anyone off. The one in Cecil Road out at Seaforth was quite nice, but you thought there was a problem with the drains, didn't you? And the last one would have been all right only the kitchen was downright poky and they'd not installed a bathroom.' Emmy looked curiously about her as the houses grew further and further apart. 'Where are we going, Mr Mac?' She laughed. 'I hope you aren't aiming to kidnap me, or send me off to South America for the white slave trade, because I told Beryl I'd probably be home by six.'

As she spoke, the taxi drew to a halt in a pretty village, where the houses crowded close to the main street, many of them very old, some with bow windows and others with plate glass. Emmy looked out and saw that the nearest cottage had a sign over the window which read: *The Lilacs – Miss Ethel's Tea Rooms*. Mr Mac climbed out and went round to open the passenger door. He indicated the tea rooms with a jerk of his head. 'I can't see Miss Ethel as a part of the white slave trade,' he said, smiling broadly. 'And I don't think she belongs to a kidnap gang, either. But she does make the most delicious parkin, as well as the best scones I've ever tasted.'

Presently, Emmy and Mr Mac were seated at a window table whilst a neat little waitress, in a flowered dress and a frilly apron, trotted to and fro, carrying a heavily laden tray and placing all manner of dainties on the highly polished oak table. There was a set high tea which started off with poached eggs on toast, surrounded by crisply curling bacon, and included a plate full of tiny sandwiches with a variety of fillings, finishing up with home-made cream cakes and the famous parkin. Emmy sighed with admiration; all the china was Royal Albert and the cutlery was silver-plated and gleaming. This was the sort of place to which Peter had introduced her, years ago. She smiled across at her companion and took a sip from her teacup. 'This is absolutely lovely,' she said appreciatively. 'Doesn't it make you want to own something similar, Mr Mac? After all, there's nothing you don't know about catering and I'm sure you could run a place like this standing on your head.'

Mr Mac laughed. 'Look around you,' he invited. 'I couldn't afford to run a place like this, Mrs Wesley. What would the dining rooms in the city look like at this hour, eh?'

Emmy thought of the dining rooms at around this time. Every table would be full and the waitresses would be rushing backwards and forwards, bearing plates laden with steaming food and trays crammed with cups of tea, whilst someone would be wheeling a trolley full of various cakes and noting down, on her pad, which table had taken what. 'I see what you mean; but if you owned this place, Mr Mac, you'd know how to fill every table, instead of only two.' For the fact was, there was only one other table occupied in the spacious tea rooms.

Mr Mac shook his head sadly. 'Mrs Wesley, where is your business acumen? The only way to fill a place like this would be to move it into the city centre. And then, of course, it would lose almost all its appeal. No, I shan't open a country tea rooms until I'm too old to run Mac's. Now, you said you had a problem. Are you going to share it with me?'

Emmy, tucking into poached egg on toast, outlined her dilemma in a rather muffled voice, whilst Mr Mac listened thoughtfully, eating his own eggs in a leisurely fashion as he did so. After some thought, he gave his opinion with all his usual forthrightness. 'I don't believe you should make any hasty decisions, since in my opinion you aren't at all sure of your own feelings and marriage, as you must know, is probably the most important event in a woman's life – or a man's, for that matter. If you make a mistake now, I can promise you that you will regret it for the rest of your days. So don't act hastily. Take your time.'

'I know all that,' Emmy said, trying not to sound impatient. 'But I've known these two fellers for years now . . . well, I knew Johnny Frost when we were just a couple of kids . . . and I feel I can't keep them hanging about for a decision any longer. I've been visiting Johnny in Llandudno and I've been really happy there but – but I don't think my happiness comes from being with Johnny so much as being in a beautiful town and enjoying helping Mrs Frost in the guest house. Johnny's an old friend – I was going to marry him until I met Peter – but I'm not sure that friendship's enough.'

'It isn't,' Mr Mac said briefly. 'I don't mean to embarrass you, Mrs Wesley, but as you know, I'm a practical man and believe in calling a spade a spade. You have to be in love with someone to marry them and it's pretty clear that you don't love Mr Frost. How do you feel about Mr Johansson? You've scarcely mentioned him.'

'Oh! Well, he's awfully nice. He takes me about and makes a big fuss of me—' Emmy began, only to be interrupted by Mr Mac, who gave something perilously akin to a snort. 'Awfully nice!' he said scornfully. 'If you were in love with Mr Johansson, you wouldn't say he was "awfully nice". Unless you are marrying for the convenience of having a partner, someone to help you manage your life and bring up your child, then you should love him with all your heart and soul.' She saw that he was almost glaring at her. 'Why do you think I have not considered marriage until now, Mrs Wesley? It is because I regard it as the most important thing in life and want to be very sure that the woman I love loves me with equal intensity.'

Emmy was so surprised that she could only gape. She had never thought of her boss as anything but a friend and employer, but now she realised that a romantic and passionate heart was hidden behind his practical, sensible exterior. 'And – and you're considering marriage now?' she said, unable to keep the incredulity out of her tone. 'I had no idea . . . no one at work has ever said anything about – about you having – well, a friend even. Is – is that why you're thinking of moving out of the flat? But if so, why didn't your young lady accompany you today instead of myself? I'm sure she won't be interested in *my* opinions . . . she might even be cross that you've consulted me. Oh dear, if only I'd known . . .'

Across the table, Mr Mac smiled. 'She knew all about today and I can assure you she will have every opportunity to choose the house which suits her best,' he said reassuringly. 'But back to your own problem. You'll know the old saying marry in haste and repent at leisure, I'm sure. I can see you've already decided that marrying Mr Frost might be a mistake, and in my opinion at least, you are not yet sure enough of your feelings to marry Mr Johansson. In fact, you hardly know him, do you? He comes back to Liverpool, takes you out a few times, and then he's off again. I think you need to be with someone on a more permanent basis before you consider marriage.'

By now, they were at the cake stage and Emmy agreed, reluctantly, that she did not know Mr Johansson as well as she knew Johnny Frost. 'It's true that we've never spent longer than a couple of days in each other's company,' she admitted. 'And I suppose you're right. What's more, Diana really dislikes him, which does make things difficult.' She sighed, pushing a wing of bright hair off her forehead and tucking it behind her ear. 'I really envy you, Mr Mac; you haven't made a fuss or asked for advice, you've just found the right person for you and I know you've hit the nail on the head: neither Mr Frost nor Mr Johansson is my Mr Right, and it's time I told them so. And yet . . . and yet . . . I can't hang on Beryl's sleeve for ever and if I stop seeing them . . . I shall be most awfully lonely.'

'There's no reason why you should stop seeing either of them,' Mr Mac said reasonably. 'Just don't commit yourself, that's all I'm saying. And now, how about another cup of tea? I could do with one.'

When Emmy returned home, it was past eight o'clock and Mr Johansson had been and gone. 'He weren't very pleased, queen,' Beryl told her, a trifle reproachfully. 'He arrived at three o'clock, full of plans, and waited till half past four in the hope that you'd come home early. I explained as best I could, made him a cup of tea and gave him a slice of cake. And then he went off, but he come back at six, 'cos that was when you said you'd be home, an' stayed till seven. He's only in port till noon tomorrow, but he said he'd come round in the morning if he possibly could, even if he only stays for an hour.'

'Oh! Oh, but Beryl, I promised Mr Mac that I'd take a look in all the estate agents on my way to work, and pick up details of any houses that I thought were suitable,' Emmy said, dismayed. She was on the noon until eight shift and guessed that Mr Mac would await her arrival at work with additional eagerness because of the errand she had promised to undertake for him. 'Oh, whatever shall I do?' She looked appealingly at Beryl, but if she hoped for sympathy she was out of luck.

'Really, queen, you behave very thoughtless at times. You knew Mr Johansson were here for a couple o' days and you must have told him you weren't working tomorrow till noon, so you don't have no choice. I'm sorry, but you've got to be here tomorrow mornin', whether Mr Johansson turns up or not. And if he does come, you'll have some explainin' to do, I don't mind tellin' you. Oh, I know Mr Mac is your employer,' she added, as Emmy started to speak, 'but that's neither here nor there. You let that young feller down today, but you aren't goin' to do it twice.'

'Yes, I do see what you mean,' Emmy said, in a small voice. 'I'll just have to explain to Mr Mac when I get in to work. But suppose Mr Johansson doesn't come? Then I'll have wasted my morning off and let Mr Mac down as well.' She looked hopefully across the table at her friend, for they were sitting in the kitchen, sharing a pot of tea before going to bed. 'Suppose – suppose I left you with a message that I'd be in the Kardomah Café at eleven, say, or . . . or—'

'*No*, Emmy,' Beryl said grimly. 'It's time you grew up, young woman, and learned that other people's feelings matter just as much as your own; more, sometimes. You should have seen that young man's face when he left here this evening.'

Emmy began to answer but a quick glance at Beryl's expression stopped her in her tracks. She knew that she was being both selfish and cruel, and I'm neither, really, she told herself, a trifle guiltily. The fact is, I've made up my mind that I'm not going to remarry, but I'll be needing my job for a long while yet. That's why I'm behaving so badly; it's not because I'm a nasty person.

She explained all this to Beryl, who leaned across the table and patted her shoulder before heaving herself to her feet. 'It's all right, queen. I know you don't mean no harm, it's just that you've been spoiled rotten,' she said. 'Your being so ill didn't help, either. As for Mr Johansson, when he sees you tomorrow, looking so pretty and telling him how sorry you were to miss him, he'll forgive you. And now let's get to bed before I drop in me tracks; tomorrow's another day, so we might as well get what rest we can before tackling it.'

When she finally got to bed, however, Emmy found it difficult to fall asleep. Although she had tried to hide it – and thought she had succeeded – she had been dismayed, as well as surprised, to learn that Mr Mac meant to marry. It had been bad enough when he had told her that he meant to live away from the restaurant and appoint a deputy to take his place so that he could have more time to himself. Emmy remembered the rare occasions on which both Mr Mac and his mother had been away at the same time, and the chaos which usually resulted. Oh, it was not the sort of chaos that the customers noticed – the staff's training saw to that – but behind the scenes there was a good deal of shouting, tears were freely shed, orders were muddled and the cooks grew short-tempered.

But a wife would change everything. A married man, particularly one newly married, would want to spend time in his new home, and the wife would naturally come in and out of the restaurant as of right. Knowing nothing about the business would not stop her giving her opinion and trying to change things. New brooms, Emmy reflected bitterly, always swept clean, they say, and the last thing she fancied was some masterful young woman lording it over her and the rest of the staff. She could see the new Mrs Mac in her mind's eye; she would be a bottle blonde, hard-faced but handsome, probably in her mid to late thirties and fond of dressy clothes, the sort that cost a lot but don't last long.

The picture thus conjured up was so unpleasant that Emmy hastily banished it from her mind, telling herself severely that Mr Mac was far too nice to make such a dreadful mistake. No, his wife would be plump and cuddly, with a gentle expression and a sweet smile. She would potter about the restaurant being everyone's best friend and would never interfere, in any way, with the running of her husband's business.

This picture of the new Mrs Mac, however, did not seem convincing. The boss did not pick plain, plump little waitresses, so why should he go for a plain, plump little wife? Tossing and turning in her small bed, Emmy eventually decided that it was no use getting in a state over Mr Mac's intended. She would just have to trust to her boss's good sense to see that everything at the restaurant went on as before, even after his marriage. And anyway, if it didn't, and she was unhappy, there was always Johnny Frost, or Carl Johansson. They were there, standing in the wings, both equally anxious to rush to her rescue, scoop her out of the restaurant, and give her a comfortable, worry-free life.

In the other bed Diana, crammed in beside Becky, sighed and stirred, and poor Emmy realised that the light which came in round the sides of the curtain was growing stronger. The moon had risen, and if it lit up the bedroom too brightly, she might lie here awake till morning. Having decided, miserably, that sleep would never visit her, she promptly fell into a deep and dream-filled slumber in which Johnny Frost and Carl Johansson vied for her hand, bought her beautiful gifts, and took her to exotic places. Unfortunately, the three of them were always together, the two men glaring at one another whilst she tried, in vain, to keep them apart. And there was a third figure, hovering in the background, always seen through mist so that she could not recognise his features. At one point, Carl asked, jealously, who the fellow was and Emmy glanced round wildly, hating to admit that she did not know. Then the words came tripping out of her mouth without any hesitation. 'Why, it's Mr Right, of course,' she said happily. 'It's my Mr Right; he's come at last!'

Carl had been holding her left hand and Johnny her right, but now she broke free from both of them and ran towards the mist-enshrouded figure. If only she could see him clearly . . . she knew that he really was her Mr Right, that she had found him at last, and if only she could see his face—

But hands were pulling and tugging at her as

Johnny and Carl shouted that she was making a horrible mistake, that she was going to marry them – both of them. 'We'll be really happy, the three of us,' Carl said positively. 'Emmy, be ours!'

Emmy tried to fight them off, tried to reach out to Mr Right . . . and woke. Diana was shaking her shoulder impatiently and peering into her face. She was washed, dressed, and standing with her hairbrush in her hand, looking down at Emmy with both anxiety and irritation. 'What time did you get in last night, Mam?' she asked, rather crossly. 'It's half past eight an' if you don't plait me hair for me, I'll have to go down with it loose. Oh, *do* come on, or I'll be late for school. Aunty Beryl's got the porridge on the table . . . do wake up!'

Still befuddled by the depth of her sleep, Emmy lurched out of bed, plaited Diana's hair, and told her daughter to tell Aunty Beryl she would be down in five minutes. Diana clattered out of the room and down the stairs, and Emmy began to think about her dream and how extraordinary it had been. She tried and tried to remember the identity of Mr Right, but could not recall one detail. Finally, with a mental shrug, she put the whole, ridiculous episode out of her mind, and went down to breakfast.

She and Beryl were in the kitchen when Carl arrived at about ten o'clock. They welcomed him warmly and then Beryl left the couple to themselves, saying that she had not yet done her messages and leaving the kitchen with her largest marketing bag and a list, she told them, as long as her arm.

As soon as they were alone, Emmy apologised for her absence the previous day, explaining that her boss was getting married and had asked her to look at some houses for him. She did not do it on purpose, but soon realised she had given Carl the impression that she had visited the houses by herself. Still, something prevented her from admitting that she had done so in the company of Mr Mac. Carl said ruefully that, had he been able to do so, he would have greatly enjoyed accompanying her. 'For when we are married we shall want a neat place of our own,' he said expansively. 'It would be an excellent scheme to examine a number of houses so that we could see whether our tastes are similar. But I'm sure that anything you like, I shall like also,' he finished, giving her a beaming smile.

'Oh, Carl, it's not me that's getting married, it's Mr Mac,' Emmy reminded him. 'I don't think I'm ready for marriage yet . . . and then there's Diana . . . she was very fond of her daddy and can't imagine his place being filled by anyone else. But I tell you what. Mr Mac asked me to pop in to some estate agents on my way to work today. Suppose you and I go out now and visit Humphreys & Lloyd Jones and Robert Roberts in Netherfield Road and then we could make our way towards the dock, if you have to hurry back to your ship; that would be killing two birds with one stone, wouldn't it?'

Carl did not look over-enthusiastic but agreed that they might as well do as she suggested since he would have to be back aboard SS *Cleopatra* by half past eleven at the latest. 'As for your so charming daughter, I should not be marrying her but yourself,' he said, rather plaintively. 'I'm afraid Diana is a little possessive of her mother and will not like any man who looks at you twice. However, I do have a suggestion which I hope may please you. I am taking three weeks off in the summer, and would like you both to accompany me to my home in Sweden for a short holiday. You could meet my parents, and my married sister and brother-in-law. As I must have told you before, my father is a farmer and I'm sure Diana would greatly enjoy a spell in the country. My sister has three girls aged eleven, nine and four; they would be delightful companions for Diana.'

Emmy was so taken aback that she could only stare. Carl had mentioned his family, vaguely, but there had never been any suggestion of a visit and this was the first she had heard of a farm. She supposed that his reticence had been caused by the fact that she had made it clear she would not move away from Liverpool. But now she found the thought of a trip abroad both exciting and stimulating. It would be marvellous to see Sweden, to meet Carl's relatives, and to learn how life was lived on his parents' farm. But even so, she was aware of doubts. If she agreed to go with him, then she could scarcely expect to remain a widow; he would take their eventual marriage for granted. But surely it would be no worse than visiting Llandudno, which she had been doing for months?

Emmy hesitated, trying to think of a way to find out whether such a visit would commit her in some way. She began to reply, rather falteringly, that it was most kind of him to suggest it, when he broke in. 'There would be no – how do you call it – strings attached,' he said eagerly. 'After all, my darling Emmy, you told me yourself that you have visited the Frosts in Llandudno many times since leaving the sanatorium. You have said those visits meant nothing, save that you and the Frosts had been friendly for many years. I, alas, cannot claim an old friendship between us, but our friendship, surely, is of sufficiently long standing for such a visit?'

Emmy stared at him thoughtfully for a few moments, then went across to the kitchen door and took her hat and coat from the peg. She perched the hat on her smooth pale-gold hair and spoke to Carl over her shoulder as he began to help her into her coat. 'Yes, I have been visiting the Frosts, so I suppose I could visit you without – without risking a lot of talk. And I should enjoy such a trip very much, since I have never been abroad. Diana would, too, I'm sure. Only – well, you do know I could never live in your country, even if we did get married? I don't speak the language and besides, I don't want to leave Liverpool. All my friends are here, and Diana's too.'

'I understand, and I would not suggest such a thing,' Carl said, but Emmy thought she detected a touch of impatience in his tone. 'May I take it, then, that you will accompany me when I go back to Sweden?'

They had let themselves out of the kitchen and were crossing the court, Emmy with her hand tucked into Carl's elbow, but at these words she stopped short, feeling that committing herself at this stage might be a big mistake. 'No you can't,' she said baldly. 'Summer is months away. Anything might happen in that time. Now let's change the subject.'

Carl began to say that summer was not that far distant, although if she preferred it he could take time off over Christmas, but Emmy resolutely changed the subject. Very soon, they entered the first estate agent's premises, whence they presently emerged with details of two houses, both of which sounded promising, on paper at least.

'If only I had a little more time ashore, I would love to accompany you to examine these places,' Carl said, rather wistfully. 'But, my dearest Emmy, if you see a house that you really like, will you write to me, giving me all the details? After all, if we mean to marry, then we should—'

'You are beginning to bore me, Carl,' Emmy said crisply, hearing the edge in her voice with some satisfaction. 'Why can't you simply accept that it is too soon for me to think of marriage? You said if I accompanied you home, it would be without strings, without any commitment in fact, yet you are making me feel guilty because I won't say yes or no right this moment.'

'Good. That is how I wish you to feel,' Carl said, surprising a choke of laughter out of Emmy. 'Do you realise, my love, that I have been taking you about now for the best part of six years, but we have never spent more than a couple of days together? However, if you come home with me and we spend three weeks in each other's company, you will soon discover that I am a grand chap, willing to dance to your tune and to satisfy your slightest whim.'

He said it so comically that Emmy was forced to stifle another laugh. Very soon, they were saying goodbye at the dock gates and she was promising to write, though not necessarily about houses.

She stood and waved until Carl had mounted the gangway and disappeared into the depths of the ship, and then she turned and began to make her way towards the restaurant, feeling rather guiltily light-hearted now that she had waved Carl off, knowing that she would not be seeing him again for three weeks. I shouldn't really be feeling like this, she told herself, as she walked briskly along the pavement. Carl is very nice but I truly don't think I ought to marry anyone who makes me feel so impatient and cross. Though, of course, if I did marry him, he wouldn't have to nag me so.

On this thought, she entered the restaurant and was once again surprised by the rush of pleasure which came over her at the sight of the familiar room, with Mr Mac giving her a quick little smile – he was on the cash desk – and both customers and staff greeting her warmly as she went into the staff room to hang up her coat and hat. Working on the cash desk, she no longer needed cap or apron, but had merely to wear a neat black dress, with lawn collar and cuffs. Mr Mac had formed the habit of buying a fresh pink rosebud for the cashier to wear during her shift and now Emmy took it from the little vase next to the mirror and pinned it to the front of her dress. She checked her hair, her stocking seams, and her general appearance, then picked up the house details she had acquired earlier and headed for the cash desk.

Mr Mac greeted her warmly and took the papers from her, standing up as he did so, and stepping away from the desk area. 'You are a good girl, Mrs Wesley,' he said approvingly, flicking through the papers in his hand. 'I am most grateful . . . perhaps you and I could repeat yesterday's expedition on your next day off? Some at least of these houses will be worth viewing, I'm sure.'

Emmy returned his smile, realising as she did so that her expedition with Mr Mac had been one of the nicest days out she had enjoyed for years. They got on so well, had so much in common, seemed to know what the other was thinking without having to put it into words . . .

She was beginning to say that she would be delighted to view more houses with him when a revelation occurred. The Mr Right of her dream suddenly appeared in her mind's eye, but this time there was no shrouding mist, and the face which smiled into her own was that of Mr Mac!

For some while after he had left her, Emmy could think of nothing but Mr Mac. She was in a daze of happiness for, in the end, the whole thing had been so simple. She had realised, at the moment of revelation, that she did not care a fig for either Johnny or Carl, but instead cared, passionately, for her employer. He might be forty-two, and she remembered she had once thought him old, but now his age simply did not matter. Mr Mac was not as handsome as either Carl or Johnny, not as tall, not as obviously desirable, yet she knew now that she loved him with all her heart. She had tried and tried to love Johnny or Carl, and a very poor job she had made of it, because love can't be forced, nor does it come for the asking. When it does come, it is completely natural, completely understandable, and that was how she felt about Mr Mac.

The sudden recollection as she gave a customer his change and watched him slip twopence into the staff gratuities box was like a douche of cold water. She might be free, but Mr Mac was most certainly not. He had told her he was hoping to get married in the near future, and again two pictures of his possible mate – one plain and plump, one beautiful but hard – popped into Emmy's mind, only on this occasion both faces were seen through a red mist. They shan't have him, Emmy thought vengefully. They're not right for him – neither of them is – they know nothing about the business, so they'll just get in the way when they come into the restaurant, and

I don't believe they know him half as well as I do. Why, he's the kindest and best man that ever lived . . . look how wonderful he was, visiting me almost every week whilst I was in the sanatorium, and even bringing Diana with him sometimes. Oh, how I wish I'd had the sense then to try and make him love me.

The day wore on. Emmy enjoyed her work, but now, when Mr Mac came over and spoke to her, she was uncertain how she should reply. It would be dreadfully shaming if he realised she was in love with him, since he could not return her feelings. If only she knew just how fond he was of his wife-to-be! But the very fact that he meant to marry must mean he adored the woman.

All afternoon, Emmy wondered what she should do for the best. The obvious course was to tell herself that Mr Mac, as an almost married man, was out of the running as far as she was concerned. Yet surely there must still be some hope for her? After all, he had repeated his invitation to her to view more houses on her next day off. I *know* he likes me, Emmy told herself stubbornly, as her shift ended and she went to the staff room to put on her coat and hat. And if he likes me – well, you never know what might happen. I'll be so nice to him that he's bound to begin to think of me as a friend rather than just as an employee. I shall ask old Mrs Mac to tell me about his lady friend . . . I shall pretend I want to know so that I can judge her taste when viewing houses. But, oh dear, what a fool I've been! I've had a hundred opportunities to make him love me, and I've let them all slip. But I won't give in, I won't, I won't! Somehow, I'll make him see that his marrying anyone but me would be a terrible mistake.

'Emmy, if we're going to walk home together,

you'd best gerra move on. The rain's stopped, for a miracle, so if we hurry we might get back without being soaked to the skin.'

Emmy swung round. It was Dolly, who had recently moved into a house not far from Nightingale Court, and the two of them often walked home together. 'Sorry, queen,' Emmy said, hurrying across the staff room in Dolly's wake. 'I want a word with Mr Mac, though, before I leave. Can you hang on for two more minutes?'

Emmy had no idea what she intended to say but, in the event, said nothing. Mr Mac had left.

Chapter Fifteen

Diana came thundering down the stairs and burst into the kitchen. Her mother, she knew, had left for work early this morning – if she was going to work, that was. Diana thought it was her mother's day off, but Christmas was getting near and the staff at the restaurant were frantically busy, so when Diana had woken to find Emmy already dressed and about to depart, she had assumed that she was working overtime to help out.

As she entered the kitchen, Aunty Beryl looked up from her morning task of cutting Charlie's carry-out – Wally had already left – and smiled at her. Charlie had managed to get a job as a delivery boy for a local butcher, Mrs Sparks on Limekiln Lane, and usually left for work at the same time as the rest of the family left for school. 'You're early, love,' Beryl said cheerfully. 'Your mam rushed off early, too; she's probably wanting to get some Christmas shopping done before she starts work at the restaurant. Want some porridge? You'll have to ladle out your own 'cos I'm cutting Charlie's sarnies.'

Diana went over to the stove and dipped the big ladle into the black porridge pot. 'I know I'm early, and it's 'cos I wanted a word with you before Charlie and the rest come down,' she said. She carried her bowl of porridge over to the table and settled herself before it. 'Aunty Beryl, what's the matter with me mam? I'm worried in case she's getting ill again or in case she's going to do something stupid, like agreeing to marry that Carl. You know he invited us to go to Sweden?'

'Yes, I did know; but since your mam says she's going to turn down his invitation, that shouldn't worry you overmuch,' Beryl said placidly, continuing to slice bread and spread margarine and meat paste. 'What do you mean, you're afraid she might be getting ill again? Her last check-up was real good, she told me.'

'I know. It's – it's just that she doesn't always listen when I'm speaking to her,' Diana said, her spoon suspended over the porridge. 'It's as though she was thinking of something else, something more important, and though I'm only a kid, what I say *is* important – to me, at any rate. Does she do that to you, Aunty Beryl? I mean, ask you a question and then not listen to your answer . . . stuff like that.'

Beryl laughed. 'Just because someone's a bit absent-minded, a bit turned in on themselves like, that doesn't make them ill,' she said. 'And yes, your mam acts absent-minded with me as well as with you. The fact is, queen, Emmy's got rather a lot on her mind right now. For the first time in her life, the thing she wants most isn't going to be handed to her on a plate. So, of course, she's spending a lot of time wondering what went wrong and how she can put it right.'

Diana gave this pronouncement some thought as she spooned porridge, then looked up at Beryl with a puzzled frown. 'I don't understand,' she said plaintively. 'What hasn't she got handed to her on a plate? And why is she turned in on herself?'

'I telled you; because she thinks she must have done something wrong . . . no, not wrong exactly.

Oh, Diana, me love, I can't really explain but I think, in a way, your mam's growin' up.'

'Growing up?' Diana said, now completely bewildered. 'But she is grown up, Aunty Beryl . . . she's old. Well, not terribly old, but she isn't a kid.'

Beryl sighed and began to wrap Charlie's carry-out in a piece of greaseproof paper. 'Just you take my word for it, queen, that there's nowt wrong wi' your mam and she isn't going to marry anyone all in a rush. What's more, I'd bet a pound to a shilling that neither of you will be going off to Sweden when summer comes, so you can stop worrying over that as well. Want to toast yourself a round of bread?' She cocked her head as the sound of boots came thundering down the stairs. 'Here come the heavy brigade, expectin' their breakfast on the table so's they can guzzle it down an' gerroff in good time. Be a pal, Di, and dish up some bowls of porridge for me.'

Diana set about the task, aware of a feeling of relief. She did love her Aunty Beryl, who was always so sensible, so kind. She had managed to put all of Diana's fears at rest. She had as good as said that Mammy wasn't ill and wasn't going to marry anyone, either. It also sounded as though her mother meant to give Carl his marching orders, which was marvellous. Diana carried the first bowl of porridge to the table just as Charlie and Lenny burst into the room, getting stuck in the doorway and cursing each other as they jostled and shoved. 'Stop mucking about, you two, and don't you go barging into me, Charlie Fisher, 'cos I don't want porridge all down me decent skirt,' Diana said briskly, beginning to fill the second bowl. 'I dunno, boys act more like wild animals than human beings.' She smiled across at Becky as the child came dreamily into the kitchen in Bobby's wake, her cardigan half on and half off, one boot on her foot and the other in her hand. 'You two ought to take a lesson from our Becky. She doesn't shove and push or shout and swear, but I bet she's ready for school while you lads are still squabbling over who's got the most porridge.'

Since Charlie and Lenny were even now disputing who should have the larger bowl, Diana was sure she would presently be proved right. She settled Becky in her chair, having first straightened her cardigan and buttoned it correctly, then knelt on the floor and began to push Becky's foot into her boot, remarking as she did so that the younger girl could do with a new pair. 'Feet do grow at such a rate, don't they, Aunty Beryl?' she said, tying Becky's laces into a neat bow and getting to her feet. 'Now don't hurry, Becky, or you'll spill porridge on your nice clean cardy. Want some milky tea?'

Becky replied that she did and presently the two girls hurried out of the kitchen, Diana's arm looped affectionately round the younger girl's waist. As she had prophesied, the boys were still at the table, eating bread and marge, talking with their mouths full and occasionally taking a pull at their tea.

'I 'spec they'll be late, Di, like you said they would,' Becky remarked, as they crossed the court and turned into Raymond Street. 'The boys is nearly always late, ain't they, Di? They doesn't seem to care like us girls does.'

Diana chuckled. For all Becky was so slow in some things, she was sharp as a needle in others. She was still in the infants' class, painfully learning to read and write, though she was making big strides at both, and Diana reflected that another good thing about her mother's not marrying was that she would be able to remain with the Fishers. Diana still admired

Charlie very much and was on excellent terms with Lenny, but now that she was growing up she got enormous satisfaction from taking care of Becky, and teaching her as much as the child's brain would hold. As they hurried along the street, she began to teach Becky a little poem which her mother had taught her when she was four or five. Becky was ten now but Diana knew that her mental age was a good deal less – knew also that she would enjoy learning the poem. 'I'm going to teach you a little verse, Becky, as we go to and from school,' she said instructively. 'It's a lovely poem, all about flowers . . . and you love flowers, don't you, queen?'

Becky nodded. 'Yes, I does love flowers; an' I loves you, too,' she said, in her flat little voice. 'Tell me the poem then, Di.'

Diana was touched by Becky's affection and gave her hand a squeeze before beginning to recite the poem. 'It goes like this:

Little brown seed, oh little brown brother,
Are you awake in the dark?
Here we lie cosily, close to each other
Hark to the song of the lark.'

Becky listened intently, then began to repeat the words, and Diana, nodding encouragement, thought how nice it was to have a little sister who loved you and looked up to you, even if she wasn't your real sister. Becky came to the end of the second line and stopped short, and Diana gave her a hug. 'You *are* clever, Becky,' she said admiringly. 'Why, you said those two lines just as good as I could. Say 'em once more and then we'll start on the next two.'

*

Beryl watched the two girls leave the kitchen, a smile hovering. She reflected how Diana's attitude to Becky had changed over the years and told herself that it was not only Emmy who was growing up. Diana might be only eleven but she was a real little mother to Becky. Once, Beryl had worried a great deal when she had agreed to let Becky start school. She had known how cruel children can be and knew, also, that Becky would not know how to complain to authority if she was bullied, beaten or mocked. On Becky's first day, however, Beryl had wandered along at playtime and had been delighted, and relieved, to see Becky and Diana, their hands tightly clasped, queuing up for a turn at hopscotch. She had watched as Diana showed Becky how to throw the slate into the square she wanted and how Diana had squashed another girl who had tried to shoulder in first. When the children had come home that afternoon, she had asked Becky what she thought of school and the child had replied, with her usual transparent honesty, that it were nice. 'Teacher were kind to me. I chalked on the board and made a castle of bricks,' she had said. 'Can I go back tomorrer?'

'Mam, me shoelace has bust. Is there a bit of string in the drawer?' Bobby's voice broke into Beryl's thoughts, and for the next ten minutes she was far too busy getting the boys off to school to think about anything else. Charlie got himself off to work and was never late, because he brought his delivery bicycle home each night and cycled off at top speed each morning.

'Young Diana was right; you're going to be late, as usual,' Beryl scolded the other three, bundling them out of the door when they would have lingered. 'No, Lenny, you can't come back for that tatty old football.

You aren't supposed to take it to school, anyway. Now, off wi' you, and you'd best run because I don't want no more complaints from Father Ignatius that the Fishers is always late.'

Returning to the kitchen, Beryl got out her flat irons and stood them in a row by the fire to heat whilst she cleared away the breakfast things and washed up. Then she put a blanket on the kitchen table, covered it with an old piece of sheeting, and went over to her laundry basket. It was warm in the kitchen and the top tablecloth was almost dry, but the rest were nicely damp still and would iron up a treat. Beryl picked up the first iron and spat on it; yes, it would do nicely. She shifted all the other irons up one, tucked the almost dry tablecloth beneath the others, picked up the second cloth, and set to work, reflecting as she did so that she could have done this job in her sleep. The long, smooth sweeps of the iron continued until the cloth was finished. Then she folded it neatly, placed it carefully in her big wicker basket, and began on the next. She glanced, a trifle anxiously, at Freddie, playing with the wooden cars Charlie had made for him, but he was absorbed, so she continued with her work, letting her mind wander. She had suspected for some time that Mr Mac was sweet on Emmy and had been truly astonished – and dismayed – when Emmy had told her that Mr Mac was going to get married. At first, she had felt quite angry with Emmy for never really noticing her boss as a human being. He had confided in Beryl once, when they had travelled back from Llandudno together on the train, that he blamed himself for Emmy's illness. 'I knew she was in difficult financial circumstances and thought that the best help I could give would be to employ her for more hours.

Evening work is better paid so I saw to it that she was given evening work, never even suspecting that it was too much for her. Of course I cursed myself for a fool when someone pointed out how thin and pale she was getting, but when I tried to reduce her hours she seemed more upset than delighted. So I thought . . . I thought . . .'

Beryl had nodded, understanding Mr Mac's dilemma. 'Yes, I know what you mean,' she had said. 'She were that difficult and bad-tempered, not like her usual sunny self at all. Why, she even fell out wi' me, her closest friend, took Diana away from me, wouldn't let me so much as pass the time of day with the kid. Naturally, I were cut to the quick, but instead of trying to find out what the trouble were, I took offence. I thought two could play at that game and when we passed in the street, or even in the court, I kept me eyes to meself. I knew she were meetin' that Carl pretty reg'lar and I telled meself that now she'd got a feller she didn't want her old friend no more. So you see, if anyone was to blame, it were me. And when I did see her – after she'd collapsed, I mean – you could ha' knocked me down with a feather.' She had smiled at him across the railway carriage. 'So don't you go blaming yourself, Mr Mac. Why, she's had no more reg'lar visitor than you since she's been in the sanny, and she enjoys your visits that much, I've been quite jealous at times.'

Mr Mac had made some non-committal reply and changed the subject, but Beryl had noticed how his eyes had softened when he spoke of her friend. She had thought him to be merely taking a fatherly interest in Emmy, for she knew he had no kids of his own, but lately she had begun to suspect that his affection for Emmy was a good deal warmer than mere friendship. After all, no matter what he might say, there was no reason for his taking Emmy house-hunting if, as Emmy had said, he intended to marry someone else. Beryl knew enough about human nature to realise how bitterly a fiancée would resent her intended's taking another woman round the property in which she meant to live.

Beryl finished another tablecloth, folded it and laid it on the first. The trouble with Emmy was that she was incapable of putting herself in anyone else's shoes. She might conjure up horrible pictures – or even pleasant ones – of the woman her boss meant to marry, but she would simply never wonder how such a woman would feel if she found out that Mr Mac was asking another woman's opinion on the house they were to share. Neither would it occur to her, in a million years, that Mr Mac was acting completely out of character. After all, why should he take one of his employees into his confidence over such a personal matter? Why should he hire a taxi to facilitate their days out? For that matter, why should he treat her to delightful meals, trips out into the country, and other nice things, if he was truly planning to marry someone else? No, the more Beryl thought about it, the more she suspected that Emmy's employer was playing a rather clever double game. Because Emmy had only thought of him as her elderly boss, he had been unable to court her as Johnny and Carl had. Mr Mac probably imagined that any attempt on his part to appear interested in Emmy as a woman would have resulted either in her trying to change her job, or in great embarrassment to them both. And he might well have been right at that, Beryl concluded, finishing off another tablecloth and spreading out the next. The truth was that Emmy had never even considered Mr Mac as a suitor because to her he was simply her boss. When visiting her at the sanatorium, he had behaved with great decorum, making sure of her comfort, treating her, in fact, like a favourite niece. Beryl assumed this was because, had he behaved otherwise, it might have made things very difficult when Emmy returned to the restaurant. Beryl imagined that he had not, at that time, fully realised the extent of his own feelings towards her friend. That had only come upon her return to Liverpool and now Mr Mac was making up for lost time, treating Emmy as a beautiful and desirable woman, hoping that she would begin to see him not just as a friend and employer, but as a lover.

Beryl finished the tablecloth and pulled out the next one. It was worn and old, with a tear quite a foot long right across the middle. I'll make it into four table napkins, she decided, rough ironing the material and laying it aside. Ella, from Bonner's Tea Rooms, was always grateful for any little mending jobs Beryl might do, and would pay a bit extra for the task. Beryl began to iron the next tablecloth. She was pretty sure that her friend no longer intended to marry either Johnny or Carl, and she was equally sure that Emmy was jealous as a cat whenever she thought of Mr Mac's marrying someone else. She also believed that Emmy was regarding Mr Mac more and more fondly, was probably already a little in love with him. What she did not know was whether Emmy understood her own feelings. In Beryl's opinion, her friend had never known the sort of breathless, helpless love which she and Wally had shared when they were young. Emmy had been dazzled by Peter's good looks, position and experience. Oh, she had loved him in a way, but had always been a little in awe of him. When he died, she had been heartbroken, but her loss had not blighted her life. Now, Beryl wondered irreverently if Emmy would recognise love if it jumped up and bit her on the nose. If not, she found herself pitying Mr Mac deeply, because a little butterfly who flitted over the surface of life, never soaring to the heights or plumbing the depths, would be a poor mate for a man of strong passions like Mr Mac.

Beryl stood her iron back by the fire and picked up the next one, astonished by her own thoughts. Emmy was her best friend; she had known her all her life, knew that there was a great deal of good in the younger girl. It had taken courage not to accept an offer of marriage from someone with money and position, like Carl, she reminded herself. At one time, Emmy had been desperate for any sort of financial help, which was why she had taken the job in the restaurant. For a girl brought up to believe that she was a cut above everyone else in her neighbourhood, working as a waitress had been a brave thing to do as well. And despite the difficulties, Beryl knew that Diana had never wanted for anything which Emmy could give her, and that included both attention and love.

On the hearthrug, Freddie crashed his cars together and got to his feet. He wandered over to the table and jerked at Beryl's skirt. 'Goin' out?' he enquired hopefully. 'Mammy goin' out? Freddie go too?'

Beryl smiled at her little son, but resolutely continued to work. 'Presently, old feller,' she promised. 'We'll do our messages as soon as I've finished the Bonner tablecloths. You play with your cars till Mammy's ready, there's a good boy.'

Freddie, a placid, sweet-tempered little boy, nodded

solemnly and returned to his game on the hearthrug. Beryl leaned over the fireguard and changed irons once again. She had told Diana that her mother was growing up and now she realised that the remark had been very true. Part of Emmy's undoubted appeal had been her innocent acceptance of male admiration. Now, the fact that Mr Mac seemed, to Emmy, to be immune to her charms was causing her to be a little more self-critical. Perhaps it's good for everyone to have doubts, Beryl told herself. Emmy's brave, bright, pretty as a picture, but not her dearest friend could call her modest or unassuming. Now, because she does have doubts, she's a far nicer person than she was.

Having decided that a little uncertainty was actually good for her friend, Beryl put the whole matter out of her mind and finished the rest of her ironing in record time. She packed her work carefully into the long basket, covering it with a stout piece of American cloth. Then she dressed Freddie in his outdoor clothes, put on her own coat and hat, and carried the small boy and the basket over to the rickety old pram. I'll kill two birds with one stone, she decided, tucking Freddie under the waterproof cover and erecting the hood. I'll deliver my work and then do my messages, and after that, I'll pop into Mac's and see how Emmy's getting on; if she's working, that is. I told Diana she might be Christmas shopping, but the truth is she were in such a rush to get off this morning that we scarcely exchanged a word. I might treat myself to a pot of tea while I'm in Mac's, because by then I'll need a sit-down.

Beryl did as she planned, popping into the restaurant at eleven o'clock, and finding it crowded with Christmas shoppers. She looked towards the cash desk and was only slightly surprised to see that Emmy was not there. Old Mrs Mac, very erect and smiling, sat by the till.

Beryl hovered for a moment, then decided to have a cup of tea anyway, and waited until a plump woman in a scarlet headscarf vacated her seat. Beryl, with Freddie in her arms, hastily took the woman's place, and asked Freda for tea for herself and a biscuit for the baby. 'I see Emmy's got her day off, for all you're so busy,' she observed. 'Good thing the old lady's fit again or you'd ha' been scrattin' around to find someone to mind the till.'

Freda beamed at her. 'It ain't only Emmy what's off, of course; Mr Mac's not in now, on a Tuesday,' she said. 'D'you know he's house-hunting? He wants a place in the country where he can relax from time to time, so whenever Mr Mac's off, the feller he's employed to help out, his cousin, comes in for practice, like.'

'Oh, I see. What's he like, this other chap?' Beryl asked curiously, as two more customers left the table and Freda began to clear the used crockery on to her tray. 'Emmy's not said much.'

'He's awright,' Freda said, resting the laden tray on her hip. 'If you look towards the office . . . that's him, the feller what just come out. He's learnin' fast; took to it like a duck to water, you might say. But I can't stand here chattin' 'cos you know the rules. Shan't be a mo.'

Beryl sat back in her chair; Freda had given her considerable food for thought. The staff clearly didn't know that Emmy had accompanied their boss in his search for a house, far less that Mr Mac and Emmy were probably together today. Beryl smiled to herself. Lately, Emmy had said more than once that she did not mean to marry either Johnny or Carl. Beryl had taken this with a pinch of salt, but now she decided Emmy had been speaking no more than the truth, even if she herself did not know it. Another clue, now that she thought about it, was that Emmy had not mentioned Mr Mac's cousin, and that was because Mr Mac's cousin came in when Mr Mac was out and when Mr Mac was out, Emmy must be out as well. Beryl's smile broadened; the plot thickens, she thought gleefully, just as Freda arrived back at her table with her pot of tea and the boy's biscuit. Oh aye, the plot thickens all right!

It would be an exaggeration to say that Emmy and Mr Mac had seen hundreds of houses, but they had certainly viewed most of the properties being offered for sale at the moment. Emmy was beginning to get confused, so when they climbed into the taxi after viewing the third house of the day and Mr Mac suggested that they should have a break, she gladly agreed with him. 'They're all beginning to run together in my head,' she said apologetically. 'I find myself trying to visualise the kitchen in so and so street, or the master bedroom in what's its name street, and finding that I'm probably really thinking of a house over the opposite side of the city.'

She laughed, and Mr Mac laughed with her. 'That's why I suggested we have a break,' he told her. 'I thought we might go to Chester, take a look at the shops – do some Christmas shopping, if anything takes your fancy – have some lunch, and come back so you're in time to help Beryl make the tea. Does that appeal?'

'Oh, it does,' Emmy breathed. Then her eye was caught by the address on the next house they would have visited. 'Oh, but . . . I wonder if we might view just one more house, Mr Mac? Only it's in Sydenham Avenue, which is next to Lancaster Avenue. We lived there before my husband died, you know. It's a good neighbourhood and this house might be just what you're looking for. There's Prince's Park and Sefton Park just a short walk away, and you can catch a tram into the city centre on Croxteth Road, which is even nearer. Only of course it's up to you, Mr Mac.'

The taxi driver, an elderly man who usually took them house-hunting, turned in his seat to gaze at them a trifle reproachfully. 'Well, what's it to be?' he demanded. 'Sydenham Avenue ain't far; you could see that one house and then go on to Chester, if you want.'

Mr Mac ferreted in his pocket and produced some keys. 'Right, Sydenham Avenue it is, driver.' He turned to Emmy. 'The house is empty but the agent gave me the keys, so we shan't be held up by a chattering householder, or an agent eager to influence our decision.'

They reached Sydenham Avenue. The trees which lined it were bare, but Emmy was immediately struck, as she had been struck so many years before, by the peaceful atmosphere. She and Mr Mac climbed out of the taxi and walked up the short garden path, Emmy grateful, suddenly, for the pale winter sunshine. She found she desperately wanted Mr Mac to like this house, to say that he wanted to live here and would actually make an offer for the place. She realised that she had always 'hedged her bets', so to speak, when they discussed the properties they had seen. She had felt awkward, not wanting to influence his decision, wondering all the while if his future wife would blame her should the house prove less than satisfactory. Now, all these doubts and fears had left her. She had always thought Sydenham Avenue even lovelier than Lancaster, and now she was actually going to take a good look at one of the nicest houses.

Mr Mac unlocked the heavy front door and pushed it wide, and she followed him in so eagerly that she almost trod on his heels. They went first into a large and airy living room; the floor was of polished oak and, through the window, they could see the avenue and the front garden. At this time of year, it might have been a cheerless scene, but the sunshine falling on the silvery trunks of the trees, and a splash of scarlet berries and the yellow flowers of a jasmine, seemed a promise of things to come.

'Nice,' Mr Mac said briefly. 'Well-proportioned room.' Then he turned, and led the way into the rest of the house.

To Emmy, it was just as she had imagined; larger than the house in Lancaster Avenue and with a bigger garden at the back, but even empty, and with the December chill upon it, she thought it a welcoming house. It had been a family home and wanted to be one again, she thought wistfully. Perhaps Mr Mac would not like it; after all, he was looking for a home for himself and his future wife, for old Mrs Mac did not intend to move when he did. He had told Emmy, a week earlier, that his mother had decided to stay in the flat. 'I thought she would enjoy living in pleasanter surroundings, with a garden to cultivate and less interference from the staff, but apparently I was wrong,' he had said ruefully. 'All her friends live in the Scotland Road area; she knows every shopkeeper, every stallholder and almost all our customers. She told me that she would be lost away from the dear old Scottie and, naturally, I respect her point of view, even though I can't share it. But it has to be her own decision and perhaps, when I decide to buy, she may change her mind.'

When they had examined the house from attic to cellar, Mr Mac produced the keys again and unlocked the back door, and they went into the garden. Whoever had owned the house before had clearly either employed a gardener or been keen on horticulture himself, for there was a fruit cage, in which Mr Mac said he recognised blackcurrants, gooseberries and raspberries, and a sizeable patch which probably held every sort of vegetable during the summer months, though now it contained only cabbages, sprouts and a long rectangle full of what Emmy took to be golden ferns, dotted with brilliant red berries, which Mr Mac assured her was an asparagus bed. There were two apple trees, a plum tree and a small lawn, as well as a potting shed and a brick-built outhouse in which logs and other items could be stored.

Having examined everything minutely, they returned to the kitchen. It was a large, airy room, whose big window overlooked the back garden, but it was terribly old-fashioned, the sink at knee level and the range so old that it must, Emmy guessed, be an antique. The floor was quarry-tiled – easy to keep clean, Emmy thought approvingly – but the white-washed walls were in sad need of attention and the light bulb which swung from the ceiling was so tiny and so badly placed that, at night, the kitchen would be a very gloomy place.

Emmy, however, knew that all this could be put right with very little outlay; probably the fact that the kitchen would have to be rebuilt would be reflected in the asking price. So she faced Mr Mac, almost challengingly. 'Well, what d'you think?' she asked. 'I know it's winter so the garden isn't looking its best, and you're going to say the kitchen's a mess and the geyser in the bathroom must have been installed by Julius Caesar, but, aside from all that, what d'you think?'

To her surprise, Mr Mac, who had been standing by the window, crossed the room in a couple of strides and took both her hands in his. 'What do *you* think?' he asked her, his eyes very bright. 'This is your old territory. How would you like to live here again?'

'Oh, well, you must have guessed that I think it's a lovely house,' Emmy said slowly. 'But I suppose it's really a family house and you're looking for something smaller. Only if your mam did agree to come here . . . and you might have guests . . .'

'I might have children,' Mr Mac said quietly. 'I dare say you think I'm far too old, but I'd love to have a family. I think this would make a wonderful home in which to bring up two or three children, don't you agree?'

Emmy stared into Mr Mac's dark eyes and what she read there brought the hot blood rushing to her cheeks. She said unsteadily: 'Why, you aren't old at all, Mr Mac, only you've never said you meant to start a family, and . . . and . . .'

Mr Mac's hands slid gently from hers to grasp her by the elbows. 'It isn't the done thing to ask a young lady if she would like a family before proposing marriage, you know,' he said, and to Emmy's astonishment his voice, too, was rather unsteady. 'But let's do things the wrong way round, shall we? Would *you* like a family, Mrs Wesley?'

Emmy stared at him, knowing that her eyes were getting rounder and rounder. 'I – I've already got a family,' she said huskily. 'But I've always thought it a shame that Diana is an only child. If – if I married again—' She broke off, and pulled away from Mr Mac, facing him resolutely. 'Just who *are* you going to marry, Mr Mac? Only – only I do wish it were me.' She took a deep breath and gathered up all her courage. It was now or never. 'Will you marry me, please, Mr Mac?'

Mr Mac gave a triumphant shout of laughter and gathered her into his arms. 'I thought you'd never ask,' he said, a smile tilting the corners of his mouth. 'I know I'm ten years older than you but I do believe I fell in love with you the day I interviewed you for a job in the restaurant. Then, as I grew to know you better – visiting you in the sanatorium – I began to see that you were the woman I'd been waiting for all my life. Only you were wrapped up in Johnny Frost and Carl Johansson, both young men of your own age, and didn't give me a thought. I might tell you, I was near despair, deathly afraid that you would make a snap decision and marry one of them whilst I was still wary of chancing my arm and losing you altogether. Then you asked for my advice and I did my best to put you off the pair of them and—'

'How devious you are,' Emmy said, marvelling. 'And telling me you were going to marry someone else – how I hated her – when all the time . . . all the time . . .'

'All the time it was you I wanted,' Mr Mac said, smiling down at her. 'And of course there was no other woman, there never has been. But I thought, if you got to know me better, not just as a boss or a sick visitor, but as a man, you might begin to like me a little.'

'I like you a lot,' Emmy said shyly. She looked down at her feet and then up at his face. 'Well, like isn't really the right word. I – I didn't know I was in love with you, I thought I was just jealous of the woman you meant to marry. Only I was beginning to see for myself that neither Johnny nor Carl was the right man for me. Then I had the weirdest dream, one of those really daft dreams that don't seem to make sense at the time, and it's only later that you can begin to interpret them. I dreamed that Johnny, Carl and another man were all waiting for me to make up my mind which one I wanted, and I knew that Mr Right . . . that's what I called him in my mind . . . really *was* right – for me, I mean. Only I couldn't see his face because it was sort of misty and vague. I tried and tried to see him clearly, tried so hard that I woke up. Then, of course, I came into the restaurant and gave you the house details, and you stood up and smiled at me. It – it was just like magic. At that very moment I saw Mr Right's face clearly, and it was you, and I realised that I'd been in love with you for weeks and weeks, but hadn't let myself see it.' She looked ruefully up at Mr Mac and then, on an impulse, threw both arms round his neck and nestled her head into the hollow of his shoulder. 'It sounds as though I'm making it up, but I'm not,' she mumbled. 'Oh, Mr Mac, I'd want to be with you even if you lived in Sweden, like Carl Johansson, or were weak-willed and easy to boss about like Johnny Frost. I can't remember ever feeling like this before, not even when I first met Peter. Oh, and I still don't know your first name!'

Mr Mac laughed, boisterously, and hugged her a

little more tightly. 'My first name's Ted – Edward, really – and since we've decided to get married, I think I ought to kiss you, otherwise we'll be the only engaged couple in the whole world who have seldom even shaken hands.'

As he spoke, he bent his head, and their lips met. It was a long kiss and a passionate one, and it left Emmy feeling dizzy with delight. I must have been mad, she told herself, not to have realised before how wonderful he is. And we're going to get married! I'm the luckiest woman in the whole world!

They did not go to Chester after all, but got the taxi driver to take them straight to the estate agent's, where Mr Mac made an offer for the house in Sydenham Avenue. 'My fiancée and I prefer it to any of the other properties we have seen,' he said grandly, giving Emmy's hand a squeeze. 'There is quite a lot that needs doing – the kitchen and bathroom both want modernising – so as soon as the contracts are signed and the money has been paid over, I shall get the builders in to do what's necessary. That is, if the owner accepts my offer,' he ended.

From the estate agent's, they went on to a jeweller's, where Mr Mac insisted upon buying a beautiful sapphire surrounded by diamond chips, though Emmy assured him that the only ring she really wanted was a plain band of gold. 'I shall wear Peter's rings on my right hand,' she said, as they left the shop. 'Diana shall have them when she's old enough, but until then I would like to continue to wear them.' She looked anxiously at Mr Mac. 'You don't mind, Mr Ma— I mean, Ted?'

'I don't mind at all,' Mr Mac assured her, steering her across the pavement and back into the taxi. 'And now, my love, we must discuss your daughter, our plans for the wedding, where you would like to spend the honeymoon . . .'

'Diana! Oh, good lord!' Emmy said, a hand flying to her mouth. 'She has no idea . . . I've never said . . . oh dear, I do hope she isn't going to be difficult.'

'I don't see why she should be,' Mr Mac said mildly. 'I know she didn't want you to marry Mr Johansson, or even Mr Frost, but neither of them lived in the city, so whichever one you married Diana felt she would be moved away from her pals and the area she knew. She was happy in the local school when you lived in Lancaster Avenue, was she not? I dare say it won't be long before she's as friendly with the other girls in her class as she was the first time round. No, I don't see why she should object to our marriage, particularly as I am sure you will want her to be your bridal attendant. Most little girls like the idea of a frothy-laced dress, with yards of tulle, flowers in their hair, and everyone admiring them.'

'I do hope you're right,' Emmy said fervently. 'But I'm afraid her opinion isn't going to affect my decision in the least. If she loves me – and I'm sure she does – then she'll be happy because I'm so happy. I'll make sure that she's the first to know . . . in fact, it might be a good idea to meet her out of school. We could take her somewhere nice for tea and break the news over a strawberry ice cream cone and a lemonade; she'd like that.'

'And then we could run round to Sydenham Avenue and show her the house,' Mr Mac suggested, as the taxi headed out towards the suburbs once more. 'But right now, I think we'll give Chester a miss, my love, and have a light – and rather late – lunch. And then we'll really have to start planning our future together.'

Diana had been satisfyingly amazed when her mother had revealed that she was engaged to be married and that the man of her choice was neither Johnny Frost nor Carl Johansson, but Ted McCullough. At first, Diana could not think who Ted McCullough could possibly be, but Mr Mac had put her right on that score.

'I know it'll be a surprise to you, Diana, but I hope it won't be a disappointment,' he said gravely, though Diana thought that laughter lurked in his eyes. 'You see, your mother was so popular, and had so many admirers, that I didn't think I stood a chance, and I wasn't going to put myself forward to be knocked down like a perishing skittle. Only then she told me that she had decided neither Mr Frost nor Mr Johansson was right for her, and of course that gave me hope. I decided to pop the question and your mam has honoured me by accepting. We've put in an offer for a house on Sydenham Avenue and we're hoping to get married in April, because that's such a pretty month. Well, what d'you say? Do you approve?'

Diana had stared up at Mr Mac. It was on the tip of her tongue to ask if he were kidding her, because he was Mam's boss, not a foolish young feller carried away by Emmy's pretty looks. Also, he was old. To be sure, his hair was thick and dark, but there were silver streaks at his temples and there were tiny lines round his eyes. But then she looked deeply into those eyes and somehow she knew at once that he was not kidding; not only was he going to marry her mother, but he was in love with her, and in love in a much steadier, more sensible way than either Johnny or

Carl had been. To her own secret astonishment, Diana realised that she would welcome Mr Mac – she could not yet think of him as Ted – as a step-father. He would not pretend to play games with her, as Johnny Frost had done; nor would he treat her with the sort of amused, though veiled, disapproval that Carl had shown. He would be exactly the same on the inside as he was on the outside, Diana concluded, rather confusedly. If he disapproved – or approved – he would say so at once, and she knew he would take good care of her mother; he was that sort of man.

But best of all, she thought, he would leave Diana herself alone. He would not interfere or try to become a father figure. She thought he would leave Emmy to decide how her daughter should behave, and because she liked him, Diana told herself she would behave well. Emmy deserved that much from her.

'Well?' That was Emmy, sounding distinctly anxious. The three of them were sitting in a small teashop, Diana with a large dish of ice cream and a glass of lemonade, the adults with a plate of fancy cakes and a pot of tea. 'Well, Diana darling? What do you think? Only I must warn you, love, that much though I want your approval, it won't affect my decision. Mr Ma— I mean, Ted and I are going to get married and I know we're going to be happy.'

Diana took a large spoonful of ice cream and beamed at her mother across the table. 'I'm really glad and I'm sure you will – be happy, I mean,' she said. 'And I do think you were right to give Johnny and Carl the elbow; they really weren't right for you, Mam. As for me, I guess Sydenham Avenue will be almost as good a place to live as Lancaster was. If you give me my tram fare, I can get to and from the city pretty easily, and my friends from school and the court will come out to me, I'm sure. And if I remember right, we're ever so near Sefton Park; it's as good as the country, is that. I bet Charlie – and the other kids, of course – will be happy enough to spend days in the park, and to have their dinners at our house. Why, we've had enough dinners at their house to feed a fighting army, as Uncle Wally would say,' she ended.

Mr Mac laughed. 'Aye, you're right there, queen,' he acknowledged. 'Your Aunty Beryl has been marvellous to you and your mam, so I reckon she'll visit you whenever she can. And now look lively, young lady, and finish that ice cream because it's getting dark and we'd best be on our way. Tomorrow, we'll take you to Sydenham Avenue to see what you think of the new house.'

Diana, gulping ice cream at a great rate, assured both adults that she was longing to see the house. 'But what am I to call you, Mr Mac?' she asked, rather plaintively. 'I can't call you Dad, because – well, because I've got a dad of me own, even if he is dead. But just "Ted" sounds rather rude, somehow, coming from a kid like me.'

'Ted would suit me just fine, but if you feel it sounds cheeky, I'd settle for Uncle Ted,' Mr Mac said gravely. 'Of course, Edward is my given name, but hardly anyone uses it; it always makes me feel as if I've done something wrong, because the only time my old mam calls me Edward is when I've annoyed her in some way. Still, if it would make you more comfortable . . .'

Diana hastily assured him that 'Uncle Ted' would be just fine, and presently they set off for home.

*

If Beryl was astonished by Emmy's news, when the three of them entered the house in Nightingale Court, she hid such feelings very well. Wreathed in smiles, however, she rushed to the front room and brought back a bottle of sherry, so that they might drink to the future happiness of the engaged couple.

'You don't seem very surprised, Beryl,' Emmy said reproachfully, as the three adults settled into the rather stiff and uncomfortable parlour chairs. 'I know I told you I wasn't going to marry Johnny or Carl. But I don't remember giving you any sort of hint . . . well, I couldn't, because I didn't know myself until Mr Mac – I mean, Ted – popped the question.'

'And I must tell you, Mrs Fisher, that it wasn't me who popped the question,' Mr Mac said. He looked serious, save for the lurking twinkle in his dark eyes. 'This forward young hussy put it to me straight that I needed a wife and that she would suit me best.'

Emmy choked over her sherry and began to giggle, but presently, mopping her streaming eyes, she said indignantly: 'It wasn't like that at all, Beryl, he's having you on. Oh, I admit I asked him to marry me, but he had asked me, very improperly, if I would like a family. So then, of course, I felt I had to mention marriage, to make things respectable, like.'

'Well, whichever. And whether you knew it or not, I've known for weeks that you'd fallen for Mr Mac,' Beryl said comfortably. 'You never were one who could hide your feelings, Emmy, my love. Every time Johnny or Carl were mentioned, you'd look that worried and anxious that I felt downright sorry for you. But every time Mr Mac's name came into the conversation, your eyes went all dreamy and soft and half the time you stopped listening to a word I was saying, and drifted on into some dream of your own. Oh aye, *you* may not have known you'd met your Mr Right, but I knew, I'm telling you straight.' She turned her gaze on to Mr Mac, smiling slightly at him. 'And as for you, Mr Mac, it weren't difficult to put two and two together and make four, not after our conversation in the train coming back from Llandudno that day. I haven't lived in this court all me life without learnin' a good deal about people. I thought you were in love with our Emmy, but I weren't sure whether you knew it yourself or not. Not until you come round askin' her to go house-huntin' with you, that is. Then I were pretty sure.' Mr Mac and Emmy stared at Beryl, goggle-eyed. Then they both smiled, their expressions so similar that Beryl laughed aloud. 'You'll do,' she said. 'You're two of a kind, you are. And how did young Diana take it? I guess the reason she lit out without waitin' for her tea was so's she could be first with the news.'

Diana would have found Charlie, if she could have done so, but it appeared that he and Lenny had gone off on some errand of their own. She could have told the other kids but wanted Charlie to be the first to hear her news. So, having scouted up and down the area for him, she decided she would go to Mrs Symons first. After all, the old lady had been a good friend to her and would be delighted that Emmy had chosen someone she both knew and liked. Of course, Mrs Symons had known Johnny Frost slightly, and had shared Diana's opinion that he was weak, but she had not known Carl Johansson at all and had accepted Diana's view of him, especially when Diana had told her that Carl might well carry his wife and stepdaughter back to Sweden with him. 'And I'd miss all of you dreadfully, Mrs

Symons,' Diana had said mournfully. 'So I do hope Mam comes to her senses. Aunty Beryl says there's as good fish in the sea as ever came out of it, which I *think* means that Mam might meet someone really nice one day. Still, there's nothing I can do about it; I'm only a kid.'

So, knocking briskly on the Symonses' front door and going in, Diana was confident that her old friend would share her feelings, and so it proved.

'Mr Mac is a thoroughly nice, thoroughly good man who will make you and your mam very happy,' Mrs Symons said positively. 'And you say you're to live in Sydenham Avenue? That's an excellent area. When I was a little girl, we lived for a while in Buckingham Avenue. I was really happy there; my mama used to take me to the park and I had a great many little friends living nearby.'

'Why did you leave?' Diana asked curiously. 'We left because my daddy was killed; if it hadn't happened, I'm sure we would still be there.'

'My papa was in business with a partner, a Mr Phillips,' Mrs Symons said. 'They had a company which imported fine china from all over the world, and were doing very well. Mr Phillips, however, was not an honest man, though my mama said many times that he could charm the birds out of the trees.' She sighed sadly, looking back down the long years. 'But my mama did not take to him and she was proved right when he disappeared one morning in early summer, taking with him all the profits from Gregg & Phillips, as well as all the orders which were waiting to be honoured. The receivers were called in . . . you won't know what that means, dear, but it was the end of Gregg & Phillips – and we were forced to sell everything, our beautiful house, all the horses and carriages, even the cottage in the country where we had spent our holidays.'

'Oh, Mrs Symons, how dreadful,' Diana breathed, awestruck. 'Did the police ever catch up with Mr Phillips? Did your family ever get their money back?' She stroked the old lady's hand. 'I am *so* sorry.'

Mrs Symons laughed and pinched Diana's cheek. 'You're a kind little soul,' she said. 'No, Mr Phillips disappeared like a raindrop in a puddle, but my papa managed to revive the business, though in a much smaller way. We lived in a far humbler house and, naturally, in a far humbler style, but we never went hungry, and very soon there was enough money coming in to enable us to live comfortably once more. And then, of course, I met Adam Symons. It was love at first sight and, even though he was only a clerk in a shipping office, we married almost at once.' She beamed at Diana. 'And lived happily ever after,' she ended.

Diana smiled back. 'Well, if Mam had married either Johnny or Carl, I'd have gone away from Liverpool, but now I'm safe because we'll stay here,' she said. 'Mr Mac – I'm to call him Uncle Ted, by the way – is going to buy a car, so if he sends it to fetch you, would you come out to Sydenham Avenue and visit us? Mam and I would be delighted and I'm sure Mr Mac would, too. And now I must go and find Charlie. I wonder what he'll say when I tell him we will be moving out.'

What Charlie said in his head was 'Thanks be to God', but his mother gave him a glance so loaded with warning that he bit back the words, saying neutrally: 'Well, ain't that grand, queen! I've heared Mr Mac's flat is pretty large, so no doubt you'll have a room to yourself.'

Diana, alight with excitement, told him about the house in Sydenham Avenue and Charlie mentally revised his feelings; it would be rare nice to be able to spend all day in the park, playing footie, muckin' about by the lake, and going in and out of the palm house. They could pop in to Aunt Emmy's for their dinner and though it would mean having to let Diana share their games, it was a small price to pay for the freedom of the park.

So Charlie approved of the wedding plans, though he was satisfyingly astonished to hear that Emmy was to marry Mr Mac, instead of Johnny or Carl. 'But he's *old*,' he had said, when he and Diana had gone for a stroll along the Scotland Road. 'Don't you mind him being old, Di? An' wharrabout Aunt Emmy? Don't she mind?'

'He's not *that* old,' Diana objected. 'But I don't think it matters, Charlie. Look at Mrs Symons. She's old as the hills – older – but she's me best friend, after you.'

Charlie did not argue the point; he had no intention of putting a rub in the way of the Wesleys' leaving. They were all right, both of them, but the house was crowded enough without them, and anyway, he would be glad of a respite from Diana's constant presence. So he agreed that Mr Mac was probably just right for Aunt Emmy and began to look forward to moving-out day.

Christmas came and went. March arrived and Diana bounced around the house, talking excitedly about the gown she would wear for her mother's wedding. The house had been bought and Emmy and Mr Mac had enormous fun furnishing it, though Diana rapidly grew bored and opted out of such shopping trips. The wedding date was fixed for 9th April. Mr Mac had closed the restaurant to ordinary customers on that day, in order that the wedding breakfast might be held there, and when the day dawned, bright and sunny, the excitement amongst the staff and the wedding guests was intense. Wedding breakfasts in the courts were entirely dependent on the weather, for the houses were far too small to allow for a party to be held indoors. That was why weddings were mostly held in June, July and August, when at least the weather was warmer and there was a good chance that the 'two penn'orth of sky' above the rooftops would be blue.

Emmy, dressing in her room, with her daughter dancing excitedly around, a vision in pink and white lace and tulle, found herself aflutter with nerves. Her first wedding had been wonderful, but she acknowledged now that the way she felt about Peter had been puppy love compared to the way she felt about Ted McCullough. She knew, without a shadow of doubt, that Ted was indeed her Mr Right. She supposed that Peter had been exactly right for the fluttery little butterfly she had been at nineteen, but now that she was a woman who had had to learn both strength and independence, she needed someone altogether different. In fact, she needed Mr Mac.

'Emmy, time's getting on, queen. I know they say brides always ought to be a bit late . . .'

Emmy's heart gave a little jerk; the words Beryl was saying were the very same that she had used to hurry Emmy to her first wedding. For a moment she saw Peter's face quite clearly as he had looked on that long-ago day, and she felt tears come to her eyes. Poor Peter, her first love . . . but not, thank goodness, her last. Life had to go on and she knew that her happiness would have been Peter's first concern. So she banished the tears, because they were for a past which could never return, and turned to smile resolutely at her friend. Beryl was looking her best in a bright blue skirt and jacket and a pink cloche hat, and, beside her, Diana looked sweet in rose-pink. Emmy was dressed in a cream linen suit with a string of amber beads round her throat and tan-coloured court shoes on her feet, and on her dressing table lay a modest bouquet of dark yellow roses. She picked up the flowers, then glanced in the mirror to check that nothing was amiss with her appearance. She could not regret leaving the little house in the court, though she would always remember the wonderful kindness of both Beryl and Wally in offering her a home at her time of greatest need.

'It's all right, Beryl, I'm ready to leave,' she said, and reached up to give her friend a quick kiss on the cheek. 'You've been wonderful, queen, better than any sister, and I've been very happy under your roof . . .'

'Oh, go on with you,' Beryl said, returning the kiss. 'Now let's get this show on the road. I dare say Mr Mac will be as nervous as a kitten, because though you're an old hand at weddings, this is his first. Emmy, you look like a girl again, pretty as a picture. Why, Diana might be your sister.'

As she spoke, she was ushering mother and daughter downstairs, and presently Emmy stepped into the court, glancing upwards as she did so. 'Oh look,' she said, clutching Beryl's arm, 'the two penn'orth of sky that Mam talked about is all blue and gold. Oh, Beryl, it's a sign, isn't it? We're going to be the happiest little family in the whole world!'